THE GLASS BUTTERFLY

A.G. HOWARD

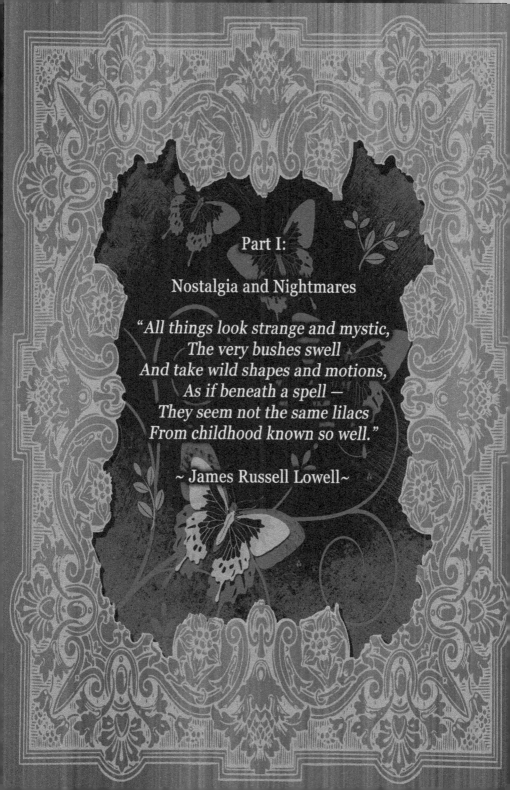

Part I:

Nostalgia and Nightmares

"All things look strange and mystic,
The very bushes swell
And take wild shapes and motions,
As if beneath a spell —
They seem not the same lilacs
From childhood known so well."

~ James Russell Lowell~

CHAPTER ONE

Province of Ulster, Northern Ireland
May, 1907

Breaking into a wealthy estate should never be this easy. No night watchmen posted, no dogs sniffing around ... it was as if the grand countess wanted her enclosed garden to get robbed. Butterfly consortiums were all the rage back in London. A symbol of wealth and prestige second only to Orchid collecting. Perhaps such a hobby wasn't quite so prestigious here in Ireland.

Or it could be that she's relying upon the ghosts to protect her.

Nick Thornton had heard rumors aplenty from the townspeople of Carnlough of the haunted castle in the hills. Peering through the iron bars where it rose in the distance from a well-kept courtyard of shrubs, vines, and lattices, he could see how such talk began. The estate was isolated— ghoulish even, especially on such a foggy night. Unfamiliar sounds added to the eerie atmosphere. A constant hum of katydids and the occasional call of some night bird or frog grew faint each time the cool wind rattled the trees with a keening whine.

1

His gaze settled on the castle's turret where mist draped the tip like an otherworldly nest hoarding an un-hatched batch of specters. A sane man would be unnerved by the sight. But it called to him, in more ways than one. He had grown up in a fortress of stone similar to this, and was, after all born of a ghost story, as was his twin brother and little sister. Also, he'd long since bid sanity farewell, having seen much ghastlier vistas when he used to dance with opium every night.

He looked over his shoulder to assure his faithful companion—a one-eared pit bull terrier—still waited quietly behind him. Careful not to disturb the large brass bell hanging from the top of the gate, Nick wedged his carving knife between the fence's iron frame and the lock. He would've preferred a diamond pick or short hook for this particular mechanism, but he'd sold his entire set of picklocks piece by piece to fund a ferry trip across the Celtic. So now he had to resort to more primitive methods.

Utilizing the shy patch of moonlight that illumined his gloved hands and the turn-style latch, he jiggled the blade to force the metal bar into its socket, bypassing the locking component. The gate swung open with a creak.

The sound uncoiled through his spine—a tangible warning. He tucked his knife away then sunk several steps back into the shadowy firs of the surrounding forest that filled the air with a crisp evergreen scent. Piney needles poked through his coat's collar. He brushed the branch aside. A familiar whimper sounded as his dog pushed between his knees. Nick caught the eager pit bull by the scruff as he tried to lunge and muscled him back from the courtyard's entrance.

"Easy there, Johnny Boy," he whispered and untangled his legs from around the dog's ribcage. He knelt down, rubbing Johnny's one good ear. "You know the rules. We wait to assure no one heard us. You're as rusty as those gate hinges, old chap."

As if in apology, the dog licked Nick's nose and panted, lips curled upward.

Nick grinned back—a genuine smile. Not the one he'd been sporting over the past two years. Not one of concession to assuage his disappointed father. But an expression of hope: an emotion that had eluded him ever since.

Despair knotted in his throat before he could finish the thought. He swallowed and the lump metastasized in his chest, an ache so intense he had to force himself to breathe. Adjusting his hat, he absently touched the earring in his left ear—a diamond stud—the deficient remains of a wedding ring.

He *had* to reach Mina. To beg forgiveness for his unforgivable sin. It was the only way to live again.

His thoughts strayed to his belongings hidden in the forest ... the pocket-sized almanac on spiritual folklore from around the world. He'd stolen it from an eclectic bookstore in London almost a year ago. Thus far, the pages' contents hadn't helped in his quest.

If things went well tonight, that would soon change.

He scanned the shadowy courtyard. Seeing no movement other than snaky wisps of fog, he eased within the gate. Johnny Boy loped a few steps ahead, nose to the pebbled path and ear perked.

Catching the dog's attention with a tongue cluck, Nick hedged toward a glass enclosure to the right. Sporadic glimpses of moonlight reflected off the panes, capturing his image. Seeing himself dressed in thief's garb brought back memories. None of them good.

A black coachman hat hid his plaited shoulder-length

blonde hair; black trousers hugged his thighs; and an ebony rifle-frock coat swung open to reveal the dark shirt buttoned-up to the edge of his golden beard. The coat's hem skimmed his shins when it should have grazed his ankles. Nick had broad shoulders and stood taller than most. *Such strapping lads.* His deaf mother used to sign the words with pride—about him and his twin, Julian. A pride that was all too short lived in Nick's case.

He stalled at the greenhouse door, pleased to find the entrance unlocked. Just as he'd hoped, the dowager was unaware of the invaluable treasure harbored within. If she knew of the spiritual quality of her butterflies, she'd no doubt have them under lock and key. She was a superstitious woman, judging by the stories surrounding her estate. A fact substantiated by the haunted romance novel she'd dreamed up. He'd read passages himself, as his sister Emilia had been the coauthor.

Nick left home, almost three years back while they were still writing. Surely the duo had finished by now. He hoped the ending was a happy one. At least happier than his own tragic tale.

Kneeling to cup Johnny Boy's muzzle, he met the dog's soulful gaze. "Stay here and watch my back. Warn me if anyone's coming."

Snorting, the dog turned around and planted his haunches in front of the door, ear at attention and eyes trailing the length of the courtyard.

Nick's heart warmed. Johnny always managed to awaken a burst of fondness when no other human could evoke anything but shame and regret. Granted, the dog wasn't technically a person, but he was the closest thing to a friend in this foreign land. And he was more human than some people Nick had known in his life.

Stepping into the greenhouse, Nick sealed the entrance behind him. He removed his gloves and tucked them in his pocket, reaching in the darkness for the slick glass he couldn't see but knew would be there. Duel doors were standard in butterfly conservatories and enclosed gardens—one to enter, then the other to provide passage after the first one shut—to prevent escape of any insects or birds.

His family had a greenhouse much like this one, though larger, at their Manor of Diversions—a holiday escape replete with hot water springs, shops, and amusement rides. A butterfly garden had been his father's most recent addition to their estate, though Nick never saw its completion. Another change he'd missed out on in his absence, though more forgivable than missing his beloved sister Emilia's sixteenth birthday, and the birth of his nephew to Willow and his twin.

There was no way he could've faced that healthy, perfect infant, after what had become of his own.

Clenching his jaw against a goring sensation in his chest, Nick slipped through the second door and secured it, the familiar tang of dewy plants and humid soil welcoming him with a bittersweet nostalgia. He glanced over his shoulder through the transparent entrance. Though difficult to make out much detail, the silhouette of Johnny Boy's intent vigil bolstered his resolve.

He hadn't planned to come here unannounced. He'd first thought to introduce himself. His name would've been recognized. No doubt he would've been cordially received and put up for the night. His family had been buying pupas via post for three years, which had evolved into his sister's writing correspondences with the reclusive dowager.

However, after rethinking, Nick opted to sneak in quietly for some reconnaissance, and leave out his family entirely.

He'd done enough damage to the Thornton name in London ... had no intention of repeating those mistakes here in Ireland.

It wasn't the dowager he was here to see anyway. He intended to gain audience with the visionary lepidopterist who worked for her: Professor Jasper Blackwood.

Unlikely the scientist would be in his garden this late in the evening. However, if the special breed of tropical butterflies were here, Nick would present himself at the castle door under an alias to see how much the professor knew. According to Nick's stolen almanac, the insects had the ability to connect with spirits and cross into the afterlife. So ironic, that his only hope for peace and redemption depended upon these creatures with fragile glasslike wings...

Taking tentative steps forward in the darkness, he used random spills of moonlight to piece together a view. Fog and clouds drifted above the glass roof, causing the ground to appear to move. He planted his feet apart to steady himself. Dust motes swirled in the soft beams, draping the flowers and foliage in purple-blue shadows. The gloomy artistry could've been a landscape wrought in one of his drug-induced states.

Leaves rustled at the far end of the glass house. A dark sweep of movement caught Nick's attention. His pulse jumped. Before he could react, there was a sharp crack. The sensation of something wrapping below his kneecap sliced through his trousers.

His flesh peeled back to expose a glimpse of bone as his knee tugged out from under him with a harsh jerk. Losing his balance, he hit the ground and banged the back of his head. Warm liquid oozed from his leg and saturated his torn trousers. A potent odor laced the air. He felt dazed ... dizzy and disoriented. Losing his grip on reality, he drifted into the past—his clothes soaked with blood that was not his own.

Johnny Boy's bark dragged him to the present again. The dog threw himself against the glass, desperate to get in. Gasping air to clear his mind, Nick attempted to stand on his good leg. The lasso beneath his left knee tightened, gored deeper into the wound, and held him down. His fingers curled around the leather binding. He gritted his teeth, head pounding and nausea twisting his gut.

The leathery rope grew taut at his touch. Someone held the other end.

Cursing, Nick searched out his knife with one hand and jerked the cord with the other. He misjudged the lightness of his captor. The assailant flew into him, crashing atop his body with a grunt as if caught off guard by the strength of his pull. As they wrestled, a faint citrusy-spice filled the air.

Situating his free foot against a mound of dirt, Nick flipped to straddle his attacker, breaking the man's hold on the whip in the same move.

Propped on his elbow, Nick caught the lapel of his opponent's tweed jacket. He slanted his knife beneath their jaw line, puckering the skin. The man gasped for breath and stopped fighting, frozen. Sweat beaded on Nick's forehead. Fuzziness swarmed him as his wounded leg shot pulses of fire up through his kneecap.

"What the hell're y'doing? Y'drugged mmmeee ..." Nick slurred. He couldn't make out his opponent's face for the darkness and his blurred vision, but the man felt slight—his bone structure delicate beneath his clothes and hat. It must be the professor ...

The bind on Nick's leg tightened as his attacker caught hold again and whispered breathlessly, "At long last we meet, *Dark Raven.*"

Unsure if he'd heard the cryptic words clearly, Nick

7

grappled for his waning concentration.

His opponent leapt into action. One hand slapped away Nick's knife as another covered his nose and mouth with a linen handkerchief. A scent akin to rubbing alcohol gushed into his lungs.

Ether.

Gulping shallow breaths, Nick struggled to turn his chin, but the more he fought, the more he inhaled. His whiskery chin snagged on the fabric and he rolled off to escape the hanky, but it was too late. His pain numbed and he fell to his back, floating ... floating in his mind toward the strands of moonlight washing over his face.

Fingertips as soft as petals smoothed his temple—encouraging him to fade away.

Against his will, Nick's eyes fluttered shut.

As the hanky slid free from his nose, he heard his attacker whisper: "No. Not you. How could it be you?"

Then a black, snowy emptiness seeped into Nick's head, muffling the sound of crashing glass and Johnny Boy's agonized yelps.

CHAPTER TWO

"What were you thinking, Dove? Executing a reconnaissance alone. You're shaking like a leaf in a hurricane."

"Posh. I'm fine. And I haven't a scratch." Felicity Lonsdale brushed past her groundskeeper and strode toward her room at the end of the candlelit passage. Clooney was a dear old friend, more like a father than a servant, with a tendency to over-worry. She couldn't admit to him why she was shaking ... why her heart thundered like a storm had broken loose in her chest.

"We've got our Dark Raven," she managed. "Tis all that matters." Peeling off her hat, she shook her long hair from its pins and added, "Do we know how he got here?"

"The stable hands heard a horse nickering in the forest. They're searching for it now. I'll have them put it in our stables."

"Fair enough. So, are our intruders settled into their bed?"

Clooney rubbed a knuckle along his wiry white beard and moustache. "Aye. Binata is tending them."

Felicity smiled at that. The Nigerian nanny's authoritative manner and maternal instincts would keep the man and his dog in line, should they start feeling spry enough to cause trouble. "Will they be all right?" She loosened the cravat from around her neck. Her boots scuffed along the marble floors.

"The hound is whimpering," Clooney answered, "none too happy with the seam I made in his throat. I removed the shards, but one came nigh to severing his windpipe. The valerian and passion flower oil you had on the whip worked well enough to slow down the man. So, I used some on the dog to help with his pain."

"Never have I seen a more faithful pet," Felicity said, her heart softening despite herself. "Bursting through the glass to save his master."

She'd always been grateful for Clooney's past walk as a physician. There had been countless times he'd saved the life of someone she cared for, herself included. It also gave her great relief that the castle had an abundance of bedchambers. Since her captives were on the fourth floor, she and her nieces could sleep through the night in their second story rooms without hearing the dog's whimpers. She didn't want anything waking up her girls and scaring them.

"And our Raven?" she asked. Remembering how gruesome her captive's leg had looked as she staved off the bleeding, Felicity winced. She hadn't meant to injure him to that degree. She'd been driven by anger and righteous fury; had thought he was ... someone else entirely. "How is he?"

"Still asleep. I stitched his ripped skin. Your whip damaged some muscle, too. Oh, and he has some bruised ribs and a bump on his noggin. Pretty busted up for a ghost."

Clooney smiled, but Felicity couldn't bring herself to share his levity. She straightened a painting—red velvety butterflies on a black background—as they passed through the corridor. She couldn't seem to assuage the guilt turning in her abdomen. "He must be in a lot of pain."

"That ether you gave him is keeping him oblivious. But

he'll be feeling it in the morn. Hope you're right about him being Donal Landrigan's sidekick. Otherwise..." The groundskeeper's thin body stiffened as he walked alongside her, boney shoulders hunched beneath a plaid gardening shirt.

He tucked a hand in the trouser pocket where he always kept his pipe. He rarely lit up due to his allergy to tobacco smoke. Chewing on the stem was often enough of a comfort to him. But judging by the scent of smoke emanating off his clothes and the moisture glistening in his bloodshot eyes, he'd given in to temptation earlier. He was obviously worried for her and the girls.

"Otherwise nothing," Felicity tried to reassure him, if not herself. "A stranger broke into my estate. What other reason could he possibly have, if not to aid Landrigan's schemes? Tomorrow, we'll get to the truth. And once he admits to being our culprit, I'll march the girls up to meet their ghost and put an end to this Dark Raven nonsense once and for all."

Clooney chomped on his pipe. His lower lip jutted out— an expression Felicity had grown fond of over the years. He often pouted when he was feeling fatherly. "That crashing glass was ear shattering. We don't need the Royal Irish Constabulary sniffing around."

"You well know the RICs never patrol out this far. We'll have the stable hands escort the man back to town before they get wind of anything."

Clooney took out his pipe and thumped its bowl against his chin. "You have doubts. You have doubts he's working for Donal, or you would've already had Tobias and Fennigan dump him out in the forest to bleed to death."

"You truly think me so heartless? Perhaps had he *been* Landrigan." She feigned a wry laugh. "No. I assume this man was an ingenuous pawn. That even if he isn't innocent, he was misled."

Her mouth dried on the words. She wasn't prepared to tell Clooney the real reason the wounded man deserved the benefit of the doubt ... how she'd recognized him when she released the hanky and saw his face in the moonlight. The earring, the beard, and his brawny build had thrown her at first. But his features...

She'd been eighteen at the time, and he couldn't have been much more than two years younger than her. For these seven years hence, she'd fantasized of him ... playing out his kindness and bravery behind closed eyes. Even drunk to the gills as he'd been, he still managed to be a hero. Now, those features were indelible in her mind. An unmistakable beacon in a past otherwise filled with bleakness and despair.

But Clooney wouldn't see him as a beacon. He'd see him as a threat to her identity and would insist they send him away. Though a part of her shared this concern, a bigger part knew she owed this man shelter and nurturing, at the very least.

"Donal." Clooney spat the name again, narrowing his eyes and pointing the pipe's stem her way. "He'll be here at week's end for his monthly call."

Felicity regrouped her thoughts. "Yes, and the good dowager will be ready for him as always. Should be interesting to see his reaction when he finds I've out-maneuvered him once again."

The longcase clock in her room began to strike midnight. Her gaze made a sweep to the shadowed and cobwebbed stairway on her right—the one that led to the castle's highest turret.

"Are you feeling one of your headaches coming on?" Cloony asked, his attention following hers to the stairs.

"No." Her nights hadn't revolved around said headaches for some time. Ever since she'd finished writing that romance novel with young Emilia Thornton and put a stop to their correspondences. As incapacitating as those megrims had been, and as confusing as the missing time was, some part of her felt incomplete without them. "Are you going up?" she asked.

"Aye," Clooney answered. "My final check before bed."

Felicity stepped backward across her threshold. The smoky beginnings of a fire crackled in her hearth—set into play by her maid who was now retired for the night somewhere within the servant's confines on the first floor.

The clock's sixth gong sounded.

"I suppose since you've captured our factitious ghost and your headaches no longer plague you, you can catch up on your sleep now," Clooney said before walking away.

Without answering, Felicity shut the door and strode to the window to study the black landscape beyond the castle's stone walls, though couldn't see a thing for the fog clinging to her panes.

Clooney was mistaken. She wouldn't sleep so easily. For this man who slumbered in a chamber two stories above hers was in fact a *genuine* ghost—from a past as dark and binding as the clouds which had swallowed her beloved estate whole.

Felicity awoke to the crack of dawn and a clap of thunder.

She rolled out of bed still bleary, having wrested insomnia and bouts of restless dreams over the past several nights.

Their wounded trespasser had been here for three days, yet had not fully awoken once. Clooney was keeping him in a valerian haze so he wouldn't damage his leg further by moving too much. It had been no easy task keeping her nieces out of the room, but Felicity had managed with the help of the servants. Today, however, Clooney planned to wean the man off the sedative so he could answer for himself, and Felicity needed to prepare for the altercation.

She stretched her cramped muscles and twisted her waist length hair into a bun at the back of her neck.

Looking down at her gown, she reminisced of those nights in the past, when she used to awaken each morning wearing the same clothes as the night before, with the pen in her hand and her lantern still burning. Each time she'd find herself at her rosewood desk, head craned at an awkward slant, cheek flat against the parchment spread out upon the surface.

The lapses in her memory when writing to Emilia had started some months after their initial correspondence about butterflies. Felicity fell asleep at her desk trying to respond to a letter. When she awoke, the letter was answered, though not in her handwriting. However, she did recognize the script, for it was as familiar to her as her own would have been. She'd seen enough of her brother Jasper's scientific scribblings to know his hand.

As she tried to decipher the messy words, her head had started to pound. Due to the uncomfortable sensation, she couldn't read what she'd written at all. Yet, a compelling force enticed her to mail the response to Emilia, and she deigned it best to obey, lest the headache return. The routine continued on a nightly basis, the megrims hitting at midnight. She tried twice to break the cycle by not going to her bedchamber or by opening the chapter before the clock struck twelve. But such rebellion only resulted in a horrendous head-splitting buzz that caused bouts of vomiting and incapacitated her for hours.

Felicity tightened her jaw on the memory. She'd heard of people with dual personalities living within them; dark, disturbed individuals who had lost their sense of self due to some trauma in their past.

Her past was indeed filled with ugly thorns; and it terrified her to think that they had pierced her sanity and allowed dementia to seep within. But there was another explanation: a spirit using her body to enact correspondence with the living. That possibility had filled her with hope, especially since the pen was always in her left hand. Though she was right-handed, Jasper wrote with his left, and to be connected to her beloved brother on any plane meant she hadn't truly lost him.

However, it was unbelievable for so many reasons—too farfetched. And her optimism fell away when the writings stopped altogether.

Felicity never admitted any of those details to Emilia, for if the time lapses in her memory were ever to become public, she would be deemed unfit to raise her nieces.

Felicity was so afraid to that end, she hadn't told anyone in the household but Clooney, and only he knew because he'd been treating her symptoms during that time. Also, he was the one who mailed the letters to Emilia on his trips into Carnlough. He'd been the one who had suggested the possibility of Jasper using her hand, trying to keep himself among the living through automatic writing. But he knew as much as Felicity how unlikely that was.

Some three months ago, when the final chapter was written and mailed off, everything simply stopped. Felicity's nights were hers once more ... and her memory no longer had spotty patches. Since every following letter would be written by her hand—her *right* hand—Clooney took over the business correspondence so as not to reintroduce the different scripts. He wrote the note breaking off Felicity's contact with Emilia and asked to continue any interactions via Master Thornton, the girl's father. Felicity felt guilty for not giving Emilia any reason, but protecting her family was of utmost import.

At the thought of protection, Felicity went to her desk and pulled out her top drawer, withdrawing the knife she'd found among the shattered glass in the greenhouse—the blade that belonged to the wounded man now slumbering on the fourth floor.

The few times she'd managed to sleep the past few nights, she'd dreamt of him. A stranger, yet not. His youthful face, so filled with compassion and rage. Then the contrast of seven years—a man now, whose body straddled hers in the greenhouse, a heavy and potent sensation which took her breath in a way that was far from unpleasant.

She would never have imagined him mixed up with someone like Landrigan. For him to be in Ireland instead of London boggled the mind even more. Until she had some answers, she deemed it wise to hide his weapon. She knew too well the damage such a blade could incur.

As she ran a finger along the handle, tracing the initials *N.T.*, she wondered what the letters stood for. So long reminiscing of her knight in shining armor, and still no name to assign him.

At her picture window, she opened the black brocade curtains which matched the cushions on her window seat. Bluish light streamed in through the water-tinged glass and caused the flocked patterns on the crimson wallpaper to appear to dance. It must have started raining hours before sunrise. Typical. Dawns were rarely anything but misty and hazy here in Ireland. But it was unusual for her to not have even heard the drops hitting the window.

She put the knife aside and gathered up her gown, placing a knee on the seat's cushion. With both palms splayed against the chilly glass, she wiped away the condensation and stared out at the thick, needled canopy that blocked most of the gray sky. A thousand pines, firs, and coniferous trees surrounded the castle—green, lush, and isolated. A foreboding and shadowy beauty which had taken years for her to grow accustomed to. Now, she wouldn't know how to survive anywhere else. This temperate rainforest, tucked along the outskirts of Carnlough where steep coastal mountains and cliffs bordered the North Atlantic Ocean, had become her home. A sanctuary she had secured at great price.

She unbuttoned the front of her gown and ran a finger between her breasts to her abdomen, tracing the ugly scar ... bidding a memory as dark as the underbelly of the marshes and bogs hidden within the forest.

In all these years, she'd never once braved looking at it full-on in a mirror. She only knew the disfigurement by touch; and by the flash of its angry red flare in her peripheral at times she almost forgot to avert her eyes.

As she traced the trail of thickened skin, her wounded guest's face came to mind again.

A knock on the door startled her.

She forced her gaze from the view outside just as a flock of vivid yellow goldfinches began to leap about in the canopy. Buttoning her placket, she pulled a shawl around her shoulders. After securing the knife in her drawer, she padded in her stocking feet to her door and unlocked it.

Clooney waited on the other side in an orange plaid shirt and green trousers. With the addition of his balding head and hunched back, he looked like an underfed pumpkin.

"Please tell me Landrigan hasn't arrived already," she said.

"Not yet. But our patient is up. And he's asking ... no ... *demanding* to see you. He wasn't very happy to learn we kept him sedated for three days. I'm thinking it might've been a bad idea to wake him. He's strong as an ox, injuries notwithstanding. We're having a difficult time keeping him abed."

Clooney's breath hinted of tobacco, and Felicity imagined he'd already been out in the courtyard for a calming smoke.

"Well, I should see to him then." A phantom stitching sensation tightened the damaged skin between her breasts. This overwhelming desire to meet her rescuer unsettled her, awoke a fascination she had never contemplated being faced with. *Ever.*

She started to step out of her room.

Clooney stuck out a boot, holding her back. "Forgetting something?"

Remembering what she wore, she bit her lip. "I should wash up first. And dress."

"Among other things." He gestured to her face. "He is expecting a forty-year-old dowager ... not a young beauty. Better age that skin."

Felicity touched the outer corner of an eye. "Oh ... yes."

"And there's something you should know. I managed to get his name last night while he was still groggy. He doesn't realize he told me yet. But it's Nicolas. Nicolas *Thornton*. Of the London Thorntons."

Felicity gulped, stunned by the coincidence. That's what the initials on the knife meant. How could it be? The boy who had once been her hero had lived under the roof of one of her patrons. Almost within reach ... and Felicity had never known.

"Well, what are your thoughts?" Clooney pressed. "The son of a patron. Brother to your prior mailing correspondent. This poses a bit of a problem, aye?"

"Indeed it does." More than Clooney could conceive, because she'd yet to tell him that this was the boy ... the man ... who had saved her life years ago. Felicity's fingers drummed the door frame in an effort to hide her nerves. "That must be why he was in the greenhouse. He was sent by his family to check on their missing shipments."

"Missing?"

"Last months' have yet to go out. My pupas have been dwindling."

A swift intake of air whistled through Clooney's lips.

Felicity stared at him. "What?"

The old man blushed in fits and starts—little blossoms of red on his cheeks and neck. "I-I had no idea the shortage had become so serious."

"How could you? I haven't yet told you of the fungus." She stepped back into her bedchamber.

"You've found a fungus? Where?"

"On the passion vines. I believe it's what's causing the butterflies not to breed successfully, and I'm sure Donal is responsible. It is the reason I was in the greenhouse last night. I meant to catch him, to show him he wasn't the only one capable of subterfuge and violence." Her eyes met Clooney's. "If only Jasper were with us still. He'd know how to cure his butterflies."

Clooney visibly tensed. "We'll talk more about the pupas later. Make yourself presentable and I'll meet you upstairs. Together, we can smooth things over with Lord Thornton."

She caught the groundskeeper's hand, still not prepared to tell him the whole truth of their guest's identity. "No, Clooney. This is one introduction I wish to make alone."

The old man's white-bearded chin tightened in reluctant resignation. "Then there's one thing more you should know."

Sighing, Felicity steeled herself. *What else could there possibly be?* "Go on."

"This man is a professional thief. He had a cascading wallet. By the imprints in the leather, I'd reason it once held an entire set of picklocks. They're gone now. But he left no trace or scratch when he jimmied that lock on the gate, so he apparently doesn't need them. And ... and I've heard talk about town of a widow missing her horse. What struck me, was that someone would steal a hobbie."

"A *bog* pony?"

"Which is what our guest had tied to the tree last night."

"Incomprehensible. For a man of his stature?"

"Exactly my point. The pony's eight hands high and looks to be almost fifteen-years aged. Far too small and old to appeal to any honorable English nobleman."

Felicity was speechless.

"He obviously just needed it to carry his baggage on the walk up the mountain." Clooney thumbed the pipe in his pocket. "We found his bundles tied to the horse. Humble supply, really. Only a lantern, a flask, a threadbare change of clothes, and two blanket rolls. One blanket belongs to his dog, judging by the hair shed upon it. Oh, and he had a journal about spirits. Considering the book's content, there could be something to your theory about him working for Donal."

A slow breath slipped from Felicity's lips.

Clooney clasped her hand in both of his. "I don't know why a nobleman's son would lower himself to scaring a woman and children and stealing decrepit ponies. But you've had enough dealings with reprobates in your life. I don't wish to see anything disrupt the semblance of peace you have with the girls here. Find out why he came, then let me patch him up and send him on his way."

He squeezed her hand before striding down the corridor, leaving Felicity to contemplate the unexpected chinks in her knight's shining armor.

CHAPTER THREE

"Cranky old snoot. Telling me to stay abed." Nick shifted to his right side beneath the canopy and gazed into Johnny Boy's soulful eyes, thrilled to see him awake and responsive. Of all the destructive messes Nick had made of other people's lives ... now he'd managed to pull his dog into one.

At least Johnny appeared quite happy at the moment, sharing the plush quilts and pillows in the dimly lit bedchamber.

"Who does this Binata think she is?" Nick asked, falling into the old habit of talking things over with the hound. "She takes my clothes and leaves me here naked. If she thinks that will stop me, she's in for a ripe surprise."

Johnny tilted his head and gave him a slimy, smelly lick on the nose.

Nick tried to emulate the dog's one-sided smirk. Who but Johnny could make him feel better after that conversation with the groundskeeper earlier?

The old man said he'd found the little mare Nick brought and stabled her, but then he outright accused Nick of stealing her. Didn't matter that the groundskeeper was right. He shouldn't be one to judge. After all, he'd either lost or stolen Nick's knife.

That blade had been a gift from his father in his youth, to encourage Nick's innate talent for carving beautiful things out of wood. A talent he used to help build a herd of carousel horses for his brother's amusement park set upon his family's estate. Nick's artistry was the one thing he'd ever accomplished that made his father proud, and the one thing that made him feel close to Julian.

Yet in the end, the razor-sharp edge of his knife had been used to destroy beauty.

His gut clenched on the memory. Perhaps it was better if the blade remained lost. Then he would no longer be tormented by its part in his wife's brutal death.

Johnny Boy blew a puff of hot air in Nick's face, once again rescuing him from bitter thoughts.

"Well, you seem to be in high leg this morn," Nick said. "How about some breakfast? What say?"

Johnny's tail wagged, but Nick knew the dog had a long recovery ahead. A three-inch seam marred his throat and clusters of raw, pink wounds mutilated his white coat where bits of glass had been worked free. The dog had lost a lot of blood, and was still quite weak.

No. Johnny wouldn't be going anywhere for a while.

Nick, on the other hand, had a mission. He'd already lost three days to sleep, so had little time to spare. He fingered his earring. The man who attacked him so viciously the other night must've been Jasper. He was frail and delicate with hands as soft as rose petals, just like one would expect of a man who spent every waking hour with his nose in journals and books.

Nick rubbed his beard in an effort to calm himself. He wanted to pound the mouse. But he couldn't blame him for trying to protect what was his. Still, at the very least the little professor owed Nick a tour of the butterfly conservatory after what he'd done. There was such a thing as etiquette, even among the reclusive. Who executes an attack before asking questions, after all?

One thing Nick knew: he would get more of an apology by using his surname, but he refused to bring his family into this. They couldn't know his whereabouts, for they would stop at nothing to bring him home. As much as he missed the manor, he no longer belonged there.

A chill raised the hairs on his bared legs and torso as he slapped off his covers and rolled to his back. He made the mistake of kicking aside the sheer voile curtains that draped the bed's four-poster frame. Nerve centers combusted in his leg and ribs—angry and hot.

With a hiss, he cradled his left knee and jerked when a halo of stitches pricked his fingers. His ribs caught where a bandage cinched him like a woman's bustier and a dull ache pounded his head. Easing back to lie down again, he left both legs hanging at the knee over the mattress, his feet flat on the slick floor. The bed curtains had wound around his chest, doing nothing to hide his lower extremities.

He moaned, considering covering up but too woozy to care. Let the old woman return and see him in all his glory. She was the one who took his clothes and refused to bring any replacements.

He resituated to a more comfortable position. Head propped on a lump of covers, he scowled through the sheer curtains at his surroundings. Faint daylight filtered in from beneath the drapes—just enough to illuminate the room to a grayish haze. Floral fabrics and laces bedecked every window and wall.

A white wicker vanity along the north side showcased glass containers of every size along with a silver hair brush and some glistening hair pins. He recognized several of the perfumes by their bottle shape and labels: Lily of the Valley, Magnolia, and Lavender. They were of a rather cheap quality, and most of the bottles were only half-full. Three had toppled to their sides—no doubt leaking their innards to spawn the noxious flowery scent stinging his nostrils.

Feathery scarves and plumed hats were thrown about, and a mismatched assortment of fancy shoes peppered the luxurious rug running down the middle of the tiled floor. Like a lacy waterfall, a petticoat draped a wing-backed chair next to a desk where a pink crystal clock ticked a rhythmic tune.

"Aw, bloody beautiful. A man and dog at death's door and they put them up in a hoity-toity lady's parlor."

Johnny Boy shoved his nose into Nick's hair and snorted. Nick smiled. One of the things he'd always loved about this dog was his impeccable sense of humor. Nick raised his voice an octave. "Yes Johnny old chap. Let us discuss the latest hairstyles and fashions in *Harper's Bazaar*. Perhaps for breakfast they'll serve us tea and crumpets on tatted lace napkins."

"There might be a rather ... *substantial* problem with your breakfast plans."

Nick snagged a pillow with his good hand and planted it firmly in place between his legs. *Too little too late.*

Pulling a sheet around to replace the pillow, he forced his mutinous body up to a sitting position. He bit back a growl at the resurgence of pain but took heart the dizziness had subsided. Glancing through the filmy voile, he could make out an elegant silhouette in a flowing black dress standing at the door. Though he couldn't see her face clearly, there was no doubting who she was by her carriage.

He groaned. Dandy way to make a first impression on the countess.

"A traditional Irish breakfast"—the flared hem of her form fitting skirt swished around her ankles as she stepped inside— "consists of sausage and black and white pudding."

"So what might the problem be?" he asked through gritted teeth.

"Well, we're out of sausage." She bent to pick up some scarves and hats, stuffing her arms on her way to dump them in a trunk in the furthest corner. Passing the window, she coaxed the drapes open with a gloved hand and tender light blanketed the room. "But it appears you've brought your own. An excess, in fact."

Nick flicked the bed curtain away to get a clearer view of her back, impressed and surprised by her impropriety. "I'm perfectly happy to share."

From behind, she looked like any other dowager with her silver-blonde hair wound to a knot at the base of her neck, gleaming like the polished blade of a brand-new carving knife.

The countess bent down to pick up a pair of mismatched lady's shoes. Her waist was petite, hips small yet nicely curved. The hips of a woman who had never given birth. An unusual aspect for one of her class. Most noblemen married for no other purpose than to perpetuate their line through heirs. Other than that oddity, she could've been any forty-some-year-old widow.

Until she turned and their gazes met. In that instant, the clock on the desk ticked so loud Nick felt it in his pulse, for that's where all conformity ended. Her eyes were so unique—mystifying. A deep sadness lurked beneath those long lashes ... lashes so dark and thick, they could've belonged to a child ... and her eyebrows boasted the same dark hue—not a hint of white or gray within them.

Nick ran his fingers through his scruffy whiskers,

wondering at the strange niggle of attraction awaking within him. Surely he'd been too long without a woman to be seeing a dowager in such light.

Speaking of light, the lady stepped into the gentle radiance splaying from the window and her irises took on the color of mahogany, warm and rich. He saw a familiarity in that gaze ... but couldn't place it.

A lacy black scarf hid her neck, secured with a glistening butterfly brooch. The jewels reflected tiny sparkles of light upon her face, dancing along her skin. Her wrinkles could've been made by the etch of a knife—inscribed for character yet sanded to subtlety. As an artist, he couldn't help but admire the intricacies. Were he carving a woman's maturing face of smooth white pine, he couldn't have done a more masterful job.

He absently rubbed Johnny's velvety head, too confused by his piqued interest to even care that an uncomfortable silence wreathed them. She was indeed a contradiction; for though a fringe of lines skimmed her lips, her mouth was plump and shapely and smooth. He wanted to trace it with his fingertip, to see if it was as soft as it appeared.

"Generous of you to offer."

Her words shook Nick out of his fantasizing. It seemed she'd read the direction of his thoughts. "Offer?"

"To share your"—those tragically expressive eyes wandered to the sheet at his nether regions— "*provisions*. But I'm partial to scones and Devonshire cream. I find them much more satisfying."

Nick smirked. "Ah. You obviously haven't sampled the right sausage."

Without even blinking, she took back the reins. "There is a change of clothes for you in that wardrobe." She gestured to the wall behind him as she reached for a key looped around her waist on a delicate chain. "But before I give you the means to open it ... I must first demand an answer as to your appearance here three nights ago. How long have you been working for Donal Landrigan?"

The query forced Nick away from a surreptitious appraisal of her breasts—pert and nubile beneath the sheath of her full-coverage bodice. She wasn't wearing a corset, which further shocked and intrigued him. It was apparent this woman had never had babes to nurse.

He ceased petting Johnny. "Donal Landi—what?"

"He's a snake, in case you're unaware."

Nick frowned, baffled by the direction of her query, but enjoying the wordplay. It had been some time since he'd kept company with such a witty and well-spoken woman. "I thought Ireland was the land of no snakes," he baited. "There are tales of your blessed St. Patrick taking care of that."

"St. Patrick merely took care of the legless variety. There are still vipers aplenty roaming our land. See that you don't become one by association."

Nick clenched the sheet around his waist, no longer amused. She had every right to disparage and doubt him. He'd broken into her grounds. But ever since his youth, it had always grated on his last nerve to be reprimanded like a schoolboy. This lady assumed that just because she was his senior, she had lived more life and gleaned more wisdom than him.

Well she was bloody wrong.

In the past, he would have lured her into his bed. He would have stripped her of her stodgy attire and lay her out beneath him, disproving those notions of inexperience. He'd always had a way with the older women. It's what made him both rich and poor, all in the same breath.

Caught off guard by that thought, he ground his teeth.

He should never have sworn off bedding the ladies after his wife's death. Two years gone by without any sort of physical interlude had left him at the mercy of his libido. Until now, he'd had no desire to seek companionship again. Strange that this aging woman with a shattered gaze had reawakened it.

Too bad she was as frigid as sculpted ice.

"Do not speak to me as if I'm your son, madam. You are a stranger. The solicitudes of which are as useless and forgettable as a clouded sky that never swells to rain."

As if to disparage his comment, the room grew darker and droplets began to spatter on the glass. A flitter of some unnamed emotion—smugness perhaps—swept over the widow's face then faded with the change in lighting. "But we are hardly strangers, Lord Thornton. Considering your father has been buying pupas from me for years."

Nick felt his surname like a punch to the jaw. *Hell.* He'd been found out. Come to think, he vaguely remembered his attacker recognizing him the other night. Or had he dreamed that?

The dowager shifted her feet and ruffled her hem. "Again, I'll ask. How long have you been working for Donal Landrigan?"

"I'm not working for him ... whoever he might be. I've ne'er even heard the name."

"Then why were you lurking in my greenhouse? Was it at the behest of your father? Or perhaps your sister, checking up on me?"

"Certainly not. My family and I have been ... out of contact for some while." His head lowered. Better it stay that way. Better they think him dead or missing. They didn't need his constant shadow of misery and missteps darkening their doorway.

"So, your purpose here?" The key pendulated from the tips of the widow's fingers in time with the clock beside her.

She pursed her mouth at his silence.

"I see," she said. "This is a game to you. You rather enjoy being bared and on display. All right then. I shall wait for the novelty to wear off." With that, she eased gracefully into the winged back chair, not even bothering to move the petticoat draped over it. The lacy slip bubbled out around her, offsetting her black ensemble as if she were a chocolate candy laid out on a white doily.

Nick licked his lower lip at the imagery, thinking she'd be a bit more bitter than sweet to the tongue. "Perhaps"—he rubbed his palm across the tender bump on his nape— "if you were to stop staring, my penchant for nudity would lose its appeal."

"Perhaps, were you to tell me of your purpose for being here, I might be inclined to stop staring."

Although more verbal jousting was tempting, he had to come up with a feasible explanation. This courtly lady had allowed him to stay in her home for several nights. She'd had his wounds tended even after he violated her privacy. "Before I tell you anything, I ask for your word."

Her dark eyebrows lifted in interest. "My word on what?"

"That you'll not involve the RICs about the pony. I fully intend to give her back to her owners. I meant to all along."

Glancing thoughtfully at the window, the dowager shrugged. "Well enough. You *should* be the one to return her. Besides, I harbor no allegiance to the Constabulary. My only loyalties are to my loved ones ... the souls that are here, in my care." The key slid through her fingers, still dangling on the chain. "Which leads us back to my original query. Why would you break into my estate when you could simply introduce yourself at the gate by ringing the bell?"

"I wanted to see Professor Blackwood's work."

She paled as if her blood drained to her feet, then quickly schooled her features to a serene mask. "What do you know of the professor?"

Nick squeezed his thumb and forefinger around the jagged gem set within his ear. "I read a newspaper interview with him a few years ago, about a special breed of butterfly he's raising. I was in the greenhouse last night to explore in solitude before announcing my desire to invest. I realize now I went about it the wrong way—"

"You have money to invest?" she interrupted. Her long lashes trembled anxiously.

"I do." The injuries on his body blossomed to heat, as if lit afire by the blatant lie. He couldn't imagine where such a reaction had come from. Lying to women had never bothered him before. "But I must admit. I feel at a disadvantage, speaking business with you, the lady of the house, while in less than my skivvies."

She stood and smoothed her skirt, once again drawing Nick's attention to her enticing figure. "Then by all means, let us amend that." She stepped toward him and held out her down-turned hand. The wardrobe's key had been freed of the chain and wedged between two fingers for a tradeoff.

Nick carefully stood on his good leg, holding the sheet in place with one hand as he took her palm with the other.

She barely came to his collarbone when they were both standing. She looked up at him, her fingers stiffening in his grasp.

Again, he noticed something familiar about her. Her delicate size for one.

His gaze trailed the shape of her face, the poetry of her neck's curve beneath the scarf. Faint notes of orange blossoms and spice swirled around him at her proximity, making his mouth water. He'd smelled such a scent in the greenhouse ... when he was wrestling with his attacker.

His very soft attacker...

As the key passed between them, Nick let his fingertip brush the tiny snippet of skin peering out where her glove dipped low on her inner wrist. She sucked in a breath and he savored the reaction, surprised to find her skin as supple as rose petals.

"I was mistaken," he said. "We're not strangers at all. No. We've met before. Though under much different circumstances. Isn't that right?"

CHAPTER FOUR

Gaping, Felicity stepped back, but her obstinate guest refused to release her hand.

Her heart butted against her sternum, competing with the clock and the rain. He couldn't possibly remember what she had once been, couldn't know her from their encounter all those years ago. It had been too dark that night; he'd been drunk. Only *his* face had been lit up, just like the other evening.

And now ... her disguise should at the very least throw him off the scent. The wrinkles, the hair.

"You're mistaken, Lord Thornton," she intoned. "Other than my association with your family, we've not met. And I'd like you to relinquish my hand."

"Not until you address me properly. Lord Thornton is my father's name. I am Nick. Nothing more." His lips curved to a half-moon grin. Felicity's own lips trembled in response. No man should have a mouth so full and sensual. It was too distracting.

She jerked free, taking back the key and knocking him off balance. He put his full weight upon his injured left knee then lost his sheet trying to compensate with his good leg. Felicity froze for an instant, taken aback by his impressive ... physique. His only frailty appeared to be the mottled bruises beneath his dusting of golden hair. It had been so long since she'd seen a man in the raw, much less touched one. It left her rattled to the bone.

He cursed and grabbed his sheet, trying not to topple. Felicity gathered composure enough to rush to his side. She held his sheet around him as he propped his arm on her shoulder, limping the three steps back to the bed with her help. He groused all the way, displeased with having to lean on her. "What the hell is wrong with my leg?"

She eased him onto the bed's edge, surrounded by his scent—clean and earthy—like cool water beaded upon leather. She watched as he unwound his hair where it had caught on his earring. The strands glistened like sunshine. "Your muscles have been torn. It will take some time for them to mend. I'm sorry."

His eyes met hers—as gray and soft as a wolf's winter coat, yet with enough hardness they could drift to steel in a blink—every bit as unpredictable as a wild beast's moods. "Why should *you* be sorry? It isn't as if it was your doing."

Felicity swallowed against the bramble of nerves in her throat. She busied herself by strolling to the wardrobe with the key and opening the door. "I … I simply meant—"

"The man who attacked me with the whip. Where is he?"

Felicity procrastinated answering. Instead, she rifled through the clothes in the wardrobe—outfits once worn by her late husband that smelled of moth balls, cedar, and dusty terror. Stumbling upon a lawn shirt the color of cornflowers that would complement her guest's eyes, she tamped the ripple of emotion his touch and proximity had inspired.

How could she be feeling this way? She wasn't some inexperienced ingénue.

It was just that she'd admired him in her memory for so long, she reasoned. All these years she'd idolized him … like a dream-stricken virgin, laughable as that might be. Now here he was, in the flesh. A thief and possibly a liar.

The scar upon her chest and abdomen stretched rigid and unbending beneath her clothes as she dug deeper within the wardrobe, pulling out a pair of brown trousers and a union suit.

"Your Ladyship..."

The reverberations of his deep voice spread a tingling, warm flush of sensation through her pelvis and breasts. A resurrection of yearnings better left dead.

She did her best to ignore him. After finding a pair of canvas y-back braces to help hold up the trousers—to compensate for the difference in girth between her late husband and her guest—Felicity stopped at the trunk to fish out some men's stockings, black and ankle-high, then joined Nick beside the bed. She was relieved he'd tied the sheet around his waist to prevent any further accidental unveilings.

"There. These should suffice until the maid washes your other clothes and repairs the rips and tears." Felicity laid them out on the mattress, her gaze passing over the sleeping dog. It had warmed her heart when she first stepped in, to see Nick teasing with the pit bull as if he were a friend. His affection for the forlorn creature was apparent. "Can I get anything for your dog?"

"Some beef or chicken broth. Clooney said he couldn't eat solid food for a few days yet. But first ..." Nick caught her wrist. "You can get something for me." His fingertip found the opening in her glove again—a hot, erotic pressure against her throbbing pulse. Her thighs weakened as he nudged deeper inside, finding her life-line while his remaining fingers clasped tighter around her wrist. "I want to meet the man I encountered in the greenhouse. We have unfinished business."

The rain had stopped and the clock echoed in the resulting silence. Breath shallow and shaky, Felicity glanced down at her companion's bare feet—long, large, and powerful. Just like the rest of him. His finger continued its pressure along her palm, winding her stomach into dueling knots of discomfort and pleasure.

"He's ... indisposed ... at the moment," she mumbled.

She expected an argument, but Nick was no longer even listening. He was too intent on trying to peel off her glove. She jerked free and put some distance between them.

"Really, Lord Thornton." She resituated her glove and rubbed her wrist. "Such familiarity is highly improper."

He smirked, having the gall to look pleased with himself. "*Nick*. And you have the softest skin I've ever touched. I shan't apologize for wanting to see it bared."

Felicity made the mistake of glancing at the sheet gathered between his thighs and found him every bit as aroused as her.

"A pole," she blurted.

Nick looked at his lap. His tousled hair draped over one broad shoulder as he tilted his head to meet her gaze. "You flatter me."

Biting her tongue, Felicity whirled around and strode to the trunk, unwilling to give him the satisfaction of seeing he'd disarmed her. "I mean you *need* a pole ... a cane. So you might walk about." She dragged a stick-horse from the space between the trunk and the wall then returned to him while forcing her eyes not to stray again. "This should be perfectly suited for you. Seeing as you like miniature horses so much." She held it out, tamping a smile as she thought upon the bog pony in her stables.

Amusement danced across his face and he took the plush horse's head in his hand and propped the stick end on the floor between his feet. Gold and silver ribbons streamed out from behind the white stallion's ears to resemble a mane.

Nick twirled them around his forefinger. "I must say, Lady Lonsdale. You are a queen among hostesses."

Felicity stifled the stubborn giggle wanting to flourish, envisioning her lips bolted to her teeth.

"And I suppose this makes me a princess among guests, aye?" Nick asked, holding up the girlishly embellished horse. A grin spread over his face, stealing Felicity's breath. His white teeth shone like a luminous beacon breaking out from the dark gold whiskers.

Felicity's scar, which so often was chilled and numb, seemed to melt into the skin around it—a tickly sensation. She couldn't stop herself. Her own smile broke free. And it felt wonderful ... foreign and intimate.

Acknowledging her reaction with an appraising glance, Nick looked around the room. "So, you play with toys. Do you play dress-up as well?"

Felicity gulped. Was he referring to her past? Had he indeed recognized her and was baiting her? "I-I am not sure what you mean."

"The room. It looks as if someone has been playing dress-up. The shoes, the trappings." He gestured to the opened trunk brimming with hats and scarves.

Felicity exhaled, relieved. "My daughters. They live here with me." She couldn't resist the urge to test against an association with Landrigan one last time. "Although you already know that, don't you?"

He narrowed his eyes. "How could I? I've not seen anyone but you and your servants. You have daughters? I don't remember you sharing such information with my sister."

Measuring the sincere confusion in his expression, Felicity continued. "One is thirteen and the other is about to be seven. It's the youngest girl you have to thank for your cane."

"Hmm. So … why would you put a wounded man in their playroom?"

"It is the biggest bed in the castle; and Clooney wanted you next door to his chambers, in case you needed him in the night. You might prefer to stay up here today and let the servants tend you. You will have a difficult time getting down the stairs, being on the fourth floor."

Grinning, Nick batted the stick-horse's ears. "Well, I'll make myself at home, then. I've forgotten how much I enjoyed living in a castle."

The thought of him becoming an everyday fixture left Felicity's confidence flailing like a drowning child. Already she'd been fantasizing of him coming to her rescue again. The longer he stayed, the more fanciful she would become. And fancy only led to weakness. Who could trust a thief, after all?

"You shan't be here long enough for it to feel like home, Lord Thornton. I would ask that you leave as soon as we conduct our business, when you and your dog are physically able. My girls have been lacking a father for some years now. I won't have them getting attached to strange men who would but leave their hearts broken." Though she secretly wondered if it was her nieces she was worried for.

"As you wish, Your Ladyship." There was a pinch to his voice that hadn't been there earlier.

Felicity started for the opened door but paused at the threshold, fighting a remorseful tug in her chest. "There is a hip bath and water closet down the hall, and some gauze for bandages. If you require help washing off and dressing your wound, I shall send Clooney in." She stared at the corridor's swirling blue walls, awaiting an answer.

"Why send Clooney? I think the lady in men's clothing—who left me in need of bandages to begin with—should be the one to help me dress them."

Her guest's pointed challenge set her pulse hammering. She stepped out and shut the door behind her, leaning against it. So, he knew it was her that night in the greenhouse. That's what those innuendoes had been about. He'd been trying to get her to admit it. Well better he know that, than her real secrets.

Before she could even contemplate the effect he'd had on her nerves, she noticed Clooney waiting at the end of the corridor next to the stairway, holding her shawl.

"Donal is here," he said from one side of his mouth, biting his pipe as she joined him. "He's in the Doll's Garden with Binata and the little knots."

Felicity slung the shawl around her shoulders, taking the stairs two at a time. "I've already asked Binata not to let him in the greenhouse. He could be planting more fungi as we speak."

Clooney picked up his pace behind her, silent.

"And I don't approve of him being around my nieces. You and Binata both know this. Do my solicitudes mean so little?"

"He has every right to visit Binata. What am I to do?"

Felicity came to a full stop, gripping the railing lest her calm exterior shatter. "Next time, bring the girls inside with you."

Clooney shook his head, sliding out his pipe. "Their hands were soiled. They were busy planting things. You know you can trust Binata. She'll not leave them alone with him."

Felicity's descent resumed. "I would like for you to go to the stables. Stand guard over the horses until Landrigan is gone." She tied the shawl in place at her neck. "And later this morn, I want you to go into town. Wire some of your acquaintances in London. Be discreet ... but find out what you can about our Nicolas Thornton. He's offered me capital, but I doubt without his father's purse he can afford even a flagon of ale. I need to know if he's truly estranged from his family, and why."

Swearing an oath, Nick left the buttons open on the lawn shirt's placket, deciding the union suit beneath could suffice for modesty. Just below his pant leg, his bandage bulged at his knee. He'd done a careless job of dressing the wound, not even bothering with the salve set out for him. But his mind had been preoccupied.

He knew the countess had been the one that attacked him in the greenhouse. Yet there was something beyond that. A familiarity which he just couldn't place.

He winced at the needling desire he'd felt upon touching her soft skin. Was this how desperate he'd become? That he'd be craving the attentions of a woman almost twenty years older than him like he had in his youth?

In truth, he *was* desperate. Coming here was a mistake of which desperation had been the driving force. For two years he'd been celibate while trying to reach his dead wife and baby. He'd disconnected from any healthy human interactions, obsessed with the afterlife instead, in hopes to reconnect with what he'd taken for granted ... to make up for his mistakes by any means possible.

He'd carried Mina's ring with him ever since the funeral. Most supernatural folklore suggested that having something treasured which belonged to the deceased could help bridge the gap. It had just seemed simpler to make it into an earring, so he'd have it on his person always.

But after countless disappointments with counterfeit séances and fraudulent soothsayers, he'd fallen prey to the darker side of obsession, dabbling in the very drug which contributed to his wife's death.

The delusions he had while under the laudanum's influence—though some were macabre and terrifying—were for the most part a sweet and delicious torment. He could touch Mina's face as she kissed him. He could hold his son as he cried with a burst of healthy lungs. Using opium brought Nick closer to his wife and child in death than he'd ever been in life.

The addiction had almost destroyed him. Until his father found Nick at his lowest point—about to sell his body to a reputedly abusive man just for one more fix.

He'd been at a seedy tavern moments away from going into a back room, his mind a confused haze, his body taut and nauseous, heart racked with guilt and degradation. Nothing had mattered but finding oblivion. But his father found him first—came in and laid out Nick's would be supplier with a fist to the jaw. Then he dragged Nick to a hotel and weaned him off the drug. So quiet ... so passive.

So deeply disappointed.

His gentle condemnation still stuck in Nick's mind to this very day: *"I would rather see my son dead, than beneath that man's thumb."* Granted, Nick had been going through withdrawals—muscle cramps, cravings, nausea and anxiety—and couldn't remember the exact wording of the statement. But that was the gist of it. And it made sense, as his father had been beaten and abused by his own step-father years before.

In Nick's case, however, it wasn't abuse his father referred to. It was Nick's selfish and weak choices.

A shudder, laced with shame and revulsion, jolted Nick's spine on the memory. He would never again feel worthy of his family's love or forgiveness. No matter how many years cushioned the downfall. When his father had tried to get him to come home, Nick couldn't face his gentle mother, his aunt and uncle, and most of all his sister and brother. Julian had everything Nick had lost. Willow, the girl they'd grown up alongside and both pined over, was now his wife. Together they had a healthy, growing son and were expecting another child very soon. Although Nick wanted such bliss for his brother, he wasn't a strong enough man not to envy it. Not to be bitter.

So, Nick had run, farther and faster than ever before, to escape it all.

But now ... *blast it.* The dowager somehow knew his name. No doubt she would report his presence to his father, along with his unscrupulous behavior. That's all he needed, for his family to find out where he was so he could disappoint them once again.

Perhaps he could fix things by being charming and asking the dowager for her discretion. It wouldn't be easy, considering that each time he touched her skin or smelled that fragrance she wore, he wanted to be a hell of a lot more than charming.

Growling, he limped to the window with his infernal princess stick. His father walked with a cane and a limp ... all he needed was another reminder of him and how monumentally Nick had failed in his eyes.

His gaze swept across the landscape where a stone fence enclosed the estate, including the stables and henhouse to the east. Outside of the fence, a roof of emerald conifers, ancient oaks, and needled pine trees surrounded the castle and spanned beyond vision, unlike the meadows and clearings in which Nick had grown up.

The Thornton estate had been vast and open. Other than sparse thickets here and there, some harboring hot water springs or ponds, the only greenery other than shrubs grew within a garden surrounded by glass. Yet the townhouse and castle bloomed with life, always thriving with galas, gaming, and social events.

Nick's every action had been under the scrutiny of a thousand monocles. And he'd resented it. In truth, it had inspired him to be a rebel. Why not give them a show, after all? Why not seduce each and every woman with enough cushion within her bodice and purse to soften his self-hate.

After the tragedies stemming from his marriage, he'd developed a new appreciation for quiet and privacy. It would be heaven to live in a natural fortress such as this. So far away from the outside world, in a sanctuary of anonymity with no one to play judge or jury.

Some movement below caught his eye and he saw Lady Lonsdale and Clooney striding along a dappled path toward her greenhouse where the stable hands were polishing the new panel glass they'd installed.

Nick glanced over his shoulder at Johnny Boy. The same young men had come in earlier and carried the dog downstairs while Nick washed up and dressed. Due to Johnny's cumbersome weight, they utilized a canvas stretcher with the edges sewn to casings through which wooden poles were slid. They kept him on the first floor long enough to lap up some broth and relieve himself. Now the pit bull laid on the mattress, content and sleeping on fresh-changed bedclothes.

One thing Nick had noticed this morn: being small in number, the dowager's servants took on double assignations—the housekeeper was also the cook, and the maid served as the laundress. There was no butler, but the two stable hands made good substitutes. In fact, when combined with Clooney and Binata's efforts, the countess's domestic servants had woven their variant talents into a tapestry of proficiency which ran the large estate without a glitch.

At the moment, since they were all busy with their tasks, this would be the perfect opportunity for Nick to have a look around.

He wanted to learn more about this dowager. Such a shock that she'd borne children; her body didn't bode the markings of a mother. Least from what he could tell with her clothes on. Perhaps they'd belonged to the Earl from another marriage.

Regardless ... the woman had an air of sadness about her. A wounded bird knows its own kind. And she appeared to be in some sort of financial straits. She'd certainly warmed at the prospect of money.

And now he was to help her with his grand fortune.

A muscle in his jaw jumped. He would've laughed at the irony, had he not felt so unsettled about the lie.

But why should he be? This woman was nothing to him.

So what if he hadn't a punt to his name. *She* didn't know that. All she knew was that his family was wealthy. That would sustain his claim.

Catching sight of her slender frame as she slipped into the greenhouse, Nick scowled. The lie need only last long enough to gain him access to her colleague, Professor Blackwood.

His first order of business would be to convince Lady Lonsdale not to talk to his family or give away his whereabouts until he could glean the information he needed from the professor. Then he would disappear once more.

This time for good.

CHAPTER FIVE

Nutmeg wagged her tail and licked Felicity's shoe as she stepped out of the chill morning air into the humid two-and-a-half-acre greenhouse. "Good morning, sweetheart." Felicity bent to nuzzle the Irish Setter's cold, wet nose. How fortuitous that the dog slept with the girls three nights ago. She shuddered to think what would've happened if their gentle pet had been roaming the grounds.

Felicity pulled tiny leaves from the setter's silky, spice-colored fur. "My, you're so aromatic today. You've been in the basil again, haven't you?"

The dog's tongue lolled out from one side of her grin. Her petite feet pranced as she tried to wrap her tall, lithe body around Felicity's legs and thighs. The hound had been the runt of a litter four years ago, and was adopted by a cat when her mother abandoned her. Nutmeg now lived under the perpetual delusion that she was herself a feline. It was how she had won her name, as she loved to come into the herb garden and trundle through the spices while her "mother" rolled in catnip. The two animals were inseparable, and an odd pairing considering the disparity of their sizes.

Two yellow eyes peered out from a cluster of orange nasturtium.

"Hello, Dinah," Felicity said. The plump grey tabby pounced out, whiskers and tail twitching. Nutmeg butted her mother with her long muzzle then dropped to her back in a submissive pose. They wrestled around Felicity's feet.

Felicity stood and giggled, trying to stay balanced against the onslaught of affection. With a start, her furry companions bounded off in the direction of the Doll's Garden on the far south side of the greenhouse. Felicity looked over her shoulder at the butterworts, their purple blossoms crushed where Nick had landed last night.

If he was telling the truth, and wasn't working for Landrigan, then the Dark Raven was still at large. But why had Nick been carrying that book on spiritual folklore, if he weren't involved somehow? How else would the supernatural tie-in with his presence here? For him to break in, it had to be more than a passing interest in the rumors that abounded about the haunted castle.

She inhaled a deep breath and followed the shaded path behind her pets, wishing the heady perfume of flowers and herbs could tamp the storm within her.

The greenhouse was divided by glass walls and wrought iron gates into three separate conservatories: the herb garden, where she trudged now; the caterpillar sanctuary to the left, wherein she bred and raised her butterflies and the passion vines that sustained them; and the Doll's Garden, which she had made after her brother, Jasper, and his family had come to live at this castle six years earlier. A few months into their arrival, Jasper's wife, Isabella, birthed their second daughter.

Isabella was built like Felicity—dainty and fine-boned. But she was much frailer physically. Jasper had hoped her health would improve upon their arrival, putting faith in the humid environment and clean air to suppress her tuberculosis ... but Isabella died only months after Lianna's arrival.

Felicity did her best to step-in for Jasper and be a mother to his girls. It was the least she could do. He had come here to help her run this estate; to help her make a living off of his expertise as a lepidopterist who specialized in rare butterfly breeds.

Though some of Felicity's patrons—Nick's family for one—pursued butterfly gardens simply as a hobby, others made a profit charging admissions into their living exhibits. They had earned the title of Butterfly Boomers. It was through Jasper's training and genius that Felicity had capitalized on the said "boom", and came to be known as the most successful caterpillar breeder in Ireland. If only Jasper were with her now to help solve what was happening with the butterflies.

She'd learned so much from him in those first four years. Until he had his stroke and left her angry and alone, locked in her mourning clothes and perpetually grieving...

Glancing through the rain-spotted glass roof, Felicity studied the castle's looming tower. Sorrow mingled with bitterness and surged through her veins. She thought upon the urn of ashes—the sad remnants of a once-functioning human being—sitting up in the highest turret within that dark and foreboding room.

There had been too many tragedies in this castle those first few years. Too much loss and cessation of life. Hell would be a rose garden before she'd let Donal take over and bring his own brand of infestation here, now that she'd finally managed to turn it into a haven for her family. She would get to the bottom of his latest scheme.

He would not better her.

Stepping through the open gate into the Doll's Garden,

Felicity glared at Donal on its farthest end. She could only see his profile as he knelt beside Lianna, the youngest of the girls, helping her place pebbles for a miniature pathway. He was showing her how to curve it around to meet the doll-sized gazebo Felicity had made out of an abandoned and repainted birdcage. A tiny porcelain horse sat in the cage. Felicity had never seen it and knew it must be a gift from the Irishman. Or rather a bribe. Watching him with her niece was like watching a spider teach a fly how to spin a web.

Biting back the impulse to rush into their midst and send him on his way, Felicity swung her gaze across the dwarf marigolds, zinnias, and forget-me-nots that lined the stone walkways, seeking Binata. She found the nanny crouched beside a patch of rosemary plants. Felicity's oldest niece, Aislinn, had her back turned, helping the old woman cut the herbs' branches and tie together their remnants, shaping them into topiaries which resembled miniature trees. Nutmeg and Dinah had found refuge in the leaves beside them, nestled amongst Lianna's collection of dolls.

Felicity tried to see things from the nanny's perspective. Donal had never been anything but kind and attentive to his aunt. And Felicity had no proof that he was behind the bad luck that had encumbered her over the past year. The lost pigs ... the damaged stables ... the missing chicken eggs. All she had was her gut instinct. It wasn't enough to accuse him outright; not yet.

As far as Binata was concerned, Donal came to visit once a month for two reasons: because he believed this estate was his birthright, and because Binata was family.

The nanny must have felt Felicity's stare, for she looked up. The scars on her face—two vertical lines beneath each eye and one perpendicular across her nose which formed a veritable "H"—crinkled around the edges with her frown.

Her gaze hopped from Felicity to Donal and back again.

"I'm sorry," she mimed the words across the way. Her ebony-sheened hand smoothed the scarf tied around her head as she started to stand. A new brooch, silver with a speckling of blue jewels, glittered at her neck. Apparently, Donal had been generous with the gift giving today.

Felicity motioned for Binata to stay put. "It's all right," she mimed back, wanting above all else not to upset the girls.

Her oldest niece, Aislinn, turned and glared. No telling what she was angry about today. Just once, Felicity wished they could see eye to eye—on anything.

Straightening her skirt, Felicity strode toward Donal and her smallest niece, her disfigured chest feeling cold and stiff against the inferno combusting behind her sternum.

Lianna's shimmering blonde braids flung about her shoulders from beneath her hat as she flounced toward Felicity. "See Auntie! See what Uncle Donal brought me!" She held out the teensy horse no bigger than a grasshopper.

"Ah, I see it." Felicity took the toy and stroked the bumps of Lianna's braids as Donal stood to wipe leaves and dirt from his trousers.

He tipped his hat and grinned, his white teeth glaring. He wore a lavender pinstriped vest over his dress shirt with matching cravat and trousers, resembling any other wealthy aristocrat ... on the surface. But he'd accumulated his small fortune by scraping the underbelly of society—dirtying his hands with everything from extortion to gambling. He might resemble a gentleman, but there was nothing *gentle* about him.

Felicity remembered the first time she'd met him a year ago. He looked so much like his father, her heartbeat had faltered. Except that where his father had been pale and thin with a protruding belly out of place on his tall stature, Donal's skin was a creamy tan with a toned build perfectly proportioned to his impressive height. He also had his mother's plump lips and cropped black corkscrews, traits intrinsic to the Nigerian side of his heritage. He was an elegant man ... beautiful in the same way a swaying cobra must be while mesmerizing its prey.

Felicity held his appraising gaze—those dusty gold irises, like a wheat field in a windstorm with dark, predatory shadows behind the fray. He always appeared to be hiding something.

"He is not your uncle, Lia." Felicity flung out the words so Donal could catch them. "Regardless what he says. And it is unbefitting for him to give you gifts when it's not your birthday or Christmas."

"Awww." Lianna's vivid blue eyes slanted up at her from behind straight, whitish-blonde lashes so thick they made her lids look heavy with sleep. "Please, Auntie. My birthday comes soon."

Having always had a soft spot for this youngest child, Felicity suppressed the urge to give in, determined to make her point more for Donal's benefit than Lianna's. Her fingers tightened around the horse. "It's a month hence, little goose. He can put it away somewhere and send it via post when the time is proper. Now go help your sister and Binata. I wish to speak with Mister Landrigan alone."

"You're not my mum, Auntie." Lianna's plump cheeks reddened. "But I still let you give me hugs and kisses." She stared up at Felicity with her mouth turned on a frown—an obvious effort to appear sagely.

"And I am so grateful you do." Felicity knelt. She traced the small, dirty handprints on her niece's gardening apron, tickling her belly until she burst out in giggles. "I love you, Lia. I've known you all of your life. Mister Landrigan hardly knows any of us."

Lianna's laughter clipped short. Her smudged hands captured Felicity's gloves. "Bini's his aunt. Like me, you, and Aislinn. And he knows *you* enough to want to marry you."

"The snapper makes a point, Felicity." Donal's Irish bass reached across to her, making the hair along her nape stiff. "Wise beyond her years, aye?"

Felicity kissed Lianna's button nose and stood. "Do as I say. No more stalling. No more arguments."

Huffing, Lianna turned, her apron swirling with the motion, and tromped off toward the rosemary topiaries.

"Sharp as a cutty knife, that one." Donal watched the child settle between Binata and her sister. Aislinn cast another turbulent glance Felicity's way, then turned back to her work.

Felicity gestured for Donal to follow her out of the greenhouse and into the courtyard where a cool breeze raised gooseflesh along her neck and the blissful trills of birds mocked her foul mood.

She leaned against the hitch wagon that stood beneath the shade of several coniferous trees so thick with moss they appeared to be molting. The scent of pine needles and wet wood stung her nose.

Keeping distance between herself and her unwelcome guest, Felicity used her shawl to hide her right hand as she reached into the wagon, surreptitiously lifting the stockwhip which was coiled up on the squab. She drew it back beneath her shawl.

"A coward's ruse, Mister Landrigan. Making me out to be the ogre."

An amused smile curved Donal's lips. "Ye chose to be selfish all on yer own. Bit insecure, are we, Felicity?"

"I've told you time and again, I am *Your Ladyship* to you. You've long since forfeited any right to call me by my first name. And I shan't allow you to hand out poison to my children, in any form."

"Yer children? I thought they were yer dead brother's."

His insensitivity stung like a snakebite. "I am the only parent they have now. And the only mother Lia has ever known." With her free hand, she flung the porcelain horse at him. "What is this, another bribe to gain her good graces?"

He caught the toy against his chest, that blasted grin deepening to incite his dimples. "Go way outta that. I've no need to bribe. The little skirt likes me enough already. She wants ye to marry me."

"She's too young to know why you're pushing for this farce of a union. I cannot believe the conniving lengths you've gone to in hopes to send me running to you."

"I've been tellin' ye all along. I've nothin' to do with yer troubles. This land is simply dangerous for a woman and her nits—unprotected and unattached. Ye need a man."

Felicity's fingers tightened around the whip.

Tucking the toy horse into his jacket, Donal dug out a peppermint stick from a parchment bag. He slid the candy into the side of his mouth. The end hung from the corner of his lips, glistening white. "Yer takin' a chance out here. There are nawful fellas gummin' to get their mitts on pretty little English skirts for slave trade. These girls are vulnerable. We both know how easy it would be." He held up the peppermint—studying it in the soft light. "Them bein' so susceptible to bribes."

In one fluid, split-second motion, Felicity freed her right arm from beneath the shawl and flicked the whip's handle. Its tail cracked, snapping the peppermint out of Donal's hand without even grazing his fingers.

His surprised gaze followed the broken candy as it crumbled to the path beside his foot. "Powerful fine, Felicity. Ye've improved."

"Not really." She rolled up the leather cording, quelling her temper with the action. "I was aiming for your nose."

Smirking, Donal scraped the peppermint beneath his boot's toe, coating the pieces with dirt. "This might be a bright time for ye to reconsider my proposal. Now that yer becoming insolvent."

Felicity blinked. "I haven't any idea what you mean."

"Your littlest nip told me yer caterpillars be goin' missin'. Dyin' too young to breed or some such."

The urge to call him out for causing this newest dose of bad luck was strong, but Felicity knew enough about poker not to show a bloodthirsty opponent her hand. "My caterpillars are robust and thriving. Lia has a grand imagination. It would appear you do, too. This 'ghost' you've conjured certainly has the girls stirred to a frenzy. But I plan to put an end to that soon enough."

The man had the nerve to look confused. "Yer the one that spread the rumors of hauntings to keep out the world. Mayhap yer own cock-and-bull stories are comin' to life. All I know is it takes funds to run an estate like this. Not to mention the cost of raisin' a family. And if yer not careful, these girls will end up in an orphanage. Is yer pride worth that?"

Felicity winced. The man knew right where to hit her.

Landrigan baited her again. "Despite what ye think of me, I have a care for Lia and Aislinn. I won't watch them starve or be deprived of the things they need. I'll go to the RICs before I let that happen."

Fear surged through Felicity, chilling her blood. The law could never be involved. Though Landrigan didn't know, she was not legally the girls' guardian since her brother never finished a will before his stroke. That was the very reason she had lied to Lord Thornton about the girls being her daughters. Unfortunately, Donal had found out the truth about their lineage months ago.

"Oh, for heaven's sake!" she said, taking up the gauntlet he'd thrown at her feet. "No one is being deprived of any necessities here."

"Not yet. But with yer caterpillars dyin', that'll soon change."

"You care nothing about the girls, so don't try to pretend otherwise. Your only concerns are your aunt and this land."

"Whatever ye think, bird. But it ain't no matter. Without yer business, ye'll have to marry me. Ye have no other way to meet expenses."

"Oh, but she does."

Felicity turned at the velvet-deep scrape of Nick's voice. He limped out from a curve in the path where trumpet vines formed a fragrant hiding place—their red blossoms clinging by their roots along a tunnel-shaped trellis.

An uneasy twinge tightened Felicity's chest as she wondered how long he'd been standing inside the trellis ... how much he'd overheard.

Noting her guest's intensely curious regard of Donal, and Donal's glare of mistrust at him, she at last accepted his claim of not being acquainted with the man. Nick's armor once again glistened in her eyes.

Even using a toy horse for a cane, he still looked virile enough to make her heart flutter like a caged bird. He'd left his shirt unbuttoned and it flapped in the cool breeze, revealing the union suit beneath. A flash of sun-colored down peeked out from the half-opened placket at his chest, matching the hair on his head that drifted in waves around his shoulders. Felicity's fingers curled around the whip's long, stiff handle in remembrance of his naked physique. Desperate to redirect her thoughts, she placed the braided leather cord back on the wagon.

"Bang on." Donal's attention held Nick. "Looks like ye found a man after all. Or mayhap more of a Molly." He sneered at the effeminate stick pony.

Jaw clenched, Nick passed his grey eyes over Felicity once, warming her cheeks, then stepped closer to Donal. She was taken aback by how close in size they were. Although Nick was more muscular—a utilitarian body, created to give a woman protection ... and pleasure.

"I've come to tour and invest in Her Ladyship's butterfly conservatory," Nick said, inches from Donal's face. "And I'll be dealing directly with Professor Blackwood, so don't be spreading any slander."

Donal crushed the peppermint pieces beneath his foot. "Cracker that! Should be an interestin' affiliation, considerin' the professor be dead. Did ye forget to tell him that about yer brother, Felicity? That yer raisin' his nieces in wake of his passing?"

Nick turned to give her another once over. Discomfort crept up her neck, frosting her vertebra like ice-tipped spider's legs.

"I'd be dog wide if ye plan to deal directly with this one," Donal said. "She's shrewd. Popped into existence seven years ago and convinced old Da to marry her on his deathbed. All so she could inherit this pretty piece of land. Isn't that right, *Step-mum*?"

CHAPTER SIX

Nick intensified his study of the widow, making her squirm. He almost couldn't swallow for the snarl of disappointment in his throat. The professor he'd come all this way to see— who held Nick's one hope for redemption in his hands—was dead. Such news cut sharper than the spasms in Nick's injured knee.

The dowager's face flushed, lashes shading her eyes. She wouldn't meet Nick's gaze. Instead, she rushed her gloved hand over the whip, as if debating whether or not to pick it up again.

Remembering how it felt to be on the receiving end of that snapping cord, Nick opted it best to return his focus to Donal.

He would never have guessed this man was the Irish earl's son. They didn't share the same surname, and his coloring alluded to a mixed nationality. Whatever the case, Nick had heard enough of the conversation between Lady Lonsdale and Donal to know that she was being bullied. Perhaps that's why she'd lied to him about her nieces, claiming them as her own—to protect them somehow.

The fact that she was raising those girls all alone, that she still wore black so many years after her husband's death, all attested to deep emotions. Nick suspected she'd married him for more than this property. It could've been to help her hold onto her nieces. Whatever the case, it wouldn't do his cause any harm to get on the woman's good side. Win her trust.

He sharpened his gaze on Landrigan. "Get the hell off of this estate before I escort you off."

Quirking his mouth again, Donal glanced at Nick's frilly cane. "Ye and who's army? Humpty Dumpty's?"

Nick allowed a threatening smile to play over his lips. He'd been in his fair share of brawls over the years. Even in his present state, he could get enough punches in to give this weasel a run for the crown. "Did you not hear? I broke Humpty into pieces. Just like I'm going to do to your eggshell of a head."

"Well, ride yer little pony over and we'll have a go at it."

Nick thrust the stick-horse to the ground and took a step forward on his good leg, clenching the Irishman's lapels. He and Donal stood in place, muscles coiled, staring one another down until the dowager shoved an arm between them.

"Mister Landrigan, you claim you're here to visit your aunt. Then by all means, go spend time with her. But stay away from my nieces. They are off limits to you. Are we clear?"

"Clear as an Irish morn." Donal glanced up at the misty sky and low hanging clouds as he tipped his hat and strode toward the greenhouse. "I'll be back next month for yer answer to my proposal."

Cued by the rustle of her skirt, Nick plucked up the stick-horse and faced the countess. "You're not seriously thinking about marrying that dolt, are you?" She didn't answer, so Nick altered his tactic. "I assumed your late husband was

English, considering his surname."

She stroked the wagon's side. "Hayes was of English descent, though his title was based here in Ireland."

Nick glanced in the direction of Donal's retreat. "So how did your stepson come about, if you don't mind my asking?"

"Binata's younger sister—Donal's mother—was a servant at this castle, years ago, long before I married Hayes. The earl was a very religious man ... and appearances were everything to him. So when his servant ended up pregnant with his seed, he sent her away." She paused, as if unsure she should continue.

"How did she find her way back?" Nick prompted.

"She didn't. She married an Irish fishmonger in Larne who raised Donal as his son. Eleven months ago, Donal wound up here after finding out the truth about his paternity from his mother on her deathbed. Since the earl was his father, he wants what he deems is his birthright."

"Ah. And since he's only half-aristocratic blood, and a bastard to boot, the only way he can have such an inheritance is to marry you."

Felicity nodded. "He's been trying for months to charm me into a legal union and acquire the estate. Now that he's realized I'm not one for charms, he's resorted to goading me."

Nick watched her palm trail the leather cord, impressed with her bravery—the way she'd handled Donal's threats. "You're a master with that strap, Your Ladyship. To which my leg can attest."

Running a finger over her shawl along her sternum—a gesture Nick had come to realize was completely unconscious on her part—she blushed. "You may call me Felicity. You've earned the right to address me casually, considering." Her gaze fell to his wounded knee.

With a dismissive nod, she grasped the coiled leather cord and started down the path that led along the stone fence toward the stables on the lower end of a hill.

Pony-cane in hand, Nick fell into step beside her, concentrating on the birds overhead to distract himself from the jabs in his leg. "So, you're admitting it was you wearing the trousers and jacket the other night. I must say, you're much more approachable in a dress." He regarded her delicate profile.

She lifted her chin. Soft daylight peered through the tree branches and swept shadows across the lines in her face. "I'm sorry for your injuries. I was protecting my home."

"After meeting your stepson, I can see why."

She swept away a lock of hair the wind had captured and slung across her cheek. Judging by the strand's length, it appeared to stretch beyond her waist. Nick wondered what it would look like all taken down, hugging her curves and soft skin like a swathe of silvery-gold satin. His gaze slid further and he made an effort not to notice the bounce of pert breasts beneath her shawl as she moved. He failed miserably. He'd already gauged that the woman didn't wear a corset. He'd like to know what other proper articles might be lacking beneath those mourning clothes.

"So." He reined himself in with the question burning his throat. "How long has Professor Blackwood—your brother—been dead?"

"Jasper's been gone for three years."

"I'm sorry for your loss." He tried to hide his own despondency by forcing his gaze to the roof of trees which thickened to a wall in the distance.

"You sound disappointed yourself." The countess stalled on the path. "Does this dampen your willingness to invest, the fact that a woman now runs the business alone?"

He stopped beside her, curbing the desire to come clean with his true intentions. Only a fool laid his cards on the table without having an ace in hand. "No. I am curious about something, though. You called me 'Dark Raven' the other night. It's the last thing I remember before blacking out. And I heard you mention something about a ghost to Donal."

"Hmm. Surely you've heard the rumors about this place." She melted him with those tragic brown eyes—their soft depth a contrast against the stony gray of the sky overhead.

"I have, but something tells me it's beyond rumors at this point."

"Let me put your mind at ease. There've been sightings by my eldest niece of some shadowy man. Though she never gets a good glimpse of him, she's dubbed him the Dark Raven because his silhouette flutters as if he's made of feathers. She's convinced it's a ghost, and has her little sister believing it now."

"And you think it's your brother's spirit?"

Her expression flashed from startled to scowling in less than two blinks. "Absolutely not. I put no stock in the superstitious sagas of the afterlife."

Nick rubbed his whiskery chin in thought. "The novel you penned with my sister would say otherwise."

"That was a one-time farce. I've long since put such frivolities behind me to present a good example to the girls. They need pragmatism in their lives. Bad enough they have Mister Landrigan pulling their strings. He's either hired some cretin to wear a costume or is playing the role himself." She took up walking once more, casting Nick a sidelong glance as he moved with her. "Contrary to the whisperings you've heard of this castle, there is no one, or nothing, haunting it."

"Tis a shame. I rather hoped there was."

"Why?"

"Macabre curiosity," he blurted the half-truth. "I venture it's more than a passing fancy to you, considering that book my groundskeeper found with your possessions."

A barbed jolt shot through Nick's leg when he put too much weight on it. He stopped in his tracks, digging the stick-horse into the ground for balance.

Felicity hesitated a good three steps ahead of him, back turned. "From what Emilia said, your mother's family came from Catholic stock. Would you care to inform me"—she looped the whip around her shoulder—"why her son would be indulging in something as pagan as supernatural folklore? Or perhaps this is the influence of your father's Romani side? Ghosts, curses, and superstitions?"

Nick stiffened his jaw. "I'm willing to exchange truth for truth. First, you tell me the real reason you married the Earl. And why you lied about the girls being yours."

Inhaling deeply, Felicity started forward again. "Make yourself at home in the dining hall, Master Nicolas. My family and I will join you to discuss our business over breakfast."

As she left, Nick observed the sway of her hips—graceful and unassuming, yet undeniably seductive. He cleared his throat, unwilling to let their conversation end on such a curt note. "So, it's to be a mixed company gathering. I suppose sausage is out of the question then."

She continued her stride, but he could tell by the easement of her shoulders that his comment had had the desired effect. "Feel free to indulge on your own while you await us. You strike me as a man well versed in servicing himself."

The path declined on a slope, and he smirked at her descending back before turning toward the castle.

He needed something to carve.

Nick sat in solitude on a cushioned chair, ankle propped atop a pillow. His hands jittered, itching for creation. His muse had reawakened. For over a year, he'd thought it dead. Each time he drew out his knife to create something, Mina's blood-drenched nightgown tainted his mind's canvas.

Now all he could see was Miss Felicity's face, her delicate wrinkles around a jaw set to an angle of grim grace as she cracked that whip at Donal. Nick wanted to make a rendition of her magnificence in that moment. But his knife was still at large.

Glancing around the room, he struggled to relax. He felt out of place at the head of the table even though the cook had directed him to sit there. He courted the idea of going up to visit Johnny Boy, but his leg throbbed relentlessly. Taking the short staircase just to get inside the castle had been bad enough. He wondered how he'd ever made it down the flights this morning or would ever make it up again for bed tonight.

Clooney had told him he should stay off of his feet for a couple of days. Now he wished he'd listened.

He took in his surroundings. Compared to the dining hall at home, this one was twice the size though much less formal, obviously not here to impress guests. The table appeared to be set for ten, which in Nick's count, included all of the servants. The domestics were treated like family. Nick liked that idea. It reminded him of his own upbringing and seemed magnanimous on the part of Miss Felicity.

The cook had mentioned earlier that breakfast was a casual meal here, implying that everyone wandered in and out at differing intervals until all had eaten.

It was obvious Donal wouldn't be attending. Mulling over the countess's reaction to the Irishman—Nick wondered what their past entailed.

Thumping his palm on the table, he rattled the silverware at his place setting. He'd overheard Donal bait her about dying caterpillars. Nick wondered if it could be the Heliconius butterflies he'd read of in his almanac. If so, his sojourn here was now even more pointless.

A dead professor, he could reconcile. But dead butterflies? That would be the end of his quest, and his hope.

For an instant, he allowed a glint of altruism to enter his thoughts. The dowager was in financial straits. And he had given her false courage with his trumped-up investment plans.

Nick gave the table a final thump, trying to shove the thought from his mind.

This wasn't his problem. Now that he knew Jasper was dead and the Heliconius were dwindling, he shouldn't care one way or other what happened to the countess or this estate.

He ran his gaze over the room again. It was actually a combination of rooms: a dining area and a parlor woven into one. Winged-back chairs and settees curled around the fireplace to form a large sitting area. Generous windows stretched from the ceiling to the floor along three walls. Sheer drapes invited any available light to glaze the wooden floor. When paired with the strings of miniature white electric bulbs strung from one end of the ceiling to the next and the cheerful fire in the fireplace, the room boasted the radiance and warmth of a sunny meadow—not a shadow anywhere in sight.

Children's drawings graced the windowless wall with bright color and vivid imaginings. Some were of butterflies and tulips, some stick animals, and then one grouping of collages made with real flower petals and leaves. Those must have been crafted by the older girl, for they were more sophisticated. They had words scripted at the bottom of each paper—scientific names which suggested they were specimens put on display. Around the hearth, an assortment of dolls sat wearing their laciest dresses with miniature tea cups in their laps.

Nick smiled, realizing that this room, and no doubt this entire estate, had been styled around the needs and wants of the two young girls that lived here. It was obvious Miss Felicity loved them, catered to them even. He found himself curious as to the story behind her dead brother. Did a guilty conscience bid her service as a guardian to these girls? Is that why she felt so responsible for them?

In the right corner sat a desk where a dusty phonograph, its wooden case not much bigger than a shoe box, shared space with stacks of books. Apparently, the music player served as more of a prop than entertainment.

Most of the books appeared to be study related: arithmetic, literary tropes, and an introduction to the Gaelic language. He recognized one—a translation of the French work *The Book on Mediums,* by Allan Kardac. It poked out from the bottom of a pile. Being a study on the theory of spiritism and the basic methods of joining the physical and spiritual worlds, it seemed strangely out of place among the secular reads.

Nick tilted his head thoughtfully. It appeared Miss Felicity hadn't been forthcoming after all. Someone was indeed preoccupied with the spirit realm in this castle, and he'd venture it was her.

Perhaps *she* was the answer. Her brother, Jasper, had surely left behind journals of his findings. It was possible the dowager had taken up his studies considering they had the same blood running through them.

He straightened in his chair as the maid, Rachel, and the old cook bustled into the well-lit room. They nodded to him, busy with the arrangement of fragrant pudding, scones, and jams along with steaming kettles of coffee and tea across the long dining table. From beneath her lashes, Rachel glanced at him several times.

When the cook left the room, Rachel's gaze caught on Nick's earring. He tipped his head and she blushed, dropping a china cup. Leaning forward, he caught it before it hit the floor.

As he handed it back, their fingers touched and she batted her lashes, too tongue-tied to say anything other than, "Thank ye, Yer Graceship."

He smiled at the grandiloquent title—perhaps a byproduct of her Irish upbringing. Rachel was a pretty piece, with green eyes as warm as a spring meadow, bright red tendrils of hair falling from beneath her mop cap's pleated edges, and fleshy curves waiting to be plucked like ripe fruit. A few years ago, he would've already been planning a way to get under her skirts and wouldn't have had too hard a time getting there.

But now, all he wanted was information.

"Rachel, is it?"

She nodded, pressing her shapely lips together as she settled the cup and saucer on the table.

He smoothed the linen napkin where it wrinkled beneath the dish's placement. "Rachel, I'm embarking on a business venture with Her Ladyship. I'd like to buy her a gift—a gesture of goodwill. I was hoping you might offer some insight into her hobbies and personal interests. Could you help me with that?"

Gaze darting over her shoulder to assure the cook hadn't returned, Rachel smiled. "Aye, sir. I'd be happy to."

"I see she likes to read." He gestured to *The Book on Mediums.* "Is the spirit realm of particular interest to her?"

"Well, that one used to belong to her brother. She don't read much for pleasure, mind. Too busy with the upkeep of the place. She could use a good romance or two, if ye ask me—" The maid cut herself short and swallowed hard, polishing some silverware with her apron.

Nick frowned. Obviously the maid knew nothing of her proprietor's dalliance with the pen and the sweeping romance she'd written with Emilia. It seemed Miss Felicity kept everything close to the vest, even from those she lived with; he knew that feeling all too well. He also knew how lonely locking away every secret could be. "So, I should buy her a sweeping romance, aye?"

Rachel traced her trembling fingertip around a saucer's edge, making its cup rattle. "Not sure that would be an appropriate gift, Yer Graceship."

Grasping the maid's hand to still her fidgets, Nick issued his most charming smile. "No need to worry. I shan't tell her what you said."

Smiling back, the maid's features relaxed. She stared at their joined hands, her cheeks pinkening again.

The cook waddled in. Upon seeing them, a scalding fury lit her green eyes.

"I've told ye time and again," she scolded the maid, "not to bother the Lady's guests. Remember the trouble it got ye in last time? There's work to be done in the kitchen. Pots to scrub." The cook snagged Rachel by the elbow.

Nick stood, leaning on his good leg. "I initiated the rapport. She tried to leave but I wouldn't let her. Please … I did not intend for her to be punished."

Rachel cast him a grateful glance, but the cook was unconvinced. She dragged the young maid out without another word.

Shaking off the episode, Nick's attention fell back to the book as he sat again. So the dowager-ice-queen needed some romance in her life. At one time, he could've used that to his advantage. He would've been just the man to melt her. He'd honed his skills of seduction on older women bred of wealth and loneliness. Much to his parents' utter shame, he'd once made a career of fornication, earning gifts of fineries and wardrobes by satisfying the lusts of his adulterous lambs. Vanquishing older women came easily to him. But upon meeting Mina, he'd abandoned such pretense.

However, this widow seemed different than any he'd ever met. Her wounds ran deep. He could see it every time he looked in her eyes.

Where he to regress back to those old ways, just for a short time, that vulnerability could be his way in.

The sound of shuffling boots distracted him as the stable hands came in from the corridor connecting to the stairs, carrying Johnny Boy on the stretcher. Clooney walked behind them with a wide pillow. The moment the pit bull saw Nick, he started struggling to get free, his tail thumping against the chest of one of his escorts.

"Whoa there." Nick laughed. Using the table for leverage, he stood. "Careful with his throat."

"Sit down, lad." Clooney dropped the pillow on the floor at the right side of Nick's chair and motioned the stable hands over to ease the dog onto the cushion. "I told you to be giving that leg a rest today. I can see pain all over your face." The old man walked over to a pine sideboard and started to jiggle a key in the middle cupboard's lock. "You need some laudanum."

"No," Nick answered, more abruptly than he'd intended. Sitting again, he rubbed Johnny Boy's ear while the dog smiled and snorted contentedly. He opened his palm so Johnny could lick it in the hopes to ease his nerves at the mention of the drug. "No laudanum. Johnny is all the medicine I require." Nick glanced up to meet the old man's suspicious gaze. "Thank you for bringing him in."

Clooney gave up trying to unlock the cupboard. He put his keys away and took the seat to the right of Nick so Johnny Boy was between them. "Had nothing to do with it. It was Miss Felicity's request when she saw the boys out letting the dog relieve himself. Seems to think you two need to be together, to heal proper."

Nick smiled, surprised by the depth of her insight. He nodded his gratitude to the stable hands as they left the room.

"I, on the other hand"—Clooney poured some coffee for himself and Nick—"think the dog's better off as far from you as possible. You're to blame for this. Bringing him along for a theft." The old man's watery eyes turned on Nick.

Nick looked down at the dog's injuries. "I wasn't planning to steal anything. I assure you."

The groundskeeper rolled his eyes, obviously not convinced.

"But you're right about one thing," Nick continued. "I very well am responsible for my dog's present state." The admission numbed his tongue, remembering the many heists he'd taken Johnny on in the past. The pit bull had lost his ear trying to defend Nick against a guard dog during one such interlude.

"Don't care what deal the lady plans to make with you," Clooney said between sips of coffee. "I want you gone. I'll have the baggage we found on the hobbie returned to you tonight. Then the minute you're healed, go back home to your family and leave hers alone."

Nick jiggled the loose, velvety skin beneath Johnny's chin. How to tell the groundskeeper that this dog was the only family he had left? He scooted back to the table and pulled his coffee beneath his nose.

Steam drifted up and burned his eyes, making them water. Clooney was right not to trust him. He was lying to his hostess. Was considering seducing her for his own purposes. And that was nothing compared to the sins he'd committed against his own wife.

His future was as dark and bitter as the liquid swirling in the cup. He'd rather enjoyed having other people to talk to over the past few hours; a glimpse into another world which hadn't been tainted by his failings. But he was to always choose the wrong path; destined to be on the run and alone for the rest of his life. He'd long ago accepted those facts.

A murderer couldn't ask for any future brighter than that.

CHAPTER SEVEN

Fabric rustled in the dining hall's doorway, rousing Nick from his cup of self-pity.

Miss Felicity stood on the threshold with a blonde, blue-eyed angel clinging to her skirt.

Nick started to stand with Clooney, but Felicity waved them both to stay seated.

"Lord Thornton, I should like you to meet my youngest niece, Lia. My eldest niece is otherwise occupied. She'll be breakfasting with the servants once the morning tasks are done."

"Of course." Nick tipped his head at the tiny beauty. "A pleasure to meet you, my lady." Something about her eyes, the way her pale lashes fanned to shadows on her cheeks, drew him into her sleepy gaze. He grinned at her.

She crinkled her forehead. "Why are you sitting in Auntie's chair?"

Humbled by the accusing strains of her tinkling voice, Nick glanced down at his lap. "Oh, is this your spot, Miss Felicity?"

Felicity took the child's hand and led her to the seat beside Clooney. "I asked that you be seated at the head. You need room to prop up your leg. Lia..." She helped the child into place. "Do not ask rude questions. And stay to the topics we discussed on the way here. Those appropriate for dining conversations with guests."

Wiggling her nose, the sprite waited for her aunt to walk to the other side of the table and take the seat next to Nick. As soon as Miss Felicity had mumbled a token Catholic blessing over the food and opened a napkin to arrange her silverware, Lia raised on her knees in her chair.

She banked one dimpled hand on the table and the other on Clooney's shoulder then stared over the groundskeeper's lap at Johnny Boy. "What happened to your dog, Mister? He's quite ugly."

"Lia!" Felicity started to stand.

Nick caught the countess's wrist and coaxed her back down. "It's all right."

Felicity stiffened beneath his grasp and he released her, managing only to stretch out the tension between them.

He refocused on the little girl. "Did you not hear of his collision with the greenhouse?"

Her tiny mouth pinched tight. "I mean his ear. Why is there only one?"

"Ah. My dog fought with another dog. Some while ago. He lost his ear in the scuff."

"Lia, from this moment on you are to address Lord Thornton as My Lord or Sir." Felicity pointed to the cushion on the child's chair. "Now sit down properly, little goose."

Lia grumbled and rearranged her orchid-colored skirts as she sat back.

"You might carry a sausage in your pocket next time," Lia said to Nick, nibbling on the scone Clooney had handed her in hopes to silence her inquisition.

Felicity snorted and covered her mouth with a napkin.

Nick suppressed a chuckle. "Should I now?"

"Dogs like sausages. We feed them to Nutmeg. Might save your dog from another's teeth if it has something else to bite."

"Tis right good advice, my lady." Nick spooned some apricot jam on his plate, his lips trembling from holding back a smile.

Felicity shook her head and plopped a dollop of Devonshire cream atop her scone.

"Think you might be done with my pony soon, Mister *Sir*?" Lia's attention had strayed to the stick-horse propped against the side of Nick's chair.

"Needing it back, are you?" he asked before Felicity could scold the child for her intentional butchery of his title.

"Yes. I should like to have a carousel for my birthday gala and he's the only pony I have." She gave her aunt a pointed glare. "And you're the only man I've seen that likes to play dress up."

"Lia, *hush*," Felicity hissed from behind her tea cup.

The sprite stared at her aunt wide-eyed. "He is! He wears jewelry like a girl!"

Nick tweaked his earring. "What, this? It's holding my ear on. You see, the same dog got me."

Felicity's brow lifted on an amused slant as she sipped some tea.

Nick nearly burst out laughing when Lia glared up at him, obviously too sharp to buy a word of it. "So that's why auntie's sweet for you. Because you're jolly."

Nick smiled at Felicity's exasperated moan. Seducing her could be easier than he thought. "She said she likes me, aye?" he asked Lia.

"Nope." The child nibbled more of her scone. "I just know. The way her eyes get bulgy like a frog when she looks at you."

Felicity made a gargling sound, as if she were choking on her tea.

To salvage his hostess's waning dignity, Nick returned to Lia's original query. "As to my earring, I wear it for sentimental reasons."

"So, it's rather a keepsake?" Lia asked.

Nick nodded.

Satisfied with his answer, the sprite looked away and started to smear jelly along the rim of her tea cup. After she'd slathered it on, she leaned forward and lapped her tongue along the sticky edge.

"Oh, for heaven's sake, Lia." Felicity set down her cup with a loud clink.

"I'm eating like the butterflies. With my tongue."

"You well know they do not have tongues. They have proboscises. And your antics are unacceptable at the table, most especially with a guest present."

"You're just cross that your caterpillars are sick," Lia groused.

Nick wiped his whiskers with a napkin. "I should like to discuss these production issues, Miss Felicity."

The countess and Clooney exchanged a murky glance. "That is not your concern, Lord Thornton," she said. "It shouldn't affect our business transaction. Your funding will help rebuild the caterpillar populous." Then she sharpened her attention on her niece. "And where are your manners, child?"

"I left them in the garden when you took Uncle Donal's gift from me."

"Fine then. You can just go up to your room until you find some new ones."

"But ..."

"Dig through your trunks if you must. Surely you have a

reserve of proper etiquette somewhere. Now scoot."

Brandishing a woeful pout that nearly melted Nick to a puddle on the floor, the child slipped from her chair and puttered out of the room. Her ruffled skirt flapped at her knees with each overdramatized step up the stairs.

Felicity straightened the black lace at her sleeve cuffs. "Clooney, please fix her a plate and take it up. She's bound to get hungry from all that soul searching. And then could you go into town and see to that other matter we discussed earlier?"

The old man nodded curtly. He took Lia's plate and lined it with a slice of white pudding and another scone garnished with jam before excusing himself.

Felicity felt Nick's gaze heavy on her face as she gnawed on a bite of black pudding. Even after seven years of living here in Ireland, she still had a hard time tolerating the pungent taste of the pig's blood and beef fat. She'd meant to take a slice of the white pudding since it contained minced liver in lieu of blood. But she opted to save it, in case their English guest was averse to the traditional Irish cuisine, as well.

When she swallowed, the oats and barley scratched her throat all the way down. Sipping some tea, she noticed Nick's attention still heated her skin. "I suppose you think me an ogre, sending her to her room like that." Glancing up, she was surprised to see admiration shining in his eyes.

"You handled it magnificently. I would have been on my knees, begging the little sprite to forgive all my wrongs— imagined or otherwise. She's quite irresistible."

"And she knows it. She uses her charm and wiles to get her way with almost everyone."

"But it doesn't work on you."

Felicity shrugged. "That depends on the day or the hour.

Sometimes, I get too weary to fight her anymore. But weariness is a small price to pay for having children in your life."

A pained expression crossed Nick's features. "It must be difficult, raising them on your own."

Tipping her fork in her Devonshire cream, Felicity licked the sweetness off the metal prongs, all too aware of Nick's intense observance of the action. She stopped and bit her lower lip when it started to quiver uncontrollably. "There are times I wonder if I'm simply too young to have wisdom enough to be their guardian."

He lifted an eyebrow and Felicity immediately caught her faux pas. "I—I mean to say, *they* are too young for me to understand ... to remember how they feel at this age. Perhaps, were they older..." Satisfied she'd salvaged her guise, she let the sentiment trail off.

Nick studied the quarter of a scone left on his plate, too thoughtful for Felicity's liking. "Females only get more enigmatic with age."

"Are you referring to any female in particular?" Felicity goaded.

Elbows propped on either side of his plate, he eased in close, casting a glance to the doorway to assure they were still alone before capturing her gloved hand. "A whip-wielding countess who wears men's clothing and runs an estate while raising her nieces without any outside help. You are nothing if not an enigma."

The roasted heat of his coffee-tinged breath awoke a tingle in Felicity's chest.

Nick was touching her again. *Nick* ... the gallant paladin of her dreams. It didn't help that she'd fantasized of moments such as this. To actually start experiencing them rendered her inept and weak in the knees—out of her element. And to be treated as if she were attractive again, after so long playing the role of lonely elder widow, it melted all her defenses. It was as if he didn't see her wrinkles, or think of her as a declining dowager, but only as a woman.

"Seems the little sprite was right," Nick said, tightening his grip. "Your eyes are bulging a wee bit. Though you look rather more like a doe. Far too elegant for a frog."

He squeezed her hand which roused Felicity from her fanciful musings. She stiffened in her chair.

"Master Nicolas," she sputtered, her face hot. "Release me at once."

He did, but it was a slow and purposeful liberation. His gaze on her intensified as he skimmed his nails across the lace which covered her palm, stimulating her lifeline before he stopped and held the very tips of her fingers. Finally, he turned loose and pulled back to his plate.

All of her nerves hummed with sensation. It left her reeling, that such a small gesture—with a layer of fabric standing between them—could arouse her entire body to such extremes.

As if completely unaffected, her guest slathered more jam on the remainder of his scone. "I ask that you would call me Nick. Only my father addresses me as Nicolas." A dark look crossed his face before he schooled his strong features to a blank page. "So, you're to give Lia a birthday gala with a carousel. Quite a stunning debut for a seven-year-old."

The silver teapot rattled beneath Felicity's trembling fingers as she poured herself more tea. She offered to warm Nick's coffee but he shook his head, his diamond stud casting chinks of light on his neck with the movement.

Inhaling the tea's calming scent, Felicity took up the subject he'd so graciously given her. "Living here ... well, it has some disadvantages. Lia has never had a real party.

Never even attended one. She's been begging for a gala. The guest list will include only our staff and family, since neither of the girls have been exposed to society."

"They have no interaction with other people? Do they not attend mass with you? There must be a cathedral somewhere close by."

Felicity swirled her spoon through her tea. "I have little use for religion."

"You asked a blessing over the food earlier. I assumed—"

"That's for the girls' sake. They are innocent children, and need something to believe in. Adults, on the other hand … too many use religion as a mask to hide the evil that lurks in their hearts." Feeling her face flush, Felicity tamped down her bitterness. "Besides, to attend services would be risky. We've been alone up here since my brother died. No one knows I'm raising these children without a husband. Case in point, what do you know, as a patron, of me?"

"Well, before I left home, you and Emilia became rather close. Though she never spoke of your personal life."

"As I never shared it."

Nick swigged some coffee. "All right then. All that I know of you is what I heard from strangers. In Carnlough, it's said there are phantoms protecting this place. And the story that frequents London is you're a reclusive dowager who breeds her caterpillars here in solitude, with no one but her husband's ghost for company." Nick half smiled. "Rumors that *you* started, I assume."

Felicity shrugged. "It's better this way. Both the cook and my maid are fine seamstresses. They keep our wardrobes stocked. The stable hands are orphans, and have no family or friends other than us. Clooney and those boys are the only servants with authority to leave the premises. They run any necessary errands in Carnlough for me. They do the shopping—buying fabrics, food, whatever is needed. I conduct my business via post. Thus, I can stay here to care for my butterflies and teach the girls their subjects." She waved in the direction of the books on the table. "I feed them, clothe them, love them," she finished. "That will have to be enough, for I made a promise to my brother to raise them. And to honor that, I can never leave this castle."

Nick stroked his beard, unrelenting in his ardent study of her face. Felicity had the passing concern that her wrinkles might be fading, but it was too early in the day for such an occurrence—unless the lotion was getting weaker. That was an ever-growing possibility, considering the source had been compromised.

"I applaud your effort to uphold a promise, Miss Felicity," he finally spoke. "But surely there's a better way. How can this be enough? To never know others their age ... to never have friends or share little girl secrets and games. And you mentioned a thirteen-year-old niece. Why, she's almost a lady. By twelve, my sister was already attending galas, under my mother and father's close supervision. Your niece will be old enough any day to experience the innocent splendor of young love. Would you begrudge her that?"

"I never knew such innocent splendor, Master Nicolas. And I survived." She toyed with the corner of her napkin, listening to Johnny Boy's soft snore.

Nick paused, as if digesting her statement. "I see. You are captive here in your gloom—for whatever reason. And in turn, choose to hold these girls captive as well."

She dabbed a napkin across her mouth to hide her grimace. "As you've been acquainted with us all of one morning, that is none of your concern."

"So you've told me." That pinched quality had returned to his voice.

Felicity fisted her hands on her lap as the maid came in to take their soiled plates. As always, Rachel treated her with a hint of controlled disdain. Ever since the maid's seduction of Landrigan months ago, she presented a haughty air, as if proud she'd bettered her employer. Lord knew it hadn't been much of a contest, considering.

Running her finger over the scar hidden beneath her clothes, Felicity frowned. Perhaps Rachel was hoping to better her again, with Nick. One couldn't miss the young woman's special attention to their guest—calling him "Yer Graceship," ... asking if he needed anything more ... offering to bring him a cheroot to smoke or a pint of stout to drink. Rather like the dance of a bee upon a flower's swollen stamen. Felicity's blood simmered at the spectacle.

If not for her respect for the girl's mother, Felicity would have already cast Rachel out. But Cook was saving funds to send her daughter to finishing school in America in hopes the girl would find some rich beau, since she hadn't the *"motivation or intellect to amount to anything other than a trophy or plaything."*

Cook claimed to only need a few more months of saving. So Felicity tried to cleave to patience. She supposed the maid hadn't done anything unforgivable, other than being driven by desire.

After Rachel left the room, giddy from her verbal exchange with Nick, Felicity stood from the table and tamped her jealousy. Nick followed her lead. He stepped behind his chair to avoid disturbing his sleeping dog as he garnered his stick-horse cane.

"Before we conduct our business," Felicity said, "I must ask one favor. That you honor the secret of my castle. It is of utmost import that I keep the girls safe." Felicity strolled to Lia's drawings on the wall, stopping at the child's latest attempt to sketch a carousel.

"Of course. As you said, it's no concern of mine." Nick settled behind her—far too close. His proximity pressed her skirts so they clung lightly to her hips. His body heat permeated each protective layer. "I do ask, however, that you give me something in return."

Disillusionment tugged within her. She should've known it would come to this. No man offered an alliance without a price.

She'd expected better of Nick, having built him up for so long. She thought he was different—motivated by compassion. Even more disappointing was her temptation to appease him. The battle to uphold this fragile self-respect she'd earned back over the years waned with the thrill of even the slightest touch shared between them.

"What do you ask of me then?" she mumbled in resignation.

Nick's breath surged warm on her nape. "That you keep my secret as well. That you not tell my family of my presence here. Unless you've already sent word to them..."

Felicity exhaled. That was all? He expected nothing but loyalty in return for his own? "I haven't. And I won't." She reached for the wall and her gloved fingertip traced the carousel's jagged lines and squiggly curves along the paper.

"So..." Nick stretched out an arm and banked it on the other side of the drawing, pinning her between the wall and him. "How does your little sprite know anything about carousel ponies if she's never been outside of this fortress?"

Felicity concentrated on the drawing, lest she lose all control. He smelled so inviting ... felt so strong behind her. "Lia learned of the ride when Mister Landrigan brought a picture of one that is being disassembled in Larne. He told her he'd buy the used ponies for her. I forbade it. She still hasn't forgiven me for that."

Felicity found strength enough to duck under Nick's arm

and walk toward the fireplace. She stopped there, squinting at the flames—letting the brilliant orange heat cauterize her rampant emotions.

Nick trailed her, stalling a few steps behind. "Speaking of Donal ... do you plan to marry the wastrel?"

She turned to face her guest. "Now that I have you, I've no longer any reason to feel pressured into the union."

"Now that you have me." Nick stared at her, the blinking fire and the dog's steady breaths playing harmony to Felicity's rapid heartbeat. She had heard of men undressing women with their eyes, but this was so much more. This man already had her bared and was consuming her—flesh, soul, and spirit.

"Now that you're offering to invest," Felicity barely managed to whisper the clarification.

Her companion regarded her lips, warming them with a prickly fever. "Suppose I wish to offer something *other* than money. Would you be receptive to that?" He closed the space between them. Gaze ravaging her again, he dragged a finger along her arm. "You're not at all the stuffy dowager you wish to appear to be, are you? There's passion beneath those layers ... I read enough of your chapter exchanges with Emilia to know the truth."

She didn't step away, frozen by his perceptiveness, but he was only half-right. Were he ever to learn the *real* truth behind her contribution to that romance novel ... he would think her crazy ... inept to raise her nieces. Her pulse pounded against his fingertip despite her discomfort, as if he were a magnet to her blood, causing it to flare toward his touch.

Skirts rustled outside the door and Felicity drew back in the same instant Nick dropped his hand. They exchanged chagrinned glances as Binata rushed in, dark face fraught with worry.

"Miss Felicity, there's been an accident. Aislinn fell from the trees. Clooney is with her outside, checking if she can be moved. She ain't seem to wake up!"

CHAPTER EIGHT

The stable hands and Clooney clambered up the steps, carrying Aislinn on the same stretcher they'd used for Johnny Boy. Nick had wanted to follow them outside but everyone scrambled away so fast—Miss Felicity at the head— he thought his purpose better served apprising the other servants of the situation. Helping them prepare for the injured girl's arrival to the castle. He knew a few things about aiding the wounded, both animals and humans, having learned from his father's example in his youth.

As the rescuers crossed the threshold, Nick noticed the younger of the stable hands, the sandy-haired Tobias, had a very strained and pallid expression on his face. He kept craning his neck to look at the patient, appearing almost sick with worry while carrying the stretcher's front end.

Nick wondered if Felicity had any idea of how that boy felt about Aislinn.

"Sissy!" Lia held her sister's fingers where her arm dangled from the edge of the stretcher. She rubbed the back of Aislinn's hand across her wet cheeks then kissed her palm. "Sissy, wake up. I'll give you water to sip and sing rhymes to you and tell you fairytales. Just wake up!" She sobbed—a nursemaid with sleepy eyes and a heart of gold to match her plaited hair.

It inspired Nick to awe, how that self-absorbed and outspoken little creature from breakfast could metamorphose into the epitome of benevolence without so much as a blink of her impenetrable lashes.

Felicity intervened, prying the girls' hands apart.

"I want to help!" the blonde angel cried.

"You can help best by saying a prayer for her, Lia." Sending the sprite to the kitchen with Binata, Felicity added, "Have the maid gather clean cloths. Tell Cook to boil some water."

"We've already done all that," Nick said, falling into step with Felicity behind the stretcher.

Appearing surprised, Felicity cast him a grateful nod then eased forward to take the hand Lia had been holding. "Aislinn, if you can hear me, squeeze my fingers."

Nick caught some movement between the clasped hands, then he saw the girl's eyes flutter open. They held a pained depth, their violet hue deep as blueberries at harvest.

Felicity gasped. "Thank God! She's awake."

Aislinn favored her younger sister, aside from the fact that her hair and lashes were jet black. Their bone structure and facial shape were similar, but on Ailsinn the plumpness of childhood had surrendered to the fine-boned softness of a young lady. An angry red gash stretched across her forehead, bleeding profusely. Head wounds often did. Yet the sight was unsettling on one so delicate and fairylike.

"The Dark Raven..." she whispered. "He can fly..." Then she wailed, favoring her left wrist.

"She's in so much pain she's babbling nonsense," Felicity said to Clooney, worry tightening her lips. "Is it broken?"

Clooney shook his head. "I believe merely sprained is all."

Nick craned his neck to hear better, but everyone hushed as the girl lapsed into unconsciousness again.

Clooney looked over his shoulder, leading the boys carrying the stretcher up the first flight of stairs. "I need to wrap the wrist, staunch the head bleeding, and watch for signs of brain injury. Which room?"

"The playroom. I want her next to you." Felicity glanced from Clooney to Nick, the fear in her eyes gripping his heart. "We will move you to either Lia's or Aislinn's room on my floor. Though the upper levels have dozens of bedchambers, we only have five that are furnished. Lia will wish to be with her sister for the night, so their rooms will be empty."

Nick nodded and stayed at the bottom of the stairs as they made their way up. Tearing her anxious brown gaze from his, Felicity followed the others.

He hated that the child was hurt. Hated even more that he was already thinking of ways he could use it to his advantage. The countess had nearly swooned beneath his touch earlier. He'd venture that no one had bedded her since her husband died. She was vulnerable now. Being on the same floor as her chamber, he'd have ample opportunity to charm his way into her bed and in turn, learn where her brother kept his scientific findings. Then it would just be a matter of stealing them.

As much as he despised himself for it—almost hearing Julian's scolding voice accusing him of being a cur as he had in their youths—he knew now what he'd been too proud to admit back then: He would never be the man his twin was.

Nick winced at the tug of remorse within his chest. Old habits die hard, and his need to reunite with Mia and his son trumped all else.

The seduction would begin tonight.

The next week passed in a blur of medicines and hushed concerns. Nick groused over his foiled plans for seducing Felicity but had no one to blame but himself. Though his ribs and head were healing up nicely, he won a slight fever due to his negligence with the salve, and his leg worsened. Unable to climb to the second floor to sleep, he spent each night in the parlor with Johnny Boy, dozing beneath quilts.

Clooney applied yarrow and blackberry leaf poultices to Nick's stitches to "strengthen his torn tissues and curtail the infection." Every other waking moment, the old groundskeeper ran into town for supplies or tended to Aislinn's recovery.

Nick tried several times to get up, worried for the young patient. He wanted to assist in some way, but the maid would not allow him to move from his spot. *"Yer Graceship mustn't aggravate his inj'ries."*

Rachel waited on him exclusively, smothering him. Thankfully, he was blessed with reprieves when the stable hands helped him to the water closet set off of the servant's quarters. Or when little Lia scrambled in to pet Johnny Boy—pitying the dog's ugliness and prattling on about her upcoming birthday. She ended each visit with her pert nose held high as she gushed over the bog-pony put up in their stables, convinced Nick had brought it just for her.

The highlight of his days came when Miss Felicity stopped to take tea with him, offering updates on Aislinn's recovery. The countess had so many walls erected around her, it was refreshing to see her show real emotion about something.

Nick was moved by her concern for her niece. It spurred a pang of sympathy and guilt which threatened to overplay his plans of seduction and reconnaissance. Why the hell did she have to be so bloody human?

Even in her worry for Aislinn, Nick sensed tension between her and her eldest niece. It seemed as if something hung there, unspoken. It cut familiar to Nick, as he had always been the outcast in his home. He hated to think Aislinn might feel the same.

Unlike his parents, Felicity had reason to be proud of Aislinn. The collages in the dining hall were hers—as Nick had first suspected. From what Felicity said, Aislinn inherited her father's inquisitive mind and superior intellect. The girl had been studying the tropical passion vines in the greenhouse, convinced the blight upon them would harm Felicity's caterpillars.

It was to that end Aislinn climbed to get another sample of the unusual fungus she'd observed growing upon the caterpillar's fodder. It had surprised her to see the same fungus leeched upon the highest branches of a dying coniferous tree about five yards south of the greenhouse. Had the limbs not been so weak and brittle, perhaps she would have accomplished her task.

On the eighth day, as dusk came to settle in a purple haze throughout the parlor, Nick found his leg much improved and his fever abated. He slipped from beneath the lovelorn maid's thumb while she helped the cook wash dinner dishes, then ascended the first two flights. He planned to look in on the room he'd be sleeping in and, if he felt able to climb to the fourth floor, visit Aislinn afterwards.

While scouting the second level, he came to a stop at the bottom of a dusty and spider-infested stairway at the end of the corridor closest to Felicity's room. As he stood there, looking up at winding steps which faded into darkness on their climb, the hair at the back of his neck lifted. He curved his fingers along his nape to stave off the eerie sensation. Being so isolated, this turret would've been the ideal place for a scientist to contemplate his studies. Perhaps Jasper's notes were up there.

Footprints wound up and down the steps, stamped in the dust—one set small and one larger. Yet everywhere else, the powdery film was intact along with the cobwebs. As if someone made the effort to leave the passageway with an atmosphere of abandonment—a deterrent, perhaps. A deterrent that only exacerbated Nick's desire to explore. He regarded the winding steps. He'd seen the tower from outside ... knew there were too many flights to even contemplate trying to conquer in his injured state.

He was just about to attempt going up anyway when the cook appeared behind him.

"His Lordship mustn't wander any further," the plump woman's nasally voice warned. "The turret stairs are off limits to everyone. They're impassable up top."

Nick kept his hand on the railing. "Impassable. How so?"

"The upmost flight was leveled upon the professor's final request."

"Why? What's up there?"

She scowled. "Nothin' but death, sir. An urn and some ashes."

Meeting the servant's wrinkled gaze, Nick frowned. He wondered if they were Professor Blackwood's ashes. "Scientists are an eccentric lot," he said, thoughtful. "I suppose he wanted to be locked away with his findings even in death." Nick tapped the stick pony on the floor, awaiting the cook's concurrence.

"Her Ladyship is a private woman," came the cryptic response. "A gentleman would respect that."

"A gentleman." He smirked. "That's the one thing I've never been accused of being." Nick offered the boxy servant a nod then strode toward the main stairway. He limped up the next two flights to the playroom, determined he would get the answers on his own later when there weren't any spies about and his leg was closer to mended.

Arriving at the playroom door, he propped his left shoulder against the frame, watching Binata tend to the bandages on Aislinn's head. Clooney had gone to run some errand in Carnlough before dinner and had yet to return. He'd left the nanny in charge of the patient.

Only one lamp lit the room along with the flames in the fireplace, enough to provide adequate illumination without being too bright. The patient had been sensitive to light ever since the fall. Even the slightest glare caused her head to ache to splitting proportions.

Nick didn't see Lia or Felicity anywhere.

"When can I go out again?"

Binata unwrapped the girl's wrist. "Soon enough. Let's see if the wrist is good without it's bandage, then once the headaches stop, you'll be right as a rainbow."

"I need to find the Dark Raven."

Nick dipped his head into the room to hear Aislinn's hoarse voice more clearly.

"He flew up into the branches beside me," she said, staring imploringly at the nanny who coaxed her to lie back on her pillow. "I saw him clearly. He's not made of feathers at all ... he's made of butterflies."

"Hush child." Binata placed a compress on her head. "Ain't no kinda man made up of butterflies." The nanny had a strained quality to her deep, rolling voice.

Aislinn groaned, her eyes closing. "Not actual butterflies. Just their shadows. I know what I saw."

Binata sized up the child with a concerned expression.

Nick could read the doubt behind it. Everyone assumed Aislinn delusional from the bump on her head. Everyone but him. He believed her, considering his family's own experiences with ghosts and the afterlife. Nick's own uncle had been murdered ... and it was his ghost that had brought Nick's father and mother together, and in the end, aided in their falling in love.

Even without that, Nick couldn't refute the sensation he'd encountered while standing at the turret's stairwell moments before. There was something decidedly otherworldly and unnerving about that tower.

And he hoped that very *something* would lead him to Mina.

Feeling a tug on his trouser leg, he glanced down. Lia stared up at him. Assuming her aunt close behind, Nick edged out into the corridor, but Felicity was nowhere in sight.

"Mister Sir." Lia followed him into the hall, her fingers still gripping his trousers.

Wet curlicues draped down to her waist. Her skin glowed pink, scrubbed from a bath. She obviously had something important to say.

Nick attempted to kneel, holding out his bad knee at an odd angle. "Yes, my lady." As she released his trousers, her scent enfolded him: vanilla custard and rose petals—purest innocence. It sent a trickle of tenderness through him.

She crossed her arms. "Now that you're better, Auntie says you and your ugly dog will be sleeping in mine or Aislinn's room tonight."

"That is correct."

"If you choose mine, I should ask that neither of you slobber on my pillows."

Nick bit back a chuckle. "I vow to sleep with my mouth closed. But my nose is feeling a bit drippy ... might you have a clothespin I could borrow?"

Lia scowled viciously. "You can use your earring to hold it shut."

Nick laughed.

"And if my ghost visits," she continued unfazed, "I should ask you be a good host and entertain him. He likes tea parties. Or you may direct him to the playroom. I fear he must be missing me."

Nick turned her words over in his mind. "Your ghost, you say? And what does this ghost look like?"

"Did you not hear my sissy? He has a body made of butterfly shadows."

Nick considered the sincerity behind her eyes. Either she was piggybacking on her sister's description—craving attention—or she had seen the mysterious silhouette for herself. "Oh, right ... right. The Raven. So, you've seen him often?"

"He comes to play every night."

Nick frowned, discomfited by this turn of the tale. "Does he enter through your bedchamber door?"

Lia rolled her eyes. "He's a ghost, ninny. He doesn't need a door. He simply ... swishes."

"Swishes."

"Yes, like the wind. Swishing all about, knocking things out of place. He's rather clumsy."

Nick's jaw twitched as he crossed the line from cynicism to concern. "Has he ever knocked you over? Hurt you in any way?"

"Oh no. He is a proper guest. And he always leaves early enough so I might sleep."

"Hmm." Nick narrowed his gaze. "I don't suppose you've introduced him to your aunt?"

"No, my ghost is too shy to even meet my nanny. He swishes away when she comes about. And Auntie doesn't like such nonsense."

Nick prodded at a knot forming in the back of his neck. "I see. Could you tell me where your auntie is at the moment?"

"She's in the greenhouse. Watching the butterflies make babies. She's to tuck us in later."

Nick nodded. He needed to apprise Miss Felicity of this new wrinkle ... that her niece might be receiving nighttime visits from someone or something she couldn't identify. Selfishly, he welcomed the opportunity for reasons other than just the child's safety: To be alone with the countess in her element would give him a chance to confirm the existence of the butterflies at last—to ascertain if they were the same species he'd come all this way to see ... the mystical Heliconius who could bridge a spirit to the living world, or vice versa.

Tonight, he would get some answers.

"Thank you, Lady Lia." He caught her eyeing her stick pony and grinned. "And thank you for sharing your chamber and your things."

The child clasped his left palm as he started to stand, holding him down with a touch like a feather.

He glanced at their joined hands—hers so tiny and intricate, every little knuckle and every little line a map unwinding toward the future. Then his, so large, so rough ... every callous and bulged vein stalled to an impassable past of tragedy and loss. He squeezed her fingers gently. He always wondered what it would have been like to hold his little boy's hand ...

The sprite released his grasp, slamming Nick back into his childless present.

"See that you take care of them," she demanded.

"Them?" Nick asked, his son's and wife's faces crowding his mind's eye and clawing through his chest.

"My things."

Using the princess cane for leverage, Nick stood against the weight behind his sternum. "Ah. Understood."

"Treat them as if they were your very own," Lia scolded, then trounced over the threshold and into the playroom on a swirl of delicate fabric. As he watched her hover over her sister like a nurturing hummingbird, Nick fondled his earring.

"No, little sprite," he whispered, amending her request. "I'll treat them *better* than my own."

CHAPTER NINE

Felicity leaned her shoulders against the cool glass of the caterpillar sanctuary and inhaled the humidity inundated with flowers, greenery, and dirt. The moon struggled to pierce the canopy outside, gracing the plants and butterflies with random sparkles of silvery light.

Her shoes had been shed. She wriggled her toes in the moist soil, just as she'd done as a young girl. The butterfly brooch pinned to her scarf felt cold beneath her fingers, but she gleaned comfort in its familiar weight.

She needed comfort this night, and a place to hide.

She'd spent more time with Nick over the past few days than her injured niece and felt weak for avoiding the playroom. But each time she looked upon Aislinn lying in that bed with a bandage around her crown ... it stopped her heart to think of what could've happened.

How often had she told that girl not to climb so high? Not to be so inquisitive? Her curiosities always, *always* ended up hurting her. Felicity had nearly screamed when she saw Aislinn inert, bloody, and battered beneath that tree. She'd fallen to her knees, sobbing the most heartfelt prayer a heretic could manage. Thankfully, this once, God had listened.

If Felicity would've lost that child ...

Tears burned behind her eyelids and she pressed against her lashes, holding them back. Lord, she couldn't even think it.

She loved her. Loved her as her own—every bit as much as Lianna. She only wished she could make Aislinn believe that. Felicity battled constant guilt for her and Lianna's easy rapport. She knew it left Aislinn feeling slighted at times.

But the strain between her and her oldest niece couldn't be helped or resolved. Aislinn would always hold a grudge against Felicity for the secrets shared between them. And she would always resent being forced to uphold silence ... to keep those secrets from her little sister.

Felicity had made a promise to Jasper, and the cost of keeping it was her oldest niece's love and respect. Sometimes Felicity hated what he'd asked of her, why they had to stay at this castle. Sometimes it seemed too steep a price.

Felicity eased into a faint strand of moonlight where it glazed a budding passion vine. The fragrant flowers had opened lush and purple just this morning, and already they were shriveling and setting to orange fruit.

It was a trait unique to this genus. Their blooms lasted one afternoon. One day of indescribable beauty before they surrendered themselves to function and practicality.

Perhaps this had earned them their name ... this passion for propagation; a desire to give birth that was so all consuming, it burned like a flame from the inside out until nothing was left but the seeds—the genesis of new life.

Felicity rubbed her scar from atop her bodice, all too familiar with the sentiment.

Although she often fought the bitterness Jasper's secret had left her with, he had left her blessings as well. She could never birth children of her own but she still had a family. And she was grateful for that. If only she didn't feel as if she were damaging them with this isolation from the outside world.

Nick's pointed accusation the other day had cut her to the core. And to use the word captive so blatantly, as if she were a wicked stepmother punishing her unwanted wards. For him to grasp her own misgivings and drag them to the surface ... well, it spoke highly of his powers of intuition to say the least.

But this was not his battle. Nor was it his decision. For heaven's sake. She wasn't about to let a man infiltrate the barricades she'd spent years piling up—no matter how his body called out to hers. However, there was more to Nick than brawn and sensuality. He had wit and a discerning intellect. And any man who would wear an earring for a keepsake had an endless well of depth. She wondered who the earring reminded Nick of ... a past love? A beloved family member he'd lost?

The last few afternoons, he'd listened to her prattle on about her concern for her ailing niece with a patient sort of empathy she hadn't expected. In fact, every moment spent with him brought to light yet another layer she'd like to explore.

Felicity groaned. What was wrong with her? After so many years of solitary independence, why did she suddenly yearn to trust a thief of all things, to open up to him? All because of a drunken heroic deed seven years ago that he likely didn't even remember.

The logical side of her was adamant about keeping her defenses intact. Although having Nick with her during the most recent Raven sighting exonerated him of being in league with Landrigan, she still couldn't trust him.

Especially after what Clooney had learned on his venture into Carnlough.

She didn't know what to make of the information, didn't want to agree with Clooney's summation of it all, and opted not to think of it for the moment.

She had other things to concentrate on. Like how to stretch her wrinkle lotion when the next set of passion flowers weren't due to blossom for another month.

Because of the recent excitement, Felicity had forgotten about the flowers blooming today and missed her window of opportunity to make more of the special face cream. The butterflies' saliva could only be harvested shortly after they fed off of the blooms.

Jasper had been the mastermind behind the concoction which gave Felicity the wrinkles. Before he'd come to stay, Felicity had used makeup and worn veils.

Her brother's jeweled longwings—a family of Heliconius butterflies from the orient—were the unsuspecting donients of the potion. As Jasper bred and studied them, he discovered that the insects supplemented their nectar diet by feeding on pollen—a rare trait for any Lepidoptera.

They would wait for the flowers to bloom, then collect pollen with their long proboscises. When the pollen came into contact with the butterfly's saliva and the digestive enzymes were released, it initiated the degradation of cells in the passion flower, enabling it to age and wither within hours, speeding along its reproductive cycle.

Those enzymes worked much the same when applied to human skin, once combined with a few choice ingredients easily accessed in the forest. The wrinkles—no matter how genuine they appeared—were only temporary, lasting twelve hours at most. They couldn't be washed off with water or even soap. Only time wore them away.

A mixture of the nectar-tinged butterfly saliva could be harvested without harming the insects by using tweezers, beads, and airtight vials; but it had to be gleaned from their proboscis within the first half hour after their contact with the flowers. Any later, and the air compromised the potency. Felicity's shortage of face cream had resulted from her shortage of butterflies. Many of her caterpillars had been dying prematurely before they even reached the chrysalis stage and metamorphosed into adults, so they'd been unable to breed. She'd been finding less and less pupas hanging on the plants and had yet to see any improvement in the numbers.

She'd spent twenty minutes earlier scraping that foreign purple fungus off of the plants—the very fungus that had lured Aislinn into the rotting tree from whence she fell.

Felicity frowned. She knew Landrigan was behind it. He had infected her greenhouse. If she could only prove it before his determination to win this estate got out of hand. Or perhaps it already had. Through some trick of light or costume he'd startled Aislinn from the tree and she'd lost balance.

Felicity's throat stung dry at the thought of him hurting her girls. Protective fury rose within like a storm cloud, dark and menacing. She glanced down at the ground next to her discarded shoes where a set of discarded pruning shears lay.

Her stepson would have to be dealt with.

Felicity's breath caught when the glass-inlaid gate creaked open from the herbal side of the greenhouse. Squinting at the velvet darkness which swallowed the entryway, she could only make out the rustle of clothing and a man's shape—too tall to be Clooney or a stable hand. The gate closed behind him.

"Landrigan," she seethed the name and lifted the shears

by their handles, snapping the blades. "You're a dead man."

"I prefer death by whip over a blade. Less messy for us both."

Felicity nearly toppled backward at the sound of Nick's voice.

"But you might wish to reconsider altogether," he said. "We don't need two ghosts running about to contend with, do we?"

Felicity suppressed her dancing heart. Its rapid pulse had jumped from hatred to contained excitement within one breath. A dizzying conversion. She set the pruning shears aside, picked up her shoes, and hedged out of the moonlight, all too aware her wrinkles were fading. She had hoped to sneak into the castle via the back way, say goodnight to the girls, then lock herself in her bedchamber without being seen. Now she'd have to rely upon patches of darkness to mask her youth.

"Ghosts are non-existent," she said.

Nick's earring caught a fleck of light and glistened in the moon's glow. "I see. It's a subject better left to fiction. Haunted romances, spectral love affairs. Tis all fodder for readers escaping reality."

"Precisely." Felicity stammered, frustrated by the obviousness of the comparison. Her constant avoidance of the novel Nick thought she wrote with his sister was getting exhausting. "Ludicrous and impossible."

"I suppose you don't believe in folklore, either."

"Such as?"

Nick gestured around the sanctuary. "The Heliconius butterflies are said to be a link to the afterlife. A living man's spirit can connect with them somehow, and ride into the afterlife to visit those who are dead. I doubt even your brother was familiar with that claim."

"In fact, he was." She heard an intake of breath. Obviously, Nick hadn't been expecting that. "Jasper wasted many months trying to..." She cleared her throat before she said too much. "He believed butterflies were a metaphor for the soul. That their emergence from entombment within a cocoon was a parallel for human resurrection. For a scientist, he had some very irrational thoughts."

"Some might call that faith, Miss Felicity."

"Faith, bah. More like foolishness."

Chuckling, Nick lifted his good leg and tried to weave around the invasive plants that stood as a barrier between them. Passion vines had a tendency to take over their surroundings. These had formed a labyrinth of curling leaves and stems on this side of the caterpillar sanctuary. Felicity knew the way through the maze by heart, but Nick had to feel it out—no easy task in the dark with a cane.

She offered no assistance, needing time to regroup her thoughts. Taking a seat on an overturned bucket, she scooted it against the glass wall away from the moonlight. After getting her shoes back in place, her gloves followed suit. Then her fingers clenched her knees over her skirt.

Nick had managed to find his way to her side while taking care not to disturb the vines' leaves and their fluttering occupants. He was preoccupied with the butterflies now, glancing across his shoulder at them as he loomed over her. When he turned back, only his full lips and whiskered chin were illumined by a swatch of light.

He pulled up a crate in front of her and took a seat. Its height matched the bucket's so he still remained taller—an imposing presence. "So, you have no use for religion and no use for superstition. What *do* you believe in, Miss Felicity?"

"My own strength and hard-earned wisdom, Master Nicolas. That and nothing more." The lie tasted bitter. She wouldn't dare admit how many superstitions once flourished within her soul, before life experience had plowed them all to chafe and waste.

"And you're convinced Donal is your ghost."

"I am."

"You won't even entertain the notion that it's an actual spirit." He raised his hand before she could answer. "Allow me to play Devil's advocate. Just for a moment."

She forced a huff, having already given up on such hopes. That Jasper had indeed possessed her at one point. That he walked among them even now. No. For there were barriers he couldn't possibly cross. "All right. Who would it be?"

"Your husband."

The mere thought of her husband returning in any form caused a prickling frost to creep up her spine. Felicity shivered. As if sensing her unease, Nick reached out and clasped her hand.

"I'm sorry. I didn't mean to introduce such disturbing imagery." A dragging sensation raked across her features as she sensed him straining to see her. "You're afraid of the afterlife."

"No, not exactly," she offered the half-truth.

"No? Then why are you trembling?" His hand stroked hers.

The friction of his skin against her glove prompted a rasping rhythm in the hushed surroundings. She warmed with a familiar fuzzy comfort. He'd been her support these past few days—a rock. So attentive. Always ready to touch her hand ... to listen. Sitting patiently as she yammered on and on about her beloved family.

Lia had fully captivated the man. He obviously adored children. And why wouldn't he? He was kind, with a generous soul.

Felicity, stop baiting yourself. He's a red-blooded male. A thief. He wants to steal his way into your bed then cast you off for the next conquest.

Nick's flirtations with the maid validated the harsh surge of logic. Felicity knew better than to be duped. To court any nobler motive would only slice her scar open again, start the bleeding anew.

She jerked her hand from beneath his, her elbow thumping the glass wall behind. Waves of hot and cold tingles spanned from her funny bone to her wrist.

She rubbed her arm and the tension stretched between them as taut as a violin's string. Nick sat unmoving—his expression unreadable in the darkness. Only the sounds of their breaths could be heard. It became so quiet that she forced herself to speak.

"My husband didn't die here. Why would he haunt this place?"

"Then your brother."

"You said that once before. You seem determined to make it a real ghost."

Nick's clothes rustled as he pulled out something from his pocket. Hearing pages flip, Felicity guessed it was the small almanac he always carried.

"In the Romani culture"—Nick placed the book face-down upon his lap— "it's believed that after death, any soul with unfinished business can freely retrace its steps to make things right. During this time, the soul maintains the body's physical shape; therefore, the body must remain intact. If something happens to disrupt this ritual, if the body is dismembered or otherwise destroyed within that year, the spirit must find another form and in turn becomes chained to this world. For we must all leave in the same vessel we arrive in. Often, the spirit stays close to the place of its demise, seeking its body. My father and mother had a personal experience with this phenomenon."

Felicity clicked her tongue in feigned derision.

Nick turned the book over, undeterred. He tilted a page into a spread of moonlight to see the words. "This book validates the same belief in other cultures. Perhaps your brother became one with the butterflies when he passed, perhaps his faith wasn't so foolish after all." He tucked the almanac away again. "Your cook mentioned something about an urn being kept upstairs in the turret. Jasper was cremated, correct?"

Felicity swallowed the urge to tell Nick how preposterous his ramblings were. "What you're suggesting ... is impossible."

Nick took his cane and twined a vine around its base, rattling the leaves—an eerie distraction. "Implausible, perhaps. But never impossible."

"But Jasper wasn't..."

Nick let the vine slide back into place, intent on her. "Wasn't what?"

Felicity wound her gloves in knots. "Wasn't the sort of man who would've haunted his own children. He would never have terrorized Aislinn, or caused her to fall from a tree. He loved the girls more than anything in this world. Too much, perhaps."

After a thoughtful pause, Nick crossed his ankles. "Could it be he didn't intend to startle her? He could've meant to warn her. He might have feared she would fall and wanted her to get down."

"Nonsense. This is Landrigan's handiwork. I know it is."

"Well, then he has mastered the art of transcendence. For he's somehow sweeping into the castle at night without even using the door."

Felicity's pulse took a tumble. "What are you going on about?"

"Lia informed me that she's been having moonlit tea parties with the Raven in her bedchamber."

Felicity nibbled the leathery tip of her glove, tasting soil and dust as she fought a wave of panic. "Lia is a storyteller. She must be pretending."

"Hmm." Nick propped his left elbow on his knee, leveling his face with Felicity. "I guess we shall see tonight. I've decided to sleep in her chamber, despite the tiny bed. And I promise you this: If Donal makes a midnight call to that little angel's room, I'll kill him myself. With my bare hands."

Felicity fought the burn beginning behind her eyelids. This was all she needed. Another damnable mystery in a castle already rife with them. "If you experience anything inexplicable, you must go to Clooney and tell him immediately."

The silhouette of Nick's head tilted. "Not sure I'll be able to make the two flights of stairs fast enough. I assumed I would come down the corridor and get you."

"You can't." She touched the fading wrinkles at her eyes. "I-I have trouble relaxing ... I often take sleeping drafts." The lie tasted bitter on her tongue. "I'm difficult to awaken. Perhaps one of the stable hands could sit in a chair in the hall; then you can send him sprinting up the stairs for Clooney, should the fiend make an appearance. I believe Tobias would be choice. He has the longest stride of the boys."

"Miss Felicity." Nick's voice sharpened to a scolding pitch.

Shaken out of her musings, Felicity glanced up. "Yes?"

"Do you think it prudent to invite Tobias out of the male servant's lodge and into the castle to spend the night, knowing what's happening between him and your niece?"

"Lia? I know she's harsh with him ... but he takes it good-naturedly."

"*Aislinn*. Tobias is infatuated with her. And I would venture the feelings are reciprocated."

"That's ludicrous. Those children are not of the age—"

"Tobias looks close to fifteen. I was already visiting brothels by then."

Thank goodness for that. Felicity clenched her teeth against the thought, willing Nick to get on another subject. He was dancing too close to their shared past.

"And Aislinn is a young lady," he continued. "Not a child. There's a romance blossoming under your nose, and you can't see it for your preoccupation with Donal and your caterpillars."

Felicity shoved to standing, moving with such force she nearly toppled Nick from his perch. Her fingers tugged at the scarf around her neck. "You're judging me? You who know nothing about my life or family ... or how hard it's been to manage this estate without a husband. Or how difficult it was to play mother to two girls heartbroken over their father's tragic choice."

"Choice? He died of a stroke. Where's the choice in that?"

Felicity touched the brooch at her neck. "Enough pontificating about my brother." Vying for a distraction, she kicked the cane out of Nick's hand. It clacked onto the floor then slid out of his reach beneath the vines. A flutter of butterflies burst upward with the disturbance, settling again in a matter of seconds. "And dare not presume to tell me how to raise my nieces when you are nothing more than a thief and a liar." Clooney's ugly hypothesis began to glide like a shadow over her rattled psyche. "I know the truth about you, Lord Thornton. You are here to ruin my life."

CHAPTER TEN

Nick stood with surprising grace and balance for one who'd lost his cane. "What the deuce do you mean, ruin your life?"

Felicity stiffened her spine. "You were sent to spy on me."

"Are you mad? I was with you when the 'ghost' showed up last. And you're still linking me to that Irishman. What do I have to do to prove my innocence in this matter, fall from a tree myself?" He was so close his warm breath veiled her face with the scent of berries from their dessert earlier.

Ignoring the strange hunger this awoke, Felicity continued on her tirade. "That article you mentioned ... the one my brother wrote. You said it drew you here. I remember it now. It was about his skill with raising rare butterflies, published by a newspaper in London five years ago in an effort to garner my business some publicity. And it worked, in spades. Your father and brother bought that newspaper recently. I'm surprised they could afford such an investment, after your careless dalliance with some woman nigh caused your family's manor to fold."

Nick leaned in, face dark and unreadable. "How do you know any of this? Did Emilia tell you?"

"As I said, she and I are no longer corresponding. Once we finished the book, she became too familiar ... asking personal questions I wasn't willing to answer. All you need know is I have my own resources, and I know enough to surmise why you're here. This is all a plot to infiltrate my estate ... your father put you up to this, to earn back his good graces by bringing him something that can give his recent investment an edge over the others. A news-worthy story. The truth about the reclusive dowager and her haunted castle of horrors. That's why you brought your blasted book. To either disprove all the theories of specters and spirits and expose my lies, or to prove me insane." Her vocal chords squeezed tight against a sob. "How could you put my family on display like this? You'll break down all the defenses it's taken me years to build, in one sweep of your bloody pen. You may not be working for Landrigan. But you are for your father. You're under his thumb."

Employing a lightning-fast reflex, Nick caught the ties hanging around her neck before she could step away. The scarf scraped her nape—a sensual shackle of lace and thread.

Trying to put some distance between them, Felicity pressed her shoulder blades to the wall, nearly tripping over the bucket. "Master Nicolas!" She caught his wrists where they dangled at her chest. "Release me at once."

"It is *Nick*." There was a wounded rasp in his voice, as though her words had been a slap. "Simply Nick." He nudged the bucket from between them with his wounded leg. Holding her taut by the scarf—completely unaffected by her efforts to force his release—he bent down until their nose-tips touched. "And I am under no man's thumb."

A molten awareness pooled within Felicity's breasts at the proximity of his hands. She could fight him. She had the advantage of an able body. With his gimp leg, if she were to push hard enough, he would topple like a castle of cards. But she was taken aback by how convincing his touch could be, how persuasive his pain when it fell from lips so close to hers.

Clawing within herself ... grappling for her waning resolve, she flattened her nape against the cool glass, putting space between them. "So, are you angry at me for overturning the truth? Or your bastard father for forcing you to win back his love?"

"Your assumptions are dead wrong, *Your Ladyship*." Nick's deep voice rolled through her like a rumble of thunder. "And do not disrespect my father. He rescued me from laudanum. In spite of how I'd shamed him, he helped me break free. He has no idea I'm here, that I snuck into your greenhouse like a fool ... seeking forgiveness from my dead bride through some preternatural butterflies. And he's been a loyal patron to you, even during his near loss of the family business. He deserves your respect for that, if nothing more."

Nick released her scarf and his features appeared strained in the dimness, as if just realizing the confession he'd sandwiched between the noble defense of his father. Felicity watched him, awed. This was why he carried the almanac. Why he was drawn to the butterflies.

Clooney had been terribly mistaken. Nick was here because he somehow thought he could make peace with his own ghosts. Make amends for some past mistake, whatever it was. But what a sad, hopeless way to go about it.

She wanted to help him, to comfort him ... but did she dare?

As if reading her thoughts, he murmured. "I would ne'er put you in the public eye, nor hurt you or your girls." He lifted her gloved fingers to his chest.

She fell into the scent of his skin—leather and rain. Her staccato breaths hit his face and rebounded into hers in a smothering rush of moist heat as he drew her closer. She didn't refuse him, but she did turn her head.

"Trust me," he whispered in the ear closest to his mouth.

"Trust you? I-I don't even know you," Felicity said, trying to distance herself from her body's melting betrayal.

"All you need to know is that I understand wanting to hide away from the world better than anyone could." His lips skimmed her earlobe—the gentlest of touches.

She gasped at the soft contact. All these years she'd longed to thank him ... to touch him. To tell him how he'd changed her life. How he'd given her the means to escape a hopeless life and find her own haven. She could never say the words ... never admit it aloud. But she could give him this moment, a silent offering of gratitude. Against her better judgment, she turned into him and tilted her face, pressing their mouths together. She broke their clasped hands and reached for him, fingers brushing across his shoulders to sculpt the ripples of muscle hidden beneath his clothes.

His lips parted on a stunned breath, and she drank of berries and maleness and heat. His beard tickled her skin— leaving delicate traces of sensation like a caterpillar's silken stream upon a leaf. Her hands wove through his hair and she wished her gloves were off so she might feel the strands there, too. Insistent yet gentle, Nick trapped her chin to shape her mouth to his, coaxed her tongue to touch his. He moaned.

She felt his potency building—the tense coils of his fingers around her jaw, the tautening of muscles in his nape and shoulders as he held himself in check. His fingers skimmed down her neck.

"You're silk," he mumbled, a sentiment filled with wonder. His hand trailed further, loosening the scarf at her collarbone. The warmth of his touch permeated the fabric and seeped into her scar like a living salve.

She arched into him with a whimper and he smiled—a scintillating curl of lips flush with her mouth. Sweeping more whisker-rough kisses across her jaw, he allowed his palm to traverse her clavicle. His fingers skimmed the bodice's neckline—only inches away from the tip of her scar hidden underneath—her hideous deformity.

Felicity snapped into action. "Nick ... stop!" She pushed him backwards.

He tried to salvage his stance but his leg gave out, sending him sprawling into the passion vines below.

"You pushed too far," she scolded from above.

"You're the one who pushed." Entangled in ivy and flat on his back, Nick winced from the ache in his jostled bones and the agonizing reminder of torn muscles and screaming nerves from wounds not yet healed.

She straightened her clothes and fondled her scarf. "Are you hurt?"

"No more than I already was." His pride especially. Her accusations of him being under someone's thumb had cut too close to home; it had sliced so deeply, he'd nearly lost his mind. By God, the woman riled him into confessing everything about Mina and his reason for being here. She now knew he was an addict *and* a superstitious fool.

He couldn't believe all he'd said in that bumbling mind spill, not to mention the clumsy way he went about it. But for her to kiss him afterward ... where had that reaction come from? A place of pity? If so, it had been short-lived, because the moment turned into something completely unexpected. Something intimate and binding. She had to have felt it, too.

He focused on her, sure that he saw stars floating over her head. After a few hard blinks, they came into focus as a dozen butterflies fluttering around her with moonlight gilding the edges of their wings, filmy and transparent.

Lord, they were beautiful. Their color spots—red, lavender, and gold—stood out like embedded jewels on the glasslike splay of their wings. Only one word could describe these creatures: *celestial.* Surely there must be something to the folklore. Felicity had as much as admitted that Jasper believed it. Now all Nick had to do was convince her to let him read the late professor's journals.

Peeling away curly stems and leaves from his clothes, Nick concentrated on nothing but Felicity's face. She hadn't yet noticed that she stood in an errant strand of light. She'd made an effort to stay hidden earlier. Now that he could truly see her, the moon's glow seemed to soften her wrinkles, coloring her even lovelier than before.

Felicity offered a gloved palm to help him stand. He considered pulling her down on top of him for a closer look but waved her off instead.

"Allow me *some* dignity." He found his cane, and his entire body ached with the effort to stand, yet it was nothing to the taste of Felicity still heavy on his mouth.

He wanted more. He wanted her naked and wanton beneath him, begging him to satisfy her. He'd bet his sorry life this woman hadn't been pleasured by a man in years. He recognized the ravenous tremors of her flesh beneath his mouth and fingertips ... the way she arched into him, clung to him as if her very breath depended on the completion of that one act.

There was an emptiness deep within her that made him feel necessary. It had been so long since he'd felt needed by anyone other than Johnny.

"I did not intend for you to fall," she said, disrupting his inner musings.

He stood and fought the urge to snarl. She'd retreated

into the shadows again. "Least you finally got my name right."

"About what happened..." She stepped around him to lean over the vines, searching each leaf with her back turned.

"You mean the kiss you initiated?" At his mere mention of it, she nearly toppled over into the ivy herself.

She regained composure and shook her head. "It gets lonely here; and I've been so anxious of late. You were kind and listened. I-I felt gratitude, and let my defenses down, you must understand. It will not happen again. Nor will we speak another word of it."

Nick bit back a growl. He had a mind to oblige her; to wrap her in his arms and show her how delightful an evening without words—with only touches and sighs—could be. A jab shot through his ribs, reminding him if he tried anything else, he'd be risking paralysis. Damn his uncooperative body.

She wound across the enclosure, following the labyrinth of vines.

"What are you doing?" he asked, lagging behind her with his cane leading.

"The Heliconius are most active this time of night. If all goes well, they're going to mate. Unless you've ruined it with your buffoonery."

"*My* buffoonery. You were the one so afraid to give in to a moment of abandon that you shoved a wounded man into a nettle of thorns and briars."

Felicity glared at him over her shoulder, and he saw her again—exposed and unkempt in a spill of moonlight. Long, silvery strands of hair had fallen from her bun and framed a face where there was barely a wrinkle in sight. Was it that unfinished kiss wreaking havoc with his imagination? His desire painting her in a softer bias?

"There are no thorns in passion vines," she hissed.

"But there are thorns aplenty in passion. And you fear getting pierced by them."

She paled in the hazy glow. "I need to study my butterflies' breeding cycle. It is private. So please leave."

"These butterflies are the very reason I'm here. You'll have to physically drag me out. Think you have the muscle to do it?"

Felicity held silent, a defeated scowl upon her face.

A sporadic rush of movement along the vines claimed their attention. Along a slim, twisting tendril of green, two butterflies climbed atop one another, slapping wings in a heady rhythm.

"They're mating?" Nick asked, intrigued by the spectacle.

"They are fighting," she answered.

Nick grinned as she eased down on her knees for a closer view.

"Their courting rituals aren't so different from those of humans, then," he teased. He imagined Felicity's eyes rolling—a mannerism he'd seen tied to that petulant flick of her head.

"They are both males." Her voice strained to a whisper. "They're fighting over *her*." Careful not to disrupt the event, Felicity pointed to a cocoon hanging by a silken thread on a leaf. The casing was almost as transparent as their wings. "She has released her pheromones to attract them."

"But she's not yet hatched."

Felicity glanced up at him again, her pretty mouth smirking. "Hatched? She's not in an egg. That is her pupa."

Nick knelt to one knee so they were almost eye level, using the stick-horse for balance. He grinned back. "Right. Where she morphs into her adult form. And she's not there yet, or she would've already broken free. Their timing seems a bit off."

Felicity studied his face. "It has nothing to do with timing. The attraction is so intense they cannot refrain or wait a moment longer once the process has begun."

Her lower lip glistened in the moonlight. Nick thought upon the taste of her. How the flavor had smoldered between them ... an ember that could've ignited a blaze hot enough to burn down the surrounding forest.

She might not want to talk about that bloody kiss, but talking was the last thing he wanted, too. He wanted to sample her lips again. And he wanted it *right damn now.*

She still held his gaze, so he leaned in. Her chin tilted up as if to surrender, but at the last minute the two butterflies broke free in a distracting rush of movement.

Nick cursed beneath his breath then watched one of the insects flutter to the other side of the room, defeated. The vanquisher took his place atop the cocoon. Nick assumed the male would wait for the female to emerge. Instead, the insect penetrated the exoskeleton of his mate's cocoon with the tip of his abdomen.

"Impatient little crank, isn't he?" Nick glanced over Felicity's shoulder, catching a hint of her citrus-spiced scent. He debated if burying his nose in the hair bundled at the back of her neck would be worth the beating that would ensue.

"He knows that heaven's waiting beneath that calloused exterior, and he'll stop at nothing to get at it." Felicity spoke with a far-away reverence, as if she'd fallen into a trance.

"Poor deluded fellow," Nick mumbled.

Felicity didn't seem to hear his sarcasm. She crept forward on hands and knees, watching as the female emerged from her pupa. Even as the fragile creature began to unfold and dry her wings, she remained linked to the male. Nick had never seen a more profound depiction of how all-consuming the need to merge with another soul could be.

His awareness of the countess heightened, even more than when he'd had her pinned to the wall. He admired the curve of her neck, the swan-like turn of her profile in the dimness as she watched, mesmerized by the phenomena.

She fascinated him. This delicate lady with the mind of a sage, the body of a seductress, and the soul of a nurturer, all wrapped within a shell as tough as granite.

"In the morn, she shall be flying." Felicity's voice still had that ethereal quality. "She'll be flying ... and inhabited with new life." At the end of the statement, her vocal chords released a plaintive rasp—an audible ache.

"Are you all right, Miss Felicity?" Nick grasped her shoulder, but she raised to her feet, forcing his release.

"You asked earlier what I believe in? I am not blind to the creation around me. It begs rumination ... such exquisite loveliness boasts an artist's touch. I do believe in a higher power. I simply feel that at times, we humans are forgotten. Set aside for the brighter and more beautiful aspects of His handiwork." She brushed off her skirts, still facing the butterflies as Nick stood up behind her.

The back of her hand lifted, wiping something from her cheek. "When I was a little girl, I spent every waking moment outside with my brother, searching for bugs and plants and flowers." Her words drifted on a far-away tremor, as if she were lost to the memory. "Until one day, I saw a creature that appeared to be all three. Wings the shape of leaves, colors so vivid they rivaled any blossom, all springing up from the body of an insect. It was a butterfly ... and I wanted to be one. Oh, how I prayed to be something of such exquisite design. When Jasper told me I would never burst from my cocoon, that my metamorphosis was already complete, I cried for hours on end to know I would never have wings. My mother gave me this brooch"—she touched the glittery pin at her neck— "to tender my heartache. But wearing it was never the same as seeing wings splay out from behind my shoulders. Never the same as being a butterfly myself."

Nick felt the need to contribute, to keep her talking before she realized her barriers were down. "So, you were the superstitious one. Not your brother."

She shrugged. "Funny, how life ... and death ... changes a person."

Nick raked his cane's tip along the ground, humbled by that truth and this glimpse into the sacred place where her little girl fancies still lived. She was beautiful and fragile in her soft reminiscing, all aglow with dreams and moonlight. It had been worth him spilling his heart to her, if this was the result of that moment of vulnerability. He squeezed the plush horse beneath his hand to stave a blinding rush of compassion, overcome by the communion between them. By the alikeness of their souls.

Composing himself, he spoke. "What if there were someone who could give you your wings, Miss Felicity? Would your faith be renewed?"

Her gown rustled as she turned to him in the darkness.

A moment of intense unspoken emotion passed between them as they held a stare.

"Not only would such a person have my faith. They would have my heart."

Silence wreathed the moonlit chamber.

Nick made a move toward her but Felicity bounced to life. "'Tis late. I should go inside. The girls are awaiting me."

"May I walk you to the castle?"

Felicity fell back into the shadows. "I prefer to walk alone." She stooped to scoot the pail and crate back into their perspective spots, her shell in place once more—aloof and blunt. "I suppose I'm correct in assuming you never meant to invest in my business? You must be cut off from your father's funds after your falling out."

Nick helped her with the crate, then glanced outside where mist and stars draped the turret. Her cold abruptness reminded him he was a temporary guest, only welcome if he could offer financial aid. The shame of his lie shocked him out of his emotional euphoria like a cold splash of water. "Have you no money left of your husband's estate?"

"Most of it went to debts he'd accrued before he died. For the past three years we've been living off of my butterflies and livestock. But no matter. It isn't your—"

"It is my concern," he growled, interrupting her. "We can make a trade. If you let me read Jasper's journals, I'll repay you. I can get funding. Just give me a little time."

Felicity grew quiet as she hung the pruning shears on a standing hook next to the wall. "And how would you win this grand purse? By stealing it, like you no doubt did that book you're so fond of?"

Nick's skin heated at her blasted perceptiveness. That's exactly what he planned to do. He would need some means to fund his trip out of Carnlough anyway, once he healed enough to leave the castle. He would need something to tide him over until he found a new location. "I steal mostly from the rich. Those who won't miss a pearl here or a ruby there. Or sometimes, I take things no one will miss at all. Junkets."

"Like an arthritic, knotted up bog pony? What appears to be junk to you, Master Nicolas, might be their heart's dearest treasure. Sentimental value. One cannot put a price to that." Her gaze fell on his earring in the same instant she touched her brooch.

He felt as if he shrank three sizes. "A man has to make a living," he said—a last ditch effort to save face.

116

"Yes. I daresay he does. Even at the expense of another man's misery."

Her high and mighty manner left an acrid aftertaste. "I wouldn't think a woman who holds her nieces hostage would have the brass to accuse anyone of bringing people misery." He regretted saying it the moment it slipped from his lips.

The air frosted between them, and all the progress they'd made this night crumbled at his feet like shattered ice.

"Goodnight, *Lord Thornton*," Felicity said.

Clenching his jaw, Nick left her where she stood without looking back.

CHAPTER ELEVEN

The door creaked as Nick stepped into the dark chamber. He swayed—dizzy from his indulgence in bourbon, still tasting liquor at the back of his tongue. He mentally questioned why no fire burned in the fireplace, why no lamp was lit to greet him.

Shutting the door, he stumbled along until his foot kicked something. The lump moaned and moved against his boot tips. An odor—sickeningly familiar—stung his nostrils. The scent of rust and copper. He stalked to the window, throwing open the sashes to bid moonlight over the surroundings. Upon turning back around, he crashed to his knees on the hardwood floor.

"Oh ... Lord, no." He crawled toward the whimpering body where a shiny pool of liquid reflected his movements in the half-light. "No, no, no. Mina..." He reached out with a trembling hand to stroke his wife's back. She was face down, but dread stayed him from turning her over.

His carver's knife laid next to her, its blade sticky and glinting red in the moonlight. An empty bottle rolled away at the touch of Nick's hand. The words Opium Tincture *came into view on each revolution.*

"I tried to get him out." Mina's words were weak and

muffled—her face buried in her hair as it was. She sobbed. "He's still crying inside of me." She brought her blood-stained hands up to her ears, covering them. "Make him stop crying!"

Battling a hot flash of nausea, Nick gently eased her onto her back. Blood had caked on her gown's skirt between her thighs.

"Mina, what have you done?" He wailed, already knowing. Her pale face became a blur of white with black smears in place of her eyes, a subtle transformation until her features melted back to clarity to become Felicity's: flawless and youthful. Her tragic eyes stared up at him, unblinking.

She reached for him, her abdomen sliced through, seeping blood. A pair of butterfly wings appeared, swishing along the floor behind her shoulders. "Help me..." she begged. "Please, help me."

The wings swished again.

Aghast, Nick shoved backward and tried to stand. His feet slipped in blood and he fell, a spinning fall which cast him in a fetal heap upon the billowing softness of his sheets.

With a jolt, Nick sat up, gasping—his nightshirt soaked in a clammy sweat, his bare feet tangled in blankets and bedlinens. Darkness veiled his surroundings. He shivered, anticipating the convulsions and sneezing. They always came next.

His breath hitched as he heard the swishing of wings against the floor again. So, he hadn't imagined that?

Johnny Boy whined and nudged Nick's leg with his cold, wet nose, grounding him. Nick inhaled deeply. The scent of roses and vanilla eased through him as he remembered where he was.

Lianna's room.

He wasn't coming off of an opium high at all. He'd been asleep.

"Mina." He groaned, scraping his face with his palm. How he wanted to forget. It had been months since the memory had taunted him in the guise of night terrors.

Though this one was different than the others. Somewhere within the fuzzy dredges, Felicity had appeared. Gutted and winged.

Nick threw off his sheets.

Why? What could the parallel be between her and his wife?

Guilt.

His harsh accusation of earlier came back to slap him: "I wouldn't think a woman who holds her nieces hostage would have the brass to accuse anyone of bringing people misery."

His fingers tightened around the pillow beside him. He shouldn't have spoken to her that way. She'd only been trying to grant him some wisdom, no doubt hard-earned by her own mistakes. She wanted him to see the selfishness of his choices. And she was right. The little pony he stole had belonged to an elderly couple. And they no doubt loved it just as much as he did Johnny. But he'd really only borrowed it. Planned to return it all along.

Felicity didn't understand. He needed to steal. The rush of a heist, however small, filled his loneliness ... gave him power over an addiction that even now courted him with the promise of amnesiac nirvana. Poverty had a way of making a man forget his resolutions—especially the tender, recently acquired ones. Each and every day he craved a substitute for the opium.

His fingers slid to Johnny Boy's head. During his recovery, Nick had found company and solace in the pit bull. So many nights, when the laudanum called, Nick sat up and told jokes to Johnny. The dog would listen intently and laugh in that clown-like way, his black lips drawn up nearly to his eyes. Invariably, his enthralled attention carried Nick through until the temptation passed. Other times, when Nick would wake with a start from a nightmare, the dog's snores would lull him back to sleep. The sound was more of a sedative than a dreamy drizzle on a rooftop.

Johnny Boy's companionship had granted Nick the strength to stay away from the drug during his recovery. But over the past few days, Nick had found himself craving a new kind of companionship: the purr of a voice, soothing and feminine yet biting with a wicked wit ... the touch of a hand soft as rose petals yet strong enough to crack a whip ... eyes as brown and glossy-deep as a polished mahogany chest, and holding just as many fragile secrets.

Tonight, he'd seen that Felicity's shell wasn't impervious at all. And he'd rewarded her for sharing that vulnerability by being a pompous brute. No wonder she'd thought him in league with Donal. Nick had the same self-serving motivations as the Irishman, in many ways. He'd been planning to seduce Felicity for his own purposes from the very beginning.

Well, no more.

This attraction ... connection ... whatever it was he felt for her was very real, and it begged exploration if for no other reason than his own peace of mind.

He eased out of the small bed. Johnny Boy smacked his lips and stretched out across the mattress, obviously pleased to have the extra space.

Nick pulled his trousers on beneath his nightshirt—surprised at how much better his leg felt. After fastening his waist's clasp and tucking the shirttail in as best he could, he felt around in the darkness for the stick-horse he'd propped next to the nightstand.

He wasn't sure how much time had elapsed since he'd come to bed. He hoped Felicity was still up. Because he wouldn't sleep another wink until this was settled between them.

Felicity slipped into the cool folds of her chemise. The brush of linen raised gooseflesh along her sensitized skin. Having just returned to her chamber after washing in the hipbath, she smelled of flowers and orange blossom soap.

She contemplated whether to pull the pins from her hair or just fall into bed and give herself over to nocturnal oblivion. Her soul ached from what Nick had said in the greenhouse, and she wanted to forget it all, if only for a little while.

Her nieces meant everything to her. She yearned to do right by them. But thus far, she'd failed miserably. Her eyes filled with tears as she remembered earlier when she'd tucked them into the playroom after prayers.

"Please Auntie..." Lianna had begged. "Lay abed with us. Tell us a story."

Coaxing Nutmeg and Dinah off the bed to make room, Felicity had crawled beneath the covers between the two girls. Touching their bare feet with hers, she curled her toes around theirs. The blanket where the animals had laid smelled of fur and spices. "What story, Lia?"

"Tir-Na-nOg."

Propped on pillows, Felicity wove her fingers through both of the girls' hair, an action that had always soothed her. "Ah. The Land of Ever Young."

Beaming, Lianna closed her eyes. Her lashes fringed the top of her cheekbones like sandy-blonde ferns. Felicity shifted her gaze to Aislinn's and found her older niece studying her intently, waiting.

"In Tir-Na-nOg," Felicity murmured, her forefinger tracing the edge of Aislinn's bandage along her forehead, "the leaves never wither or die. The trees are always green. One never trades the scent of blossoms for stale snow or mildewed moss. It is spring forever, and anyone who is fortuned enough to live there will never age."

"Like you, Auntie," Lianna whispered.

"Dear child. I'm aging constantly."

"But your wrinkles fade every night. You become young again."

Aislinn intensified her glare at Felicity and tightened her jaw as if struggling to hold her mouth closed. An uncomfortable heat gathered in the base of Felicity's throat. "I've explained that to you, Lia. I only look different because the light is dimmer and your eyes are sleepy."

Lianna yawned—her breath tinged with milk and mint leaves. Her lashes remained shut. "All right. More, Auntie. Tell me of their dishes and clothes."

Felicity tore her gaze from Aislinn's accusatory frown. "Tir-Na-nOg has a stream gurgling through the green hills. The water is magic, and can be spun into crystal threads so shimmering and fine they resemble crushed diamonds. The fairies who live there wear gowns and suits made of the special, sparkling fabric. And when they are hungry, they eat off of solid gold lily pads and drink wine out of silver-lined tulips."

Lianna's tiny snore preempted the rest of the telling. Felicity turned to find Aislinn's deep blue eyes boring into her face.

"Now that your sister is sleeping, Aislinn, tell me of the Dark Raven. You're convinced you saw him in the tree with you, that he's made of butterfly shadows?"

Aislinn rolled to her back. She drew the sheets to her chin and looked up at the sheer canopy. "I think it's father."

Felicity's throat clenched shut. "You know that is impossible, dearheart."

"Only to someone so narrow-minded as you."

Felicity met her niece's turbulent gaze. Every time she looked at this older child, she saw Jasper—the dear brother who had come back into her life after so many years only to fade away again.

It was in part Aislinn's features and coloring that brought to mind his image ... but so much more. The speckling of freckles on her nose which crinkled when she smiled ... the eyes that opened to wonder and fascination, then in a blink shuttered, holding back a savant's temper. And the hair that when brushed swirled across her shoulders and back like a starless sky. All of these were reminiscent of Jasper.

Even more, they shared the same thought processes, the same amenable mind—so open and willing to believe the impossible. Felicity often wished she hadn't lost that ability herself. Though it was hazy, she did remember a time...

Perhaps these likenesses were what made it more difficult to be close to her older niece. Felicity feared, were she to let down her defenses and need Aislinn too much, she would vanish from her life, just like Jasper.

"I shall tell you what I think," Felicity said, trying to banish the tension between them. "I believe Mister Landrigan is playing games with us. Games that have gone too far. When he left the other morning, he told Binata to contact him immediately should we have any *episodes*. How would he have known there were to be any episodes lest he planned them himself? He's toying with us. And you need to accept that. You have your sister making up stories about the Raven now."

"Of course you would be concerned for Lia. All she need do is invent another imaginary playmate and you analyze her every move. But you never listen to me." Aislinn sat up, the sheets tugging against Felicity's torso with the movement. "Every night when you pray with us, you never mention Father."

Felicity's lips pressed tight at the accusation.

Aislinn scowled fiercely. "It doesn't matter. I do. In my private prayers. And now they've been answered. I've tried to tell you for months. I think I have found a way to bring him back to us. You ignored me. So I took care of it on my own."

Balancing her weight on her elbow, Felicity grasped her niece's hand. "What do you mean by that, Aislinn? Have you been visiting the turret again? You know you aren't to go there without me or Clooney accompanying you." She searched the girl's face for any hint of emotion.

"*You* accompany me? You never visit. Other than wearing your black all the time, it's as if you've forgotten he ever existed." Aislinn's porcelain complexion stretched pale over features as regal and deadened as a statue's. She shrugged. "I'm tired." She pulled free and laid back, tucking the bedclothes around her once more.

Felicity's heartbeat bounced like a pounded drum, echoing between guilt and annoyance. She'd had enough of this talk of the supernatural. Landrigan knew how much Aislinn missed her father. The girl spoke of Jasper constantly to Binata. It made sense the pig had overheard, considering he always dug his snout into things that didn't concern him. Landrigan used Aislinn's grief, just as he did Lianna's penchant for bribes and Felicity's own fear of losing the girls. Nothing was sacred to him. He would exploit anything he could in order to acquire this estate.

Tears edged Felicity's lashes. Was she truly going to have to marry him, just to protect everything she loved? Had it come to that? He seemed to suddenly be holding all the cards.

Perhaps it wouldn't be so bad … she had already been married once to a man that spurned her, a man she hated with equal venom. She'd endured through silence. Although that was only for a few days. How would she survive a lifetime of such quiet agony?

Wiping moisture from her face, Felicity shoved the excruciating possibility aside. Right now, in this moment, she needed to be Aislinn's guardian. And that entailed more than protecting her physically. Felicity needed to address the subject of the stable hand with her niece. She herself had taken the path of sensual awakening at a young age—however unwilling it might have been—and stumbled into a tangle of emotional briars. She wouldn't stand by and watch Aislinn make the same mistakes, watch her future fall away to shreds.

She chewed the inside of her lip, unsure how to broach the subject. "Tobias seemed quite concerned about you earlier."

A blush blossomed on Aislinn's porcelain cheeks. "Wasn't everyone?"

"Certainly." Felicity tightened the sheet around her stomach, trying to staunch its nervous upset. "But he seemed … unduly concerned. For a servant. Fennigan helped carry you in on the stretcher as well, but his actions were methodical. Whatever was necessary and nothing more. Tobias waited by the playroom door until you were settled in. He was—"

"Tobias *is* a friend. He has been assisting me in my study of the fungus. A girl must make friends where she can. You allow me no other recourse than the servants. Who else is there close to my age?"

"It is my experience that friendships between young men and maidens rarely remain … chaste."

"Please. You've already apprised me of the origins of babies. I'm not so stupid as to go bumbling about and get with child."

Aislinn's words hit too close to Felicity's truths. Truths Aislinn didn't know—could never know. She'd once accidentally seen Felicity's scar. But Felicity claimed the carriage accident that left her and Jasper orphans was responsible. Aislinn could never know of the wretched life she'd lived before Ireland, or the results of her mistakes.

Felicity and her niece stared at one another in the soft echoes of light which radiated from the dying fire.

"I do not wish for you to spend time with Tobias alone anymore," Felicity finally spoke over Lianna's heavy breathing. "You must always have a chaperone. Be it Binata, or Clooney. Even Lia. Just not alone."

Aislinn rippled the feather bed with her shift in position, scooting to the furthest edge. "You fear I'll tell him your secrets," she hissed.

The fire sputtered its last breath and the room grew dim.

Felicity slipped from the bed, knowing Binata would be coming in to sleep with the girls soon. Nutmeg hopped back up on the mattress, curling into the warm indention where Felicity had been laying. Dinah rubbed Felicity's shins, purring.

Shrouded in shadows, Felicity kissed Lia's drowsing eyelids and squeezed her eldest niece's hand. "Understand, Aislinn. These restrictions are not for me. They are for your heart's protection."

Aislinn surprised her by squeezing her fingers back. "One

does not protect her heart by building a wall around it. Our hearts are like flowers ... they must be fed with love and light to survive. Yours is withering away, Auntie. You have so many secrets, you fear letting anything penetrate them. I shan't allow that to happen to mine."

Felicity was taken aback by the words. Her thirteen-year-old niece was no longer a child at all. Just like Nick said, she'd become a young woman with romantic thoughts and ideals. Ideals that Felicity had once shared ... which the world would one day crush beneath its merciless feet.

In that fragile instant, something passed between them— an opportunity that Felicity almost grasped but waited a moment too long. Once Aislinn released her and turned over into her pillow, the connection had severed.

It didn't matter. It would've done little good to explain for the hundredth time that Lianna was too young to understand the secret of Felicity's true age, and that's why she kept it from her. Aislinn hated withholding things from her little sister. And this secret was nothing compared to the other one Felicity had forced Aislinn to keep.

The one about Jasper's death.

Regret roiled through Felicity's veins. No wonder Aislinn despised her. Felicity's entire identity was a lie. Other than Binata and Clooney, none of the servants knew the truth about her age. When Felicity walked the corridors at night, she always wore a veil or stayed to the shadows.

It had been this way since her arrival in Ireland that first year. She had justified it then. She couldn't have come here and claimed this estate after the Earl's death in London looking the part of a young, damaged courtesan. The servants would never have honored her ... they would've suspected foul play. Clooney had come with her—her physician and confidante—to help her heal physically and uphold the charade of her age so none of her domestics would stumble upon her true identity.

All along, the ruse had been easily justified. It had freed her to live this new life devoid of any repercussions from her past; it had freed her to love and care for the girls without anyone's intervention. But with each passing day, this masquerade came to feel more like a restraint than a liberty, for everyone involved.

Aislinn was right. Felicity had forgotten how to trust. Covering the truth came too easily now, second nature. What was she doing to her nieces by hiding them in a fortress of secrets? Nick's incrimination in the greenhouse had stung with honesty; perhaps that's why she'd reacted with such venom. It unsettled her that he could see into the core of her conscience. But this insight was only natural since he battled his own demons ... lived in his own prison.

She'd heard that laudanum could chain itself to a man for life; and then there was the loss of his bride. Perhaps that's why he stole things. To fill those empty spaces. Nick was obviously no stranger to guilt and loss. It was this shared baggage that enabled him to read her, and in turn made her feel so drawn to him.

Birds of a feather...butterflies of a wing.

A knock on Felicity's bedchamber door brought her back to the present. She wiped tears from her cheeks and rushed to unlatch the lock, expecting to see Clooney. Her heartbeat gave a flutter, wondering if he might have something to report about his nightly excursion to the turret's broken stairs.

When she opened the door, her heart took on an entirely different rhythm, for it was her handsome thief's face staring down at her instead.

CHAPTER TWELVE

Felicity swallowed her shock. "Master Nicolas."

An annoyed frown met her greeting. "*Nick,*" he corrected.

He looked tired—dark circles carved beneath the shadow of his long lashes, his blonde hair tousled and his beard scruffed up. Somehow the disorder of his appearance made him even more charming. Afraid he might get a glimpse of her in the glow of the corridor's sconces, she drew back, shrinking the door's opening until only a small gap remained.

He'd already seen her once tonight as the wrinkles were fading. If he got a good look now, when she had barely a trace of them, he might start to remember her from his past. Any spark of recognition could shatter this fragile illusion she had built her present and future upon.

"Did your ghost visit you?" The comment came out more caustic than she'd intended.

"No." His eyes narrowed. "You're the only one haunting me at the moment."

His response took her aback. She studied his mouth in the gap of space between them, remembering those lips pressed to hers, soft and hot on her skin, casting her awash in sensation. The hungry intensity of his touch had surprised her. She assumed him a rake by their risqué exchanges. Considering Rachel's constant attentions, he didn't appear to be a man that would have any trouble bedding his choice of ladies.

But that kiss had felt desperate ... raw. He'd been reaching out to her ... just as she had to him. She knew why she wanted him, how she craved the protection he'd given her once before. Still, logic begged the question: what could she possibly offer him that he couldn't get from some lustful toffer at a rookery? Or her maid, for that matter.

What, but perhaps a portal to the netherworld, to the wife he'd lost and sought. He was using her. Just like every man she'd ever had dealings with other than Clooney and her brother.

Hearing the clock's tick, she started to close the door. "It is late."

He jutted his foot between the door and its frame, holding the slight opening. "All I ask is one moment of your time."

"I believe you've already used more than one."

Unfazed, his foot shoved harder against the door. "Might I come in ... or you come out here? Tis rather awkward speaking through a crack in the wall."

"I am in my sleeping attire. It would be—"

"Unseemly." Nick propped his wrist on the door frame outside and pressed his forehead to the back of his fist, peering into her dimly lit room.

Felicity considered the irony of upholding social strictures after what they'd shared in the greenhouse. Her companion no doubt had the same thought but proved himself the gentleman and removed his toes from between the door and its frame, allowing her the choice to shut him out or hear him out.

She chose the latter, hoping she wouldn't regret it. "Please, be quick."

He grated a knuckle against the wall. "You told me something about your childhood tonight, so I wish to reciprocate."

"I'm sure it can wait till morning. I just took a sleeping draft and—"

"I was never a good son," he blurted, startling her lie to silence with the unexpected confession. "Even as a child, I used to break my parents' hearts, often. I stole from their guests, pulled pranks to ruin their fancy galas, anything to shame them. I suppose I wanted them to pay more attention to me than my perfect twin or their darling baby girl. But one time I went too far and ruined a hat my mother had made for a patron. The customer accused her of not understanding their instructions, their requests. They blamed her deafness, then stormed out. My mother was a strong woman, but I heard her crying later that day in the sitting room." He shook his head. "She'd put so much work into that piece, weeks and weeks of effort. I wanted to apologize but was too much of a coward. So, I crept into the garden and picked some flowers called mouse's ears. They're colloquially known as forget-me-nots, but I chose them for the ear reference. I was trying to give her what she'd never had. I laid them behind her on the floor. I hid and watched, hoping she'd find them. She walked over them instead, crushing the petals beneath her shoes before she realized they were there. When she bent to pick up the mess, I slipped out without telling her I'd left them. To this day, she doesn't know why the flowers were there. And she'll never know how much I've always regretted breaking her masterpiece, and how I would've given anything to put it together once more."

Shamed to silence for her earlier terse remark, Felicity clutched the gown over her scar as the longcase clock began to strike eleven.

"I know I was harsh in the greenhouse," Nick spoke over the gongs. "And now I find myself standing here with a deplorable lack of flowers. But damned if I'll be a coward again." He swallowed. "I'm here to say I'm sorr—well, that I'm an insensitive lout. Perhaps you might open the door a bit ... just enough I can see for myself that you're no longer broken."

His sweet apology softened to a caress, so kind and heartfelt Felicity ached to open the door so she could invite him in—into her room *and* her arms. She wanted to tell him thank you for sharing such a beautiful memory, and that she suspected his mother knew it was him all along. However, in lieu of the clock's gongs, all the things she wished to say lay stillborn on her tongue. For her wrinkles had worn off, and she was the coward now.

She couldn't tell him the truth. That there was no fixing the parts of her that were broken. If she dared even one word, every defense would come tumbling down. She'd confess everything ... all her lies, all her secrets. Clenching her eyes shut, she slammed the door in his face instead, locking it upon the eleventh strike.

In the morning Nick awoke late and in a foul mood.

Lianna's bed was decidedly too short. His ankles and calves had hung off the end all night. Each time he'd moved, the bloody frame creaked as if it would split beneath his weight.

Soft sunlight streamed beneath the edges of the floral drapes, casting the chamber in a pinkish hue. As if it wasn't feminine enough already.

He slapped off the lace and satin covers, flattening his feet on the peach rug which ran like a plush path from the door to the bed and warmed the white tiles underneath. Through bleary eyes, he glanced at a vase of fresh-cut flowers on the nightstand next to him. He rubbed his eyelids, inhaling deeply. The heady fragrances branded his senses, reminding him of Felicity's intoxicating scent when she had answered the bedchamber door last night: hair hanging like satin all about her shoulders, aglow in a crisp white gown, and fresh from a bath.

Damn. He'd wanted to run his lips and hands over her damp skin. When she'd backed into that dark room, it had taken all of his restraint not to bust the door down, enfold her in his arms, and kiss her breathless. Instead, he'd tried to be a friend. To be sincere.

Next time, he would push his way in; he knew by her response in the greenhouse that she wanted—needed—so much more than a typical companion.

He wove his fingers through his hair, regrouping his thoughts. What was he thinking? *Next time?*

No. There would be no next time. He would play the fool only once. And that he had. Spilling that ridiculous memory about the forget-me-nots. Telling her his juvenile name for the flowers. He doubted she could even recall the details this morning. He doubted she'd even listened. She believed him nothing but a petty thief, after all. To think he let down his defenses just so she could slam the door in his face without even a goodnight tossed his direction. She'd claimed she'd taken a sleeping draught but didn't seem the least bit drowsy when she'd shut him out so abruptly.

Well enough. Let her self-righteousness comfort her on cold nights. Let a pristine conscience be her lover. Better he realize now what an unforgiving shrew she was, before he invested anymore restless dreams in her behalf. She should marry Donal, the Irish beefwit. Both of them were cut of the same cloth—cold and self-absorbed.

Nick was done with this madness. The sooner he left, the better. But he wasn't giving up what he'd come for. He would be taking a few Heliconious butterflies with him so he could contact Mina on his own. His reason for coming had seemed to fade somewhat over the past few days, replaced by the drama with Felicity and her family. He wasn't sure if he liked her ability to dominate his thoughts to that degree. Small matter. He now knew the nightly routines well enough to find the perfect moment to sneak into the greenhouse before leaving.

Nick's gut cramped. Once again, he would shame his family; this time by stealing from a widowed countess. Yet he knew himself well enough to know it wouldn't stop him. He'd turn his back on his sins as he always did; turn his back and walk away, as soon as Johnny Boy was well enough to travel.

Nick's ponderings stalled at the thought of the pit bull.

He glanced around the bed. The dog wasn't there. Nick rolled to the other side to assure his canine companion hadn't fallen off in the night. He leaned down, hanging over the edge. Blood rushed to his head and his hair swept across the floor as he gazed under the frame. He knew the stable hands hadn't come to take Johnny; Nick would've awakened at such a disruption.

He stood, not seeing the dog anywhere.

It registered then, that the pain in his leg and ribs had faded to nothing more than a faint throb. Before he could contemplate the anomaly, he heard a thump from beneath a child-sized table set with china, tatted napkins, and silverware. A tablecloth draped the top and hung all the way to the floor. At one edge, Nick caught sight of a tail sticking out from the fabric.

"Johnny?"

At the sound of his voice, the pit bull burst from underneath the table. The cloth caught on his back and tottered half of the dishes. They cracked as they hit the tile floor. Johnny Boy bounded over to Nick and jumped up on his thighs, his tongue lolling and his smile wide.

Nick dropped to his knees, holding Johnny's muzzle to escape a slobbery greeting. Disbelief shimmied through him, tinged with shock. It appeared Johnny was already well enough to travel. How could that be possible, when his injury had been so grave?

"All right, boy. Lay down now, c'mon. Roll over."

His entire body wagging, Johnny flopped to the floor and rolled on his back. His legs stuck up, feet dangling at the joints. He barked, waiting for Nick to pet his belly.

Nick obliged, scratching the soft fur on the dog's chest and stomach as he searched for the wounds he'd had the day before. Most of them had started to scab over. But today, he almost couldn't find them. They were nothing but scars. Even the stitch on his throat appeared to be closing—the skin rejoining, as if it'd been healing for months as opposed to ten days. Then Nick noticed a bright purple residue in the middle and around the edges of the wounds.

Had he not known better, he would've thought Clooney had doctored the dog. But this looked more like something that would grow on a plant ... a fungus, perhaps.

Fungi usually decomposed other organisms ... they didn't heal them. It made no sense.

Nick released Johnny. The dog catapulted to his feet and shook his fur before trotting about the room, exploring. Upon finding the stick-horse, Johnny Boy clamped his teeth on the ribbons. Nick wrestled the toy away, leaving the ribbons frayed. He was awestruck at the dog's strength. It was as if the pit bull had never been at death's door.

Remembering his own injuries, Nick set the stick-horse out of the dog's reach and lifted his leg, propping his foot on the bed's edge. That same queer purplish fungus lined the seam below his knee where his own gash had closed.

Stunned, he scraped away some of the residue. It flaked off easily, like a powder.

His stomach flipped. No one could mend this quickly. And could this be the same fungus Aislinn and Miss Felicity had been so concerned over? If so, it was indeed a mystery. For what sort of fungus spontaneously sprouted upon someone's flesh during the night?

Finding the basin he'd used the prior evening to wash off, he scrubbed at the spores until they flaked away, unsure if he should be disgusted by the infestation or grateful for it.

He dressed quickly, shrugging into a sage green shirt the maid had brought in as he slept. After stepping inside trousers still wrinkled from the day before, he braided his hair in a slip-shod fashion, in too much of a rush to care.

Just as he gathered up the tattered stick-horse and threw open the bedchamber door, he ran smack into young Tobias. Johnny Boy bolted toward the opening. They both jumped out of the way to keep from getting bowled over.

The young man regained his balance and raked a lock of thick, sandy hair off of an intelligent forehead. He was tall for his age, coming up to Nick's nose.

Appearing nervous, he adjusted his gray vest and trousers over his white shirt—a typical stable hand's uniform. Dark eyes, glistening like a muddy creek in the sunlight, turned upward to meet Nick's.

"Pardon, Lord Thornton. Her Ladyship asked that I should help take out the dog." Short, thick lashes wavered as he glanced in the direction of Johnny Boy's escape and then at the stretcher he'd propped in the hall, obviously befuddled by the dog's improvement.

"And where might Her Ladyship be?" Nick asked, trying to staunch his annoyance at her. Of all the mysteries and enigmas in this castle, Felicity was indeed the most binding. The more he tried to remove her from his thoughts, the more she preoccupied them.

"She's gathering eggs in the henhouse with Lianna. And she plans to cut you a branch for a new cane. She—*we* never expected you to be walking so soon ... you or the dog."

"Yes. It appears we're swift on the mend." Nick thought upon the queer fungus, determined to know if it was similar to the one in the greenhouse. "You are friends with Miss Aislinn."

A flush of color filled the stable hand's neck and ears. "I-I don't know what you mean, sir."

Nick held his gaze. "I saw your concern when she fell."

Beads of sweat formed on Tobias' brow. He hesitated before nodding.

The boy was honest. Nick's respect inched up a notch. "I would venture you're familiar enough to know that she's been studying some sort of fungus of late, in connection to her aunt's sickly caterpillars."

Tobias' Adam's apple bobbed and his hands gripped in front of his waist. "Please, sir. It is nothing improper. We merely talk ... sometimes. Rarely even. I-I have helped her gather specimens once or twice. You must understand. She has no friends her age."

"I'll not get you in trouble with Her Ladyship, as long as your intentions remain honorable. I just want an answer to the fungus. Does Miss Aislinn know anything about it? Has she made any discoveries?"

Tobias' chin twitched—devoid of even an echo of

whiskers and smooth with the sheen of youth. "She's been seeking information in her father's journals. She has them with her in the playroom this morning, spread out on the bed."

Nick offered a stern scowl. "And you would know that, how?"

"I ... oh, no sir. No. Nothing like that. I took up some baskets of flowers for Lianna. Binata was there. We had a chaperone."

Nick tipped his head. "See that you always do. If you truly care for Aislinn, her reputation and virtue should be your utmost priority." He moved into the corridor alongside the stable hand. "I suggest you catch Johnny Boy before he makes hash of the fancy drapes in the parlor." He held up the stick-horse. The threadbare ribbons swayed with the movement. "He's in high spirits today."

Tobias nodded; he lifted the stretcher and strode away, stepping aside as Lia passed him in the corridor. She stopped him when the stretcher raked the bun pinned high atop her head, causing some loose tendrils to stick to the canvas. After a firm scolding, Tobias was allowed to proceed.

As Lia turned to Nick, he leaned the damaged stick-horse against the wall behind him in hopes it would elude her slumberous gaze. He had no time for explanations. He needed to speak to Aislinn, to finally get a look at Jasper's notes.

But Lia was on a mission. She held a tray in her hands and the scent of cinnamon and coffee wafted through the air as she stationed herself directly in Nick's path. Nick's stomach grumbled. He supposed he could take the breakfast upstairs in the playroom.

"Mister Sir." She curtsied. Her blue frock—the same luminous hue as her eyes—grazed her ankles with the movement.

"Good morn, my lady." As Nick bowed at the waist, he noticed several errant strands of straw sticking out from between her dusty, bare toes, completely at odds with the refined image she was trying to present. He couldn't help but grin.

When he straightened, an indignant scowl met him.

"A suitor should never laugh at his lady."

"Forgive me." Nick dragged his palm down his facial hair—from lips to chin—wiping away the smile. "It was a twitch actually. Yes. My lips were twitching."

"An itch more probably. From all that hair you wear on your face."

"Or could be I'm allergic to hay." He gestured to her feet.

Her chin dropped. "Oh! We use it to pad the buckets." She wriggled her tiny toes. "It keeps the eggs from cracking."

"I see." Nick noticed a book tucked beneath the napkin on the tray. "Is that for me?"

"Auntie sent it. She said you might like to read as you ate." She held it out to him.

He thanked her, balancing the platter on one palm. Pushing aside the cinnamon pudding and coffee kettle, he peeled back the napkin to reveal the book—a compilation of famous authors' quotes. A soft blue petal peered out from the middle of the pages. Nick worked his finger into the space and nudged the spine open.

The bookmark was a forget-me-not, freshly picked and pressed. Nick ran his finger along the stem. Skimming the print on the page, he found a Mark Twain quote lightly circled in pencil: *Forgiveness is the fragrance which the violet sheds on the heel that has crushed it*. The word "violet" was marked through lightly and replaced with the handwritten: *mouse's ear*.

Dazed, Nick stroked the flower's silky petals. Felicity had been listening, after all.

Perhaps her slamming the door hadn't been intentional. Maybe she didn't look down upon him. Judging from the tragic depths of her eyes and that repeated clutching of her chest—it was possible she had been so wounded by something in her past that she'd lost the ability or courage to ration out her emotions.

Nick started to close the book but noticed in the white space beside the verse that Felicity had scripted an invitation to meet her at noon beside the greenhouse for a picnic.

He smiled. A picnic ... what a splendidly ordinary suggestion.

Closing the book, Nick tucked the flower into a buttonhole on his shirt's lapel. He looked up to find himself beneath Lia's inscrutable long-lashed gaze. He'd almost forgotten the little sprite was there.

"You don't seem very brightened," she said.

"Brightened?"

"When people wake from a long sleep, they should look brightened. All but Auntie. She always looks darker in the morning ... it's her wrinkles that make it so. They get better at night."

"Do they now?" Intrigued, he resituated both hands to hold the tray, hardly aware that his chin grew warm from the fragrant steam rising from the kettle's spout.

Lia shrugged. "She doesn't like me to speak of it. But I don't care. Not today."

"Why is that?"

"She won't let me play with your bog pony. Even though it's just the right size for a carousel horse. So I found a new pet in the chicken coops." She stomped a foot. "But Auntie killed it."

Nick measured her accusation carefully. He had seen Felicity's tenderness with animals firsthand. She would never intentionally hurt one.

"Did my ghost visit last night?" Lia blurted out before Nick had a chance to delve further into the pet mystery.

His mind spun with the unexpected shift in conversation. "Not that I remember."

"You didn't hear any swishing?"

It occurred to him then, that the butterfly wings he'd heard in his dream hadn't stopped swishing when he'd awakened.

"Yes. In fact, I did." This revelation left his logic swimming. There had been no one in his room; Johnny would have barked at an intruder. Did that mean he'd had an otherworldly visitor? If so, it validated that a human and spirit could make contact.

His hope to contact Mina flickered brighter in his chest.

Lia started toward her door. "I shall check the flowers on my nightstand. My ghost always leaves his mark there."

Nick widened his stance, trying to keep the damaged stick-horse hidden from her view. "His mark..."

She paused. "He dots the flowers with purple moss—" Her focus sharpened on him. "I thought your leg was to be resting."

Nick felt like he was playing hopscotch, bouncing around subjects chosen by the rolling pebble of her little girl sensibilities. He saw the inevitable slide of her gaze to the stick-horse behind him and his stomach sank. "Oh, actually ... my leg is much the better. I suppose you would like to have your horse back."

The words had barely left his lips before she'd stepped around him and had the stick in hand, covering the stallion's muzzle with kisses. "Have you missed me, Snowbell? Have you?" Then her dainty fingers ran through the torn ribbons and chew marks at its neck. Her gaze met his, wide with accusation. "What did you do to him? You promised to treat him as if he were your very own! Are you so sloppy with the things you love?"

The question punched him in the gut, resurrecting memories better left buried. "I have been known to be."

She stormed across the threshold into her room, vanishing from his view. Trying to think of the right words to soothe her, Nick stepped inside to find her tiny body kneeling beside the broken china set Johnny Boy had knocked to the floor.

"Daddy's china!"

Nick set the breakfast tray on the bed, cursing under his breath. He would never have imagined her father had given her those dishes. He pulled the flower from his button's placket and knelt down, offering it to her. "Please forgive me, my lady. I never meant—"

"I'm not your lady, *Sir*," she whispered the declaration, but paired with the tears streaming from those sleepy eyes, it gouged his eardrums like a scream. She took the forget-me-not from his hand and crushed it between her fingers. "And I hate you."

CHAPTER THIRTEEN

Nick sat in the playroom on the bed's edge, digging fingers into his knees to keep himself from pacing.

Binata stood outside in the hallway, trying to calm Lia's sobs. The sprite had raced up the stairs to the fourth floor after his encounter with her. When he arrived behind her, she was already in her nanny's comforting arms.

Aislinn turned from her place at the window, studying Nick. She smoothed the bandage that covered her forehead. This morning, her irises looked more like gliding shadows deep within the sea than a blueberry harvest. The sun streamed in from behind her, glazing her bluish-black hair with shivers of light. He was glad to see her sensitivity to brightness had abated.

"She won't soon forgive you," Aislinn said.

Nick nodded, his jaw clenched. "She said she hates me." It amazed him how that juvenile phrase cut when coming from such a tiny angel. He'd never once been disarmed by a female. But being in this castle full of them in variant stages of life was becoming entirely too unsettling. He'd even lost his appetite for breakfast after the episode with Lia.

"She believed you were her beau."

"I gather that," Nick groused. "Damn it all."

"You've not been around many little girls, have you?"

He opened his hand to glance at the crushed flower Lia had thrown at him. "Only my sister, and I was young myself so wasn't much for coddling her. Is it that apparent?"

"Well, for one, most adults try not to curse around them."

Tucking the sad wilted stem in his pocket, Nick glanced up, chagrinned. "Oh, right."

"It doesn't offend me. After all, I'm not a child." Aislinn gave him bright smile, lightening his mood a bit. Only then did he notice the freckles spattering the bridge of her nose— as if that one babyish quality refused to be conquered by her maturing appearance.

"Perhaps, if I give your sister a bouquet of flowers?" He awaited Aislinn's approval.

Aislinn gestured to the baskets of blossoms on the floor. "She already has a garden full of them."

"Oh, of course," he said, dejected. "I shall think of something else, then."

"It will have to be quite spectacular to make up for Father's china set." Aislinn strolled toward the bed. A periwinkle dress of soft muslin flowed to her ankles and rustled with her movements. "You wished to ask me something, in reference to your swift recovery? Should you not speak to Clooney instead? Or Auntie, perchance."

"I suspect Clooney doesn't believe in the supernatural. And I know your aunt doesn't." Nick had been thumbing through Jasper's journals but couldn't make heads or tails of the terminology or the messy script. However, it looked familiar. His sister Emilia had mentioned how Felicity's handwriting had changed over time, shown him how messily written her correspondences were once they started to exchange chapters for their novel. Nick might've suspected it a fluke, had he not seen the neatness with which Felicity

145

wrote his picnic invitation earlier. An odd anomaly, to say the least.

"You're right." Aislinn's freckles disappeared within a pucker of crinkles as she wriggled her nose, recouping his attention. "Auntie doesn't believe in anything beyond what she can see. She's not one for fairytales, either."

Nick rubbed the back of his hand along his bearded chin, surprised at how this saddened him. "That must be why she's considering marrying Mister Landrigan. Why she still wears black in mourning for her earl. Because she's given up on happy endings."

Aislinn regarded her bare feet. "Auntie wears black in honor of my father."

"Is that so? And why don't you?"

"Because he's still here ..." Aislinn's voice trailed as she touched the books around her.

Nick understood. For Aislinn, her father lived on through his scripted words, just as he lived on through some shattered china for Lia. Nick shook his head, wishing he had some magic wand to wave over the tea set and mend it.

"As for Auntie," Aislinn continued, "her hope dies more every day. With her business dwindling and all of the upkeep ... well, perhaps she believes that having a husband might proffer some glimpse of life." She looked up. "But she doesn't trust Mister Landrigan. I think if a man came along who could free her spirit of its doubt ... she would marry him without hesitation."

Nick considered this silently. "A man who could give her wings," he mumbled.

"Pardon?" Aislinn asked.

Nick glanced at the window behind the young lady, his eyes burning from the sunlight—unusually bright for an Irish morning. "Nothing." He clenched his jaw. "Tell me ...

that fungus in your aunt's greenhouse, did it appear before or after the shortage of caterpillars occurred?"

Sweeping aside the books, Aislinn took a seat on the far end of the mattress. She placed a pillow in her lap and fluffed it, stirring the lilac scent of clean bed linens. "After. Why do you care?" The response seemed almost defensive.

"If I solve this mystery, perhaps it will help salvage your aunt's caterpillars, and she won't feel that she has to marry Mister Landrigan."

Aislinn gently batted at the pillow.

"Your sister told me—" A heartrending wail from the hallway stalled Nick's statement. He clutched the book in his lap until Lia had silenced. "She told me that when the Raven visits her room, he leaves behind trails of purplish moss on her flowers."

Aislinn's dark brows hitched to sharp lines. "Purple?" Her posture stiffened, as if just grasping what he'd said. "The Raven has been in her room? When?"

"She has not informed you of his visits?"

"She mentioned a new friend. But I thought him like her other imaginary playmates. She never gave a description." An expression of complete wonderment crossed her face, as if she'd had an epiphany. "So, the moss ... or rather the fungus ... is connected to our Dark Raven. That's why I saw it in the tree before he appeared." Biting her lip, she flipped erratically through the journals.

She was alight—beaming as if the dawn rose within her and streamed from her eyes and the pores of her skin. Her cheeks flushed, her freckles danced, and her lips brightened to the crimson shade of a poppy. It was as if, in that moment, she lost the icy trappings of a statue and melted into life again. No wonder Tobias liked to help with her scientific meanderings.

She skimmed her fingertip along selected pages, casting

one book aside for another. Finally, she found what she sought and looked up at Nick, her gaze piercing. "What does your recovery have to do with any of this?"

Nick rolled up his trouser leg, showcasing his mending flesh. "The fungus healed me. It was on my wounds when I awoke this morn, on my dog's as well. He ran down the stairs earlier as if he were a pup again. And here I am walking with not even a limp." He pushed his hem back in place.

Aislinn turned the book around so it faced Nick. Her finger tapped one of her colored sketches where bright purple patches gathered like pygmy cauliflowers on a rose's stem. "Is this what the fungus looked like?"

Nick nodded.

"Why did I not make the association?" Aislinn smiled, but not at him. This smile was reserved for another man, the author of the scientific journals tumbling across her bed. She poured through them again, not even looking at Nick. "You were right. The pupas worked ... but different than we expected. Somehow you're—" She stopped herself, sliding her gaze up to meet Nick's.

He had once heard that savants could plummet so deep into their introspections they would forget anyone else occupied their space. He'd never experienced it until now. "Do you know who this shadowy man is, Miss Aislinn?" he asked her point blank, meaning to catch her on the cusp of her mental daze.

"No." Her eyes belied her answer, lashes fluttering down to hide the hope within them. "But I do think that the fungus is not a detriment. Instead, it is counteracting whatever ailment has befallen those plants. That's why it appeared on the dying tree, and on Lia's flowers in her room. They were withering from being plucked from the ground ... and the fungus is trying to heal them. Just like—"

"Just like it healed me; like it's healing the vines. Which

in essence, links our 'ghost' to not only the fungus, but also the butterflies."

"Yes."

Nick had a passing curiosity as to why the Raven hadn't visited Aislinn in the night over the past week and fixed the gash in her head—especially if this spirit was who he once more suspected it might be. But then he remembered Binata had been sleeping with the girls. Hadn't Lia said something about her tea party companion being shy of the nanny?

Nick stood. "Thank you, Miss Aislinn. I'll leave it to you to explain this to Clooney. And see that he treats your wound with some fungus." He started toward the open door, poking his head out. Relieved to find Lia and Binata gone for the moment, he stepped into the corridor.

"What will you tell Auntie?" Aislinn asked, coming to stand at the threshold.

"That she should leave the growth on her plants."

"And the Dark Raven?" Aislinn's query had a sharpened edge to it. The look on her face confirmed Nick's suspicions. She also believed her father was the ghost.

"I'll not say anything of him. Not until we have some tangible proof. No need to upset her unduly." Nick nodded goodbye and headed for the steps leading to the second flight, resolved to search while the servants were occupied with their morning duties on the ground floor.

It was time he found out what was hidden in that turret, and if it could lead him back to his dead wife and son.

Standing within the henhouse as chickens clucked and feathers floated like snowflakes, Felicity coiled the dead snake into a bag.

The limp orange body curled upon itself, black lines spinning around its two-foot length. She stuffed hay atop the scaly corpse then tied the bag's mouth shut. Placing the back of her glove over her nose, she staunched the raw meaty stench to ease her stomach.

Some twigs popped behind her and snapped her focus to the doorway.

"Japers! What happened here?" Landrigan's tall, toned frame blocked the sunlight as he leaned against the threshold. His teeth clacked against a stick of peppermint, moving it from one side of his mouth to another. A slight breeze stirred the hay and feathers beneath his feet.

"Back to harvest the fruits of your labor?" Felicity accused from behind her glove, trying to contain her rage.

"Aw, rabbit on. Aunt Bini sent word that Aislinn fell from a tree. I would've been here sooner, but I've been preoccupied in town. I'm here to seek about ye and the wee lambs."

"Ah. There's nothing more comforting to lambs than a rabid wolf in a bloodied sheepskin." She cinched the twine in place on the bag then met his cocky gaze, wishing she'd brought her whip.

Landrigan slid his candy from his mouth and offered a half-grin. "For once would ye stop the effin' and blindin'. Admit yer happy to see me."

Using her sleeve, she swiped some dirt from her forehead and left a dusty streak on the black fabric. "All right. I'm *thrilled* to see you." With a shove of her boot, she scooted the heavy bag his direction, watching as blood seeped through the weave. "I intended to send your snake back to you via post. You've saved me the trouble."

Smirking, Landrigan sucked on his peppermint again and dipped a hand into the dried corn sacked next to the door.

He strode inside with all the grace and alacrity of a hungry fox, stepping over the dead snake while he kept Felicity in his amber-gold sights. He crouched among the clucking chickens. His dapper gray suit looked out of place as he sprinkled the feed on the ground—like a prince posing as a pauper. "That a real snake then? They be as scarce as hen's teeth here on the bonnie green. Need to keep yer eyes sharp, it would seem."

"Should I? They're unheard of ... lessen someone brings them over illegally by ship." Felicity held back a snarl. "It was about to strike Lia's bare feet."

"A corn snake nayn't have harmed the tiddler."

"And how would you know what kind it was?"

The candy twirled along the curl of his plump lips as he looked up at her. "I saw ye tuck it in the bag, didn't I? Ye needn't have killed it."

Felicity tightened her jaw. "It was in the shadows. I acted on the assumption it posed a danger. As of late, all the snakes I've dealt with have been venomous." She cast him a pointed glare as he stood to his impressive height.

His eyes narrowed. "Damn, Felicity." He slapped his palms together to dust them before taking off his hat and raking through his black, cropped curls. "Yer always accusin' me of bein' on the maggot." He replaced his topper, smoothing the brim with all the suave of a true gentleman.

Felicity glanced at the hoe next to her feet ... the one she'd used to sever the snake's head. She swooped down to snatch its handle. The blade—glistening with smears of blood—paused in midair as she held it steady and straightened her back.

A cautious spark lit Landrigan's features but he didn't budge.

"Twice now you've tried to hurt my girls. The threats end

today!" Felicity took a swing at him. Landrigan caught the hoe's neck, halting it just short of slicing his cheek.

He spit out his peppermint which now had droplets of red sprinkled across its tip to match the bloody spray on the pink silk cravat beneath his chin. He wrestled the tool from her— twisted her wrists until the ligaments came close to snapping. Taking the hoe, Landrigan cast it to the ground, sending several chickens squawking.

"Are ye loopers, woman? *If* I'm responsible for this, Tis only one time. And the tiddler was in no danger."

"You made Aislinn fall from a tree!" Scalding tears burned behind Felicity's eyelids and blurred her vision.

"Away with ye. I'd nothin' to do with that. I told ye, I've been out of pocket."

"Lying swine!" Felicity kicked up some hay in his direction.

His chest rose and fell in rapid succession as he rushed her. A dangerous grimace showcased teeth as white as the peppermint he'd cast away.

Backing up, she nearly tripped over several flustered chickens before her shoulder blades met the wall, giving her balance.

He had her pinned against the wood beneath his hot, hard body before she could take a breath. Her heart pecked at her sternum in a fit of panic as pointed and sharp as a beak.

"Every time I see ye..." His minty breath scorched her forehead. "Yer knickers are in a twist 'bout somethin'. High time someone loosens the knot a bit, aye?"

His hand started a descent over her bodice from her chest to her stomach. Felicity managed to wedge an arm between their bodies and catch his wrist. "You're not man enough to do it."

He didn't force her grip free. Instead, he let his palm rest on her belly, a hot pressure against her scar, a warning of how easily he could dominate the situation.

"Yer only one step from givin' in. I can feel it."

"I will never give in."

"I'll provide for ye. Ye'll not want for anythin'."

"I'll want for dignity and peace of mind."

"Nay, now. We had some bright times. All those talks beneath the moonlight. The kiss..."

"That slobbery tongue-grope you forced on me an hour before you bedded Rachel in the hayloft?"

He flipped his hand to weaved his fingers with hers and smirked—an ugly, mean, tangle of lips. "Ah, that's cracker! All this time, yer punishin' me for goin' at it with yer scrubber of a maid months ago." He leaned close, trailing his free hand down her temple. "I was tired of waitin' for ye to let me into yer icy heart. Ye want I should make up for that now?"

Felicity swallowed against the bile in her throat. "You can never make up for the things you've done."

"Well. Ye must not be too narky over them. Ye ain't even telled me Aunt."

"I've aired my suspicions. But without proof, she won't cast judgment. She wants to believe the best in her only nephew."

"Ah. Mayhap ye do, too."

Felicity fought back as he dragged her hand along his thigh.

He forced her palm to his crotch. He was fully aroused. She'd always suspected he gleaned some sort of perverse gratification from their altercations. To have it validated only made him more repulsive ... more dangerous. Lust had a tendency to inspire depraved men to a state of malicious hysteria. She'd seen it for herself, firsthand.

"Ye know, that tryst with yer maid, I wanted it to be ye all along. She's six o' one, half a dozen o' the other. But ye..." He pressed her fingers around his hard length.

She squelched a gag, grateful for her gloves lest she retch from the contact.

"Yer like no other dowager I've e'er met. Damned well preserved."

She flipped her wrist and clamped her fingers around his bollocks, pinching the vulnerable spot just hard enough that he wouldn't dare move. A startled whimper broke from his throat and his whole body stiffened.

"Here's how this will play out, Mister Landrigan. You're going to leave my estate and take your bloody snake with you." They both flicked a glance to the seeping bag on the ground.

"On second thought," Felicity said. "Take both of them." Her fingers gouged into him again for emphasis. "Lest you want *this* one to end up headless and limp in a bag, as well." With that, she tugged hard before pushing him off.

Stumbling backward, he clenched his crotch and doubled over in a coughing fit. But when it evolved to a throaty chuckle, a fresh wave of terror crashed over Felicity. He uncurled his spine—face deepened to the color of elderberry wine—looking well and ready to murder her. A stab of nostalgic terror sliced through Felicity's scar, for in that moment he looked more like his father than ever before.

Her windpipe compressed until her breath came out in whistles. The stable hands were only a scream away. They were good boys, both of them. And loyal. But neither had the matured physical prowess to match Landrigan should he decide to force his wrath on her.

"That fiery spirit's o'yers is bleedin' deadly." He sneered. "I'm gonna take great pleasure in snuffin' it out." He licked his thumb then pinched it to his forefinger, mimicking putting out a candle's wick. "Yer hidin' somethin' in yer past. Why else would ye imprison yerself up here? I'm close to figurin' out what that be. And when I do, ye'll beg me to marry ye." He took a step toward her. "What say ye practice bendin' yer knee now?"

Felicity couldn't move, nailed by the undercurrents of the cryptic threats. She'd hoped all along he hadn't inherited his father's temper. But if she kept pushing him, she might very well bring it out, just as she had in the earl.

She whispered a prayer that Nick would come and be her hero again—right at this moment—and level Landrigan to the ground.

As if by her willing it, an angry masculine voice carried over the threshold.

"Donal. What are you doing here?"

CHAPTER FOURTEEN

Felicity had never been so glad to see Clooney.

She met Landrigan's gaze and watched the angry blush fade from his face before he turned to greet the groundskeeper. He always put forward his best foot around Clooney, as he knew the old man would report back to Binata without hesitation. If there was one thing the Irishman cherished, it was his aunt's good graces.

"Aye there, Clooney. Nothin' more than some tomfoolery. Ain't that right, *yer ladyship*?" He glanced back at Felicity, a yellow flame aglow behind his eyes. Whether born of lust or rage, she didn't know. She was beginning to think the two walked hand in hand with him.

"Suppose I'd best quit pullin' me plum and find me aunt. Tell Aislinn I was here to seek about her." He tipped his hat to Felicity then shoved the snake-filled bag out of his path with his heel before passing Clooney and disappearing into the sunlight.

Felicity shut her eyes and took a deep breath, trying to calm her jittery heartbeat.

"You all right?" Clooney came forward to catch her elbow.

Still overly-sensitized from Landrigan's intrusive touch, she pulled free. "I'm fine." She rubbed her abdomen.

Noticing the bloodied peppermint stick on the ground, she strode over to grind it to crystals beneath her boot. It gave her a small thrill of pleasure to imagine it was Landrigan's skull. "How is Lia?"

Clooney swiped a palm over his beard. "She told me about the snake." He glanced at the bag. "You suspect Landrigan had a hand in it?"

"I've no doubt. But Aislinn was his alibi for being here. Is Lia still angry at me?"

"Lia is a child, Dove." Clooney bent to lift the bag's mouth and dragged it with him to the entrance. He paused. "Her emotions are always on her sleeve. She'll forgive you soon enough."

"Like she has for the carousel ponies? Every day she draws a new picture of the ride. Even when she doesn't speak aloud of her grudge, it's still there. It seems that with each new trick Landrigan pulls, he drives a bigger wedge between me and the girls."

Clooney's forehead burst into wrinkles. "Then you should go to the RICs, Felicity. Enough of this."

"He's been too careful. I've no proof of his guilt. And to bid them to investigate would only invite trouble. They'll see me living in this castle with children I have no real claim to. And I have little ground to stand on without a husband to complete the family portrait. Tis what Landrigan is counting on." She let out a shaky breath.

"Wish you'd reconsider bidding the law, Dove. Desperate men do desperate things." Clooney stared at the trees outside, the back of his head turned toward her. "I never want to see you gutted like a rabbit again. Couldn't bear to see it..." His voice broke and he left, dragging the bag behind him.

Alone once more in the henhouse, an insidious unease

crept over Felicity. Moving like an automaton, she tottered around the busy chickens and picked up the hoe, carrying it to a white enamel bucket filled with water. She dunked it in, sloshing until the blade came out clean and the water retained a pinkish tint. Propping the tool in a splay of light, she left it to dry.

As she looked about the shaded enclosure, she wondered if Landrigan had planted anymore fanged surprises. The shed provided too many nooks and crannies where a snake could hide. The seven coops raised on timber perches and the straw thick upon the ground would be the perfect camouflage for any slithering predator.

She shuddered, then squared her shoulders, unwilling to let her disquietude get the better of her. She would simply have to be alert. She should have been more suspicious when the eggs started going missing. She should've been more vigilant. She should never be caught off guard by anything Landrigan did.

Up till lately, his warnings had been artfully planned to frighten without inflicting violence on her or the girls. He'd even been gentlemanly in his treatment of her for the most part. But now...

Had his desire to win spun out of control? He said he was close to learning her past. But that was impossible. Clooney had been so very careful covering their tracks.

If she was wrong ... her fate was sealed. Landrigan would finally have the upper hand. For she would not let Jasper's daughters know the truth of her past. Not for anything in the world. She had a reputation to uphold now. The girls looked to her to do the right thing and make moral choices.

For a split second, she considered taking her nieces and running away. What Landrigan really wanted was the estate, after all. But she had no means for an income. Not to mention, because of Jasper, because of her promise to him, they were well and duly trapped here.

Yet what a haven to be trapped in.

Felicity stepped out of the henhouse into the sun, letting the light's warmth calm her as a chill breeze—flavored with spruce—cleansed the mustiness from her lungs. The songs of birds trilled all around. She glanced over her shoulder at the henhouse. It had once been a simple whitewashed shed. But Aislinn and Lianna had asked to repaint it the summer before Jasper's stroke. Now it was bright pink with white shingles. Felicity smiled, thinking of that day. The four of them had worked on it together and ended up covered in pink splotches. When they'd returned to the castle in the evening to clean up, Binata had thought they'd all stumbled into poison ivy and threatened to give them oatmeal baths.

Felicity's heart sank on the memory. She missed their closeness ... the family they once were. But even with Jasper's absence, she still loved this place. She knew herself here, accepted and understood herself in a way that she never had in her prior life.

The solitude, the serenity. Such a contrast to her self-loathing, chaotic walk in London where she was always on display for wealthy men looking to satisfy their animal urges. She would never go back. This estate was her livelihood, her means to make an honest life for the girls and take pride in her daily accomplishments—however humble they were.

She supposed, even were she to marry Landrigan, she would still have that. She could insist on the union being in name only. And if he pressed, at least she would only have to give her body to one salacious man, as opposed to a dozen or more. She needn't worry he would ever harm the girls due to Binata's constant presence, and his respect and love for his aunt. Felicity's biggest fear was how she would keep her brother's secret protected with Landrigan living beneath the same roof.

Feeling more lost than ever, Felicity wandered down the path toward the castle. Pebbles crunched beneath her soles. The trail wove in and out of the shade and the air fluctuated between warmth and coolness. Nick's face flashed through her mind—teasing the same shifting sensations in her heart. His intense eyes, his expressive mouth. That glistening diamond in his ear. After hearing his story last night, she wondered if the gemstone was somehow tied to his mother. Or, more likely, the dead wife he still sought.

Senseless postulating, Felicity.

She'd lost the opportunity to find out now, lost any chance of an amicable relationship after her horrible mistreatment of him. He'd opened his heart—a gesture which managed to melt the ice around her own. Then she'd slammed the door in his face.

What did it matter? Nick would soon be gone. He'd found nothing spiritual to keep him here. No ghosts other than Landrigan. He'd be leaving within another week or so, once his dog had healed enough for travel. After the loss of his wife, the last thing Nick would want was a widow and her nieces monopolizing his time.

She could only hope the forget-me-not she'd sent him with breakfast this morn would merit some clemency, that he would put aside any resentment for her actions and meet her at the greenhouse for a picnic. It appeared all he'd known in the years since she first met him was loneliness and regret. He deserved pleasant company and quiet moments, and she would see that he experienced at least a portion of that before he left.

An outbreak of nickering shook Felicity from her thoughts and stalled her footsteps. Curious as to what could've stirred the horses into such a frenzy, she took the left fork going away from the castle toward the stables. The path led through a shaded passage where coniferous branches and moss hung from the other side of the tall, stone fence.

Vines dragged across her head and shoulders as she stepped out into the sunlight. Tugging some needle-like leaves from her upswept hair, she squinted in disbelief.

Johnny Boy ran along the outside of the stables, as spry as a springtime pup. If not for the missing ear, Felicity would never have guessed it was the same dog. Tobias was attempting to catch the pit bull. Even Nutmeg had joined the chase.

In a daze, Felicity approached the queer scene. Unexpected sadness slowed her steps. However implausible it was, Johnny Boy was fully recuperated. And that could only mean one thing.

Nick would be leaving sooner than anyone had anticipated.

Nick took the first three flights toward the turret carefully. He stayed within the imprinted footsteps already there and tried to leave the spider webs intact. He wouldn't risk getting caught. If he failed finding some sort of proof that this Raven man existed, he would only further alienate Felicity by going behind her back to the tower.

The stairway's slim winding corridor triggered a stagnant, claustrophobic heaviness in the air. Square windows—no bigger than a folded hanky—spiraled upward with the wall's climb, providing soft bursts of light along the way.

Heady excitement pumped through his veins. The closer

he came to the top, the more his hair prickled on his arms and neck, an otherworldly rush luring him onward.

At the end of the fifth flight, he stopped dead and clamped his grip around the iron stair rail affixed to the stone wall. He had to hold his lantern high here, as the windows had ended. He stared up at the turret's door far above, unblinking, taken aback by the extent of damage to the final flight of stairs.

The cook had not exaggerated. Where there should've been steps in a straight run upward, there was instead a jagged downpour of broken rock and fragmented stone—some even ground to pebbles and dust. It reminded Nick of a layered cake that had been sat upon so it slanted to mismatched slabs of worthless crumbs. The damage was irreversible and, being so isolated, he would venture manmade. Who had done it; and why?

There wasn't even enough of a step here or there to provide footing for a mountain goat. Whoever ruined the stairs wanted to ensure no one would ever be going through that door again.

Cursing, Nick backed downward, forgetting the loose pebbles beneath his boot. He took a bad slide and twisted off his step, catching himself with the railing. His knee banged on the stone below and stopped the fall.

He hissed from the jab shuddering through his thigh and he watched the dizzying depths where several pebbles bounced downward along the stairs.

The scene shook something loose within him ... a lost memory. Blurred and enigmatic, but very real. He'd once watched a man fall down a flight of stairs much like these— narrow, steep, and made of stone.

Standing up, Nick sucked in a sharp breath as the flashback hit him full force, making the pain in his knee as insignificant as a bee sting. He hadn't thought of the tragedy in years. Partly because he'd been so drunk at the time, he sometimes thought he'd dreamt it. But even more because his part in the violence was more than anyone would wish to remember.

He'd visited a famed brothel in London's Rotten Row with some friends for his sixteenth birthday. They'd managed an appointment for him to spend an hour with the renowned Jasmine—the reigning courtesan who could leave men sated with merely a touch and a taste.

After he and his friends drank enough bourbon to float a passenger liner, Nick had meandered upstairs alone to find her. A woman's heart-rending cries burst from the room as he arrived.

The door was slightly ajar, and Nick paused beside it, hearing the words: "You won't leave me, Jasmine. You feckless whore!"

Nick peered within. When he saw the man stabbing his victim in the shadows, he snapped. Bursting into the room, he wrestled the attacker into the hallway and to the top of the stairs. He lost his grip on his opponent's waist, sending the stranger hurtling to his death.

Nick had returned, numb with shock, to comfort the mangled woman on the floor. She'd been encompassed in darkness, a line of moonlight illuminating nothing but the gaping slash from her chest to her abdomen and those tragic eyes—unblinking. Just like the eyes in his dream last night.

Felicity's eyes.

Nick dropped the glass lantern to the steps with a crash as he remembered vividly her words in the greenhouse that first night: *"No. Not you ... how could it be you?"* She'd recognized him, despite his beard. And her coldness to him, how she constantly pushed him away at the last minute ...

she'd been fearing he would recognize her.

Now it made sense: that habit of touching her chest, as if subconsciously recalling some trauma from her past. She bore a scar—and not just an emotional one. No wonder she couldn't trust men.

On that tragic night, he had whispered her name. *Jasmine.* He had smoothed her tangled, black hair and spoke gently, asking her not to die. He'd held her cold hand until her lashes had closed.

A hand softer than rose petals.

When his friends found him, they forced him to leave lest he be accused of murdering both the man and the courtesan. They had all thought her dead.

By God, she had lived. Not only that ... she'd taken a new identity.

But what of her age? It was wrong. That was seven years ago. It didn't add up. Jasmine was only eighteen at the time. Her youth was her trademark.

Then again ... what was it Lia had said about her aunt's wrinkles? That they faded with the night. Hadn't he seen that for himself inside the greenhouse, and blamed it on a trick of moonlight? And hadn't Felicity slipped up and said something about being too young to raise the girls? Not to mention those dark lashes and eyebrows without a hint of gray.

Jasmine's hair had been dark as night ... not so difficult a thing to change with washes made of herbs, of which she had plenty here.

The countess was not at all who she seemed to be and wasn't nearly so old as she would have everyone think. That explained the youthfulness of her body, of her mind. And if she was lying about her age, what else was she lying about?

Had she even been married to the earl, in truth? Why

would a man of such power and wealth have taken a scarred courtesan to wife?

Nick's innards quaked as he picked up the broken glass from his fallen lantern, finally understanding that dark terror which kept her so isolated and distant.

He eased down the stairs, staying within the existent footprints despite his burning desire to rush out of the castle to find her. If Felicity was the woman from the brothel … and he felt sure she was … no way in hell was he leaving.

He held her secret in the palm of his hand, and she knew it. But what she didn't know was that she held his hope in hers.

All he wanted was a quiet life. The chance to start over anew without the threat of shaming his family darkening his every thought. He could have security here, hidden away from the world. Away from its temptations. The past that had always haunted him would become as indistinct as the dust in this castle full of mysteries.

He could still search for a way to seek forgiveness from Mina, yet that didn't seem so pressing at the moment. Not when he'd be reacquainting the beautiful and beguiling Jasmine—a courtesan every bit as broken and damned as him.

CHAPTER FIFTEEN

Felicity cradled Dinah in her arms, trying to soothe the hissing tabby cat.

The moment she'd wrapped her mind around Johnny Boy's burst of energy, Felicity had joined in Tobias's chase of the dogs. She'd managed to save Dinah in the process. It had been no easy undertaking, and she suspected she looked as much of a mess as the cat—covered in dirt with her hair unkempt and dress rumpled.

The shredded scarf at her neck fluttered in the breeze, barely covering the rip in her bodice's neckline. She secured Dinah between her breasts in the hopes to hold her dress in place, worried that the tip of her scar might show through her thin cotton chemise.

As she followed Tobias and Johnny Boy along the path with Nutmeg in tow, the castle came into view. Her nerves eased upon seeing no sign of Landrigan's carriage. She and the stable boy walked silently with the animals, all of them panting—weary from their run. Overhead, clouds had come to settle, darkening the sky to an ominous gray and making the air humid and heavy. So much for her picnic plans.

Or so she'd thought.

Before they'd even climbed the first step to the castle

door, she saw Nick on the threshold—muscles accentuated by the tightness of the shirt he wore—holding a lidded picnic basket. He no longer had his cane.

She glared pointedly at him, meaning to ask about his and Johnny Boy's swift recovery, but her tongue numbed to silence. He had shaved off his beard and looked again like the boy who had saved her so many years ago. Yet, not a boy at all. The dim daylight underscored the strong angles of his face with shadows, rendering him beautiful in a dark and dangerous slant. The sage hues of his shirt reflected in his irises. The result was a liquidized greenish-gray, like puddles of rain mirroring a tree's leaves.

After greeting Johnny Boy and inciting a tail-wagging of epic proportions, Nick instructed the stable hands to take the dog in, citing Clooney wished to examine him. Once they left, Nick turned his full attention to Felicity.

He tipped his hat, his earring glittering in the faint light. "It appears Johnny has been making himself at home."

Dinah's answering mewl ended in a growl, as if she were tattling on the dog.

Nick grinned, reaching out to rub between her gray ears, his finger coming dangerously close to touching Felicity's chest. Her breasts tingled at the proximity.

"Sorry little sweeting," Nick murmured to the cat. "I shall have to teach Johnny how to treat a lady. Glad to see you came through better than your mistress, though."

He met Felicity's stare and something new rushed from his gaze to hers. A knowing look. It was as if he plunged into the depths of her heart and fished out her secrets, holding them up on a silken line to appraise them in the daylight. She tore her gaze free, afraid everything she'd been hiding would surface on her face beneath his intense study.

Her arms jerked around the cat and won her a scalding

hiss. Felicity set the tabby down and held the scarf in place over the small rip in her bodice. Dinah darted across the threshold, diving between Nick's legs on the way in. Nick stepped out of the way so Nutmeg could follow.

"You accepted my invitation?" With her free hand, Felicity tried to smooth her hair into some semblance of order but decided it impossible and gave up.

"Yes. And the mouse's ear was a fine touch. Thank you." Nick's sexy half-smile appeared.

She had to stifle the dotty grin that wanted to bubble up in response. Giddiness ... that was an emotion she'd never had the luxury to embrace before. How did he make her feel secure enough that such a silly sensation would even rear its head?

He lifted the basket. "Are you ready then?"

"I'm a mess..."

"You're no more disheveled than me."

Felicity studied him. The rest of his appearance didn't quite match up to his freshly shaved face. Dusty and wrinkled trousers, hair strands fallen out of his queue. He must have been in a hurry to get ready this morning. Was it because he'd been anxious to see her?

Felicity, don't play the fool. This is to be a picnic between platonic acquaintances, nothing more.

Loose strands of gold at the edge of his hat caught the wind and flailed around the square lines of his jaw, bringing her focus to his lips. In that moment, it hit her full force. This man could erase all memory of Landrigan's hands on her skin. All memory of the men throughout her life who'd defiled her for their satisfaction, leaving her without any of her own.

It startled her to realize she didn't want to take a proper lunch with Nick. She wanted to *be* his lunch—to feel his mouth on her once more, tasting every inch of her body ... every inch except her scar. "I-I should wash off and change." She squeezed the torn scarf at her neck and tried to contain the trembling in her vocal chords.

Nick's attention shifted to the sky as several droplets plopped to her forehead. "No time for that," he said. "There's a blanket in the basket ... you can use it for a shawl once we're settled. And the rain will wash you off well enough. Best be on our way before any weirdness impedes us."

"Weirdness?"

He surprised her by descending the stairs, snagging her wrist, and pulling her onto the path without answering. A soft mist began to patter on the trees.

She tried to keep up with his long stride, her legs still tired from her chase at the stables. It had been one thing to be alone with Nick when his body was less than functioning. Today, he was unbridled potency and vigorous determination, without anything to weaken him and offer her balance.

How had he healed so quickly?

"Your limp..." She couldn't manage better than bare-boned remarks, needing to preserve her breath for the brisk stroll.

"Yes. Some of the weirdness to which I referred. My untimely recuperation is tied to that queer fungus in your greenhouse."

Felicity strained her ears, unsure she'd heard him clearly over the rainfall. He proceeded to apprise her of his talk with Aislinn about the fungus. The weakening in Felicity's legs seeped into her abdomen, causing it to jitter. "How do you think it got on your skin?"

He paused abruptly and turned to her. "Perhaps when I fell into the vines last night, some of it clung to my clothes ... and somehow spread to Johnny, as well."

Felicity panted, catching her breath. "And Aislinn believes it's a curative?"

"An exceptional one, that works almost overnight it would seem. Your caterpillars and passion vines will soon be thriving once more, if you let nature take its course."

Gratitude spread through Felicity. As spry as he was feeling, Nick could simply have taken Johnny and the pony then left the castle without a word to anyone. Instead, he went to Aislinn and solved the caterpillar dilemma. Was it possible that he did want the best for her and her nieces? "Thank you for telling me. For helping us."

Nick nodded, then resumed their walk, his hand still holding hers. "I truly want to help you. I hope you can believe that now."

Offering a smile as tremulous as the wind rushing her hair, Felicity followed his lead, ducking down as they burst out of the trumpet vine and latticework tunnel and turned off in the opposite direction from the greenhouse. She'd planned to retreat inside the glass enclosure. It would be ideal in this kind of weather. But her escort apparently had other ideas, so she followed along, curious. Her heart danced on a bizarre mix of excitement and disquietude. She hadn't done anything so spontaneous in years and drank in the feeling—finding it every bit as sweet as the mist glazing her mouth.

"Where are we going?" she asked, resituating her gloved hand within the comfort of his large palm.

"Well, now that I know your brother's wife is the one whose cremated remains are gathering dust in the turret, we're going to visit Jasper's grave." He locked his fingers through hers, no doubt anticipating her reaction.

Felicity railed against him, stiffening as they approached the iron gate that opened into the surrounding forest. "Who told you?"

"Tis amazing, the things a man can glean from an infatuated maid."

Felicity broke from his grasp, her cheeks growing hot. "*Rachel.* That little trollop. And what did 'Yer Graceship' offer her in exchange?"

Nick turned around, grinning. "Why Miss Felicity, you're flushed. Are you jealous that I spent time with the maid this morn?"

"I care nothing of what you do or with whom you do it."

"Of course. Words speak louder than actions, after all."

Scowling, Felicity reached up and knocked the hat from his head. "You wish me to trust you, yet you go behind my back for private details about my family all so you can reach your precious wife."

Nick bent to retrieve the hat, securing it on his head as he studied her. "You're too damned suspicious for me to find anything out any other way. If you were to open up, even a little, I might be able to solve your ghost mystery, as well."

Felicity hardened her jaw. "You can find the grave alone. I'm not accompanying you."

She'd only taken one step back toward the castle when Nick dropped the basket and caught her around the waist. His hand was hot against her abdomen—a stern eroticism that could be felt even through the layers of her skirt and petticoats. Before she could escape, he twirled her toward the gate. Her shoulder blades pressed against the slippery iron bars as his hands secured her wrists over her head—gentle, but commanding. His sudden change in mood took her aback, excited her...

He bent down to level their gazes. "Not a very cordial attitude for a hostess. It seems you've misplaced your manners. Perhaps Lia can lend you her reserve."

Felicity tipped her tongue out to taste the mist drizzling

her lips, trying to cool the mixed sensations afire in her belly. Nick watched her mouth with open fascination.

"You know nothing of manners or propriety," she mumbled, every erogenous zone begging his attention— pitting passion against jealousy. "You who would bed a woman simply for petty misinformation."

A wry smile rolled over his lips. His skin glistened with moisture on the movement. "I believe Rachel's facts to be quite credible. And it took nothing more than a comment on the loveliness of her hair. She was butter after that." His hands glided from Felicity's wrists to her elbows, an intimate transfer of heat that hitched her breath. "Sweet, creamy butter."

Felicity shoved his hands away. "I *knew* you were like him." Tears burned her eyes. She thumped Nick's chest with her fists.

"Him?" Nick didn't topple as he had last night in the greenhouse. Instead, he tightened his stance and leaned in, his hands cupping her nape. "Are you speaking of Donal? Is this why you despise him? Did the Irishman have a tryst with Rachel?"

Sometimes Felicity hated his perceptivity. "Men are all the same. Always lusting ... searching ... for some woman other than the one standing right before them. Someone younger or prettier. Or deader, in your case. Let me go!" She couldn't break free.

Thumbs at her temples, Nick forced her to look up at him. She fought back, but her efforts only entangled her more.

"Calm down." Nick's voice lowered to a deep, sensual purr. "I didn't touch Rachel. Do you hear me?" Felicity froze as he pressed his mouth to her ear. "The only connection I'm seeking is with the woman in front of me, my darling Felicity. Whether she be living or dead, twenty or one hundred years old."

His whisper warmed the shell of her ear. Her breath caught, a gut reaction. She knew he'd meant nothing by the relativity of age ... but to be so close to the truth was disconcerting.

Then it registered how he'd said her name ... so casual, yet so reverent, like the secret epithet of a lover. She pulled back and squinted in the mist, grateful for its camouflage lest he see her tears.

"I would never have teased you about Rachel had I known something took place between her and that Irish bastard." His forehead pressed to hers, lips only inches from her mouth. "I saw him leave earlier this morning. Did he threaten you again?"

Felicity shook her head on a lie.

"Good. Because I'd hate to have to pound him with the stick pony."

Taken off guard by the untimely quip, Felicity snorted.

Nick chuckled, and his breath blended into the scent of the rain. "There's that smile." His thumb traced her lower lip. "Did you know, with all the oddities going on around me, you're the one puzzle I cannot get out of my head? Your cynicism, your suspicious and fastidious nature. The woman who maddens me and infuriates me most"—his fingers cinched her hair— "is also the most enchanting creature I've ever encountered."

That's when time stopped, for his lips met hers tenderly. With his skin bared of whiskers, it was a sensation as transient and restrained as the mist.

Moaning, she relaxed into him, giving herself to his embrace. When had she ever heard such lovely words? *Enchanting.* Who would've spared such a pretty appellation for a whore?

Her mind blurred as his tongue followed the shape of her

mouth, licking away the raindrops there, as if ridding any barriers between them. Then his lips brushed hers again, a pulsing heat, sweet and gentle.

His thumb tipped her chin and positioned her face to receive his ministrations. She grew still, oblivious to the downpour which pounded around them now, dousing their clothes and hair. She didn't notice the cold wetness seeping into her skin, or the heaviness of her skirts. She concentrated only on the movement of his mouth—straying to her eyelids then her ear and her jaw line—on how it felt to be the subject of his mastery ... to be the receptacle of such meticulous exploration. No man had ever taken the time to savor her slowly, and the sensation was such a potent aphrodisiac her thighs trembled in willing submission.

Her fingers found his shoulders and grasped him, holding herself up. His lips returned to her mouth. They clung there—more insistent than before. Hands moving down to graze the sides of her breasts. Felicity's gasp leapt up to meet his, lips opening to invite him in.

A primitive sound grated his throat as he answered her supplication. His tongue sampled the roof of her mouth—a tickling pleasure she returned in kind, sweeping along the bumpy terrain then trailing the smoothness of his teeth before meeting his tongue with her own. His hands shelved her buttocks and pulled her firmly against the tensile power of his man's form.

It was only when she found herself panting from the combination of the downpour, his hands on her body, the wildfire contact between them, and his demanding kisses that Nick drew back. He worked her fingers free from where they'd woven into his hair then kissed her exposed inner wrists in the place her gloves dipped low.

He blinked in the storm. "Let us find some shelter. I

understand there's an outlook post close to the grave."

His statement shook Felicity back to reality. She'd been drowning in him and the rain ... afloat in the wonderment of his exploration—so lost in this extension of herself into another human being she'd forgotten everything else. Including their destination.

Nick retrieved the picnic basket and coaxed Felicity aside so he could unlatch the gate. Then he clasped her hand and she followed, stepping out into the wilds. The confident resolve of his touch washed away any defiance she might've staged.

Once they'd traversed deep into the understory of the trees, she took the lead, sloshing through puddles and woody vines until they came to a platform wedged between the highest branches of two conifers. A rope ladder stretched down from its midst and led up to an enclosure—the long-abandoned treehouse.

Playing the part of the gentleman, Nick helped Felicity climb onto the lower rungs before him. But she caught a glimpse of his roguish side when she looked down to find his gaze intently fixed on the ankle-length drawers under her skirts.

"Keep your eyes to the ground, Master Nicolas. I am a lady and your elder, lest you forget."

A smirk turned his lips as he shifted his gaze off to the east. A smile tugged at her mouth, too, but vanished the instant she plunged through the trapdoor into the darkness.

She pulled her legs in and stood within the enclosure, shaking out her wet skirts. Her hair nearly snagged on the low-hung ceiling. Nick would have to hunch to stand, just like Jasper used to.

She took six steps across the floor and tugged at the hinged slats covering two round portholes. Light and fresh air seeped in to tame the scent of musty wood. Beetles and spiders scrambled into holes out of sight.

The sound of the rain pattering outside revived fresh nostalgia as Felicity glanced around the small nook. Though covered in dust and wayfaring ivy which had snaked in through cracks in the wood, everything looked just as Jasper had left it. The three-legged stool her brother used to sit upon to take notes in his journals; the kerosene lantern, now deprived of oil and thick with cobwebs, hanging from the midst of the ceiling; and the pile of scientific tomes Felicity had never bothered to retrieve after his loss.

Just like everything that reminded her of Jasper, she'd shut her eyes to this place. Forgotten it. They had spent many hours up here with the girls, viewing the forest and its native wildlife. Such broken memories she preferred to tuck away in the darkness rather than hold up to the light, for fear she might see the cracks within them.

Felicity's mindset shifted as Nick held up the basket, easing his upper half through the trapdoor. She placed the food in a corner, her gaze locked to his as he climbed in. If only things were normal again, like they were when Jasper was with them. It would be so easy, here in the solitude, to tell Nick who she was, to remind him of their entwined paths in the past, of how he saved her. To thank him in ways only a woman could thank a man.

One side of her wanted the closeness, that bond with him, more than anything. But the other side—the cautious one that had kept her alive all those years as a courtesan— forbade the confession.

Nick would be going back into the world soon, returning to society ... away from this fortress and its caustic riddles. He would forget her. And better that he did. He already held the secret that she was raising her nieces. No matter what might happen between them here today, she could never tell him her true identity. Else she would risk losing the life she'd almost died to obtain.

CHAPTER SIXTEEN

Felicity settled in the corner opposite the picnic basket, watching Nick as he unpacked the food. She studied his mouth, thinking of the kiss that still clung to her lips—a weight she hoped would never dissolve.

He laid out a linen napkin, smoothing the wrinkles with large hands which had earlier raged fires in her blood. A shot of tingling warmth burst within her breasts, swollen and heavy as she relived the feel of him so close to touching her there.

Glancing up, he held her gaze and placed a small cheddar truckle—as round as any wagon wheel—upon the napkin along with black pepper biscuits, dried beef, a fresh peach, and two goblets. Uncorking a bottle of honey wine, he poured it, the purl of golden liquid as rousing to her senses as the fermented floral scent adrift on the air.

His hat sat on his head at a jaunty slant. The grayish light from outside softened his masculine features beneath the brim. If not for the earring, he'd look just like that daring sixteen-year-old who had held her hand and coaxed her to stay alive.

Little could he know that it was his words, his gentleness, which had kept her hanging on, long after he'd gone. He'd shown her kindness at a time when she believed she deserved nothing less than disdain. The moment she'd been stabbed ... everything inside of her worthy of life had died. The precious fetus she carried, that tiny, dependent soul she'd already come to love. The very reason she'd told Hayes she wished to quit selling her body.

She convinced herself that night, while her womb was being gutted, that had she not been a whore, maternal happiness wouldn't have been ripped away from her. She deserved what happened.

Or so she'd thought.

As she'd fallen to the floor, doubled over from the slash of the vicious blade, choking on the blood she'd shared with her baby, she was praying to pass into death. But then Nick came out of the shadows—young, courageous, compassionate. He showed her through his outraged concern that every human was put in the world for an honorable purpose. That everyone merited a second chance to get it right. Had she not held onto life, her nieces would be in an orphanage today, most likely growing up apart, just as she and Jasper had. Nick's bravery had made her second chance possible.

Gratitude overwhelmed her as she watched him, now a powerful man, still possessing that same ardent humanity, still driven to rescue her. She wondered why it had been so difficult for her to trust him once he'd fallen back into her life, after everything he had done for her on that fated night. In spite of his thievery, in spite of the laudanum, he was still the same person. She could see that now. The only difference was the sadness and remorse which clouded his gaze at times he didn't know she was looking.

She wished he could be as forgiving to himself—as blind to his own sins—as he seemed to be to others'.

He bent low, the blanket draped from one elbow as he

carried the goblets over then knelt in front of her. Felicity clasped her arms around her legs where they folded up against her chest beneath her skirts, trying to stave off the shivers radiating from her scar.

"You're cold." Nick set aside the wine and slipped the blanket off his arm. He wrapped the scratchy heaviness around her shoulders, pulling her slightly forward to tuck the excess between her back and the wooden slats. Next, he picked up a goblet.

"Drink this mead. You look as pale as death itself," he said as the liquid drizzled down her throat like warm nectar. "I think we should get these wet clothes off of you."

"No." Felicity hugged her knees tighter beneath the blanket, at a loss to tell him this wasn't a physical chill, but a spiritual freeze. In truth, her deformity was the one thing keeping her from stripping naked and begging him to take her. Modesty had fallen by the wayside years ago. Yet in this moment, she felt as exposed as she had the first time she'd been with a man—a different kind of vulnerability, since she'd only been a girl then.

She was a woman today. It was that hard-won experience for which she'd bartered her innocence that caused this trepidation. She knew what a man found beautiful about a woman's body: flawless skin, a perfect valley between round breasts, a stomach that curved just enough he could envision her with child at some point. All the things she'd once possessed, now foiled irreparably by a hideous scar that ran the length of her torso—deep and pitted like a dried-up riverbed.

She shivered again, a full body shake from her toes to her lips. "Perhaps"—her teeth chattered— "if I eat something. It will w-w-warm me."

Tipping his head in a concerned gesture, Nick made his

way to the food. After cutting two wedges of cheese, he placed them on biscuits then tore up some beef to sprinkle on top. He carried them over. She started to work her arm free from beneath the blanket but Nick stopped her.

"Allow me." Setting his biscuit aside on a napkin, he crouched in front of her again, eyes shaded by his hat's brim as he held out her food.

Felicity leaned forward and sank her teeth into the peppery morsel. Nick pushed the biscuit into her mouth too quickly, and bits of it crumbled then rolled down her chin.

"Sorry." Grinning, he tried to catch them with a fingertip. "I would make a shoddy momma bird."

She giggled as she chewed, but amusement quickly traded for searing desire as he fed her the fallen crumbs off his fingertips, watching her take each warm digit into her mouth and wind her tongue to lick it clean. Eyes flashing in the lightning, he offered another sip of mead to help soften her food and ate his own biscuit, stopping between bites to give her more. He made a point to touch the corners of her mouth at each serving, to capture every crumb until nothing remained uneaten, not even a grain of pepper.

Flushed from the sensuality behind his every movement, Felicity thanked him then tried to put some distance between them. She gestured with her head to the opening in the wall at her right. "If you look out that portal, you shall see it."

Eyebrows furrowed, Nick set aside his goblet. "See what?"

"Jasper's grave."

"Ah."

"Tis why we're here, is it not?"

A ruminative expression crossed his face. "I'd rather forgotten why we'd come." He crawled over to the porthole, knelt in front of it, and glanced out. "Do the girls visit him often?"

"Never alone. I worry for their safety. The bogs are dangerous, much like quicksand. Some time ago, Landrigan set my pigs loose out there. They became stuck in the peat and died."

Nick glanced at her, his gaze serious. "Thus, the shortage of sausage?"

Felicity bit her lip. "Yes. With my business in jeopardy, I've not been able to afford replacing them."

"Peat bogs." He was quiet for a moment. "Why did you bury Jasper so far from the castle?"

Felicity held the blanket tight at her neck and crept forward, walking on her knees, until she reached her companion. "Did the maid not tell you? Perhaps she's holding out for more of an incentive, *Yer Graceship*." She offered it as a tease, unwilling to acknowledge the jealousy which still sat like a mossy rock in her belly.

Taking up the challenge, Nick glanced down, warming her blood and bones with his sexy grin. "You're the only one I plan to use my incentive on."

Felicity's heart gave a leap. She forced her attention back to the porthole, to the headstone below only a few yards to the north. A deer crossed behind it—unaware of its audience—graceful and silent as a phantom. The rain had softened to mist, coating the elegant creature with sparkles.

"In Binata's culture," Felicity began, "it is believed that there are two kinds of death. A good death and a bad one. Anyone who dies before the age of fifty is prematurely departed. Since they've not fulfilled their destiny, they will be restless. Binata was terrified that Jasper would become a floating ghost. She told me, that to prevent being haunted, her people would cast those who died bad deaths far away from the village into the forest ... so they might be eaten by wild animals to prevent reincarnation." Felicity shrugged, feeling foolish for even recanting such a tale. "Or some such nonsense. This was my compromise. To appease her worries, we buried the coffin outside the castle gates. Far away in the forest."

"But you didn't leave his body to the wilds."

Felicity pressed her temple against the wooden wall, regarding him. "Leaving the coffin open and unburied is against *our* traditions."

Nick continued to look outside, his profile studious. "I see. So you do give credence to a belief system, of some sort or other."

"I may not live amongst society, but I still uphold their customs. This surprises you?"

He removed his hat and tossed it behind him. Every strand of hair had fallen from the tie now, leaving it an unkempt mess of golden waves, much like it had looked last night when he'd come to her chamber door. Felicity's fingers itched to touch it. Instead, she clenched her hands tighter in the blanket.

"When I first came looking for Jasper," Nick said, "I hoped he could offer some untapped information pertaining to death and the afterlife. But now I realize you are the expert on such things."

"How so?"

He locked his gaze to hers. "Due to the fact that you came so close to dying yourself, seven years ago at that brothel."

Felicity shot to standing at the words. He had remembered who she was. *What* she was...

Her back slid along the wall until she came to the three-legged stool. She ended crumpled upon the seat, the blanket bunched up behind her. She dragged the blanket free and stared where it piled upon the floor, unable to look at Nick for fear of what would reflect in his eyes.

Kneeling in front of her, he took her hands and peeled away her gloves before she could jerk free. Touching her palms to his bared jaw, he turned his chin to run his lips across them. "Sweet, soft Jasmine."

Mortified by the name, Felicity tried to stand. "I-I don't know what you're referring to."

"Stop." Nick clasped her hands—a counter to her efforts. "You cannot outrun a memory that haunts us both."

Felicity closed her eyes against the scalding burn behind them, refusing to cry. She knew there was no escape, and in some strange way, gleaned relief in the unveiling of this secret. "I can't help you find Mina, if that's what you're after. If you plan to blackmail me for information, both of us will lose. For I truly know nothing of death."

"No. I was hoping my knowledge might win me refuge here, in this place. Nothing more."

She snapped her eyes open. So he did mean to bargain with her. He knew that he held her fate in his hands. "If I refuse to let you stay, do you intend to tell Landrigan?" She tensed as she felt his breath hot on her face.

"Never. What must I do to convince you I'm on your side?" His finger trailed the hairline at her temple, but she flinched and pulled back, her emotions raw and wild.

"Would I have tried to help you that night," he asked, "if I intended to throw you to the wolves today? And do you not realize you have something to hold over me as well? You witnessed a murder I committed when I pushed the man who stabbed you down the stairs."

Felicity considered letting him believe his part in the crime ... until she saw the depth of guilt behind his eyes. He already seemed to have so much remorse to bear. It was within her power to relieve him of this one thing. Yet in so doing, she would lose any leverage.

But didn't she owe him this, after all he'd done for her? She would just have to give him the benefit of the doubt. Believe that he wasn't like so many other men who had passed through her life. "You are no murderer. He didn't die. Least not from the fall."

In that moment, cold astonishment washed through Nick's blood, causing his hands to spasm, to release Felicity's from his grasp. He forfeited the softness of her flesh for the splintered floor and rocked back to sit on his hips, his body numb. "I don't understand. How could anyone survive that?"

"By some miracle of fate." The dim light rendered her tragic eyes such a deep brown they appeared bottomless. "That man was the Earl of Carnlough. The owner of this estate. Had he died that day, I would never have inherited my home. I have that fall to thank for my marriage to him."

Nick clenched his jaw. Her own husband had stabbed her? Wait ... she admitted he hadn't been her husband at that point. Why would she have married him after such cruelty? Just to gain this estate? And then to inherit the trouble with Landrigan. She'd certainly won the short end of that stick.

"For all of his faults," Felicity continued, "the earl ... Hayes ... was deeply religious. It was his fear of dying in sin, of facing purgatory for his mistreatment of me, that brought him to a place of utter penitence. In the months it took me to heal from the stabbing, the earl developed pneumonia from being laid up in a bed due to the broken bones he'd sustained in the fall. During the last week of his life, he arranged for me to marry him. Our ceremony took place in a hospital with the earl propped on pillows in his deathbed. He put me in his will, so I might legally own his estate, and he might merit a place in heaven."

Felicity resituated on the stool and reached for the

blanket, quivering again. Nick came to himself enough to help her tuck the cover around her shoulders. He noticed his trousers were wetter where her skirt had pressed against his thighs, as if a part of her had transferred to him. He rubbed the dampness with his palms as he sat down again.

"Will you tell me?" he asked. "Tell me why he attacked you so viciously that night." He saw the flash of indecision in her eyes. "Felicity, I already know your darkest secret. What have you to lose at this point?"

Her lashes slanted downward. She took a deep breath and anguish paled her face. "He wished me dead because ... because I no longer wanted the life he had arranged for me. He thought me ungrateful." She gripped her chest beneath her blanket and rolled her shoulders, as if struggling to bear the weight of her confession. "Jasper and I once lived in an orphanage in London. We were separated when a couple took Jasper but didn't want me—I was just a girl, after all. I couldn't carry their name on for other generations. Some months later, Hayes Lonsdale came to the orphanage. Out of all the other children, he chose me, carried me to his townhouse in the country. In the beginning, he was kind. He bought me fine clothes and took me to mass each Saturday, claiming that I was his cousin's child. He taught me to drive a carriage and use a whip. He taught me to read and write. Then he taught me other things. Things I didn't wish to learn. He was the first man to ever—"

Nick winced as her voice broke. A growl caught in his throat. "How old were you?"

"Thirteen."

Watching the shame suffuse her cheeks in a red rush, Nick ground a fist into the floor. The gritty ache along his knuckles offered a momentary distraction from his rage.

"The earl trained me." She still wouldn't look at Nick.

"And when I'd mastered my 'skills', he dubbed me Jasmine, because the flower's fragrance is known as the transport of joy. He said that was what I was to be to men. The transport of joy. Thus was my calling in life. I was to earn him money by lifting my skirts. At the time, I was too naïve to think I could escape, for who else would want me after I'd already been spoiled? When I turned sixteen, Hayes rented me out to a brothel while he came here to Ireland to tend his estate. He promised, if I made enough money, he would return and wed me. He would bring me here, and let me pursue my dream to breed butterflies and be a mother. I thought he meant it ... I thought he loved me, in some warped way."

When she finally braved a glance at him, Nick was crushed by the stark betrayal shadowing her fragile features—the grief deepening her wrinkles. *Wrinkles that weren't even real...*

Now he understood why she spared no tolerance for religion.

He forced himself to hold her gaze. He wanted to embrace her, to caress her. To show her intimacy the way it was meant to be, between two consenting adults who wished to share their feelings. He wanted to erase her torturous past with his lips, hands, and body.

But he wouldn't. For a woman like Felicity to offer up her most vulnerable memories, after having scraped and clawed for survival for so long, she'd be feeling exposed to her core in this moment. And he would rather fight this desire to touch her ... even when it ached to the point of visceral pain ... before he would reduce her to that helpless, violated girl she once was.

Only if she reached for him would he go to her.

When she made no such move, Nick stiffened every muscle and stayed nailed to his place on the floor. "I wish I *had* killed that bastard now," he said, unable to maintain the charged silence any longer. "I wish I had another chance to do it right."

"No, Nick. I've forgiven him, for it all. Things happened as they did for a purpose. His hope for absolution enabled this new life with my nieces. Ironically, the very life he had promised me." She turned away to look out the window. "Such a break with the old would never have been possible without this castle far removed from London, and from men who could've recognized Jasmine."

The rain had started again. Nick imagined the droplets rinsing away the wounded Jasmine to reveal Felicity, the woman underneath ... the woman she had become. From a cocoon to a butterfly. Strong and independent. He was even more in awe of her than before. To bear such ugliness and degradation, yet still retain tenderness and compassion enough to forgive her persecutor then step in and care for her nieces—it spoke volumes of her capacity for love and loyalty.

A wave of shame surged through him, to have ever thought her an unforgiving shrew. Now everything made sense. Why she held herself captive here. Why she tried to look older and colored her hair so it resembled polished metal.

"Your wrinkles?" he asked, unable to curb the curiosity.

"A lotion my brother concocted. It's a byproduct of Heliconius saliva."

"Ingenious. So that's why the butterflies are so important to you, even beyond your business dealings."

"Yes."

"Who else knows of this secret you keep?"

"Aislinn is aware of my true age. But she can never learn of my past." Felicity cast him a pleading glance.

He nodded an assurance.

Felicity's shoulders visibly relaxed. "My brother. I discovered his whereabouts soon after I came to live here and asked him to make this his home. He knew ... everything. And Clooney knows. He's been with me since I left London."

Nick's ears perked. "Does he know who I am? My role in your past?"

"No."

"Hmmm. I've noticed he's peculiarly knowledgeable in medicine. What's his story?"

"At one time, he was a fine physician ... but he squandered his life away on gambling. He ruined his reputation, lost his license. Having no other recourse, he became the personal physician for the brothel. He also became like a father to me. Perhaps since I was the youngest, he pitied me most. When I was stabbed, he helped me break away. He told everyone in London, including my mistress, that I died. He'd been keeping tabs on the Earl's condition and set up the secret appointment between Hayes and me that resulted in our marriage before his death. Then Clooney came with me here for support."

"And to hide from his own demons, no doubt," Nick said. "Your servants ... do they know any of this?"

"Only Binata. But she would never betray me."

Nick cocked his head, unconvinced. "She and her nephew seem very close."

"She adores Landrigan. But not as much as she despised his father. Hayes abused Binata's sister mercilessly. The one time Binata tried to step in, she received a slash of the whip across her face."

Nick scrubbed his palm across his smooth chin. "The 'H' upon her face. It stands for Hayes?"

"Yes. He was a master with the whip. Binata and I ... we both share scars enacted by that man. We have a sisterhood, of sorts. So she will never reveal my secret to his son."

She shivered upon the final sentence, and to see her so vulnerable had the strangest effect on Nick. To even imagine her being chained for life to that bastard gouged him inside. It felt as if he'd swallowed a carving knife that was shaping his heart and soul to some monstrous form.

In that moment, the sun shifted from behind the clouds outside, fully illuminating Felicity. A shift took place in Nick, as well. Everything in this nook was dusted with age and neglect. And there she sat, a counterfeit reflection of the confinement and decay. But he could see beyond those faded lines upon her face, beyond that messy upsweep of silver hair, still wet from the rain and clinging to her dark lashes with each blink. Despite her every effort to appear otherwise—she was the touch of spring upon a winter mountain. A blossom bursting out of the snow, attempting to open its petals at each shy sprinkling of light. Deep inside, that twenty-five-year-old woman waited to live again— tender, fragile, and searching for wings. And everything that marked him a man burned to preserve that part of her.

Pulse pounding in his neck, Nick lifted to his knees. Before he could even consider the outcome, he caught her hands in his. "You are too fine a lady for Donal Landrigan. Marry me instead."

CHAPTER SEVENTEEN

Felicity couldn't believe what she'd heard. Or had she heard it at all? Perhaps she'd merely dreamed it. Thus far, this day had felt like a walk up a winding stairway of dreamscapes. It had started at the bottom step as a Landrigan-induced nightmare then ended here in the clouds with Nick—a wonderful fantasy too lovely and sweet to be true.

How could it be possible, that even knowing what she had been in her past, Nick still called her as a lady ... still regarded her with the same veneration as when he'd thought her a respectable dowager?

She listened to the rain slapping the roof, watched Nick's face lighten and darken with the shifting storm. The soft light torched his wavy hair, glazing each strand in turn, making it appear alive and dancing. The set of his full mouth was honest and determined. Such devotion from a man she'd known less than two weeks left her breathless and unable to answer.

"Did you hear me, Felicity? You need a man. That's the one thing Donal and I agree upon. Let me fill that void. Marry me."

She gulped, trying to tamp the desire to accept the proposal without a second thought. He knew her secret, after

191

all. Her hand twitched within his. Yes. He knew her secret. But he didn't know Jasper's. And were he to live with her under the same roof, eventually that truth would come out.

"You merely wish to rescue me again," she offered as a countermand.

"I wish to rescue myself. From a life out there." He motioned to the portholes, but they both knew his implication. "If I stay here with you ... I can staunch Donal's efforts once and for all. And I'll not have to return to a world that holds nothing but loss and shame for me. The arrangement will benefit us both."

It did seem ideal. He was running from a past, just like her. "Tell me about your family. Why do you wish to hide from them? Does it have to do with the newspaper?"

He started to pull back. But she kept him anchored with her grasp.

"Nick, you know my secret—why I hide. So ... tit for tat."

A grin swept over his face, so fleeting, she almost didn't catch it. "Tit for tat, aye? You drive a hard bargain." He kissed her inner wrist, warm lips gliding across her skin and leaving a hungry ache at her pulse point. Still kneeling, he rested his hands atop hers on her lap. "I once seduced a virgin—the daughter of my brother's business partner. I took her innocence without a thought as to consequence. Her family learned of our tryst. To salvage my family's holiday resort, I tried to do the right thing by eloping with her. But we were young, and neither of us truly understood what love was, or even if we shared it. A year into the marriage, we became further estranged by a very personal tragedy. I didn't know how to comfort her when the very same pain was eating away at my soul. So I left every night to wallow in liquor and strange women. I betrayed my vows ... was a bastard in the worst possible way. Mina was alone far too often. And to seek escape, she started using laudanum. Under the influence of the drug, she took her life."

Felicity captured Nick's hands, an effort to still his trembling. "I'm so sorry." Her eyes searched his downturned head. "What was this tragedy that tore you apart?"

He wouldn't meet her gaze. "The babe came too fast. Before the physician could arrive. Something was wrong. When his tiny body slipped into my hands ... I knew." He swallowed a sharp breath. "Oh, but he was perfect. Ten little fingers and ten little toes, his mouth—sweet—poised as if ready to nurse. But blue ... by God, he was the color of shadows on snow." Nick started to tremble again. Felicity tightened her grip on his wrists, though she didn't know if it was to ground him or her.

"The cord..." He shook his head. "It had wrapped around Christian's neck. Mina blamed herself, said that her body choked the life from him. She could never forgive herself after that. She said his empty cries rang in her head every day ... cries that were never born, from lungs that never took a breath."

Felicity inhaled deeply as the tragedy unfurled in her mind's eye. Tears singed her lashes. For years she'd fooled herself into thinking nothing could be worse than her experience, but she now knew. It was a gift that she'd never seen her baby. A sad, morbid, gift that her child was always to remain a genderless, nameless angel.

Nick groaned, a sound from deep within, as if he battled a demon locked inside. The same demon which roared within Felicity every day when her memories came to call.

"My wife needed a human touch, Felicity." Nick squeezed her knees to the point of pain, holding on for dear life. "*Lord help me*. Just a little compassion. A little reassurance." His broken voice pounded her skull like the rain on the roof overhead. "And I was too caught up in my own grief to offer it."

His eyes lifted to hers then, and the raw anguish slashed through her heart's outer shield like a poison-tipped thorn. "You made a mistake, Nick. A human err." The pressure on her knees softened.

"I killed my wife. Through my own selfish indulgences, I killed her. You should despise me for that, like everyone does. Like I despise myself." He glanced at the floor, tendrils of hair hanging over his eyes. Through the strands, she could see tears sliding silent down his face. His broad shoulders strained with the effort to not break down.

Felicity swiped his hair back and dried his cheeks. "I don't despise you. You did not kill her. Her heartache and the opium did. It is not her forgiveness you need to seek, but your own. Let her rest. She has peace now. They both do."

Eyebrows furrowing, Nick studied her. "Do you really think so?"

"I do. It wouldn't have mattered if you'd tried to ease her pain. A mother's grief can be inconsolable ..." Repressing the urge to tell him of her baby, Felicity altered her response. "I can only imagine what I would feel if I lost my girls. Forgive yourself and take comfort in her release."

She tugged him into her arms. His rough chin curved over the top of her head. With her ear pressed to his chest, she felt his warmth, his life pulsing through her on a strong, masculine heartbeat. She moved closer so his scent surrounded her, seeking comfort as she gave it. She turned to nuzzle his neck, to taste the flavor there—rain and salty tears.

"Thank you," he whispered. "No one's ever put it quite like that." His shuddering breath tugged at her hair.

"I understand. More than you know," she said against him.

Nick leaned back. "You do?"

"I understand shame. That's why you left your family. You didn't wish for them to find out."

Nick's forced laugh clipped the air. "If only. You mentioned my father and brother purchasing that printing press ... wondered why, or how they could afford it after I'd nearly cost them everything?"

He waited, as if for her to verify. She nodded and he continued.

"A drinking compatriot who'd been with me on that fated night sold my story to that press as a personal interest piece. They were only too happy to print it, the tale of the unfaithful husband driving his young bride to take her life after the loss of their child. My father had a friend working there, who caught wind of the story before it hit ink. Father stepped in, and with Julian contributing half the funds, bought the paper so they'd be in control of what printed. And I was oblivious, using laudanum myself, taking the coward's way while my father and brother stepped in to be my heroes. To clean up my messes once more."

Felicity touched her fingertip to his lips. "Stop. What matters is that your family survived it. They must be doing well now, to still invest in my caterpillars."

"They are," Nick spoke behind her finger—breath balmy against her skin. She moved her hand aside. "I have an uncle who's a renowned mantuamaker. He has a fine reputation designing gowns, and a long list of prior customers. My mother makes hats to complement each outfit. And my perfect brother ... he has a way with people. Went to the world's fair and managed to find new investors for the resort. But it's not so much the money as the mark on my parents' reputation, and their disappointment in me. They have two offspring who have brought them pride, then one who's brought them nothing but misery and shame. It is better they not have to think about me another minute."

Felicity cupped his face, smoothing her palm along the burr of his jaw. His eyes locked to hers, and the remorse was palpable. To carry so much blame ... to feel like he'd lost his parent's love and respect forever. That had to be such a burden upon a man. "Do you not realize they're thinking of you still? Even more so, when you're not there. They must be devastated you're gone. It would lift their spirits to hear from you. Time can heal so many wounds."

"No. My father can't see anything but my failings when he looks at me now. Even if the wound has healed, there will always be the scar left behind. It's irreversible."

Felicity's chest tightened, the truth behind the words etched into her skin. His glittering earring caught her eye—a welcome distraction. She touched the gem. "Mina's wedding ring."

Nick nodded. "What's left of it."

"So tragic."

He shrugged, a gesture Felicity ruled as a defense-mechanism to guise his pain. "Most things kept shut within the heart are tragic, Felicity. Why else would we hide them away? You know that as well as I."

Felicity placed her hands in her lap and grew quiet, pondering the child she had not yet told him of—the hollowness inside that opened anew each day.

Nick traced a fingertip over the blanket, following her disfigured chest. His voice lowered. "We both have pasts we wish to forget. Facing my father for me, would be like you facing all those men who used you. A reminder of my most repulsive and weakest moments. I want to forget those mistakes, forever. You can relate to that, can't you?"

Felicity nodded.

"I knew you could," he continued. "We understand one another on a level few others in this world do. Thus, a marriage is not only logical, but destined. We are two broken pieces. Perhaps together, we can find a fit."

Such a beautiful sentiment. Felicity closed her eyes, fighting the burn that pricked them. They shared even more than he knew. But she couldn't tell him of her deepest loss, or her barrenness. She was frail enough in his eyes already; were he to feel any more sympathy for her, it would border on pity. He might even feel obligated to uphold his proposal even if the confession changed his mind. He was a nobleman. Surely he wanted an heir one day.

No. She wouldn't tell him anything else. And she wouldn't allow him to marry her since she could never give him another child.

Determined, she opened her eyes and found her voice again. "Nick ... there is so much to consider in a situation such as this. There are two young girls who have a stake in my decision."

"Two girls whom I've grown very fond of in just a short time. Would you put them in the care of that misbegotten Irishman over me?"

The mere thought made Felicity's spine rigid. "I would put them in the care of no one but my own. I still hope to resolve this without having to marry for convenience. To have a marriage in name only—"

"I don't recall saying anything about 'in name only'." Holding her gaze, he took off his earring and tucked it in his pocket.

The profound symbolism behind the action froze her in place. Much as her mind begged escape, her body's anticipation controlled her now. Moving closer, he tugged her blanket from between them. His fingers wedged between the back of her head and the wall and dug into the edges of the bun at her nape.

"It's been so long for me, Felicity. I haven't taken a woman since my wife's death. You and I ... there's an undeniable attraction between us. There's no reason we shouldn't have every fringe benefit a marriage has to offer," he whispered.

Before she knew what he intended, Nick pulled out the pins which secured her coif. In one smooth motion, her hair flowed through his fingers and fell to her waist in a breezy rush. She gasped in surprise. Wedged as she was between his weight and the wall—his muscular thighs against her shins—she felt like a butterfly on a cork backing.

His palms followed her hair's damp cascade along her ribs, his gaze trailing the length where the ends fringed her waist. "You are so beautiful ... you don't even know."

His fingertips continued their descent to trace the curve of her hips swelling gently around the stool's edge. His touch radiated all throughout her torso and roused a humming pulse low in her pelvis—a reminder of a life once lived, of a pleasure she'd given but never fully experienced for herself.

Wrestling the urge to throw her arms around his neck again, she clenched her hands on her lap, her scar wielding a warning as heavy as a sword. "No. It would *have* to be in name only." If he would agree to this, it would prove he didn't care about having heirs.

"Do you think Donal will respect such a boundary?" Nick asked. "You're a very desirable woman. Even with your aging façade. I doubt he could resist you for long."

Felicity shuddered, remembering the pig's hands on her in the henhouse. "But I could resist him. Much easier than..."

"Than me." Nick finished for her.

Felicity locked her lips tight.

"I only want to give you pleasure," he said. "Has any man ever pleasured you, Felicity? I mean used his body to satisfy you. Not used yours as a vessel for his lust."

Not ever... She breathed the words, unable to speak them aloud.

"Is this self-flagellation?" he asked. "Penance for a past you never even wished to live? If so, stop it now. You are young and full of life. You deserve to be touched by a man who truly wants you. *You*, Felicity, not some selfish fantasy steeped in his own lechery. But the real woman. Vulnerable"—his lips trailed her chin— "skeptical"—a sweep of sensation along her jaw line— "perplexing"—a hovering caress over her ear lobe— "you. Will you rob yourself of that for all eternity?" His eased back, his mouth settled again just a hair's breadth from hers.

Her lips ached with his proximity... a bruise wanting to be healed. "This is pointless."

"Answer me," he spoke, lips close but not touching. "Answer and I'll let you go. If you still want me to."

She tipped the back of her head against the wall to put some space between them. The scent of moisture and musty wood whisked in on a cool breeze and grounded her. "We are strangers."

"After what we shared that night at the brothel and today in this place, we are allies, and so much more." His hands tightened on her hips, anchoring her with desire. "You were in my thoughts long before I came here. I used to envision your eyes. When I tossed and turned in bed trying to sleep. I had insomnia for months after that tragedy at the brothel. It killed me to think I hadn't got to you in time."

Felicity leveled her face to his. He'd dreamt of her, too? She could hardly fathom it. "I'm sorry you suffered so needlessly." *I can't have you suffering more.*

He leaned in again to whisper against her cheek. "I'm not sorry."

Felicity quivered at the tingling sensation along her skin. "Why?"

He pulled back to look her in the eyes. "Because I have you now, here in my hands. All these years, I've lived in shame for my failures. Yet here you are. The one person I put above myself. I tried to rescue you. And I succeeded. I must be worth something because of that."

She tried to curb the rush of need climbing through her like vines aflame. "You're asking me to be your charity case." She wanted his kiss so much her mouth watered.

"No. I'm asking you to be my salvation. To rescue *me* now."

"This is all part of your quest to reach Mina." She threw it out as a last-ditch attempt to curtail his sensual onslaught.

"Damnit Felicity." His jaw twitched. He gestured to his trousers where the tented fabric verified his state better than any words could. "Does this look like I'm dwelling on the past? This is desire for the woman sitting right before me. Real and alive. A desire that enflames my blood."

Felicity swallowed. The moment was so different from Landrigan earlier. Nick hadn't forced her touch, which only made her want him more. She wanted such exploration, ached to curl her fingers around this man, to know him.

Quivering with lust, she forced herself to draw back.

He gave her quarter, but his eyes weren't so merciful. They burned into hers with feral intensity. "All I'm offering is my body to you, and my devotion to the girls. I'll find some means to support us and this estate. Some legitimate means."

"And we'll all live happily ever after." Felicity balked at the stoicism behind her quip.

Nick frowned. "You're right. Roses fade with each passing day. A knight's armor grows tarnished. But what I'm proposing isn't a fairytale. Tis reality, prettied-up and polished to a lovelier shade of gloom."

A lovelier shade of gloom. Though strange and blunt, the words touched her with a stark poeticism. It was an odd comfort, that her portion of happiness might be to share the grief with one who understood self-loathing and acute loss on a level few others did.

Hesitant, Felicity leaned forward and touched his smooth face, running her fingers over every angle and line and feature. Her senses drank him in—smell and touch and sound—reacquainting him from her dreams. He sat there, quiet and unmoving, muscles coiled with the effort to let her appease her thirst.

But the instant she pressed her lips to his—an offering of sympathy for losses shared, spoken and unspoken—he snapped into motion. His mouth took hers in a deep, hungry kiss. It was as if he'd been waiting for some sign from her to open the floodgates of his passion.

It happened before she realized it. He folded to the floor, sweeping her beneath him, straddling her. Propped upon his elbows, he scooped his palms beneath her shoulder blades and molded their bodies together. She moaned as his hips wedged between her thighs, until her knees opened to allow him between the fan of her skirts.

The press of his desire, hard and hot against her abdomen even through their clothes, stirred images of his beautiful, perfect body joining hers—flesh to flesh. She'd seen him bared ... knew his splendor. Surely such grace and fire could melt her scar away to oblivion.

He ran a palm along her leg to push up her drawer's frilly hem, starting at her ankle and settling in the indention of her bent knee. He gripped her there, securing her leg around his waist. He consumed her skin with the gentleness of lips and tongue. His hips thrust in a motion remembered yet so different from the past. For his every move seemed measured and motivated by her reactions. Only when he heard a satisfied whimper or desperate moan would he evolve to another level of pleasure. As if *her* satisfaction drove his movements, not his own.

The mere thought made her weep in silent disbelief.

Was this how it was supposed to be? Wondrous and rapturous?

Lost in the feeling, she arched upward and choked on a sob—a guttural sound that would've shamed her, if not for the overwhelming need driving it.

"Am I crushing you?" His concern came on a whisper of air at the edge of her throat where tears had left wet lines.

"Yes," she managed. "Don't dare stop." She felt his lips curve to a smile on her neck in response. She laughed then, a surprising release of honest emotion deep from her soul.

"I love your laugh," he whispered, kissing her again. "I want to hear it every day. To wake to it every morn."

Her hands burrowed beneath his shirt along his perfect chest—silken hair and taut skin around thick, tense muscles. Lifting her chin to allow his mouth access to her jaw line, she tugged his shirt off. Their panting breaths became louder than the rain.

But she stopped breathing when it was his turn to undress her ... to loosen the armor so fastidiously tied, clasped, and buttoned into place each day. He had her scarf tossed aside and the rip in her bodice stretched open—fingertip gently grazing the tip of her scar beneath her chemise. She tensed, and he lifted his face to study hers.

What she saw in his eyes in the dim light struck her heart.

Adoration. Devotion. And a desire so darkly sweet she could taste it on her tongue.

She flinched as his finger delved further, following her ugly disfigurement between her breasts.

She caught his wrist to stop him.

"Felicity. You needn't ever hide yourself from me. I'll protect you. Cherish every part of you. You can harbor in my arms by day. Fall asleep in them by night. We will be a family."

The reminder came at her like a pair of snapping shears, pruning away her blossoming hope to leave nothing but hemorrhaging stubs. The depth of his emotions as he'd told her of his son ... the way he'd bonded with her nieces in such a short time. How he wanted a true marriage.

He loved children. And for her to even consider accepting his proposal without telling him of her barrenness was a tribute to how desperate and weak she'd become.

Palms banked against his chest, she edged him off until they were lying side by side on the cold, hard wood. "You do want a family, then?"

A puzzled expression passed over him as he swept strands of hair from her face. "Yes. I want everything I lost."

Eyes blurring, she scrambled to stand against the wall—a support for her jittery legs.

"What is it?" On his knees, he stared up at her.

She stumbled to the opposite side and, after fixing her bodice, began to toss food into the picnic basket. In an effort to hold back her tears, she squeezed the peach too hard. Its juice and pulp seeped through her fingers as if it were bleeding.

"I'll solve this on my own." She swallowed hard, constricting her larynx to calm her shuddering vocal chords. "Johnny Boy is healed. You're free to leave." She steeled herself for the next words, wanting rather to gore out her own heart than speak them. "I must think of my nieces. You're a thief, an addict. They don't need such an influence in their lives. The odds are already stacked against them with a whore for a keeper. I have nothing to offer in your search for Mina. There's no more reason for you to stay."

She heard him stand, heard his stilted breaths. But she didn't turn to look at him. Instead, she wiped the stickiness from between her fingers with a napkin. The sun had dropped low behind the clouds, cutting the light to a purple haze. Cook would be preparing dinner at the castle. Felicity shivered against the numbing frost rushing along her scar. She needed to be with her nieces—to feel their warmth in her arms.

Leaving the basket for Nick, she eased through the trapdoor and down the rope, knowing he would find his way to the castle once her ugly words had sunk in. Knowing he would hate her enough to leave on the morrow without ever looking back again.

CHAPTER EIGHTEEN

Stubborn, hard-shelled crab of a woman.

Nick slid his earring into place and secured it, attempting to tamp his anger. What galled him most was what Felicity had said about herself. If he ever heard her call herself a whore again ...

She'd been forced into that lifestyle. How could she forget?

So ironic. She made a point about him forgiving himself, when she couldn't do the same for her own perceived sins.

Tilting the bottle of mead upside down, he waited for the remaining droplets to trickle into his throat. He cringed—the last swallow was always the most bitter. Hissing through his teeth to tame the flavor's bite, he glanced outside. Moonlight slanted through the trees, and Jasper's tombstone cast an eerie silhouette on the ground. Nick hadn't even had a chance to question Felicity any more about the butterflies and her brother. He would never learn if there was a spirit roaming these grounds.

Not that it made any difference now. He didn't belong here; these mysteries weren't his. Felicity had made that abundantly clear. It was to that end he'd stayed in the forest until he was sure everyone had gone to bed.

He didn't want to face her after she'd made a fool of him again. He'd opened his heart about Christian's birth, shared that private, intimate ache, only to have her shut him down without a blink of her eye.

Well, that wasn't completely true. She'd been sweet. So bloody sweet and nurturing as he told her. Even understanding, almost as if she empathized. Then, when he asked for her hand, she turned on him like a trapped bobcat. How could he blame her? She knew now that he killed his first wife through neglect. Were she to ever know the rest ... the depth of his shame and addiction, how he'd almost given himself to a man—she'd want nothing to do with him anyway.

Tomorrow he would say goodbye to this dreary, rainy estate and its melancholy mistress in black. He would blot them from his mind forever and resume his search into the afterlife. He didn't believe her, not really. That Mina was at peace. So odd, that while he'd been here in a place where spirits and hauntings seemed to reign, the need to connect with Mina had faded more with each hour.

When Felicity had asked him if he wanted a family, he blurted out a yes without even thinking. The thought of a life with her, Lia, and Aislinn gave him a sense of peace and warmth he'd been missing for far too long. That's what had stifled his search for the past over the last few days. He'd began to see a future, being a part of the inner workings of a real family. He'd wanted to assure Felicity that he understood the responsibility which came with his marriage offer.

But that admission had backfired, and he didn't know why.

Aislinn and Lia's faces danced through his mental periphery, adding to the lonely ache. Such beautiful, special little ladies with so much to offer. Yet they were never to see the world—held prisoners in this castle by their aunt's damnable fear of trust. That he had to leave with little Lia still angry stung most of all. He'd planned to seek penance for breaking her father's dishes. Now, he would never have that chance. Because of Felicity.

"Get a hold of yourself, man," he snarled. "You've known the woman all of eleven days."

Almost two weeks. But it felt like more, somehow. As if a lifetime of waiting had finally been appeased, just by the appearance of this one piece from his past. What they shared all those years ago, that moment when her eyes met his and he begged her not to give up, not to die—that intense emotional connection had spun a gossamer net around them, binding them. Instead of time severing it—the passing years had cinched the snare ever tighter. And now that he'd finally met her, the entanglement threatened to strangle him.

Nick growled and scrubbed his face with a palm. The friction of new-sprung whiskers served as a reminder of the time. Everyone should be abed by now, and he needed rest himself. However, he regretted eating the entire contents of the picnic along with the wine at such a late hour. His stomach lurched—every bit as discontented as his heart. Cursing, Nick threw the empty bottle to the corner of the outlook post. The clunk of heavy glass reverberated through his dizzy head, shaking his skeleton from his teeth to his toes.

He plunged through the trapdoor with basket in hand. The rope burned his thighs and palm as he tried to slow his descent. When his feet finally touched ground, he swayed. Or perhaps it was the forest that swayed. The dark trees seemed to bend to him, reaching for him. He stumbled

A.G. HOWARD

forward, convinced they'd shoved him with their limbs. A cool breeze licked his face and a drizzle spattered his skin through the firs.

The chill, and several hooting owls, kept him sober enough to use the sparse moonlight and stay on the trail. He remembered Felicity's vague reference to bogs. *Peat bogs.* Their existence had roused an idea in him ... one he couldn't quite grasp at the moment. It was as if cotton swirled around his brain, muffling his thoughts.

He half expected the gate to be locked against him when he arrived at the stone fence, but it opened easily. Latching it shut behind him, he stopped to stroke the slick bars where he'd held Felicity pinned for one of the most poignant and thrilling kisses he'd ever experienced.

He pressed his forehead against the cold iron, hard enough to induce a dull ache. No. They hadn't merely kissed. He understood that, even in this hazy state of mind. It had been an exchange of mutual need and desire between two broken people.

She might be a master at denying her feelings, but in that one moment, he'd forced her to face them. She would remember that if nothing else.

Heat rushed from Nick's neck to his temples, pounding in rhythm with the raindrops as he turned to follow the path to the castle's front door. He scrubbed wetness from his face. No woman was worth this much misery. He couldn't wait to be gone. He only wished he'd managed just once to bed her—to leave her with a smile in place of that sour scowl. Or better yet, with a laugh of pleasure in her throat. Lord, when she laughed, the sound was like a wind chime ... and it lit up her face like a sunrise. Too bad the occurrence was rarer than a lunar eclipse.

He let himself inside the castle. After dropping the basket

in the lightless kitchen, he trudged up the stairs. Candles flickered in the sconces, illumining the mud left upon the marble tiles with each footstep. It mattered naught. The maid wouldn't mind. Unlike Felicity, Rachel liked having reminders of him about.

The way she always leaned over him to clear his dishes from the table, swathing him in her honey-scented skin; how her bright, red hair brushed across his hand as she knelt before him to prop his leg upon a pillow. Just to think upon her daunted efforts at seduction soothed his ruffled male ego.

Nick paused at the top of the second flight and clenched the railing, veering a gaze down the dimly lit corridor toward Felicity's room. He didn't want to leave. Hated that she had the power to make him. Every muscle twitched, holding back the urge to break her door down and insist she listen to reason.

Or he could blackmail her. Hell, she was expecting it, considering his greedy and thieving nature.

But he wouldn't give her the satisfaction of being right ... or the benefit of a second chance. She would soon realize just how well he could hold a secret. For he was never to utter another word to or about her again.

Gritting his teeth, he turned in the direction of his chamber, grateful he'd only have to sleep in Lia's tiny bed one last night. Every time he moved, he feared he'd break the frame. That's all he needed, to ruin something else of the little sprite's.

A few feet from his chamber, he stalled, seeing a blur of movement at the door as someone slipped out, jingling some keys. In the darkness, a woman's silhouette took shape. His heartbeat stuttered.

"Fel'city?" He cringed at the slur in his voice, defeated in his battle against the mead.

"Nay. It be me, Yer Graceship." Rachel's answer dragged over him—an erotic yet grating stroke of sensation. She came into view beside a fluttery candle on the wall which highlighted the ripe feminine assets beneath her maid's uniform. "I was seeing to the fireplace in yer room." She fondled the buttons of her blouse where it gaped to show ample cleavage. The woman wasn't wearing a chemise or corset. Nick's body responded in spite of his drunken state.

She stepped closer. "Midnight be a strange hour for wanderin' the grounds. When ye didn't come to sup, I was a bit worried ye'd left."

Nick ran a hand over his chin, letting his whiskers prick his skin in an effort to clear his head. "I'm leavin' tomorrow." He stumbled around her in the narrow hall, fighting every impulse to press her against the wall and spend his pent-up desire and anger for Felicity. Mead was a drink rumored to promote virility. He was beginning to think there was something to that particular piece of Irish folklore.

Rachel had left his door ajar. As he coaxed it open, her cool fingers clamped his bicep over his shirt, curling to mold his tautened muscle. "Why sir, yer as wet as a pickled goose."

He jerked away. "Better y'keep distance, sweeting. This goose has a scorpion's sting."

Rachel stopped the door from closing. He rounded on her—the only sounds the crackling fire and Johnny Boy's snoring from behind.

She reached for Nick's shirt placket, her honeyed scent enfolding him. "Let me help with yer clothes. I can have them clean and dry by morn." She moved closer and began to tug the tail from where he'd tucked it in his trousers. Her chill nails trailed the hairs along his bare abdomen. He groaned, losing his resolve. "And I'll help ye into bed. Bein' yer last night here, I should like to treat ye hospitable." Her sultry green eyes left no room for misinterpretation.

Nick cursed and dragged her all the way in, shutting the door behind her. The hairs on the scruff of his neck lifted, a warning he didn't have the will power or sobriety to hearken to. He shoved her against the wall, his body pressed to hers. The crispness of her apron rustled with the movement. "I'll not be thinking of you ... I'll tell y'that now. Are you still willing?"

Rachel arched into him. "I be a fine replacement for any fantasy, Yer Graceship. And I've much more stamina than the old dowager."

Nick balked at her audacity. "What makes y'think—"

"I've seen the way ye look at her ladyship. The woman is an ice queen. I can make ye forget ever wantin' her. I've done it before for another man..."

Biting back the urge to send the maid packing, Nick pushed himself harder against her. Her buxom shape and plump, hot flesh felt hearty and receptive, unlike Felicity's delicate frame, fragile curves, and softness.

Lord, how she'd felt beneath his hands ... her breasts, even hidden under the cloth as they were, her skin, her long, lithe leg wrapped around him. Somehow, Felicity was mysterious ... foreboding. Yet at the same time, a comfort. An enigma, that woman.

Bending his head, he shut his eyes in an effort to imagine Felicity in the maid's place, sobering enough to speak clearly. "How quiet can you be?"

Her palm slid up his thigh and grazed his arousal. She gasped and he clenched his jaw. "A man yer size ... I'd have to bite off me tongue to keep quiet..."

Dizziness seeped into his head at her touch. His disgust at her smugness didn't keep him from wanting to bed her. He'd been down this road many times: using women's bodies to appease his emptiness, to counteract disappointment. Never having to like the woman or care how she felt; leaving her the moment the act was over.

Exactly how those men had treated Jasmine.

Even as Rachel kissed his neck and begged his touch, that thought crashed over him like the icy-cold waves of the ocean. He couldn't be one of those men any longer. Not after learning how the Earl had defiled Felicity's innocence so blithely. The mere thought of anyone hurting her made his pulse pound in his temples. But hadn't Nick himself intended to do the same that night at the brothel, before he'd saved her from the stabbing?

Yes. He'd intended to use her. Use her like a damned drug.

Laudanum.

Nick clenched his eyes tighter at the siren's call. *God help him.* He didn't want to face tomorrow. Didn't want to go back out into the lonely world. With Johnny for company, he might last a few months before he'd trip over his addiction. Or would he? Even now, the opium's serenade swirled within—a promise of oblivion, an illusion of heaven's peace too sweet to deny.

The closest a man could come to killing himself without pulling a trigger.

His eyes snapped open. He pushed aside Rachel's seeking hand then ran a fingertip down her collarbone, between the burgeoning rolls of her cleavage, over her clothes all the way to her waist. He stopped atop her apron, just above her pelvic bone.

She tensed, mouth agape and lashes trembling—anticipant.

"When I ask for your silence," Nick said. "I mean can you keep a secret?" His fingers shifted to drop into her apron's pocket and fish out her keys. "I'd like to borrow these."

"What would ye be givin' in return?" Rachel whispered and pressed her lips against his ear, trailing to his earring.

Shaking off the heat that surged through his body, Nick held her at arm's length. "A secure position."

Shoving a fallen tendril of hair behind her ear, Rachel tilted her head. "I be secure in whatever position Yer Graceship prefers..."

Nick frowned. "I'm referring to your employment."

The maid's brows furrowed. "Her Ladyship would ne'er cut me loose. Where else would she find a maid willin' to be prisoner here in this castle? Sides, the lady is loyal to me mum."

Ah, yes. Nick had forgotten about the familial association. It's why the cook scolded and nit-picked this maid more than she did the other servants. He looked at the young woman offering herself to him, so obviously desperate for a life other than this. A parent's opinion was so much more important than she could imagine at her age. "I doubt your mother would approve of your clandestine nocturnal excursions— breaking into guest's rooms to seduce them. I'll not damage your reputation in her eyes." He squeezed the keys and started to tuck his shirt in.

The maid's jaw dropped. "Ye mean we aren't to—?"

"Ah, Rachel. You're so tempting. But..." Nick gently helped her straighten her blouse. "Some men prefer ice queens. It's the challenge of melting them, you see."

As he helped secure her buttons, the blush which crept into her face had nothing to do with embarrassment. His rejection had humiliated her.

He hadn't intended to hurt her. But it was better this way. He'd sensed Felicity's self-consciousness when Rachel was around. Considering Donal's tryst with the maid, Felicity's aged façade no doubt fed Rachel's superiority complex. It would be good for her to experience the insecurity Felicity battled every day. It could mature her, make her safer from the rogues of the world. From men like himself.

Head bowed, Rachel turned toward the door. Nick banked his palm against it, holding it shut. With his free hand, he jingled the keys in the firelight. "Which one unlocks the dining room's sideboard?" His mouth dried on the question.

He would only raid Clooney's medical supply for enough laudanum to ease the torment so he might sleep tonight. He needed to take advantage while he had access to the drug for free.

Flimsy justifications for a crime he already hated himself for committing.

Finger trembling, Rachel pointed to a gold key with a long shank and rectangular tooth at the end. "The skeleton key ... opens most every lock in the castle."

Nick stepped back so she could leave. "Hang your apron on the peg next to the pans in the kitchen. I'll assure the keys are back in place in your pocket by morning. And remember, not a word to anyone."

The maid nodded without looking up, then slipped silently from the room.

Nick stopped at the top of the second flight, an unopened bottle of opium tincture secured in his trouser pocket. He trailed the cork seal with an eager fingertip. A cold sweat washed over him, making him shudder. Dread or anticipation, he didn't know. All he did know, was that with a few swallows of the sherry-flavored bitterness, he'd be back in that familiar place with his dead wife and son ... lost to oblivion.

He shouldn't feel guilty for stealing. Clooney kept a hefty supply of laudanum. Nick suspected they were for medicinal purposes, perhaps even Felicity's sleep draughts, but they were covered with dust as if they hadn't been touched in years. Of the seven bottles, Nick had settled for one. Least that showed an ounce of restraint.

Growling, he drew his hand from his pocket. He could lie to everyone but himself. He despised how low he'd sunk, despised his weakness. Perhaps he would never escape the opium's snare. Even chewing off a limb wouldn't save him.

And he was about to prove true everything Felicity thought of him.

So what.

In the morn, after a night of swimming in delirium, he'd leave. Then it would no longer matter what Felicity thought of anything he did. As to that, why should it matter now? Why did he care what she thought? Yet, from the moment he'd met her he'd cared, however illogical it was.

Well, no longer. He was done caring—about anything.

"Holier than thou Miss Prunes and Prisms," Nick mumbled on his stroll through the corridor toward his chamber. Hearing a jingle with each step reminded him he'd failed to put the keys in Rachel's apron.

"Well, *hell.*" He turned back, about to take the first step down when a shuffling sound from Felicity's room froze him in place.

Straining to creep without stumbling, he eased toward her locked chamber. Soft candlelight flickered in the candelabra from the wall behind him, laying out his shadow to lead the way.

Somewhere on the other side of the door, Felicity

whimpered. She sounded as if she were crying. Blast it all. He wanted to be the one to comfort her. To fix her life. And he was tired of fighting that instinct.

A sharp yelp, then her whimpers grew to pleas. "What must I do to appease you?" she murmured. "Tell me."

Nick pressed an ear to the wooden barrier between them. "I know about the butterflies," she mumbled. "It isn't the way ... there has to be another way."

She sounded distraught—confused, afraid, and drowsy. Nick could think of only one person she'd accuse of disturbing her butterflies. Donal must have slipped into her chamber while she was medicated. She was unprotected inside her chamber with that maggot hovering over her.

Pulse kicking up, Nick quietly drew the keys from his pocket, sliding the skeleton's long shank into the keyhole.

Felicity wailed, fraught with emotion. "Please, use my body ... I offer it freely! Anything for the girls—"

Her plea broke off, as if someone stopped her short.

Nick's blood spiked to flame. Turning the key with a snap of his wrist, he shoved the door open.

"Donal, you son of a—" He skidded to a stop in the room's midst.

Felicity was in her nightgown, alone, her upper torso and head slumped across her writing desk. Nick eased closer. She held a quill in her left hand, the point suspended just above a sheet of paper. A lit lantern flickered, causing the ink that dribbled off the tip to appear to dance.

Was she writing another novel? Was she walking through the scene in her drug-addled mind?

"Felicity?" He leaned over her. Something about her pose made his hair stand on end. Her knuckles were white from gripping the quill so hard. But she wasn't moving ... why? Lifting her neck, he turned her chin toward him and brushed her silky hair from her face. It slipped to the opposite side in a fall of silver-gold so long it grazed her dainty bared ankle. He noted her flawless skin; not a wrinkle in sight. *So beautiful.*

But her eyes were open, in a trancelike daze. The vision brought back her helplessness as Jasmine with vivid clarity. That haunting gaze, open and unblinking, looking through him as if he weren't there. Just like the night at the brothel. Nick's stomach fell. If this was the effects of her sleeping draughts, she had no business taking them.

Dropping to his knees, he propped her up and shook her shoulders gently. "Felicity ... Felicity!"

A keening sound broke from her throat as she shoved him away, her eyes still unfocused. Nick fell back on his haunches, surprised by her strength. The laudanum toppled out from his pocket and rolled along the floor.

As he started to reach for the bottle, something whisked across his peripheral. Nick jerked his head in the direction of the movement. In synch with a swishing rustle—the same scraping wings sound he'd hear in Lianna's chamber the prior night—he looked to the other end of the room. A shadowy fog crept over the wooden floor then stood tall as a silhouette of a man, so faint it could've been a mirage. A shallow breath clung inside Nick's lungs like soggy webs. He blinked once and the fluctuation of darkness and light was gone.

Before Nick could gather his wits, Felicity sunk from her chair in a lifeless heap. Leaping forward, he caught her just as Binata freed the keys he'd left in the door's latch and rushed into the chamber.

Cradling Felicity's limp, feather-light body in his arms, Nick met the nanny's dark gaze. Her black eyes assessed the room and stalled upon the bottle next to Nick's feet. Reading the accusation and fear behind her expression, he said, "Get Clooney." When the nanny hesitated, he lifted the arm supporting Felicity's head and bent his cheek to her bluing lips. Her breath was threaded, barely discernable. His throat clenched. "Damnit woman!" he yelled to Binata. "Get Clooney now, or she'll die!"

CHAPTER NINETEEN

Felicity stretched beneath her covers. The curtain rings rattled as someone opened her drapes, coaxing a watered-down sunrise to fill her chamber.

She grumbled, rolling to her stomach to avoid the grayish haze. Face buried in her pillow, she inhaled the bedclothes' comforting scent of lilac. Awareness trickled through her slowly, like the soft raindrops pattering the window.

She flipped over and sat up with a start. "Why am I here?"

"Where else would you be at the crack of dawn?" Clooney strode from the window and urged her to lie back again. "And you're to stay put for the duration of the morning." He took her wrist in his hand to find her pulse.

Felicity glanced around, feeling out of sorts. She'd had horrible dreams throughout the night. Dreams of trying to bring Jasper back to her and the girls, of him attempting to speak but unable to reach them. She could see his mouth forming words, but could never hear his voice. It was as if a plane of glass stood between them.

"Gave us all a scare last night." Clooney laid down her hand and touched her forehead with a cool, leathery palm.

"I did?"

"You were at the desk, much like when you used to write

the novel. But there were no words on the paper. And we couldn't rouse you. You don't remember anything?" Clooney bent over her and stared hard into her pupils. His eyes were bloodshot and his breath smelled of coffee and pipe tobacco.

Try as she might, she only recalled her strange dreams, then the sensation of floating weightless.

Wait. There *was* more. When she started to drift downward, she'd heard someone calling her from faraway...

"Nick!" She sat up again, bumping her head into Clooney's.

Clooney toppled backward but regained his balance against her desk. He scowled, stroking the red place on his forehead as she rubbed her own to ease the ache. "Yes, Nick. Told you he wasn't to be trusted."

"He was in here?"

"Said he heard a noise from your room."

"But..." She remembered having her door locked. How did he get in?

"He's a thief, Dove," Clooney offered, as if reading her mind. "Not only pilfers ponies, but keys. And drugs."

A slow curl of trepidation uncoiled within Felicity's chest. "Drugs..."

Clooney held up a bottle of opium tincture. "At first I thought he'd used it on you. But it's unopened. Not a drop is gone. He admitted he stole it for himself."

Still fuzzy, Felicity tried to make sense of the groundskeeper's words. "Where is he?"

"He's assigned himself your protector. Been sitting guard outside your door all night ever since I refused to let him in again."

"Guarding me? From what?"

Clooney shrugged. "Fool wouldn't tell me. Seemed to think you were in danger from something."

Felicity wondered what Nick could've seen. It had to be extreme to unsettle him so. Anxious though she was at that thought, the image of Nick holding a vigil offered a tender counterbalance. She felt inexplicably warm and satiate to know he'd been there. She didn't welcome the feeling, or this growing dependence he seemed to inspire in her.

Clooney cleared his throat. He held up the bottle again. "What shall we do about this?"

Her eyes burned, thinking upon the horrible things she'd said to Nick in the outlook post. She'd driven him to seek succor from the one mistress who would never turn her back on him. *Laudanum.*

It was partly her guilt to bear for the theft, as well.

She had to give Nick back his dignity, and the best way was to show him he'd earned her trust. "Clooney, could you please look in the top drawer of my desk. There's a knife there."

Clooney found the blade wrapped in a cloth and brought it to her.

"Send Nick in and leave us," she said, taking the knife and setting it in the billowed sheets beside her.

Clooney's thin shoulders tensed beneath his plaid shirt. "Not sure if he's done. Went to wash off and shave. Besides, don't you need—" He gestured to the aged skin around his eyes and mouth.

"He saw me without the wrinkles last night."

Clooney pouted. "The room was dimly lit. Could've missed it."

Felicity reached for the armchair beside her bed, tugging her shawl toward her. She wrapped the soft weave to cover her gown and pulled longs strands of hair out from beneath it. "He knows, Clooney ... about everything that night in the brothel, all but the babe I lost." She smoothed her tresses in place over her shoulders so they hung across her chest and the excess coiled to a silvery heap in her lap. "He's the young man who intercepted the Earl. The one that saved Jasmine ... me ... so I could become the dowager. At our picnic, he told me he remembered."

Clooney's eyebrows drew up. "Wait. Wait..." He smacked his lips, no doubt craving his pipe. "You've known all along! Haven't you?"

In lieu of an answer, Felicity looked down at her lap and eased her bed sheets up to her breasts, a conscious effort to shield her scar.

When she glanced up again, weariness clouded Clooney's liquid eyes. "How did he find you?" he asked.

"He wasn't even looking. Fate opened her palm, and we both fell into it." She bit her lip, considering her next confession carefully. "He asked me to marry him. As a way out of this nightmare with Landrigan."

Clooney sat on her bed's edge. "You can't possibly be considering—knowing what he is?"

"A chivalrous man? A compassionate and loyal friend? He sat vigil over me."

"Hoping to win harbor here, so he might have access to our opium."

Felicity squelched the insecurity that bloomed at Clooney's logic. "He's my hero."

"Once. In the past. You have children to consider now." Clooney said it as if he truly thought Felicity could forget.

"The girls adore him. You know he worked with Aislinn to find a cure for my butterflies. He's been sincere in his efforts to help us."

The crinkles edging Clooney's eyes deepened. He handed off the opium tincture and molded her fingers around its slick glass. "He only means to stay until the free supply is gone. Obviously has a weakness."

"Who among us doesn't?" She narrowed her eyes to accuse.

"True enough. But you've a stepson who would use any misstep to blackmail you. Were you to marry an addict—"

"A recovering addict. You already noted that the laudanum was unopened." Felicity surprised herself with this sudden defensiveness toward Nick. She'd had time to think last evening after returning from the post. They had shared so much over these past few days. She considered Nick a friend. And had circumstances been different, would've wanted him for so much more. She tasted something in his kisses that she couldn't get enough of, a fount of passion and strength she yearned to draw upon. Her own had run dry years ago, when she'd lost her baby and any chance of ever having one again.

"Felicity ... whether you marry another man or no, Donal will not give up until he's won his father's estate. He's in this for greed. Things could get violent."

She frowned. "I'm not marrying anyone. I simply want to assure that Nick understands how grateful I am before he goes. That he's welcome to visit again anytime."

Clooney huffed. "You mean, anytime he's craving more of the help's hospitality."

Felicity stiffened beneath the sheets. "Whatever do you mean?"

"Those stolen keys were Rachel's. Binata saw the maid come out of Nick's chamber late last night. Said her clothes looked ... ruffled."

Before Felicity could process the information, the door swung open and Binata carried in a tray. Steam rose from a kettle nestled among thick slabs of gingerbread and sliced pudding with buttered eggs. The tea's fragrant cloud carried a scent of hazelnut and caramel. Felicity's stomach would've growled, had she not been so nauseous.

Nick stopped at the threshold behind the nanny, a powerful counterpoise to her small frame.

His palm sculpted the door frame. Steel-gray eyes swept over Felicity—intimate as a whisper and a touch. She wondered if he'd looked at Rachel like that last night when he'd...

Her lashes squeezed closed. After all they'd shared, after how he'd opened his heart to her and her to him. She had sacrificed her desires and needs so he could find another woman who could give him offspring one day. But to even imagine his hands on Rachel ... his lips swallowing her moans ...

If he'd left that maid with child she would never forgive him.

Jealousy rose like bile in her throat.

When she opened her eyes again, Nick's freshly-scrubbed skin reflected the shadows of rain streaking the window. He had his washed hair plaited in a haphazard braid, laying bare that handsome, troubled face. He wore his own clothes this morn. His trouser knee was patched and mended and the shirt was pressed and cleaned. In spite of the weariness smudged beneath his eyes, he looked the perfect gentleman—roughened around the edges just enough to take Felicity's breath.

Just as she'd told Clooney, everyone had a weakness, and hers was obviously this man's sensuality and charm. But she couldn't afford to be weak. Her family's safety depended upon it.

Felicity willed her tears not to fall. She'd send him away today with instructions never to return, as soon as she assured he would keep quiet about her secrets.

She glanced at the tray Binata laid on her desk. As usual,

Cook had been very generous, preparing more food than one person could ever eat alone. Felicity tucked the opium bottle and knife beneath her bedclothes. "Lord Thornton, please join me for breakfast."

"It would be my pleasure." Nick's gaze met hers and held as he stepped inside the door, waiting for the others to leave. He wore his earring again. A barrage of emotions threatened to break Felicity apart as she engaged in a stare down with him.

Binata clanged some silverware. The sound spurred Felicity to break her stare and Clooney stood. He shoved his hands in his pockets on his way out, bumping Nick's shoulder. Nick's jaw clenched, but he made no move to retaliate. Binata laid down some napkins and started to leave.

"Are the girls up yet?" Felicity asked the nanny, gesturing Nick to take the arm chair beside her bed. She made a conscious effort to focus on Binata instead of Nick's muscular physique as he piled gingerbread onto a napkin before striding her way.

"They still be sleepin'," Binata answered. She adjusted the expensive beaded orange scarf covering her hair—a gift from her nephew. "Want I should wake 'em now?"

"No."

Nick came to sit beside Felicity, and she smoothed her shawl over her chest.

"They were up late with me last night..." Felicity continued her answer to Binata. "When they rouse, do not allow them to come seeking me in my chamber unless Lord Thornton and I are finished. And I must have time to prepare my face."

Nodding, the nanny flashed a curious glance at Nick then left, shutting the door behind her.

Nick's full lips opened on a question but Felicity spoke first. "The things I said last night. I didn't mean for them to drive you into..." She stopped herself short of saying *my maid's arms*. Better he think she referred to the opium.

"Felicity, you are not responsible for my mistakes. But I do have you to thank for stopping me from doing something irreversible." Sporting a pained frown, he laid the gingerbread-filled napkin on Felicity's lap. The weight lightened as he took some food for himself, leaving Felicity's thigh tingling where his pinky grazed her.

Elbows propped on his knees, he bit off a corner of the spongy bread. "I understand why you said what you did. Why you were chasing me away."

"Do you?" Felicity's stomach rumbled louder than her query.

Nick frowned. "Are you going to eat, or must I feed you again? It appears I've spoiled you, baby bird."

A blush crept into Felicity's face, making the welt from her collision with Clooney swell to a hot rise on her forehead. She rubbed it.

"How'd you hurt your head?" Nick started to reach for her, but Felicity looked away and feigned interest in the breakfast on her lap. She picked up a brown crust, fighting the urge to throw it at him. She wanted him to stop being so attentive. To stop pretending as if he hadn't bedded her maid beneath her nose. Sinking her teeth into the warm spiciness, she chewed. "Had a collision with Clooney. So, you think I was chasing you away. Why would I?"

Nick's larynx bobbed on a swallow. "Your cautiousness. Your captivity. They're all a part of one secret even bigger than your past. And I finally know what it is."

Felicity's heart thumped. What had he seen last night? Had he found the passageway into the turret? Tension cloaked the room ... a silence so palpable it muffled the rain and clung to the walls like mud.

"This chamber," he shifted the subject again, dizzying her. "It does not reflect a feminine theme like the others." He glanced at the red walls and black curtains. "It looks more like a man's design. A man with tortured sensibilities and deep intellect. Did it belong to your brother?"

"I moved in here after his stroke to be closer to the girls' rooms."

"Ah." Finishing the last bite of his bread, Nick rubbed his palms to whisk away the crumbs. "Your brother is here and you're aware of his presence. Yet you hide him. Why?"

Felicity's cheeks grew warm. Sound returned to her in the form of the longcase clock tick-tocking against the far wall. It seemed to say: *He knows-he knows-he knows.* But how could he?

As if triggered by Nick's accusation, a finger of sun broke through the clouds, filtered through the window, and pointed at her face. "I-I don't know what you mean," she mumbled. "I showed you his grave."

Nick's focus shifted over her skin, following the light. "I'm not speaking of his trumped up resting place. I'm speaking of him."

The sunbeam moved to pierce Felicity's eyes, blinding.

Nick sat back in the chair, arms crossed. "At first I thought he was here to heal your scar ... but there was no residue of fungus anywhere on your gown. I searched for it when I laid you in your bed."

"What are you talking about? *Who* are you talking about?" Felicity squinted against the light's harsh glare. Nick lifted the remaining gingerbread from her lap, placing the napkin on his chair as he took a seat at the bed's edge. He positioned his broad shoulders to block the sun from her eyes. The faint scent of mead—softened with a soapy tinge—teased her nose upon his proximity. She remembered his hot, seeking tongue flavored with the drink last night. Had Rachel even taken the time to appreciate his flavor ... his tenderness? Felicity bit back a disgusted sob.

Curling her legs to her chest, she tried to put some distance between them.

"I haven't been completely honest with you." His voice deepened on the confession, causing her pulse to jump. Was he going to tell her about the maid now? That he lied when he said those sweet words about wanting only her? Felicity's belly spasmed. She didn't want to hear it and had to clench her fingers together to keep from plugging her ears.

"I left out some information about the fungus that healed me," he said. "Where it comes from. It seems to be tied to the Raven. And Aislinn believes him to be your brother's spirit. And deep down, you believe it, too. Why else would you be so defensive each time I bring it up?"

Felicity took a silent breath of relief. So, he didn't truly know the secret—only part of it. "I've told you ... it is impossible. There is no ghost. Landrigan has spawned this nonsense to feed the girls' imaginations. He's a master at manipulation."

"I saw something, Felicity. In here, last night."

Relief ignited to caution. "Describe it."

He looked down, kneading his nape with a palm. "I—I heard a swish. Had a sense of something being there. Like a shadow."

Felicity narrowed her eyes. "Let me guess: butterflies in the shape of a man?"

"More of a blur creeping along the floor then standing." He winced. "I know, it sounds ludicrous."

"It sounds like a drunken man's musings. Did you indulge

in that bottle of mead all alone last night?"

"I did, but—"

"So why should I believe ... better yet, why should *you* believe anything you saw? You were soused out of your head."

"Perhaps." A pensive expression crossed his face, as if starting to doubt the validity of his memory. Then his chin tensed in determination. "Though I've experienced enough delusions in my life from the opium to know when what I'm seeing is real or imagined."

"Or is it possible that you've experienced so many that you can no longer differentiate?"

His mouth twitched as he leaned close. "Your brother was here last night. His spirit. In this very room. He had you in a trance so deep you couldn't wake. I suspect he's been here before ... when you were writing that novel with my sister. I suspect he wrote it through you. I recognized his handwriting when I saw his journals in Aislinn's keep. They matched the correspondences my sister received. And now, he's trying to reach you again ... to tell you something."

"Enough of this madness." Stunned by his perception, Felicity shoved against him. His rock-hard muscles didn't even give an inch. She considered spilling why she had such trouble believing this *ghost* could be Jasper. Were she to tell Nick the truth behind her brother's death, it would bring this line of questioning to a screeching halt and leave him as befuddled as her.

She shifted her legs beneath the covers. The bottle of opium rolled toward her hip, reminding her again of Nick's tryst with the maid. Felicity had enough complications to deal with. She didn't need a man with *two* mistresses to further muddle things. "I don't care what you think you saw last night. I'm more concerned with what you *did*. And for that, I'd prefer you just leave and never look back."

"What I did?" A full burst of sun brightened the entire chamber—an illumination that left Felicity feeling exposed and vulnerable beneath Nick's bewildered gaze.

Felicity eased her hand under the covers and fished out the bottle, resting it in her lap. "I can't believe you were so desperate for this that you would ..." She trembled despite the rays of light heating her hair where it draped her shoulders. "I know about Rachel's visit to your room."

"Ah." Nick looked none too happy. His shoulders grew as if ready to pounce—a dark predator with his prey in sight.

But wasn't she supposed to be the predator in this scenario?

"Has it ever occurred to you that it was her seduction? A seduction which never came to pass because I didn't wish to use her like I had other women. Because I didn't want to be like the men who had used you."

Random memories from the prior night came crashing into Felicity's mind: seeing Rachel wander the halls before coming to bed; the maid asking about Nick all throughout supper; how she stood out in the courtyard to beat the rugs which had been cleaned earlier that week just so she could watch for his return. Rachel had been waiting for him like a lioness in heat. She must've used her keys to hole up in his room. Her clothes could've been rumpled from Nick throwing her out.

The tears Felicity had been holding back broke loose in a wave of relief. "So ... you simply borrowed her keys? Without being tempted to bed her?"

"Oh, I was tempted." The mattress rippled as Nick edged closer. "But I once killed a woman I cared for by being impulsive and heedless, driven only by lust. Do you think I'd ever make such a mistake again? *Ever* in my lifetime?" He swiped away Felicity's tears with the back of his hand, then trailed her hair where it laid lightly over her left breast.

Her body instantly responded, and by the hungry slant of his lips, Nick felt it.

She waited in anticipation, wanting to be touched again like yesterday in the rain. When he'd been forceful, yet gentle. Demanding, yet pleading. When he'd been focused solely on her and she believed his every word as sincere—just like now.

But he pulled back.

The movement numbed her. "Nick. I-I wish I had a forget-me-not ..."

He sighed. "We'd have to have a field full, for all the times we'd be exchanging them." He met her gaze. "Your heart will not let you have faith in me. And I'm too weak to live teetering upon every turn of your insecurities. It drives me to do things that otherwise—" His eyes locked on the opium.

You're not weak. I do have faith in you! She wanted to scream the words. Instead, they laid flat on her tongue. The one good thing that had come into her life since the girls, and she was chasing him away. She regretted it, with every piece and parcel of her being; but in light of her barrenness, it was the kindest thing she could do for him.

Nick sighed. "When I first sat down to share breakfast, I was intent on convincing you to let me stay three weeks longer. Just until Lia's birthday. But what's the use? It's doing neither of us any good for me to be here. Is it?"

Felicity took his hand and latched their fingers tight, admiring how hers felt so small in his, taking comfort in the calloused strength. "I was wrong to say those things last night."

"You were right. The girls are impressionable. They need to be reared by people with morals."

Felicity slanted her gaze to the window, convinced Nick was thinking the same thing she was: that a courtesan had no license to hold other people to such a pristine standard. Though he was too kind and noble to say it.

"Or in the least," he continued, "people who *try* to live ethically." He made a pointed glance at the opium tincture in her lap. "Obviously, I'm not yet that kind of person."

Felicity tucked his hand beneath her chin. "I believe with all my heart you are. But until you can find something that truly fulfills you, you'll never believe in your own goodness— never be strong enough to live up to it. I know this better than anyone."

He opened his hand to caress her neck, stopping at her collarbone. "The girls. They fulfilled you. Gave you the courage you needed to live a better life."

Both her hands closed over his. "Yes." *Once you have that son you want, you'll understand.* "You must find your measure of happiness."

His eyes became dark and serious as the sun slid again behind a cloud. "I was hoping perchance I had."

A hush fell on the room. He pulled free to cup her jaw, drawing her to him, then leaned in and kissed her. A rush of tears started anew, rolling down her cheeks. Basking in his scent—in his skin's smoothness and flavor—she clasped his nape, fingers woven within his damp, bound hair.

She tried to open her lips beneath his, to give him access so she might savor the hot challenge of his tongue. But he remained closed-mouthed. The effect changed everything in the kiss—made it soft and despondent—not demanding, not even persuasive. A kiss flavored with the bitterness of goodbye.

He broke contact but stayed close enough to share her breath. She sniffled as his hand glided down the curve of her neck to pluck at the shawl covering her chest.

"The peat bogs in your forest," he whispered against her. "They're the answer. You've a gold mine here. You should be selling the peat."

Felicity strove to make sense of his words, overcome by the emotions burbling up within.

Nick broke her hold on his nape and inched back, as if to help her focus. "Draw up a contract giving Donal a percentage of the peat sales. Have a solicitor help you. It can be done discreetly in Carnlough, without bringing anyone here. Just make sure the solicitor witnesses you and Donal signing the agreement. Share profit only on the grounds Donal's tricks cease and he stays away from you and the girls and off of this estate. Have his aunt make visits to him in town. Those must be the terms in writing. With the law behind you, he can never torment you again."

Felicity's mouth gaped. Sweet lord in heaven. She would never have fabricated such a shrewd plan. That Nick had been pondering her predicament—trying to find some means to help her in spite of her efforts to force him back into the world he dreaded—overwhelmed her.

So grateful for his concern, she considered betraying Jasper's secret. Her lips almost opened on the confession before she remembered the real reason she couldn't marry Nick. No matter how much she'd come to trust him, it would never change the fact that she wasn't the woman he needed.

After a pause, Nick stood and leaned forward to kiss the bruise on her forehead with strong, soft lips, stroking her nape tenderly.

"Take care, Felicity," he said against her, his smooth, shaved chin brushing her aching flesh.

"Wait..." She caught his wrist as he edged away.

He looked hopeful, as if expecting she'd ask him to stay.

With her free hand, she tugged out the knife from the sheets. "This belongs to you." She swept her covers aside and dropped her legs over the bed's edge. Nick's gaze caught on her bared knee and calf. A muscle in his jaw twitched as she smoothed her gown's hem to her shins.

Coming back to himself, he took the blade and placed a palm on her shoulder to hold her in place. "Stay. Clooney will hang me if I allow you to get up." He let the cloth fall away from the engraved handle. A line scrawled across his forehead, as if etched in place by a painful memory. "You've had this all along? Why did you keep it from me?"

"Because ... I didn't know you well enough to give you a weapon."

"Of course," Nick mumbled apologetically, eyes flashing to her chest.

Her scar drew tight beneath her gown. "But it's not a weapon at all, is it?"

He seemed to consider his words carefully. "It is not meant to be. Tis a carver's knife ... a gift from my father. Thank you for giving it back." Squeezing her shoulder one last time, he started for the door. Upon opening it, he stalled at the threshold, studying the knife as if it held some mysterious power over him.

Felicity couldn't bring herself to look at his profile. Instead, she watched his deft fingers handle the glistening blade as he slid it into a leather sheath tucked inside his pocket. She remembered how those hands had felt when they caressed her body in the rain: reverent and ravenous. She should've known they were tools of creation—for she'd been reborn beneath them, beautiful once more.

"You are an artist?" she asked, trying to postpone his departure for as long as possible.

"It has been some years since I've been inspired. But

lately, I've had the urge to start again."

"I would've loved to see your work."

"You will. I'll be sending you something in the post. I haven't forgotten your wish for wings."

His answer snapped her head up but he'd already slipped out the door. She released a shuddering breath. The fact that he remembered her childhood ache only made her want him more. She had an impulse to chase after him, and only by imagining her arms and legs were lead could she keep herself in place. When she heard his heavy footfalls clear the steps onto the first floor, she snatched up the bottle of opium and leapt to her feet.

She stared at the red walls, letting the color feed the flame of fury lapping at her core. With a growl scraping her vocal chords, she chucked the opium across the room. The glass burst and a brackish liquid formed an ugly splatter that filled the room with a distinctive odor. A scent which always reminded her of Jasper.

"You..." she seethed, regarding her surroundings through her tears—seeing her brother's fingerprints on everything. "You've asked too much of me! Locking me in this castle ... ruining my relationship with Aislinn ... robbing me of my one chance at lo—"

She cut herself short. No. She couldn't admit that. Not that. It would make Nick's absence unbearable.

Lowering her weary body to lie back on the mattress, she shut her eyes. She knew it wasn't all Jasper's doing. She was damaged—had nothing to offer a man like Nick. This was her own cross to bear.

"Jasper," she whispered. "I'm sorry. I need your counsel, dear brother. I miss you. Is it possible it was you? Did you come here last night?"

She scraped the back of her hand across wet eyes. The

instant her lashes opened, a flash of movement swept her vision. Gasping, she sat up on her elbows, seeing the tail end of a dark blur as it stole into the corridor in the direction of the turret.

A chill scuttled up her spine. "Jasper?"

She tightened the shawl around her shoulders and strode barefoot through the door. After veering a right into the empty corridor, she stopped at the tower's staircase, clutching the rail until her knuckles whitened. The scent of staleness and decay curled through her nostrils. She took one step up, then another.

Pebbles and dust caked the soles of her feet, and each footfall weighed heavier until she stopped where the windows ceased and the steps dissolved to a landslide of rubble. Searching along the cool wall for the remembered stone, Felicity inhaled a deep breath to still her jittery stomach. Finding her mark, she eased the cragged rock out of its place and fit her hand into the opening, flipping a small lever with her thumb.

With a mechanical, grating sound, a door slid open to reveal a narrow winding staircase carved out between the inner and outer wall. She pressed the stone back in place and triggered another lever on the inside to shut the door behind her.

Then she felt her way up in the darkness—one hesitant foot at a time—starting a climb she had sworn to never take again, to see a brother she hadn't visited in almost two years.

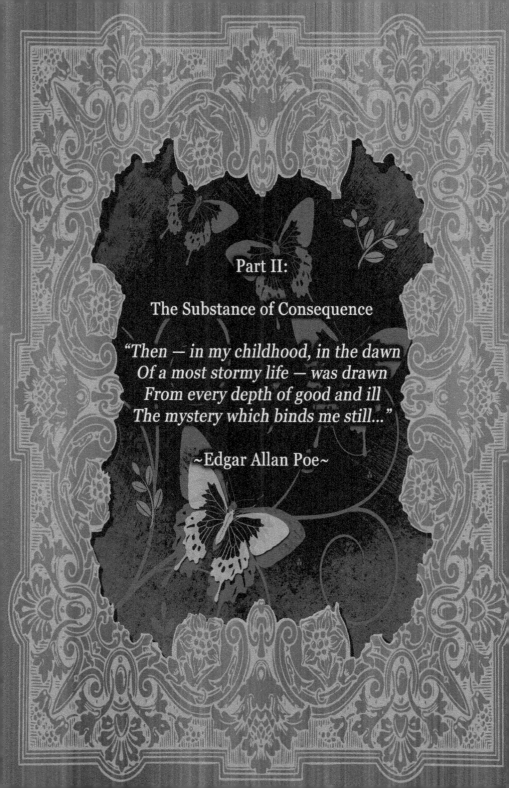

Part II:

The Substance of Consequence

"Then — in my childhood, in the dawn
Of a most stormy life — was drawn
From every depth of good and ill
The mystery which binds me still..."

~Edgar Allan Poe~

CHAPTER TWENTY

Nick paused on the first floor beside the staircase as he heard glass break in Felicity's room; he debated whether to go up and check on her. But she'd made it abundantly clear that she didn't need him ... despite that she wanted him.

He knew the latter was true. It was in her eyes, in that kiss she tried to intensify to a level he wasn't willing to surrender to.

What kind of clod did that make him? They'd been alone in there. And she'd been so beautiful: her hair fallen and messy from sleep; skin scented with lilac and orange blossoms. Not a wrinkle upon her lovely face. Sensual, vulnerable ... lying on the bed in her gown. Aside from the men's suit that first night, it was the only thing he'd ever seen her in other than mourning clothes.

All he would've had to do was lock the door. Then he could have peeled off that dowdy shawl, pushed her hem to her thighs and taken her, right there, in the pink dim of dawn—where she wouldn't have to feel conscious of her scar. He could've shown her what a beautiful, desirable woman she was.

Truth be known, he'd contemplated it.

Piss that. He'd *fought* it.

All because of his bloody pride—what little he had left. The woman was still lying to him. There was something about Jasper's death. Some reason Felicity was convinced he couldn't be haunting this place. More than just her aversion to superstitions. But she wouldn't tell him. She couldn't trust him enough.

He frowned. *Well hell.* Since when did trust figure into a one-time tryst?

A rash impulse turned him around and spurred him back up, taking two steps at a time. He would ravish Felicity despite her lack of faith in him ... they could spend all of their passion and desire in one powerful interlude. Then she wouldn't ask him to leave. She'd beg him to stay.

He made it halfway up before it registered what the breaking glass had been. It took little deductive reasoning to know she'd thrown the opium. That had been the only bottle close at hand.

His fingers clutched the railing, stalling his feet. Until that moment, he hadn't realized how much his weakness disgusted her. For her to cast aside the bottle like that. Even if she could get past his thieving nature, Felicity would never respect him because of the laudanum. Come to think, she'd as much as admitted it, pointing out that delusions must be second nature to him now.

And the most ironic thing of all? He himself wondered if she might be right. What if he'd ruined his mind irreversibly with the drug? What if he'd imagined that shadow in her room last night?

At this point, it didn't matter. What he saw—or didn't see— was irrelevant. For he had to walk away and would never know if that turret held the secret to connecting with spirits. And honestly, he no longer cared. Since he'd met Felicity, life had become so much more interesting than death.

Nick slammed his palm against the rail, cast a ravenous glare to the second floor, then turned and came down.

Tobias had the hitch wagon ready the minute Nick stepped out of the castle door with his belongings. Johnny Boy appeared with Nutmeg in tow. The two dogs had become almost inseparable over the past two days. They bounced around his legs in greeting.

He patted them then gestured to the wagon, seeing the stolen pony hitched to the back. "What is this? I planned to take the horse back myself then walk to town."

Running a hand across his nape, Tobias answered, "Her Ladyship told me last night to give you a ride. Didn't want you straining your leg, in case you have a setback. It's a long walk from the countryside to Carnlough."

Nick studied the messy pile of quilts in the back of the wagon along with the fresh cut evergreen blocks weighing them down. He started to sort through the wood, thinking it might help pass the time to carve on the trip, but Tobias rushed between Nick and the wagon.

"Her Ladyship had me pack blankets in case the rain starts again," he explained, seeming anxious to get started.

A pine-scented gust of wind clutched Nick's hat and he wedged it on his head until the brim was secure. The horses nickered, and overhead, a choir of birds worshiped the day. Dawn's pink was starting to fade, and yellow light filtered through the parting clouds.

Nick and the stable hand nodded to one another, then left without further ado.

As they pulled away from the castle, Nick glanced over his shoulder once. Yes, Felicity cared enough to see him comfortable. But the fact that he didn't see her watching through her window proved she was relieved for him to go.

The roll of the wagon rumbled through his hips, every dip

and rise of the dirt road echoing through the springs and jostling his bones. His insides felt as shaken as his emotions. He stroked his smooth chin and numbly watched the passing scenery. They were no longer in the depths of the forest but on open terrain—a landscape of rolling hills and plush grass. The earlier rains had dissipated, and he couldn't even appreciate the fresh air or the clear, dewy morning. For each time he blinked, all he could see was Felicity.

He'd never met a woman so bent on independence. She'd turned down his offer to help her financially that night in the greenhouse because she didn't want stolen funds.

But perhaps his hands weren't completely tied.

He tapped his earring. If he were to give this diamond to Tobias ... the lad could trade it for necessities at the grocer and mercantile before returning to the castle. It should provide enough supplies to last Felicity and the girls until funding from the peat bog started coming in.

She would have to accept it, knowing what that earring once meant to him.

Once meant.

Shouldn't it hurt to think of relinquishing this final piece of Mina? The fact that Felicity couldn't shed the trappings of her shattered past—being as they were etched into her very skin—he'd come to embrace his ability to part with his own as a blessing and a gift.

Incredible. The woman had changed his entire outlook on life.

In his peripheral, Nick caught the sway of Tobias' fingers guiding the reins. The youth would no doubt be glad when Nick had been dropped at the train station. He would wait until then to hand over the earring.

Then he would leave Carnlough, perhaps even Ireland, and get as far from Felicity and her mysteries as possible.

Though he had a sinking feeling she would haunt him even from across the sea's eternal span.

Seeing the turnoff they needed to take, Nick gestured Tobias to the left. The stable hand cast a skittish glance over his shoulder toward the back of the wagon. With a cluck of his tongue, he guided the horses onto the other dirt road.

Nick's original plan had been to drop the tiny mare as close to her home as possible without being seen, in hopes the owners or some neighbors would find her wandering around and lead her back. But after all those talks with Felicity, that just didn't seem good enough anymore.

The wind kicked up again. Coughing a tickle of dust from his throat, Nick patted Johnny Boy's sun-warmed fur. When they'd left, the dog had curled up on the seat and rested his muzzle on Nick's thigh as if it were the most natural place to be. Nick grinned, glad to still have his four-legged crony at his side.

Gently tweaking the pit bull's good ear, he noted the residue of lip rouge outlining the missing ear's scar with grand sweeps in the shape of flower petals. Apparently, Lia had played dress up with the hound last night in hopes to make him prettier.

"You look like a dandy boy, Johnny." The dog's eyes turned up at the sound of Nick's voice and his tail whipped the seat with a rhythmic thud. "You should be ashamed of yourself, letting Lia paint you up so. Not the way to impress the ladies, you know. I'm surprised Nutmeg gave you a second glance."

Johnny yawned, not the least bit emasculated and more than happy to be the focus of his master's undivided attention.

Nick scratched the dog's muzzle. "Should've at least offered some resistance. No doubt you laid there like a toad sunning on a rock. Surprised you didn't end up with ribbons on your paws."

"Miss Lia saved those for the hobbie's mane and tail," Tobias interrupted, looking stone-faced and straight ahead. "I took them off before tying the pony to the wagon this morn. Good thing we left before she woke. I don't think she'll be too happy to find her carousel pony gone."

Nick's spirits fell again. It was true. Lia had fallen in love with the pony, even named it.

Butterscotch.

Just another reason for the little sprite to hate him.

"There, Lord Thornton?" Tobias pointed to a thatched-roof cottage which squatted on a small hill just a few yards away. Painted red, it stood out from the brilliant green like a lone winterberry on a bush.

Nick squinted as they rolled closer, recognizing the walking bridge which curved like a dragon's scaly tail over a trout stream at the side of the tiny house. "That would be the place."

Behind the cottage, an old woman—shoulders hunched and face wrinkled like a crumpled piece of paper—hung out patched-up union suits to dry. As she pinned each one to the line, their legs and arms danced on the wind, as if performing a jig. She hadn't noticed her guests yet, oblivious to anything but her labors.

Tobias drew up close to the front door, out of sight of the woman. The home was a bit run down, but charming.

"Wait with the wagon," Nick said to the stable hand while coaxing the ratty cinnamon-colored pony to follow. Though Johnny loped close behind, offering support, Nick's pulse drummed uneasily.

The moment the old woman spotted them, she clapped her hands over her withered mouth. "Sir Roland Godfrey."

The breathless words muffled beneath her fingers. Her hazel eyes were directed to Johnny—not to the pony—as if she spoke to him.

The shock of beige-colored hair peaking from her scarf matched Johnny's spots. Her eyebrows boasted the same neutral color, making her appear as if she had none at all. She gathered her white apron and gray frock to step around the laundry basket toward them. A gust blew from behind her, and Nick caught the scent of fresh washed clothes and stewed cabbage.

Johnny Boy wagged his tail with surprising enthusiasm as she bent her hunched back to pet him.

"Aye!" she laughed with tears sparkling on her lashes. "Ye look just like Sir Godfrey, ye do! 'Cept for the missin' ear."

Being so preoccupied with Johnny, the woman hadn't seemed to notice the pony at all.

Letting Johnny lick her hand, she looked up at Nick. "Sorry for the tears." She mopped her eyes with her apron. "Me dog died just after me husband passed three months ago. Been quiet here without 'em. Yer 'bout the same size as Ian ... and to see ye walkin' up with the dog. Well ... I'm a foolish old woman, to be sure."

Feeling a fresh bite of guilt, Nick yanked the pony's reins to bid her forward so he could take his punishment. The little mare nickered and planted herself behind him, displaying that stubborn streak Nick had wrestled when he first led her to the castle. He twisted around, trying to cajole some obedience.

Johnny yipped and danced around the pony's dainty feet, not helping matters.

"There there, bonnie bones." The old woman reached down to scratch Johnny's ear. "That thief is hardly worth yer labors."

The statement snapped Nick's gaze up.

The woman's grin widened to reveal three teeth on the bottom gums, tucked far in the back. She stood, letting the pony snuffle her hand. "Yep. This hobbie is a thief. Been callin' on me gardens far too often. I tried to show her that grass is far better fare than cabbages, but she's stubborn as an ox. Can't even get her to help me with the chores. Useless as a threadbare rag, she is."

Nick patted the mare's neck, at a loss for words.

If possible, the woman's forehead crinkled more. "I fence her in to keep her from me vegetables, but she's always breakin' out. I been thinkin' of turnin' her to the hills, but don't have the heart to leave her all alone. Kind of ye to find her and bring her back." She hobbled toward the mushroom shaped cottage, motioning for Nick to follow.

Tying the pony's reins to a post, Nick caught up, uncomfortable with the misunderstanding still lingering between them. The old woman slipped through the back door which hung half off its hinges, in dire need of repair. Nick inhaled the scent of fresh baked pastries.

He ducked across the threshold beneath a queer set of chimes fashioned from a corn-cob pipe and steel gardening tools. A small three-tined cultivator caught on his hat to prompt a clanging song.

The woman chuckled at the sound. "Ian did love a smoke when he gardened."

Nick worked the tool from his brim, releasing it to collide with the others on another burst of melody.

Soft daylight dusted the tidy one roomed cottage. Glancing at the apple fritters coated with sugar and glistening on a plate, Nick nearly jumped when he saw the table's headless occupant. A union suit had been stuffed with hay to give it shape. It sat in a wooden chair at the table, as if waiting for its meal. Another union suit was stuffed at its feet, stitched up to look like a dog. Nick struggled to keep curiosity from showing on his face.

The woman turned to him while digging through a sock she'd pulled out of a drawer. "Ah, ye like me scarecrows, do ye?" A jingle of coins punctuated her query.

Nick managed a smirk. "Don't most people post them outside?"

"Depends on what they be keepin' at bay. These are to scare away loneliness."

Her confession rolled around in Nick's stomach, burning like a lump of glowing coal. Johnny's adoring brown eyes were turned on the woman, as if he found her just as interesting as a study as Nick did.

"I think three punts be a fair price for bringin' back a hobbie." She held out the coin. Unmoving, Nick regarded her trembling, work-gnarled hands. Then his gaze roved the humble little abode.

A portrait of her and her husband, and a dog just like Johnny, hung on the wall over a fireplace harboring a sadly lacking woodpile. A pair of men's gardening gloves, with the name "Ian" embossed on the faded leather, served as tie-backs for the curtains over the sink. It was as if her husband were still there, holding the draperies open to keep her connected to the outside world. A straw hat, so large it must've belonged to Ian as well, balanced on its crown and cradled a thriving potted plant. And to complete the tribute, an abundance of men's trousers and shirts were folded neatly and set in the corner, as if she couldn't bear to put them out of sight.

Felicity's words in the greenhouse came back to him like a vapor on the wind. *"Sentimental value. One cannot put a price to that."*

A sudden pang of compassion surged through Nick, imagining how very alone this woman must be to convert her cottage to a shrine of memories. He glanced her way to find her having a conversation with Johnny about the coins. She held them low for the dog to sniff.

It didn't surprise Nick to see Johnny reaching out. When Nick had been at his lowest point, the dog had burrowed his way into his heart and found something long lost—a sense of humor, a reason to get up every day—revealing that sweet spot with the proficiency of a pig rooting for truffles. Johnny had an uncanny ability to sense what any person was missing and fill that void.

Just as now, the pit bull was drawn by the woman's loneliness, staying at her feet instead of Nick's.

An uncomfortable sensation butted against Nick's sternum. "I can't accept your money," he said, forcing his gaze from Johnny.

A befuddled frown on her face, the old woman set aside the punts. "But ye brought the hobbie back. Ye deserve some reward." The pit bull lifted his front paw to dig at her skirt, distracting her. "Ah, ye like pastries, aye? Apples were Sir Roland's favorite, too." Laughing, she broke off a piece of fritter and tossed it down. Johnny dropped to the floor to lick up the crumbs then rolled to his back begging for more, as if it were some routine they had worked out.

Nick watched, baffled and bewildered. As the woman jabbered and fed Johnny another bite, Nick scraped his palm across one of the loose hinges in her skewed door. He didn't like the direction his thoughts were taking. "I can fix these for you, if you have a screwdriver. A woman needs a sturdy door, for protection."

Her face brightened, transforming her wrinkles into a hundred smiles. "That be cracker! I did feel safer when I had me dog. But now ... well, I been meanin' to fix it meself, but these old hands not be as steady as they once were." She squatted to dig through a wooden egg crate beneath the sink.

Nick took the tool she offered. Standing outside on the steps, he propped the wooden panel—every bit as heavy as the weight in his chest—against his thigh for balance. He screwed the hinges back in place. After testing the door's swing, he opened it to return the screwdriver, only to find the woman holding out the coins again.

Her watery gaze reflected deep gratitude. "For yer trouble." Johnny laid at her feet, rolled on his back with tail thumping.

Nick cleared his throat against the lump forming. He took a deep breath, hardly able to grasp what he was about to propose. "What say we make a trade instead?"

She waited, puzzled.

Nick launched into the offer before he had time to take it back. "I'll get the hobbie off your hands if you'll take my dog. He's been so long travelling with me, you see. I think he's ready for a quieter life now."

As though sensing the bond between Nick and the dog, the woman looked at them alternately. "Ye sure?"

"There's a darling little girl I know who would be thrilled to have your thieving pony." Thoughts of Lia's sleepy smile gave Nick the strength to follow through. He would send the mare back with Tobias.

The old woman's eyebrows arched to transparent rainbows. "Aye then. A fair trade that be, if ye let me throw in some of Ian's clothes." Her gaze raked over the mended tear in Nick's pant leg. "Ye look like ye could use a change or two. And take some apple fritters for the road." Smiling, she wrapped half a dozen pastries in a cotton towel then bundled it all together with several shirts and trousers. She handed him the parcel.

Unable to look at Johnny, Nick forced himself to respond in spite of the freeze upon his soul. "Thank you, Miss...?"

"Hannah," she answered.

"Miss Hannah. Nice to meet you. I'm Nick." He tipped his hat then his gaze fell to the pit bull. "And this is Johnny."

Her toothless gums appeared again. "Johnny. Fine name."

Nick nodded. "Fine dog. Perhaps I might come visit him one day? I've grown rather fond of him ... on our journeys together."

Hannah patted Nick's arm. "Ye always be welcome here."

Clenching his jaw, Nick knelt down and curved his free hand around Johnny Boy's soft head, his lips at the dog's ear. He breathed in the scent of his fur one last time, hoping to memorize it. "You be good now," he whispered so only Johnny could hear. "Laugh at all her jokes."

As he drew back, Johnny Boy licked Nick's cheek and twisted his black lips to a hearty smile.

Nick stood and turned on his heel. He shoved the door open, ascended the steps, and started toward the pony, pinching the bridge of his nose to stave the burn. He could picture it already. Within a week, he'd be the man his father despised once more. Drugged out and lying in some ditch, a worthless thieving addict. He had nothing to stay sober for now.

"Believe in your own goodness," said a voice in his head that sounded too much like Felicity's.

Wrapping the reigns around his wrist, Nick snarled. Brilliant. She'd be haunting him with colloquialisms for the rest of his days. Then again, losing his mind was preferable to being a slave to opium. He cradled the pastries and clothes like a lifeline and started toward the front of the cottage.

"If ye like the apple fritters," Hannah called behind him,

"I be glad to make ye more when ye visit Johnny. Mayhap even some supper. Jest come by anytime."

Nick turned to find the old woman had followed him to the side of the house. She wound her hands in her apron, awaiting Nick's answer. Johnny had stayed in the cottage, already making himself at home.

"Ye can chop some firewood in exchange." She grinned. "Always have tasks needin' to be done. Have lots of neighbors who do, too. So we can put yer brothers to work, as well."

"Brothers?" Nick asked.

"I saw them through the window earlier, waitin' out front. Next time, ye can introduce us."

Confused by the cryptic words, Nick nodded then led the pony around the cottage. When the hitch wagon came into view, he saw two stable hands waiting instead of one. Their backs faced him, but Nick couldn't miss how the uniform sagged on the second one's smaller, delicate frame.

Before she even turned at hearing his footsteps, Nick knew it was her ... knew she'd been hiding beneath those blankets in the wagon ... knew she'd been the cause of Tobias' earlier unease.

"Miss Aislinn," Nick scolded sharply.

Eyes as wide and deep as the ocean at midnight blinked under the boyish hat. Her dark locks were tucked into the brim and the exposed ivory skin flushed with shame. Or, on second glance, brash excitement. Her mischievous smile reminded him of her aunt when she teased or challenged him. He felt a pang, missing Felicity all the more—a void made even bigger without Johnny.

"What is that?" Aislinn asked. She reached for the parcel of clothes and pastries. Lifting a corner of the cloth, she inhaled deeply. "Mmm. Apple. My favorite."

Nick stared at her, slack-jawed and speechless.

Her long lashes fluttered. "Where's Johnny Boy?"

Tamping the stitch in his heart, Nick answered. "He's going to keep this widow company for a while. You'll be taking Butterscotch back to the castle for Lia in exchange."

Tobias and Aislinn traded stunned glances then followed Nick's gaze as he waved to the old woman framed inside the cottage window. Johnny Boy appeared next to her, his tongue lolling and his wet nose streaking the glass.

Aislinn returned her attention to Nick. "What a selfless thing for Johnny to do." Her expression tendered as she smoothed her sagging uniform. "Sir Thornton, my aunt will be worried for me. You must see us home."

"See you home?" Nick asked, still blindsided by her impromptu appearance.

She lifted her chin. "You cannot expect me to ride alone with a young man. I need a chaperone to protect my virtue. You insisted such to Tobias yourself, if you recall."

Slanting a glare to Tobias, Nick watched the boy flame red from head to toe in acknowledgement of sharing their private talk.

When Nick turned again to Aislinn, she was already climbing into the wagon. Tobias moved to help her up, but Nick gave him a scowl and the stable boy pulled back. After handing off the pony to Tobias, Nick took Aislinn's elbow and assisted her.

"You planned this all along," he said, half accusing, half praising. "You stowed away so I'd have reason to return to the castle."

She settled into place on the wagon's seat and withdrew a fritter from its wrapping. "Good thing, too. Otherwise, you'd have missed Lia's smile when she sees that gift you bartered … with your heart."

Face hot with embarrassment, Nick climbed into the

wagon on the opposite side of Tobias, placing Aislinn between them.

She handed them both a half of a fritter and licked her fingertips. "Now, let's be on our way. Can't have Auntie miffed with us."

Nick took one last look at Johnny Boy. A knot formed in his throat. "No. We can't have that." Then he bit off a chunk of pastry and snapped the reins.

CHAPTER TWENTY-ONE

"Jasper. Please. I know Aislinn's visited you. She believes she's reached you. Can you answer me?" Wincing at her resounding echo in the domed turret, Felicity laced her brother's fingers tighter and squeezed. She'd been trying to coax a response for half an hour. No matter how much pressure she exerted, his hand remained limp.

Now, the slackness became a contagion, numbing her own limbs. She tucked his arm back at his side, pulled the sheets to his chin, and sank from the edge of his bed to the chilled floor.

She had imagined it all. It wasn't her brother who'd possessed her to write the novel with Emilia. It was her own demented past that had poisoned her mind and made her insane. Just as she imagined the shadow in her bedchamber. She'd been so desperate to have him come back to her and the girls that she'd conjured these things out of thin air and dared to believe ... dared to hope that Aislinn had performed a miracle.

Nostrils stinging from an amalgamation of candle wax and ammonia, Felicity studied her surroundings through bleary eyes. Two years gone by, yet nothing had changed. Still the same cobwebs along the vaulted ceiling, glistening in the milky daylight which filtered through six dirty windows no bigger than envelopes. Still the same bare, stone walls paired with a floor carpeted by the occasional avalanche of handwritten journals and lepidopterology tomes.

The familiar pot-bellied stove in the corner lent a warm glow. Clooney kept it filled with coke. The distilled remains of coal provided the perfect means to warm the room, emitting no flame and little smoke yet considerable heat.

Her gaze skipped to the small table beside Jasper's bed where Clooney kept his medical accouterments. There, most daunting of all, sat the urn—Isabella's remains keeping vigil over her dormant husband. An eerie still-life of loyalty marred by fate's cruel paintbrush.

Jasper had been obsessed after Isabella died. So much like Nick, trying to find some way to reach his lost bride, to tell her things he'd neglected to say. Unlike Nick, Jasper had been driven by passionate love and went one step further. After he pored over the occult sciences to no avail, he turned to nature, seeking answers in his butterflies. At one point, he thought he'd found something, and it compelled him to travel to the orient for the jeweled longwings which soon thereafter became the mainstay of Felicity's thriving business. Being rare and frail, most other caterpillar breeders avoided the Heliconious. But Jasper's need to contact Isabella negated any such hesitation.

He had just had a breakthrough, was at the pinnacle of his studies, when he'd been struck down. Sometimes Felicity wondered what he'd learned, but Aislinn had that particular journal, and kept it hidden somewhere.

Perhaps, through his catatonia, Jasper had found a way back to Isabella. Fragile hope flickered in Felicity's chest; it would be a comfort to know that he wasn't the empty shell he appeared to be. That within his brilliant mind somewhere, he and Isabella were together on some level— convergent and at peace.

Shoving to stand, Felicity slid her back upward along the cold, hard wall until her shawl slipped off to puddle at her ankles. "Dear brother," she whispered. "If only you could hear me."

Jasper's black lashes fanned slowly to shutter an empty blue gaze pointed to the ceiling. The only other movement was a steady breath from his nostrils, prompting the black hairs of his moustache and beard to part slightly. The rest of his thick hair spread over his entire pillow, smooth and glossy like an ink spill. Even in his hollow helplessness, he was beautiful.

It always hurt to see him. To have these outward bursts of life—the perpetual growth of hair, the blinking eyes, the swallowing when offered water or broth. His body's mock functioning taunted her. This is why she'd left his daily care to Clooney. Why she'd stopped visiting shortly after he'd fallen into a catatonic stupor. This, and the grudge she'd held due to their rash pact.

After the initial stroke left the right side of his body paralyzed, he'd begged her never to let his daughters see him so helpless. Felicity watched him wrestle his inadequacies, saw him emotionally deteriorate to the point that he had to take doses of laudanum hourly.

Considering he'd come to the estate to help her, she felt indebted to oblige him. She faked his death, soliciting Clooney's help in making a counterfeit body filled with sand which they wrapped in sheets. They then employed the stable boys' help to carry the corpse from the turret. They assured the servants and girls witnessed them placing him in the coffin before nailing it shut. Then, following Jasper's instructions, Felicity and Clooney destroyed the final flight of stairs with the help of the stable hands, leaving everyone with the impression it had been an eccentric scientist's dying request. Only she and Clooney were left with access via the secret passageway Jasper had found years earlier. A passage no one else knew of.

But when Felicity started making plans for his "funeral" in the forest, she saw how heart-broken the girls were after losing both their mother and father and realized how wrong the lie was. Unfortunately, the very day she was going to tell Jasper that she'd changed her mind, the day she'd intended to tell her nieces that their father still lived, he'd had a second stroke which rendered him suspended in this stasis without words or communication—locked in a purgatory where he drifted aimlessly along irreclaimable minutes and hours.

She'd lost the chance to go back on her word. For she knew, if her brother couldn't bear having his children see him as half a man, it would kill him for them to see him as a vegetable. As it was, he was hanging to life by a very thin thread.

Being here with him now—his skin pale and shadowy, his once muscular tone atrophied and thin—all bitterness fell away.

So spindly and frail, he looked like a fairy prince woven from moonlight. For once, Felicity truly understood his viewpoint. Why he didn't want his girls to see him in such a state. She felt as if she'd let him down ... owed him an explanation for what had happened a few months ago.

"Aislinn had been watching Clooney and I, you see." She spoke aloud, falling back into the habit of the one-sided conversations they'd shared since the beginning of his stasis. She paced the floor, her bare feet skating along the chill stone in an attempt to keep her thoughts on track. Her gown's hem brushed her ankles.

"We were so careful with the servants and with Lia. But Aislinn..." Felicity bent to pick up a dusty picture book of butterflies. "Well, you know her, Jasper. She's inquisitive, tricky, much like you. It's a miracle we managed to keep it from her for that first year."

She slanted her gaze from a vivid monarch to her brother's motionless form. "And clever beyond her age. Beyond even mine. I assure you, she's keeping the secret from Lia. In the past two years, she's not whispered a word. And I'll not let another soul know of your condition henceforth. You can trust me."

Felicity paused, thinking she heard some movement behind her. Hairs lifted along her arms as if someone were watching her. She glanced over her shoulder and saw nothing but the wall. Shrugging off the sensation, she padded to Jasper's bed and eased down on the mattress.

Finding a picture of an Adonis Blue, she laid the book beside Jasper on the pillow and compared his empty blinking eyes to the butterfly's spectacular blue wings. She smiled sadly.

"Not only does Aislinn have your mind, she has your eyes. You know this already. You saw her for yourself as she grew. But..." Hot tears edged her lashes as she touched the freckles on her brother's straight, narrow nose. "But did you ever take the time to look? You were so busy searching for ways to reach Isabella ... I fear you lost sight of the gifts she'd left behind for you."

Moisture streaked down Felicity's face. "Lia. Oh, Jasper, you should see her now. She is so beautiful, just like her mother. And such a bold little ingénue. Her seventh birthday's coming up in a month. She wants a carousel."

Slapping at the tears, Felicity moved the book aside to stroke her brother's silken hair. "I wish you were here. I wish you could see how they miss you every day ... how very much they love you still. They speak of you constantly. They're keeping your memory alive."

The weight of those words heaved upon Felicity's shoulders, to think of how she'd shut her eyes to everything that reminded her of him. She sobbed, burying her face against his neck. "Forgive me! I never forgot you! Never forgot the memories we shared." Her strangled breaths bounced back from Jasper's skin, warming her face. "I was angry. From the moment you left, all hell followed in your wake. And I needed you here to help. And you were here ... but yet you weren't."

Resting her cheek against the sheet which covered his chest, Felicity struggled for composure. Her throat swelled with words. It was as if every thought she'd pent up for want of speaking now clawed for a turn to be free. "There's a man, his name is Donal Landrigan ... he was the earl's son. He came after your second stroke ... he means to take the estate. He's so determined, I fear he'll stop at nothing. He startled Aislinn from a tree, nigh caused Lia a snake bite ... he even claims to know something of my past..." She sniffed, letting the tears run down her face and into the sheet beneath her. "He stole the pigs and has threatened to do as much to the girls ... though he was very careful in his wording." Thoughts of the incident reminded Felicity of Nick coming to her rescue that first day as she argued with Landrigan in the courtyard.

"Remember the young man I told you of? The one who saved me years ago? He found me again. His name is Nick. He's a beautiful lost soul. He understands loneliness, and the loss of a child. He's experienced both as intimately as I have." She smiled sadly. "More so, even. Until coming here, his only friend was a dog. You should see how he talks to that hound." Her smile faded. She and Nick truly were so much alike. It was their one comfort in an otherwise lonely existence to confide in sources that could not respond verbally.

She was so thankful Nick had Johnny Boy. Otherwise, he would be alone. So utterly alone.

"I couldn't ask him to stay," she nestled closer to Jasper and whispered against the damp sheet as if he'd heard her thoughts and bade an explanation. "He wants a son one day. I'll not deprive him of things I cannot give. Things he deserves..."

The confession didn't staunch her regret any more than it lightened her worry. She closed her eyes, trying to crush the image of opium tincture in her mind. "He's strong. I know he is. He will find his way." Taking a deep breath, she smoothed the shoulder seam on her brother's shirt.

She pushed herself to sit up, wiping wetness from her cheek. She'd been idolizing her young hero for seven years. An unattainable infatuation that had carried her through her loneliest hours. When she finally met him, he was all she'd imagined and more. Not in spite of his flaws ... because of them. They'd made him human, molded her fantasy hero into a man of flesh, bones, and blood with strengths and weaknesses. Just like her.

That was why her feelings had changed so abruptly. Why they'd flourished into real and tangible affection.

Or, if she dared look deeper, something even stronger...

Trying to busy herself lest she cry again, Felicity patted the sheet at Jasper's neck, finding the fabric soaked. She folded the cover off his neck. The action exposed his chest where the nightshirt curled open and she noticed that a spattering of tiny red circles marred his skin.

"Odd." Brows furrowed, she pulled his shirt back more. A startled whimper stuck in her throat. Ten or more longwing pupas hung from his skin beneath his clothes, attached as if he were a passion vine. The circles seemed to be indicative of ones that had been pulled off or fallen away.

Her pulse stuttered. Could this be the cause of the shortage all these months?

She took stock of when the pupa shortage first began. About three months ago ... sometime after Aislinn had discovered Jasper's final secret journal. Weeks later, perhaps. And then recently, the Dark Raven had begun to make his appearance.

Nick's words in the greenhouse tangled with her reasoning. *"Perhaps your brother has become one with the butterflies, perhaps his faith wasn't so foolish after all."*

Aislinn's statement solidified the sentiment: *"I think I have found a way to bring father back to us."*

Felicity drew back in shock. Toppling off the bed, she nearly fell over. She recouped her footing and stood rigid and shivering, arms crossed over her breasts. "Aislinn ... what have you done?"

A swishing sound swept by then a cool rush of air settled in front of her. Felicity felt her life drain to her toes.

She held her breath as he appeared—a faceless man shaped of butterfly shadows—just like the girls had described. Unable to move, to even moan, Felicity stared in awe as the shadows transformed to full color until Jasper stood over her, clearly imprinted on a thousand butterflies— as if the fluttery wings were the puzzle pieces which formed his image. He reached for her.

In disbelief, she reached back.

Just as her trembling fingers almost touched him, the

door to the turret creaked open and Jasper's image burst apart into a thousand butterflies, then vanished just as quickly as it had appeared.

CHAPTER TWENTY-TWO

Clooney stood in the open door of the turret, staring at Felicity with his mouth agape. An interminable silence passed between them and she knew without a doubt he'd been hiding something monumental for months. Before she could ask him about the miracle she'd just witnessed, Clooney spoke up.

"So, you saw."

Dry-mouthed and dazed, she nodded.

Clooney stepped inside, shutting the door behind him. "Aislinn. She's been in such torment. Please understand, I never meant for it to go this far. Didn't realize how it was affecting your shipments until you mentioned it the other day. I was to put a stop to it this week, just hadn't told her yet with all that's happened."

"You've seen him, too?" Felicity asked.

"I'm responsible in part." Clooney strode to the bed, studying Jasper's chest with where the pupal barnacles tagged his skin. "Those two years ago, when Aislinn discovered Jasper's body here, she also overheard you and I hypothesizing about your odd writing stints. How you thought it impossible it could be him, since he wasn't actually dead. She came to me in secret, said that if his spirit was capable of leaving his body to enter yours, well ... we might be able to heal his body and lure him back into it, for it proved he was still here in our world, and not another plane. For months, she read his findings to no avail, until she stumbled upon his final journal. Within it was a passage that outlined the rejuvenating abilities of the jeweled longwing pupas. She begged to try an experiment in hopes to bring him back. I hadn't the heart to tell her no. But all it's done is feed the child's imagination. She's convinced now that the 'shadow' she claims to see is her father, and that he's connected to that strange fungus. We'll put a stop to it today. Obviously, it hasn't worked."

"Then, you haven't seen it ...?"

"The pupas on his skin? Yes. I helped her gather and arrange them." Clooney started to pull one off.

Felicity reached out to stop him. "You are *not* to remove them!" Her heart pounded.

Clooney dropped his chin. "But..."

"I forbid it." Childhood superstitions had unfurled within, as shy and precious as the petals on a winter rose. Nick had been right all along. Jasper was the Raven. He might not be a traditional ghost, but somehow Aislinn's intervention had enabled his spirit to materialize outside of his body—and hers—on a whole new level.

"It has worked," she murmured, her palm hovering over her mouth as if feeling the rush of words would cement the fact.

Clooney squinted and took his pipe from his pocket. "What did you say, Dove?"

On the verge of telling Clooney everything, Felicity stopped. Jasper had chosen only to show himself to his blood relatives—his family. Perhaps it wasn't her place to say anything. Not yet.

"Nothing. I'm ... I'm just babbling. But I want you to leave things as they are."

Clooney dragged his pipe along his chin, confusion etched on his aged features. "Well enough. I'm just glad to see you visiting him again. But, I'm afraid your visit must be short. We have a visitor in the parlor. Donal is here."

His announcement snapped Felicity back to the present and its miseries. "What? Why?"

Clooney stuck the pipe in his mouth. "Brute wouldn't say. Being downright cryptic. Wouldn't even speak to his aunt, other than the usual pleasantries. Wants to converse with you alone. Better hurry. He's nursing brandied coffee in the dining hall. Don't want him drunk or passed out for your interlude."

Felicity took one last sweep of the turret. Inspired by the hope that Jasper had found some way to reach her, and empowered by Nick's plan for the peat bogs, she didn't feel intimidated by Landrigan's presence for the first time in months.

She would meet him head on and put a stop to his bullying once and for all. Then—and she couldn't staunch a faint smile—she would return to the turret and visit with her brother again. Now that her faith in miracles had been restored, perhaps it would be strong enough to bring him back to them for good.

Nick looked over his shoulder and frowned at Tobias. The young man stiffened under his scrutiny.

Though the hitch wagon easily seated three, Nick had forced the stable hand to sit in back on the blankets after they'd taken a detour to Carnlough for some supplies. Nick was growing fond of Tobias. But he felt inclined to dole out some repercussion for his part in Aislinn's plan. Nick wasn't about to let either of the youths know how grateful he was for the deception, lest they make a habit of finding ways to be alone together.

Since he had a harder time being harsh with Aislinn, he directed the brunt of his punishment toward the stable hand.

"Give me that piece of wood there," Nick said roughly, motioning with his carver's knife toward the stack of evergreen blocks in the back. "The one on top." Nick had handed over control of the wagon to Aislinn after a short lesson on driving a rig, anxious to get started with his carving.

Tobias crawled across the assortment of loot Nick had bartered for his earring and handed over a misshapen block of evergreen. Nick took the wood and appraised the wagon's contents.

At the town market, he'd purchased eggs, milk, butter and cheese, that orange blossom soap Felicity was so fond of, fabrics for new dresses approved by Aislinn's discerning eye, oil paints for his carving projects, and other sundries. He also bought a handful of shimmery ribbons for Lia to use on her pony.

Nick's personal favorite, though, were the links of sausage. He'd bought enough to last the winter and couldn't help but smirk in anticipation of Felicity's reaction.

The closer they got to the castle, the more fidgety he became. He'd left Felicity with a mess without even realizing it. Last night, when he'd come up with the plan for the peat bogs, his mind had been fuzzy from the mead and lack of sleep. Today, since he'd had time to think, he saw the glitch. Felicity would have to hire workers. She wouldn't feel safe with so many strange men running about. She'd crave the protection of a husband even more. Landrigan was just sharp enough to use that to his advantage.

Nick couldn't stomach the thought of that man's hands on Felicity's body, or of him playing father to the girls. So, to that end, Nick was determined to offer marriage again himself. Now that he'd found a way to help support them, perhaps Felicity would overlook his past addiction and respect him enough to accept.

Upon speaking to the shop owner, Nick had been surprised to discover how many older folks lived in these hills. Widows and decrepit couples needing a strong, young hand. Though his intake wouldn't be a windfall of wealth, he could work in exchange for necessities. That would be enough to supplement Felicity's butterfly business until her caterpillars replenished, and funds from the peat bogs started rolling in.

Turning back around in the seat, he moved his knife in calming sweeps, shaving away slivers of the soft wood in his hand. It was the first time he'd carved in months without Mina's death weighing on the blade.

Grinning, he slid the shiny silver along the wood, leaving an excess on both sides of the curvaceous form.

"What are you carving there?" Aislinn asked, turning her deep, intuitive gaze his way. "Seems to be making you quite happy."

"Well, what do you think it looks like?" He held up his fledgling masterpiece.

"A rather lumpy rectangle."

Chuckling, Nick studied his work and had to agree. But in a few hours, he'd have a rough set of butterfly wings springing off of the woman's form he was shaping. Within a few days, it would be ready to paint. "Tis for your aunt."

Aislinn's freckles fairly jumped as she smiled. "Ah. So it

must be butterfly related. Very romantic."

Nick's head cocked at the comment. The young lady smiled and he looked away, continuing to carve.

"You're hoping to win her heart with it," Aislinn baited. "You told me yesterday that she needed a man who could give her wings."

Nick paused, amazed at her wisdom. "And you told me your father is the ghost haunting that castle."

Aislinn jerked the reins, almost dropping them. "I said no such thing." Her gaze slipped over her shoulder to Tobias. She bit her lip, some loose strands of hair flapping around her face. "Could you move to the back of the wagon?"

The stable hand's resulting scowl was nothing less than comical. "What? I'm already in the back."

Aislinn intensified her glare.

Tobias grumbled and scooted to the very end, close enough to the gate that he could reach out and pet the hobbie tied to the latch. "There." He raised his voice over the rumble of the wagon. "Should I stuff my ears with hay?"

"No. That will do. I'll speak softly." She gave Tobias a sweet smile that could've tamed a rabid badger. She then turned to Nick. "I merely said that I believed the *Raven* was real."

Nick's blade resumed its scrape against the wood. "Why don't you tell me about your aunt's childhood? How did she and your father end up at the orphanage?"

Aislinn glanced at the sky as if considering how much to reveal. "They were all on a carriage ride and had a terrible accident. My grandfather's neck broke and he died instantly. Grandmother developed blood poisoning from an injured leg and died weeks later in the hospital. Auntie was eight, and a piece of jagged wood left her scarred." The girl touched her chest and pressed her lips tight, as if she'd said too much.

Nick frowned at the discrepancy in her tale, knowing that's how Felicity wanted it. That she'd hidden the true origin of her scar because she thought it the only way she could maintain her niece's respect.

Aislinn took a breath and continued. "Father was thirteen, and only suffered a scratch or two. But the accident had other ripples. Since there was no remaining family, they both ended up in an orphanage. In a matter of months, Father was taken by a wealthy professor and his barren wife who wanted a namesake. Auntie stood in the window and watched him leave." Aislinn pressed her lips together. "It was always so sad to hear Father tell it. The last time he saw her she'd looked so destitute and abandoned, as if she thought he'd chosen them over her. Auntie was later bought by a family when she was ten."

Nick thought of the earl and bit back a growl. *Bought* took on a whole new connotation with that worm of a guardian. Obviously, Felicity's abandonment issues had started at a very young age. "So, how did they find one another again?"

Aislinn shrugged. "Auntie found him through the orphanage's records."

"And your father picked up his life and came to Ireland without question?"

"Mother was sick..." Aislinn's voice wavered. "We came hoping her lungs would rally with the change of climate. They never did."

Thinking upon the tragic losses Aislinn and her sister had suffered in their short lives, Nick started to offer condolences, but Aislinn spoke first.

"Now, I want to know something of you. Do you miss him?"

"Whom?" Nick hoped she wasn't referring to his own father or brother.

"Johnny Boy."

Nick's blade glided along the wood, releasing a long sliver to fall at his feet. "He was my best friend. Accepted me unconditionally. But I'll see him again soon."

"Will you get a new dog, to replace him? You can find a puppy who's perfect ... with two ears."

Nick leveled a gaze at her. "Johnny's irreplaceable. And frailty moves the heart in a way perfection cannot match."

Aislinn studied the road ahead. "Just as I suspected. An artist's eye finds beauty even in the broken things. No wonder Auntie is so fond of you."

Once again, Nick was taken aback by the girl's maturity. Had she been testing him, to see if he would accept her aunt's disfigurement?

He held the wood to his mouth to blow off stray splinters and inhaled the piney scent. His own chest cinched tight in anticipation of seeing his wounded Felicity again, and the hope that he'd finally found a way to break down her walls.

Felicity took her time dressing. She had to assure the wrinkles on her face were fully set in, and since it took half of the hour for the lotion to take effect, she couldn't rush.

Other than the men's suit she sometimes sported, it seemed an eternity since she'd put on anything other than mourning clothes. Come to think, her history with fashion had been sadly lacking throughout her life. She had gone from dressing in pinafores as a child to the gaudy frills and immodest décolleté of a courtesan then the languished dregs of a widow in mourning. There had been nothing to bridge the gaps in between.

But something had changed in her today, and her clothes

should reflect it. She would no longer hide behind her sorrow, or her fear. Landrigan wasn't behind the ghostly sightings. Her brother was fighting to come back, and the knowledge empowered her.

It was high time she looked the part of an honorable lady—alive and capable. She was more than Landrigan's father's widow. She was her own person ... the lady of the manor. This estate belonged to her and no other. Perhaps if she made that clear once and for all, he would respect her enough to consider the peat bog proposal.

She still couldn't bring herself to wear a corset—to be bound up tight made the skin around her scar itch terribly. But in the back of Jasper's wardrobe hung several gowns that had once belonged to Isabella, with enough stays sewn in one didn't need a corset.

After his wife first passed, Jasper had offered them to Felicity since she and Isabella were the same size. At the time, Felicity was playing the part of the mourning dowager and had no use for them.

Now she pulled one out: an elegant silk gown the gentle pink of champagne held up to a sunrise. The skirt came to her ankles, and a scalloped train dragged the floor behind. Fingerless mittens of creamed lace matched the ivory laced under-cuffs which spilled out over her wrists from beneath bell-hemmed sleeves. The bodice was pleated to fit her small waist and accentuate her bust, and the lapel sported ivory covered buttons which ran between the ribs all the way up to the high collar beneath her chin, making a scarf redundant. In spite of that, she still felt a wisp of insecurity, and chose to wear her butterfly brooch pinned in place, just above the tip of her scar. Its familiar weight reassured her.

Plaiting her silvery hair in separate links, she wrapped them high upon her crown like snakes and secured them with glistening pins. The mirror over the bureau offered a glimpse of radiance she rarely saw. The soft blush of the dress put color in her cheeks and warmed her eyes to a gleaming chocolate depth. Aside from the wrinkles, she bore a resemblance to the young girl she'd been before the earl's imprint on her life and wished with all her heart the man waiting downstairs could be Nick. Perhaps he would've melted at the sight of her, taken her in his strong arms, forgiven her for all the secrets, and never walked away again no matter how convincing her feigned rejections might be.

Swallowing a lump, she glanced down at the creamy tips of her satin boots. Just because Jasper had connected with her didn't mean she should bend to girlish whims and fancies. She had chased Nick away for his own good. Now, she would chase away her puffed-up stepson for the good of her family.

Upon this thought, a determined expression faced her in the mirror, and she rather favored herself being Medusa, off to turn her nemesis to stone with a brash baring of terrible beauty.

Before heading to the dining hall, she stopped to peek in on the girls. Dinah and Nutmeg had already been let from the room so they might relieve themselves outside. Lianna snored from her side of the bed and Aislinn was wrapped in blankets up over her head. Since their drapes sealed out the sun, and neither girl moved at the creak of the door, Felicity felt secure they would sleep through Landrigan's visit.

She took the stairs and crept toward the dining hall on hushed footfalls. Judging by the length of time her unwelcome guest had been alone with his coffee and brandy, he would either be worked up to an aggravated frenzy or drowsing. Much preferring the latter, she chose to be quiet in hopes to win the advantage of surprise.

But when she rounded the corner and stepped into the brightly lit room, she found he wasn't alone at all. Rachel and Landrigan had their heads together, whispering. Felicity inhaled deeply to ground herself. The bite of charred wood in the fireplace and the muted scent of breakfast hidden within domed silver trays tickled her nose.

Clearing her throat, she waited at the double doors. The maid startled and pushed off from the table beside Landrigan's seat. She straightened her apron over her black uniform, moving with the all the grace of a flustered crow. Then she bowed her head to Landrigan and curtsied to Felicity on her way out. The usual haughty expression on her face paled to surprise upon seeing Felicity's attire.

Felicity relished the unspoken compliment, having never been considered a peer or a rival in the young woman's eyes. She conjectured the maid's newfound insecurity was due less to the change in clothes than to the sting of Nick's earlier rejection. And she was grateful to him once more for being true to his finer qualities—those he never let himself believe in.

When Felicity shut the doors and turned back to Landrigan, he was on his feet, his glittering-gold eyes piercing her. He whistled. "Why, Felicity. Yer a vision. Such a dress could put the heart crossways in a man." He swirled a spoon in his coffee cup. The scraping-clink grated within Felicity, feeding her annoyance.

"That's *Your Ladyship* to you, Mister Landrigan. And I would like nothing better than to give you a heart attack. Such a shame I failed in my attempt."

Landrigan's dimples slapped her. "Nay. The shame is ye can't freshen yer charm with a change of clothes."

She swept to the table to pour herself some tea. "I suppose I could, should I have a care. But hatred breeds apathy, I fear."

"I still say that color is right becomin' on ye. Makes ye look least a good twenty years younger." A glint of something indiscernible danced behind his gaze.

Felicity paused sipping her citrusy brew. A shiver ran through her. She took another sip of steaming tea to tame it. He was just being his usual smarmy self. She knew better than to play victim to his baiting. "How serendipitous that you should come today. I had planned to call for you."

"Well, that right warms me to the cockles."

Felicity schooled her features to stony casualness. "I have a proposition."

"A proposition. Me morn just keeps gettin' brighter and brighter." Her nemesis abandoned his coffee but kept the spoon, licking droplets from its ladle as he strode toward Lianna's drawings on the wall. Thoughtfully studying them, he flipped the spoon so the handle rested between his lips much like the peppermint sticks he usually carried.

"Did you lose your little bag of candy?" Felicity offered the barb as she settled behind him and nursed her tea.

"I've a toothache. T'would seem there's such a thing as too much sugar. With the exception of yer sweet nieces." He stepped to the left and perused Lianna's latest attempt at a carousel. Withdrawing the spoon from his mouth, he used the handle to trace the sketched lines. "I see the snapper hasn't forgot me promise. I've purchased the ponies ... be bringin' 'em by on her birthday."

Felicity tightened her hand around her tea cup. The heat seeping into her fingers through the porcelain was nothing to the fire in her belly. "I would think a man who treasures his smile wouldn't tempt fate by speaking such folly."

He turned full around to face her. "Plan to bust out me teeth with a teacup?" His breath, hot and soured with brandy, rushed her forehead.

She looked up at him, feeling small against his height. "You wasted your money. You're not invited to her gala. The only way your carousel ponies will be arriving on our doorstep is if they gallop over on their own."

He tapped the spoon on his open palm. "Is that so? How ye plan to keep me away?"

"I won't have to. You'll stay away willingly."

Smirking, Landrigan smoothed the lapel of his suit, such a warm spiced hue it would've blended into his skin if not for the pink shirt beneath the jacket. "Now this I want to hear." He gestured to the table with the spoon, inviting Felicity to sit. She hedged into the chair he held. After scooting her in, he took a seat across from her.

A clink reverberated through the quiet room as Felicity set her cup on a saucer. She smoothed the fabric of her skirt. "I'm going to harvest and sell the peat in the bogs. And I'll give you a generous share of the profits."

Interest opened his features as he spun the spoon on the table. "Would this be yer proposition? Must say I was hopin' it was somethin' of a less ... industrious nature."

Felicity continued unfazed. "We will be in business with one another, and that will be the extent of our relationship. As partners, we will both sign a contract to that effect."

An amused grin tugged at his lips. "I sense there's to be some sort of provision on it?"

"A clause. Stating you will never set foot on this estate again and that any exchanges between us will be via post. You may visit your aunt anytime, but only in Carnlough. Clooney shall drive her into town, and you can meet her somewhere. There are cafés aplenty. Any one would suffice. Surely you can see the fairness in this. I'm offering part of your father's estate, just as you've always wanted. And this way, you'll make a steady profit without ever doing a day's work."

"And who *will* do the work?" he asked, the smugness setting in again.

"Pardon?"

"Have ye considered how many men ye'll have to hire to work the bogs? With yer private nature, I'm surprised yer willin' to let that many strangers peer into yer life."

Felicity clutched the butterfly brooch at her neck. She hadn't considered that. Hadn't had time to think this plan through at all. Nick hadn't either, it appeared. But for the moment, she couldn't worry about it. She had to keep the upper hand. Get Landrigan to agree to the contract and get him out. That's all that mattered right now. She would hone the details later.

"I shan't be dealing with the workers. Nick will. He's to marry me." The lie came easily for it slid from her heart—an unreachable dream. "He's off at the moment, getting a license in town. So, you see, Mister Landrigan, this really is the only way you'll ever have any claim on this estate, since I'm to marry another man."

She expected rage. Or in the least, piqued fury. But all that Landrigan offered was a casual lift of his dark brow. "Surprising. That ye would marry someone affiliated with London."

"Why should that surprise you?"

He startled her by sliding the spoon across the table so it teetered off the edge and into her lap. When she looked up from where it landed, he loomed over her, fists banked on either side of her teacup. "Seein' as that's where yer secrets be buried, *Jasmine.*"

CHAPTER TWENTY-THREE

"What's with the long puss, yer ladyship? Ye look like ye've seen me old Da himself. But that be impossible, don't it? Bein' as yer grounds keeper, or should I say, *physician*, killed him."

Felicity's scar cinched tight, a cold, crackling sensation which started beneath the brooch and descended to the base of her abdomen like glass breaking beneath an extreme freeze.

She had to have misheard. He couldn't know.

He could never know.

But one look at his face, and denial gave way to sheer terror.

"How...?" Her question came out on a strangled breath.

"I was leadin' the wrong way, y'see. When I stopped looking for information on yer bonny ass and turned my attention to yer groundsman and his fierce talent for medicine ... well, that brought it all about. I heard 'bout a physician from a brothel in London that my da used to frequent. The doc disappeared close to when me da died. I wrote to the madame and her return letters were chock full of interestin' stories. The most unusual one of a courtesan known as Jasmine—a favorite of me da's, not to mention of every other man she pleasured. But here be the interestin' part ... seems there was an incident that involved the whore. Da made bags o' her chest and ended up at the bottom of some stairs with a bloody knife in his hand. Least, tis the version the brothel's physician gave after the whore died. But the madam couldn't find the doc for any more questions after that fated night. I suspect he played a part in me da's death. That he was defendin' the whore and pushed me ol' man down the stairs. It's taken some money, but I finally got his name. Imagine me surprise to learn he went by Clooney and nothin' more. And ye..." Landrigan shook his head, almost laughing. "Ye look right good for a dead woman."

The sun streamed through the long windows, as if putting Felicity's entire life on display. The light was blinding and uncomfortably hot.

She glanced over her shoulder, wishing she'd left the doors open. On second thought, had she, everyone in the castle would know her secret. It was better she face this alone.

However, she'd lost all courage. Blood pounded in her ears, and the truth pinned her in place. She couldn't move even when she heard the scuff of his shoes coming around the table ... even when he knelt next to her to lift the spoon from where it had settled in the basin of her skirt between her thighs.

His hand lingered too long on her leg, scalding it. Felicity came to herself enough to shove him away, scooting her chair back in the process.

He caught the edges of the seat then spun her so the back planked the table and boxed her in. The reverberation of wood hitting wood echoed through her shoulders and shook her bones.

His hands clenched to knuckle-white tightness. The

spoon wedged between his right palm and the chair's cushion. "It be ironic really ... less a lady then me mum who was but a servant. Yet me bastard father married ye on his deathbed and cast me pregnant mum to the gutters. Can only be one explanation." His teeth gleamed on a sneer both superior and ravenous—a fox facing a rabbit trapped in barbed wire. "*Ye must be worth yer weight in gold between the sheets.*"

Deep within, hard won mettle warmed the embers of Felicity's waning spirit. "You have no proof," she spat. It was all she could think of. To dispute the details would be futile. But it was his word against hers. No one in Ireland could identify her, so he had no means to substantiate the claim.

Landrigan released the left side of her chair and laid the spoon in her lap again. From his jacket's lining, he drew out a sheet of stationary so familiar it made Felicity gasp. She reached for it, but he blocked her hand. The script captured her attention like a scream: her handwritten list of every patron's address to whom she supplied butterflies, including her London clientele.

"Can't mean too much to ye," Landrigan said, sneering. "I've had it since yesterday and ye didn't notice its absence."

"Where did you get it?" she asked.

"Mayhap, had yer betrothed been so inclined to be as generous as me, the servants would be loyal to him, and not so hungry for revenge."

"*Rachel,*" Felicity seethed the name.

Landrigan curled his lips so they opened like petals of nightshade, dripping with poison. "So, ye see I needn't any proof, *Jasmine.* I've witnesses comin' to out ye. I suspect some of yer butterfly clientele from London frequented said brothel. Tis why ye choose to live in seclusion, to never show yer face to them. Well, I've wired messages to each one to visit the estate the day after Lia's birthday—an invitation to see the inner workings of yer caterpillar business."

Felicity's mouth dropped.

"Aw. Don't look so puckish, luv. Was a cracker business move. A good faith gesture on yer part as their supplier, to show them things have improved."

Dizziness spun Felicity's thoughts. She scrambled for some way to stay afloat. "I'll withdraw each offer. Resend their acceptances in personalized notices."

"Wouldn't recommend it. Be nawful un-businesslike. Might lose some customers. Besides"—he tucked the piece of stationary behind his lapel— "I believe this be yer only copy of the list."

Felicity clutched his jacket but he pried her fingers free—sending shooting pains through her knuckles.

"I have envelopes," she said. "From missives ... with their addresses intact ... all I need do is look for them."

"Ah. But by the time ye find each one, and send off yer bonny little withdrawals, yer patrons'll already be on a ship, makin' their way to the castle." He traced the spoon's handle along her thigh. "Hmm. What will yer hero Nick think, to learn the truth about his bride?"

Her confidence wavered like a candle beneath an ill wind, but still refused to snuff out. "Nick already knows. He wants me despite it. He'll protect me if I'm recognized. To share his name will be my sanction." The lies flowed slower now—like honey, sweet but sticky on the tongue.

"Ah. But what of his family? There was another Lord Thornton at the top of yer list. According to Rachel, it's Nick's upright father. I don't think he'll support this marriage. Mayhap Nick would give up his inheritance for ye, were ye some virtuous maiden. But heroes don't relinquish treasure for scrubbers. Nay. That not be the way of fairytales, *Jasmine*."

"Stop calling me that!"

Felicity shoved him off and stood, thrashing the spoon about as if it were a sword. She backed toward the pictures on the wall, wishing she could disappear into Lianna's black and white dreamscapes. To ride away on that carousel ... never to face any music but songs of merriment and innocence.

Landrigan strutted through the shifting light where the window frames shaded his dark skin. Bluish lines moved like creeping ivy across his face. "All this time, lettin' on that yer a prim and proper widow. And everyone bought it. I wonder..." He caught her spoon wielding hand along with her other wrist and pinned them to the wall. "How do ye make the wrinkles look so real? I suspect they be exclusive only to the exposed parts of yer body."

Grinding her fingers tight around the spoon's ladle, he dragged her wrist down so the spoon's tip traced her collar beneath her chin. Using it like a button-hook, he freed her fastenings. The utensil popped at each release—a thumping pressure that trailed her scar as the buttons gave way. Felicity struggled against him, groaning with the effort as he wedged the handle between her brooch's closure and ripped it free.

The dress gaped open.

"I'll scream," Felicity breathed the threat.

He laughed, his gaze fixed on the low-scooped chemise at her neck. "Do that. Mayhap ye can explain to the help why yer skin be so soft and young, or why ye bear a knife's scar on yer chest."

Felicity's gaze probed downward reluctantly. There it was ... her hideousness ... an inch of her scar bared for the bastard to see. Mortified, she tilted her chin away and swallowed against the sandy dryness of her throat.

Humiliated tears gathered in her eyes.

"No wonder ye stopped selling yerself, Jasmine. Who would pay to touch *that*?"

Something within her shattered ... that fragile shell of self-esteem built up over the years and nurtured by the love of her brother, nieces, and friends—fortified by Nick. Memories of men using her body and casting her aside leveled the foundation to dust. Her tears broke loose, and she despised herself for being too weak to hold them in.

Her reaction fed Landrigan's torments. "Go on and marry yer crippled English hero. Least when he sees how deep the damage runs in ye, he'll have yer maid to turn to for a mistress. He'll need somethin' to pass the time, seein' as he's sure to find ye as repulsive as I do."

Sobbing, Felicity thrust her knee into his groin. He doubled over and lost his grip on her hands, cursing. The spoon clanged to the floor.

Gasping, Felicity raced to the table and clutched the teapot's handle. When Landrigan started toward her—red-faced and furious—she stood her ground, prepared to toss the steaming brew in his face.

He paused as if to measure her resolve.

So intent in their standoff, neither of them heard the door open.

"What game are you playing?" a tiny voice asked.

Felicity spun around to find Lianna behind her in her nightgown, her face pink and wrinkled where she'd been laying atop her sheets. After a body-trembling yawn, she widened her lashes. "Auntie, what happened to your dress? Why are your eyes runny? Have you been crying?"

Felicity hurriedly set the teapot down.

"Oh no, little goose. I've not been crying." She swiped her face with the backs of her fingerless gloves. "The tea's steam

... made my eyes water. And my dress ... it, it simply isn't made well. The buttons won't stay put no matter what I try. The buttonholes must be too big." She pushed the tiny covered knobs through their slitted openings and sealed the lapel.

"You should let Rachel fix them for you. She likes to fix things." Lianna's innocent remark garnered a snort from Landrigan.

"Aye," he said. "She's well and good at fixin' things, to that I can attest."

Gritting her teeth, Felicity arranged the brooch over the rip in her gown's neck. Then she knelt beside Lianna, offering her a biscuit from the table.

Lia's pretty bird-mouth nibbled at the bread. "Why are you here, Uncle Donal?"

The swine had smoothed his clothes and hair to look as fresh as when he first arrived. Grinning at Lianna, he stepped to the wall and poked a finger at her picture, crinkling the paper with the motion. "I came to tell yer aunt that I bought those ponies ye wished for."

"Oh!" Crumbs drizzled from the child's mouth upon the bloom of her smile. "Oh, I love you, Uncle Donal! I love you so!" Her unkempt hair swirled around her waist as she tried to rush to him.

Felicity snagged her around the waist. "No, Lia. You sit down and eat your breakfast. This is not the time for histrionics. You aren't dressed properly to receive company. Mister Landrigan was just leaving." She couldn't bring herself to face him. Instead, she helped her grumbling niece into her chair then loaded a plate with jam and fragrant poached eggs.

"Why does Uncle Donal have to leave *now*? I want to hear stories of my treasures!"

Landrigan came up behind Felicity and leaned over to pat Lianna's head. The hair on Felicity's neck bristled as he boxed her in beneath him where she knelt, his thigh touching her nape.

"No worries little snapper. I'll be back for yer birthday. Yer aunt is sure to be feelin' more receptive to me by then, with all the guests that will be comin'."

"Guests for my party?" Lianna asked. A dribble of jelly glazed her bottom lip.

Felicity elbowed Landrigan in the shin so he'd move. "No more talk of this now. I will see you out, Mister Landrigan."

She walked him to the double doors, stealing a glance at Lianna over her shoulder. The child swung her bare feet, pretending her biscuit was riding her fork in a circle. She hummed a perfect accompaniment to a carousel ride.

Felicity turned back around, stifling the flame in her stomach.

Landrigan held her gaze. "The little skirt has grand timing. As did Clooney yester morn in the chicken house. But in a few weeks, there'll be no one to save ye."

"You're mistaken, Mister Landrigan. There will be no one to save *you*. If you dare to attend Lia's gala, Nick will be here. And you can rest assured, in spite of all the horrible things you said to me today, he *will* defend me. He *is* my hero." With that, Felicity shoved her unwanted guest out and slammed both doors in his face.

She spun around and flattened her shoulders to the wall, trying to breathe ... trying to forget the humiliation. The bastard had made her feel like a whore all over again. Ugly, unlovable, and unwanted.

So different from the way Nick made her feel.

She pressed the back of her hand over her eyes. If only she hadn't chased him away, those lies to Landrigan would've been truths. And Nick would've told everyone the children were hers. Whereas Landrigan would assure people knew she was raising her nieces without any legal claim. Without her being their mother, her suitability to rear children would be in question as an unmarried countess. But forbidden as a courtesan.

She always knew she couldn't sustain the lies forever, but she'd been determined to manage until the girls were grown by living as a recluse. Now that Irish swine had brought the world to her doorstep, and it was too late to undo what had been done.

Too late. For Nick was gone forever. By now, he was on some train, going God only knew where. There was no means for her to find him.

Closing her eyes, she drifted atop her churning emotions. Tears nudged at her lashes. Nausea, tantamount to any bout of seasickness, mangled her stomach.

"So ... did Sissy like the eggs? Poached are her favorite."

Lianna's tinkling voice threw out a lifeline and pulled Felicity back.

"What do you mean?" Felicity asked, drying her cheeks with her sleeve before turning to face her. "She's yet to eat. Where is she?"

Lianna wrinkled her nose. "Don't know. But I wish she'd ask next time before stealing my pillows. I don't like waking with nothing but sheets to plump me."

Felicity came to the table to sip some tea in hopes it would ease her stomach. "Your sister slept on your pillow?"

"No. Just wrapped it up in blankets with hers." Lianna giggled. "I thought she was playing a caterpillar in its pupa, until I threw back the covers to tickle her. Only pillows were there. I'll not be mad for too long, since it was such a fine trick." Licking her fork, she laughed again.

Fresh terror gripped Felicity's heart.

Landrigan ... he wouldn't dare.

Or would he?

Thoughts of his threats the other morn, of young girls being sold for slaves, taunted her.

Felicity tossed down her tea and rushed to fling the doors open, nearly tripping over her skirts as she burst out of the castle and down the stairs into the courtyard.

But it was too late. By the time she reached the gate, his wagon was disappearing around the first bend in the road.

Screaming so loud her chest rattled, she took off after him on foot. Rocks and sticks slashed at her skirt's train, tearing it to shreds as she ran.

CHAPTER TWENTY-FOUR

Nick met Landrigan's gaze as they passed on the road, dust flying up between them. The Irishman flashed a smug smile and tipped his hat. Nick had to stop himself from hopping onto the other gig so he could pound the cocky maggot's face.

Nick wondered what he'd been doing at the castle ... if Felicity had proposed the plan about the bogs.

"Let me take those, Miss Aislinn." He grasped the reins and coaxed the horses into a canter, eager to learn the outcome. As they rounded the bend, he saw a figure running toward them, waving both arms. Due to the color of the gown, it didn't register that it was Felicity until they were almost upon her. The fancy shoes she wore offered no traction over the dusty terrain, and she slipped and fell.

"Whoa!" Nick jerked back on the reins. The horses snorted and Tobias almost toppled over the wagon's gate at the prompt stop. Nick leapt down and rushed to Felicity's side, helping her stand.

"Aislinn..." She sobbed without looking up, her face buried in Nick's chest—breath hot against him. "We have to get her back."

Nick lifted Felicity's chin with both hands. What he saw in her eyes ripped his heart down the middle. Helplessness, panic, and degradation. The same look he'd seen on the night he saved her at the brothel.

Tears ran tracks through the dust smudged on her face. Nick wiped them with his thumbs and started to tell her Aislinn was fine. But the state of Felicity's elegant gown claimed his attention. The bodice had been torn, gaping open where her brooch set askew. When he noted the hem waving in shreds at her ankles, he could barely contain the surge of anger scalding his gut.

"What did that snake do to you?"

Before he could get an answer, Felicity's attention locked on the wagon.

"Aislinn ... is that you?" she cried. "Why are you wearing those clothes?" Prying herself from Nick's arms, she strained to reach the wagon where Tobias was helping Aislinn down. Nick led Felicity over, supporting her elbow so she wouldn't fall again in her unsteadiness. All the while, rage lapped at his core.

He released her so she could hug and scold Aislinn, having to bite his tongue to keep from demanding an answer to his question. Her maternal instincts had taken over. She would be unreachable until her emotions were spent. Better to go to the source.

Nick glanced over his shoulder in the direction of Landrigan's egress—a hot flash of fierce protectiveness searing his blood. He could easily catch the fool on bareback. Then he'd beat the truth out of him. Or kill him trying.

Clooney, Binata, and Lia came out from the castle, sprinting through the gate toward them. Felicity would have ample assistance getting inside. Clenching his jaw, Nick strode to the front of the wagon and motioned Tobias over.

"Help me unhitch the team."

When the stable hand gave him a curious glance, Nick

started to work off the leather rigging himself, patting the horses' muscled flanks to soothe them. "I'm going after Donal."

Tobias began to help but stopped as footsteps stirred behind Nick.

Nick turned to find Felicity staring up at him, her face flushed from crying.

"Please," she said, looking as fragile and lost as a child. "Stay, Nick. Stay, and never leave us again." Then she threw herself into his arms.

Stunned, he nestled his nose and fingers into her tangled hair. The others gathered around the embracing couple, and all thoughts of retrieving Donal faded beneath the softness of Felicity's orange blossom skin and those gloriously sweet words, *"never leave us again."*

He'd lost his best friend today, but he'd finally found his way home.

The following three weeks flew by in a whirl of preparation. The playroom became Nick's sleeping quarters once more, now that he could take the four flights of stairs. He insisted that since he was healed, he should also shoulder his share of the workload. He hiked with Clooney and Nutmeg each day to learn the boundaries of Felicity's estate and the far-reaching expanse of the bogs they would harvest. He also took up several of Felicity's daily chores—helping gather the eggs under Lia's scrupulous eye and assisting with the girls' studies—so Felicity could help Cook with her maid duties. Felicity had also been spending extra time in her greenhouse. For some reason, she seemed more determined than ever to spur new growth in the passion vines and resurrect her caterpillar populace.

For Nick, getting Felicity to agree to marry him had been the easy part. Much easier than convincing her to let the girls accompany them to the parish in Carnlough for the ceremony on the day before Lia's birthday.

After so many years of hiding her nieces, the thought of taking them out in public horrified her. But he'd managed to persuade her by vowing that if she allowed them to come, he'd waive the conjugal rights he'd hoped to obtain.

It frustrated him that Felicity still insisted—even after her emotional welcome on the roadside and the furtive kisses they'd indulged in at every opportunity since—that their union be in name only.

The shyness over her scar must have spurred the stipulation. She'd seemed even more conscious of it since his return, rubbing her fingers over her chest every few minutes or so. It had something to do with Landrigan's visit. Nick didn't care that Felicity claimed the Irishman had been pleased with the peat bog proposition. That his only condition was he wouldn't sign a contract until the work had begun.

Nick's gut told him otherwise. Neither did he buy her claim that her gown's bodice had torn upon her fall to the ground.

He had every intention of finding out the truth, even if it meant tracking the Irishman down later.

For now, he tamped his quiet fury, having more pressing matters to tend. There was just enough money left from the earring to pay the fee for the license. Upon Nick's sworn declaration that there was no canonical impediment to the marriage, the archdeacon handed over the piece of paper which would defer the three-week waiting period and the calling of banns.

"The bishop will be here shortly." The small man's nasally voice echoed all the way up to the rafters in the empty sanctuary. "I'll retrieve the parish register to record the union. Ye can wait by the altar." His balding head nodded at Aislinn and Lia as he stepped into an adjoining room.

Neither girl responded, both captivated by the late afternoon sun where it filtered through the stained-glass windows to paint a patchwork of rainbows on the hardwood floor.

As soon as the archdeacon left, the girls giggled and began to slap their hands together, chanting an Irish rhyme: *Marry in white, everything's right; Marry in blue, lover be true; Marry in pink, spirits will sink; Marry in grey, live far away.*

"Just look at them," Nick said, grasping Felicity's lace clad fingers and leading her to the altar where the scent of incense and lemon oil mingled to a heady balm. "Aren't you glad you allowed them to come?"

Felicity watched the girls as they stepped in and out of the rainbows, each trying to stay within the color she'd chosen. She squeezed Nick's hand and smiled. "I must admit, it's a rare thing to see Aislinn so carefree. But Lia ... well, she's not nearly as giddy as when you brought Butterscotch back for her. You're her 'Mister Sir' again—high on a pedestal."

Nick grinned. "A precarious position. It's rather slippery up here."

Felicity's laugh sparkled. "Yes. She told me of your attempt to entertain her during your chores this morn."

He feigned a sheepish expression. "Juggling in a chicken coop is never a good idea."

"Well, I'm sure isn't the first time you've had egg on your face."

He wagged a finger at her, scolding. "Can't deny it. You're a witty one."

Laughing again, she stepped up to straighten his collar. He'd been fortunate to find a shirt and some trousers the color of coffee among the clothes the kind old widow Hannah had insisted he take. Paired with the black cravat and vest Felicity loaned him, it made a passable suit for a groom.

Her warm brown eyes melted him as her fingers smoothed his lapels. "Thankfully, you clean up nicely. You look like such a gentleman."

He grasped her hands and held them there, wanting her touch for as long as possible. "When you stare at me like that, my thoughts are far from gentlemanly."

She glanced down. "I'm just so ... what you did, giving Johnny away... and your earring."

Nick pressed his thumb to her lips. "Shhh. That's in the past. Today—this day—is only about our wedding." He let his finger glide down to tap her softly pointed chin.

A quiet thoughtfulness swept over her as she clasped the butterfly brooch at her chest. "I hope you won't have regrets."

"About Johnny, or the earring?" Nick directed Felicity to a pew.

"About anything," she mumbled. She settled beside him, smoothing the lace overlay of her powder blue gown. Her delicate fingers wound together nervously in her lap.

Dust particles swirled around her in the soft light, adding an angelic aura to her profile. She hadn't been sporting black over the past three weeks. Nick liked seeing her out of her mourning clothes. It was as if she'd finally peeled off the layers of sorrow she'd been wrapped in for so long.

Today, with her hair braided and piled atop her crown and that glow of nervous anticipation in her cheeks, the false wrinkles couldn't touch her vibrant beauty. But since he'd already commented on her loveliness—at last count, five times in the past hour—he opted to keep it to himself.

"No. No regrets," he finally answered. "Least for me. I gather Clooney's far from happy, though." The old man had driven them over in the wagon but hadn't stayed for the ceremony.

"It's not that at all. I had business for him to tend." She bit her lip. "Following up on workers for the peat bogs."

"You know I want to be the one who hires them," Nick said. "They'll need to answer to me."

"Absolutely. We're simply lining up interviews for this week. The sooner we get started, the better."

Nick studied her fidgets, suspicious something more was going on, but hesitant to dampen the mood by pressing her. "What of Lia's birthday gala?"

"We'll have the workers come the day after. That gives us two more days to schedule them."

Seeing how the subject made her uneasy, Nick decided to change it. He withdrew from his pocket a handful of flowers wrapped in a linen hanky. "Aislinn helped me pick these from the greenhouse earlier, while you were getting ready. It's your bouquet."

"Mouse's ears." Felicity's face lit up.

Nick felt a pull deep within. Every time she graced him with that smile, it nearly undid him for want of kissing her. Not only that, but she'd called the flowers by their special name, in honor of his childhood memory.

He handed her the bouquet. "These are my apology, for leaving you to deal with Landrigan alone. That will never happen again."

"Thank you." Felicity nestled her nose in the blossoms. "Lavender, too? Aislinn must have told you they're an Irish tradition."

Grinning, Nick touched the tiny purple clusters, grazing Felicity's face in the process. "To ensure a happy and long union. Though I'm surprised you would put any stock in such frivolities."

Felicity tilted her head coyly. "I'm beginning to see the charm in superstitions."

"Ah. But are you charmed enough to believe in the Raven?" He regretted saying it the moment it slipped off his tongue. The subject always seemed to sour her mood.

To his surprise, Felicity regarded him with a hint of amusement. "Let's just say, that the past week has been filled with unexpected revelations."

"Really? Revelations about ghosts, perchance? You told me you no longer believe Donal is masquerading as the Dark Raven. But you haven't told me what changed your mind."

Without looking at him, Felicity shrugged.

He tried again. "The stairs leading up to the turret ... I saw bare footprints imprinted in their dust on the day I returned." He glanced at her feet. "The size of a lady's. I hadn't noticed them there before. Why would you have gone up the broken stairs, not even bothering to wear shoes?"

Felicity clutched her flowers with her free hand. "I thought I heard something..."

"And?"

"And ... didn't you say this day is only about our wedding? Please don't make it about the afterlife ... about Mina."

Touched by the insecurity in her voice, Nick propped his elbows on his knees. He would broach the subject again at a better time. It was to be his home, too, after all. "Fair enough. Have you any other customs to incorporate in our ceremony? Stepping over a broom, crushing a glass beneath our shoes?"

Felicity smiled, obviously relieved. "Well, we could walk

through the center of town so the citizens can throw pots and pans at us—to bless the marriage."

Nick fondled the lace at the end of each of her fingertips. "Ouch. I never realized Irish goodwill was so violent."

"Not violent, really." Felicity's fingers wound through his. "Sometimes it's the most heartfelt gestures which draw blood."

He lifted her hand to kiss the back of it and her lacy glove tickled his nose. "And sometimes that pain can be an exquisite pleasure."

Holding her gaze, he turned her hand over and swept his lips across the dip at her inner wrist, touching his mouth to her accelerated pulse. Her face burst to pink, firing his passion. How a woman, who'd lived through so much degradation and shame, could still manage a chaste and maidenly flush beguiled him beyond all reasoning. He started to lean in for a kiss, got just close enough to feel the rush of her warm breath and to watch her dark lashes close in a trancelike stasis when...

"An Irish penny!" Lia spouted from behind them, breaking the moment.

Felicity jerked back fully alert, all signs of the trance lifted away. She held Nick's gaze for a moment before they both turned to the child.

Arms linked over the back of the pew so her feet swung just off the floor, Lia held out the coin. "See? I found it on the ground."

Aislinn came up from behind and helped her sister down. "I'm sorry. I tried to restrain her but she was too excited."

Nick smiled. "Tis all right. So ... what's so special about a penny?"

Both of the girls rolled their eyes, pitying his ignorance.

Felicity grinned. "For luck, every Irish bride needs five

things on her special day. Something old, something new, something borrowed, something blue—"

"And an Irish penny for her shoe," Lia interrupted, handing off the coin to her aunt.

Felicity held out the penny. "This belongs to the parish, little goose. No doubt it fell from the giving plate. Aislinn, could you put it on the pulpit please?"

Aislinn strolled to the front of the sanctuary. She placed the penny atop the pulpit and stopped to study a portrait of the Virgin Mary on the wall.

"But Auntie, what of your luck?" Lia skipped around to the front of the pew and climbed atop Nick's lap, draping him in the scent of milk and rose petals. He helped the sprite arrange her stiff skirts and petticoats then held her tiny waist to keep her balanced on his knees.

Felicity laid her bouquet on the pew so she could hold Lia's hands. "I have four of the five. That should be enough. I've my something borrowed with the rings Cook gave us to use until we can buy new ones. They belonged to her parents, so they're old as well. My dress is blue—"

"So your lover will be true." Lia grinned.

Felicity looked down, flushed again.

"I can attest that he will," Nick promised, to which Felicity's gaze lifted.

"And what have you that's new, Auntie?"

Felicity tightened her focus on Nick. "Faith. Today, I have faith in my heart."

Nick's blood and bones warmed at the sincerity in her eyes.

Again, Lia shattered the moment by wiggling in his lap. She craned her neck to pout in his direction. "Auntie's the princess of the castle. You're to be her hero. Don't you have even a penny she can use? Princes are supposed to be rich."

Duly scolded, Nick released one side of her waist and dug in his pocket for the scant remains of his diamond's intake. "Here. This one should do nicely."

Lia polished the penny on her skirt and handed it off to her aunt.

Felicity lifted her hem and lace-fringed drawers enough to tuck the penny into her ankle boots. Nick felt a stab of desire at just the glimpse of her calf. The vision took him back to the outlook post, when that very leg had been wrapped around his lower back.

It was a shame to start off the marriage with a half-truth. But he wasn't about to relinquish his husbandly rights. Felicity's effect upon him each time he saw her, much less touched her, would be impossible to ignore for a lifetime.

He thought of the carving he was making, how just running his fingers over the counterpart curves could lead his mind to dark and sweet places. She wanted him every bit as much as he did her. So, he would romance her, gently. And let her make the first move. Once she got over her initial shyness, she would realize that he desired her in spite of her flaws.

Even more so, because of them.

Hearing a rustle in the doorway, they all turned to see the archdeacon toting in a large book. The bishop entered behind him wearing flowing robes. He motioned Nick over. After gently setting Lia upon the pew next to her aunt, Nick joined the bishop—the two of them out of earshot of the others—and kissed the holy man's hand.

The bishop placed his other hand on Nick's shoulder. "I've one question before we perform the ceremony, Son. The wee ones. They can't be yers with the lady?" He was a stout man with a face like a cherub, but with enough wrinkles to attest to a long life.

Nick held true to the story he and Felicity had agreed upon. "They're the countess's. From a marriage prior to the Earl."

Nodding his head, the bishop patted down his white hair where several strands splayed out from his Mitre cap like a dove's wing. "They'll be no more, I suppose. Considering her age."

Nick cast a glance at his betrothed, watching her straighten the girls' sashes. He hadn't even considered future children. Unbeknownst to the bishop, Felicity was certainly young enough still. But Nick wasn't sure how she felt about having children of her own. After the nightmare he'd endured with Mina and Christian, a ready-made family was much more appealing to him. Besides, it was a moot point unless he and his bride made love.

"Son?" The bishop's voice jostled Nick from his thoughts.

"Yes. I mean, no. There'll be no more."

"Yer content with that, not having a son to carry on yer name? And yer prepared to love these girls, provide for them, and raise them as yer own?"

"I am."

The bishop's eyes crinkled on a smile. He squeezed Nick's shoulder. "Then let's make this family official."

CHAPTER TWENTY-FIVE

Felicity was witnessing a miracle. The third one in the past few weeks.

The first had been Jasper's appearance. She had yet to talk to Aislinn about the sighting, or to see her brother's spirit again. But he would show himself when he was ready; she had faith to that end.

The second miracle was when Nick come back out of the blue and married her without question or stipulation. Her entire body warmed at the memory of their kiss at the close of the ceremony today, and how she'd taken communion with him as his wife. Their souls were joined eternally, and nothing had ever felt more right.

Now here she stood alone in the darkened greenhouse and stared in awe at miracle number three: the blossoming passion flowers level with her knees. They were the same ones that had withered three weeks ago.

She blinked in the moonlight, watching the Heliconius butterflies flit across them in waves, feeding on the nectar. Their jeweled wings caught strands of silver light streaming through the roof. The resulting sparkles added a surreal affect.

This had never happened before. Once a set of passion

vines flowered, they were barren for months. Another set of vines had been due to bloom within the next few weeks, but not these. Not the same ones...

Purple fungus hugged the stems where the flowers were thickest. Nick and Johnny were living proof of the fungi's healing capabilities. But if it could rejuvenate wilted blossoms, perhaps it could mend scarred skin.

Fearing to hope but determined to believe, Felicity had already been using the fungus upon herself the past few weeks. She hadn't seen any change yet, but she wasn't giving up. Needing a new supply, she scooped some into a jar and sealed it shut. Then, setting the jar aside, she pulled out her tools, opting to take advantage of the blooming passion flowers and harvest some butterfly saliva for her wrinkle cream.

She'd captured enough butterflies over the years to have it honed to an art: wait until the moment just before they took flight. The insects were majestic and mystical, but their body language predictable. Their wings and antennae trembled in perfect synchrony an instant before launching. That was the best time to cup a hand around them.

Capturing the first one, she gently pinched its wings together to hold it aloft in the lantern light. With her tweezers, she took a glass bead the size of a mustard seed and pressed it against the butterfly's proboscis to stimulate the release of the enzyme-rich saliva. The thick, clear liquid drizzled over the bead, leaving a droplet balanced atop it. Before the saliva could slide off, she carefully dropped the bead into the cream she'd already prepared, then released her fluttery captive to the air. The beads would be stirred into the face cream, and later removed by squeezing the mixture through layers of cheesecloth.

Milking the Heliconius was tedious work. Each batch of

cream took twenty droplets of saliva. Upon catching her ninth butterfly, Felicity rolled her shoulders against a nagging ache. She had hoped this would get her mind off of Nick. But it didn't seem to be working.

Her borrowed ring captured a glint from the lantern. She'd had to wrap twine around it so it would fit. Nick had ended up wearing his on his left pinky, his bone structure being larger than Cook's father. But he hadn't minded a bit. He'd even made a joke about it. She knew of no other man more generous or good-natured and was humbled by the fact that he was truly hers.

In fact, she should be with him, bonding as a new family. But she'd chosen to hide instead. She could hardly sit next to him at supper tonight without wanting him. Their hands had touched once while reaching for the ladle to refill Lia's stew, and sparks of desire lit up her blood. She'd felt the glow within, brilliant enough to torch a midnight sky. She knew, just by the way he looked at her, by how his lips felt on her skin, that he could show her another side to the empty act of copulation. He could take her somewhere she'd never been—to ecstasy.

Her face heated at the thought. Perhaps, if her scar healed enough, she could one day give in to the passions they both shared.

But first, she must tell him of her barrenness. She hadn't had the courage to confess before the marriage. She told herself, if he would agree to marry in name only, he didn't care to have an heir.

Her guilt for lying—even if by omission—exacerbated the riotous tangle of emotions writhing within her.

"Need some help, Dove?"

She startled at Clooney's voice, dropping the thirteenth bead carelessly. It plopped into the cream beneath her hand and she gasped in relief.

"I could use some." She smiled at the old man, scenting tobacco on his clothes as he settled beside her to capture a butterfly.

He took the second set of tweezers and fell into a routine as familiar to them both as breathing.

"That would be fourteen," Felicity said, catching one of her own. "You've been smoking."

"I'm worried," he mumbled. "For our pending guests."

Felicity chewed her cheek. This had been the first time they'd had the chance to speak in private since the wedding. "What did you learn on your trip to the telegraph office?"

"They've accepted Donal's forged invitations. All but two."

"Nick's father?"

"Boarded a ship two days ago. It's only a three-day trip from London, including the train ride to Carnlough. He'll be here right on schedule day after tomorrow."

Blowing out a defeated sigh, Felicity released the fifteenth butterfly.

Clooney concentrated on his tweezers and butterfly number sixteen. "Lia's gala is tomorrow night, and Donal will be biting at the bit to claim his spoils."

"I'm well aware of tomorrow's agenda and our unwelcome guest, thank you."

"But is Nick aware?"

"If I'd planned to say anything to him, it would've been before the vows."

"Instead, you're letting him be oblivious in every way. You told him I was lining up workers for the bogs."

"I feared he wouldn't go through with the marriage," Felicity reasoned aloud, although it sounded hollow and petty against the quiet night. "His terror of facing his father is crippling. He harbors such remorse over past mistakes. I was hoping the elder Lord Thornton would refuse the invitation. Then I could've told Nick everything."

Nick wasn't the only one she'd lied to. She'd told her servants that workers were coming, too, and the castle's extra rooms would need to be prepared accordingly until she could build onto the male servants' lodge where Tobias and Fennigan slept. It was the one way she could think of to make arrangements for her patrons yet keep it a secret from her husband.

"The truth will come out when Landrigan arrives at the gala," Clooney said.

"I'm going to have Fennigan and Tobias keep watch at the gate. Landrigan's not getting past it."

"But when the Elder Lord Thornton appears—"

"Nick needs to make peace with his father, and if deceiving him is the only way to make that happen, then this approach is for the best. I'm hoping..." She stopped herself. Felicity wanted to see Nick reunite with his own family. Now that he'd let go of Mina and Christian's deaths, it would be the last step in burying the demons and regrets of his past. A freedom she envied yet wanted for him.

"You're hoping his affection for the little knots will convince him to stay in spite of your dishonesty."

Clooney's perceptiveness bit into her conscience. In all truth, she was counting on this strategy. "He hates to disappoint Lia. And he and Aislinn have bonded, as well."

Clooney lifted a bead with his tweezers. "It's still a lie. And it will hurt less to hear it from you ... sooner than later."

Felicity set the nineteenth butterfly free. "Weren't you the one who asked me not to accept his proposal after the laudanum episode? Now you're concerned for his feelings?"

"I've come to know him better on our walks about the estate. His fondness for you and the girls is sincere. He's obviously striving to be a better man. And I respect that. First he trades his beloved dog for a worthless hobbie to please little Lia. Then he sells his diamond to buy necessities for us all. I've a sense that was more than just an earring to him. And..." The old man took a shaky breath.

"And what?"

"He's brought something back to this place. Something that's been missing for years."

Watching the twentieth butterfly flitter gracefully from Clooney's opened fingers, Felicity frowned. "What would that be?"

"Merriment and music. After you came out to the greenhouse tonight, he dusted off Jasper's old phonograph and cranked it up. Nick is teaching the girls to dance for Lia's birthday gala. The dining hall is alight with laughter and mirth."

"They're ... *dancing?*"

After his wife's death, Jasper had shoved the phonograph into the corner and buried it beneath books. He couldn't bear to be faced with the blatant reminder of nights spent dancing with Isabella in his arms.

"The girls haven't been this happy in years," Clooney continued. "Happy, Felicity. Just as children should be." He paused in thoughtful silence. "Nick tells me he hopes you'll consider taking the girls to Mass each week, now that he's here."

Felicity rubbed her aching forehead. Yes. Nick had brought the subject up several times lately. And after hearing what Clooney just said, she could see the wisdom in such a decision. By hiding part of his relationship with Isabella, Jasper had deprived his daughters of their mother's memory on some level. Just as by hiding the girls from the world, Felicity had deprived them of memories of their own.

"I am considering it," Felicity answered.

"Good," Clooney said. "While you're at it, consider telling that man—your *husband*—the truth about his father." Clooney's watery eyes met hers. "And about Jasper's body in the turret."

She chewed her lip, thinking of how even Clooney didn't know the whole truth about Jasper yet. "I made a promise to Jasper not to tell anyone of his half-existence."

"But things are different now. Nick's living here and has a right to know. Start the marriage off on a good foot, Dove."

Felicity stroked the gold band on her finger. Nick had once asked to live at the castle for the sole purpose of escaping his family. She doubted he'd want to be anywhere near her or this place if she confessed her deception about the incoming guests.

Then again, he'd asked her at the chapel to tell him about her climb up the turret stairs. He was still intrigued by the afterlife and would be thrilled to know about Jasper's success. If she chose to betray her promise to her brother, Nick might stay just because of the butterflies. But it would also reawaken his determination to search for Mina.

Felicity had seen for herself how such an obsession could take over a man's life; how her brother had almost forgotten those who still remained living around him while seeking out the dead.

In spite of how petty it made her feel, Felicity couldn't bear to lose her new husband to a ghost.

Wrestling her conscience, she left the cleanup for Clooney and took the moonlit path to the castle, following the foreign strains of music and laughter which drifted faintly on the air.

No servant awaited Felicity as she opened the castle door; only the sound of cheerful voices in the dining hall greeted her.

She wasn't surprised. Shortly after Landrigan's visit, she'd discreetly told the cook how Rachel handed over some personal business information to Landrigan. Cook reprimanded her daughter severely. Her disloyalty had been the final straw. Using the money she'd saved from her wages, the cook packed up Rachel and sent her by train to a pious aunt in Norwich in hopes religion and strictures could set her daughter's feet on the path of the straight and narrow.

Tonight, Cook had a headache, and had gone to bed early without cleaning up the dinner mess. Felicity sympathized. Any mother would grieve her child's exile, even if it had been for the best of reasons.

Once money from the peat started coming in, Felicity would find a replacement for the young maid. Until then, everyone would have to pitch in to help the older servant with Rachel's tasks.

Ducking into the kitchen, Felicity noticed the fruit cake left on a platter from supper. Cook had insisted on making the time-honored Irish wedding dessert. Felicity scooped up some white frosting and licked the sweetness off her finger, remembering how Nick had fed her the first bite. He'd done everything in his power to ensure the wedding felt real and traditional for her and the girls.

Smiling, she washed some dirty pots in lukewarm water and dried her hands on an apron she'd tied over her powder blue gown. Then, blowing out the lantern, she headed toward the dining hall, unable to stave her curiosity any longer.

The tinkling chords of a Bach minuet wafted from the phonograph. At the far end of the room, Nick had shoved the chairs and the settee against the wall to open the floor next to the hearth for dancing. He'd lit the miniature electric bulbs strung along the ceiling and the fireplace beamed with a jolly glow.

The tang of charred wood warmed Felicity's lungs. In a shadowy corner, Nutmeg and Dinah were curled up asleep, uncaring as to the dancing and music taking place around them.

Felicity paused at the threshold, watching across the dining table still filled with dirty dishes. Her new husband—in spite of his strapping physique—twirled Lianna on his arm with all the grace of a danseur. Tobias and Aislinn twirled opposite them, then all four bowed.

"Now, you two ladies take a walk like I showed you," Nick instructed, stationary in his spot.

The girls stepped toward one another, their dress hems swaying with their movements. They met in the middle and curtsied, fanning out their skirts.

Felicity stifled a giggle as Nick took bouncy steps toward his tiny partner then clasped her hand so they could sidestep together. They were such an adorable mismatched pair.

But the intense concentration on Lia's face checked her humor. The child had never looked more like her mother than at that moment. And when Felicity caught a glimpse of Tobias and Aislinn's lovelorn expressions as they joined hands, the similarities to Jasper and Isabella during their nightly dances struck her like a slap.

The song ended and everyone bowed to one another.

Felicity clapped. "Brava!"

Nutmeg's head popped up at the sound and her tail thumped.

"Auntie!" Lianna skipped around the table and tugged Felicity into the room. The child's face flushed from physical exertion and her eyelashes were heavy with drowsiness. "Did you see me?"

"I did. You and your wonderful partner." Felicity glanced where Nick was kneeling to pet the dog and cat. She almost melted when he winked at her.

She turned back to Lianna. "And you dance just as lovely as your mum used to."

"Truly?"

Felicity knelt and raked back some strands that had fallen from the child's bun so she could kiss her rosy cheeks. "She would've been proud." Directing her attention to Tobias and Aislinn, Felicity stood and clucked her tongue. "And you two. Always have a chaperone. No more tricks like the one you pulled to bring Nick back. Understood?"

Tobias' ears flashed red and he nodded. "Yes, Your Ladyship." Bowing once to Aislinn, he said goodnight to everyone and left the room. The castle door let in a puff of cool air as he headed out to the servants' lodge.

A wicked smile teased Aislinn's pretty mouth. "It was for the greater good, Auntie. Even you can't refute that."

Felicity was about to scold the girl for her audacity when Aislinn captured her little sister's hand and whistled for Nutmeg. Dinah stood and stretched, yawning as she padded behind the dog nonchalantly.

"Come along," Aislinn said, herding her sister and the pets to the door. "Bini's drawing a bath for us. Tis time to leave the newlyweds alone."

Lianna cast a covetous glance over her shoulder. "But aren't they to dance? The prince and princess always share a dance after they're married. I wish to watch!"

Aislinn pushed her sister gently into the hall and toward the stairs, pets in tow.

"Real married couples share a *special* dance, Lia." Aislinn's voice echoed in the marble corridor. "To which no one else is invited. Someday, you'll understand."

CHAPTER TWENTY-SIX

Blushing, Felicity shut and locked the double doors to drown out her nieces' chattering. Hands clenched to a chair at the table, she watched her new husband by the fire. He stirred the logs with a poker. The movement tugged the thin fabric of his shirt, showcasing broad shoulders and rippling back muscles.

"Ready for our special dance, princess?" he asked without turning around. The amusement in his voice would've eased her nerves, if not for the husky edge behind it.

Guilt for her lies nibbled at the edges of her soul. If she told him a little about the patrons ... made it seem like she'd just found out.... "Um. Nick. I-I thought we might talk for a moment. Before we go to bed."

He tilted his head. The firelight cast his handsome profile in bold relief. "Mmm. Bed. Been looking forward to that all day."

Felicity forced her fingers to release the chair and stepped closer to the fire. Twisting her hands in the apron, she steeled her resolve. "Each in our separate chambers, of course."

Upon laying the poker aside, Nick turned to face her, rolling the sleeves down over his forearms. "I've been meaning to speak with you about that." He pursed those sensual lips, taking Felicity's mind to places better left to fantasies. "You see, this alone"—he held up his left pinky so his wedding ring glinted in the light— "isn't going to convince our upcoming guests that our marriage is real. Especially if I'm sleeping in a playroom two flights up from you."

He came to stand so close that her chin leveled with his chest. He'd taken off his vest and cravat and she couldn't help but notice the tiny glistening beads of sweat where his coffee colored shirt gaped opened.

"Our guests," she mumbled, licking her lips at the scent of him. "Precisely what I need to talk to you about."

"Ah." He skimmed his knuckles along her face, igniting all of the nerve endings beneath her skin. Then he cupped her chin and lifted it so their eyes met. "We're on the same page at last."

"Not quite. You're rattling me," she managed, feeling dizzy as his fingers curved around her jaw. She was so captivated by the way his blonde hair grazed his shoulders and shimmered against his dark clothes. If he kissed her, she'd lace her fingers through those waves and never have the presence of mind to confess anything.

His mouth curved on an almost smile. "We have to present a united front for the workers. I don't want these men thinking they're walking into a counterfeit marriage. I'd have my hands full fighting off the wolves each day. Since they're going to be in the castle with us, and Lia and Aislinn are back in their rooms on the second floor, we should both be close to them. Therefore, you and I must share a room. Not only that, but when we're out in the open, we must kiss, hold hands. All those things that lovers do spontaneously. We must be convincing in our affection. Even if, behind closed doors, I'm sleeping on the floor and we're married in name only. Surely you can see the logic in this."

Felicity's stomach jumped. Over the past few weeks, they'd indulged in sweet fiery kisses while hidden in the shadows of the courtyard and the dark corners of the castle. But the thought of touching and embracing her groom spontaneously and publicly dug a nervous pit into the center of her core. That would make everything real. And sharing her room with him ... he would see more of her than she was willing to show. Her finger tumbled across her scar. How could she allow him to look upon her most grotesque shortcoming when she herself had never once been able to face it in a mirror?

Now's the time, you ninny. Tell him the truth about the patrons ... it will solve everything. He won't want to bed you after that.

She bit her cheek. *But he might be so angry he'll leave...*

Without Nick, Landrigan would assure that her past would be exposed. And having no husband to stand up for her, her girls would be taken away. Felicity trembled at the nightmarish possibilities which could await them in an orphanage considering her own experience.

Nick held her closer, no doubt misreading her shivers as shyness over her deformity. If only her pride were all that was at stake.

"It's all right." Pressing hot lips against her forehead, he wove his fingers through her hair and stroked her scalp. "You don't have to decide this instant. We'll spend some time being affectionate for the next two days—to make our moments seem natural. Practice makes perfect, after all. And if you consider my proposal about our sleeping arrangements with an open mind, I think it will make sense to you." He kissed her nose. "Now, I've spent more time with pets, servants, and children tonight than my bride. Let's have that dance." He strode to the phonograph, leaving her bereft of his arms and that earthy, masculine scent she couldn't get enough of.

The tinkling strains of music began again.

"A minuet with just two performers?" Felicity asked, swallowing her bewilderment. "Seems rather unconventional."

"Which is why it's the perfect choice for us." Nick grinned.

Her heart hammered as he bowed while holding her gaze.

She forced a curtsy and fanned her apron—fully aware that he was seducing her. Helpless to stop it. "I'm out of practice."

"I'm a patient partner." He held out his palm.

She reached for him and her cheeks fired at the feel of her flesh sliding over his. How was it this man could bring her to tremble like a nervous virgin after all the fornications she'd committed? It had to be his artist's touch ... making something surprising and new out of even the most damaged medium. She curled their fingers together, wondering at the power hidden within those hands.

For some time, they danced without a word—twirling and bowing, stepping circles around one another, their eyes locked in mutual admiration. They were still moving when the music stopped. It didn't dawn on Felicity that their feet were keeping rhythm with the fire's crackling flames, or that the shadows around them had multiplied to an abundance of faceless spectators. Only when the fire sputtered its last spark and left just the soft lights overhead, did they stop.

They watched one another, breaths accelerating with each passing moment.

Felicity started to back away, but Nick lifted her hand to his mouth and kissed her knuckles as he coaxed her closer. "Your eyes..."

She thought upon her skin, how it tightened each night as the cream's potency began to fade. Though he'd already seen her without the wrinkles, it must be shocking to witness the actual transition for the first time.

She touched the firmness at her temples. "At least you know what I'll look like in twenty years." Her half-hearted joke fell flat as Nick pressed their bodies tight together, her breasts flush to his ribcage. She felt his desire against her stomach, a potent need in direct contrast to the tender concern on his face.

"That's not what I meant." His hands gripped her waist, sending pulses of longing through her hips and thighs. "They're runny, just like Lia said. You're crying."

"Am I?" She touched her cheeks, stunned to find hot tears streaming there.

"Are you disappointed in how things turned out today?" he asked, watching them glide down.

"No." She pressed a finger to his lips. "You've made everything perfect," she whispered. Suddenly realizing what he'd said about Lianna, she dropped her hand. "Wait. Lia told you my eyes were runny? When?"

Nick's jaw twitched. "After you went to the greenhouse tonight, the sprite and I had a talk about her walking in on you and Donal the morning I was going to leave." His tender expression hardened. "She said your dress was torn when she saw you, and you were playing a game with the tea's steam that made your eyes run. Donal ripped your dress. He made you cry."

Desperate to free her conscience of at least one deception, Felicity nodded.

Nick started to let her go, but she forced his hands to stay on her waist by clamping his wrists.

"What are you going to do?" she asked.

"Teach that Irish maggot a lesson he'll never forget." His gray eyes darkened to a storm and branded his sincerity into her soul.

A jolt of fear shot through her. If Nick went to see Landrigan tonight, he might get hurt. Or in the least, find out the truth about the guests. "You don't even know where he lives."

"Clooney will show me."

"Please don't do this. You can deal with him when he comes to sign the contract. But you must be diplomatic. He's Binata's only family, and Lia is fond of him. He was merely trying to humiliate me. Once he saw my scar ... he was too disgusted to do anything improper."

If possible, the storm brewed even more violently in Nick's gaze. He attempted again to break his hold from her waist, but Felicity tightened her grip.

"What?" she asked. "You plan to leave me alone on our honeymoon for some foolish misunderstanding?"

He hissed through clenched teeth. "Misunderstanding? He humiliated you. Violated you. I'm your husband. It's my duty to defend your honor."

Her honor. How amazing that he believed her worthy of such a charge. "You ... are so incredibly wonderful." Overcome with emotion, she eased her arms around his nape.

He stiffened, a suspicious frown tugging his mouth. "I'm not wonderful. I'm furious. What are you doing?"

"Keeping you here. I've been sampling Cook's delicious frosting. All you need is a taste of something sweet to curb your ire."

He lifted an eyebrow. "It will take more than dessert to distract me from my mission."

"That depends upon how it is served." Drawing from

seduction techniques she thought she'd shelved forever, she stood on her tiptoes. Her fingers wound in his silky hair and pulled his head down to press his lips to hers. She moved her tongue's tip across his chin then his jaw and ear with soft, sensual pulses, feasting on the saltiness of his sweat.

"I can't taste it yet," he murmured, his hands sliding to her hips. His fingernails clenched her buttocks and belied his defiance.

Determined to crush his resolve, she returned to his face and gently nudged his lips open with her tongue, savoring him in slow, pleading swaths. She dropped one hand between them. Her fingers curled around him over his trousers, learning that hard, needy part like she had longed to in the lookout post.

He gasped into her mouth.

She once she should be ashamed to use talents honed during her walk as a courtesan. But Nick was her husband. He was bound to her. Committed to protect her. He trembled with delight beneath her practiced touch. And for the first time in her life, she cared about the man she was pleasing. Which made it a delight for her, too.

She deepened the kiss, sucking on his tongue, drawing him into her mouth—into her fantasy.

That was all it took.

Cursing, he burst into a blur of movement. He locked her arms around his neck and before Felicity could react, had wrapped her legs around his waist and carried her to the table. A chair scraped the floor as he flung it out of the way with his boot.

"Say you want my touch." His voice rasped as his fingers gouged into her hips—a painful sensation, but not at all unpleasant. "I need to hear you say it."

"Yes, I want it," she shot back against his lips, hardly able to speak at all, his kisses making her drunk.

Dishes clattered as he cleared a place behind her and slid her onto the table. In the next moment he was gripping under her arms to move her with him so they'd both be on the table, supported by the wooden planks as he wedged between her legs.

She gasped at his weight melting into her body, starving for it. His mouth torched her skin, sliding over her chin and neck, then up to her lips once more. Their hips moved in perfect synchrony, so like the butterflies in the instant before flight.

Her hands became desperate—tearing at his clothes in a vital bid for contact. Yet even in the heat of passion, he took care not to expose her scar, trailing his fingers over her breasts and nipples, keeping the layers of fabric which hid her from the world between them.

His consideration only aroused her more. She dragged her palms along his muscled chest, flush with his warm skin. His heartbeat was rampant—an explosion barely contained by his ribs.

For a moment, her reasoning revisited as she opened her eyes and remembered where they were. The servants all had keys ... anyone could walk in on them.

But he consumed her mouth and any attempt at protest. She'd lost control of the seduction and no longer cared. Her palms skimmed his lower back, sculpting the firm muscles of his hips to pull him hard against her.

He moaned. One hand tangled in her braids while the other lifted her skirts and thrust them aside. His finger deftly opened the tapes of her lace trimmed drawers, finding that most sensitive place that every other man had neglected, the pearl which ached and begged to be discovered. With just one touch, he sparked a slow, rich burn in her blood.

Whimpering, she arched into him—a wanton bid for more.

A pained expression crossed his face, as if he felt the urgency of her need within his own depths. Each stroke of his finger was patient and meticulous, building upon the smoldering embers with an escalating rhythm. His mouth slanted to cover her ear, his breath scorching as he spoke. "This is how it will always be with us. Your desire, your need, your pleasure ... becomes my own."

Triggered by the beautiful promise and the skill of his touch, something caught inside her, like a parched forest lit by a flare of incandescent lightning. She smoldered hot and bright then combusted as a halo of white erupted behind her closed eyes. So unexpected and thrilling was the sensation, she cried out.

The sound reverberated off the walls.

Nick froze and glanced up at the door, jaw clenched. "Felicity, love. Did you lock the door?"

"The servants," she replied weakly, blinking. "They have keys."

He cursed and pushed her skirt in place over her thighs.

She refused to let him up. Her fingers tangled in his hair and in answer, he propped himself on his elbows and kissed her gently. She was wrapped within a fog of woozy ecstasy. Her limbs floated, as if her entire body drifted atop a placid lake. Yet just as every nerve and bone relaxed and bobbed gently atop the fray, her heart hammered a staccato rhythm in her chest. Such a conflicted and exquisite feeling—this blend of serenity and exhilaration. Gratitude swelled in her heart, that he would do this for her when she'd offered so little to him.

They laid there for long drawn out minutes, sharing kisses, Nick's skin hot beneath her hands, his heart a rapid drumbeat against her chest. She'd have to be a fool not to see: her husband was holding back to let her bask in her afterglow, all the while fighting a battle within.

"Nick," she whispered.

He pressed his forehead to hers, groaning. "I want to give you so much more. All of me."

"Then let us retire upstairs."

He drew back. "Upstairs...?"

"Yes." Still trying to catch her breath, she smiled—a promise.

He rolled to the floor and helped her straighten her skirts. A feral smile twitched his lips as he scooted her to the table's edge. He stood between her legs, hugging her against him. "You'll not regret it," he whispered in her ear, his lips nibbling her lobe.

She tucked her chin over his shoulder, was just about to snuggle into his neck when her peripheral caught some movement on the underside of the door. Several shadows seeped in slowly through the cracks and floated toward the phonograph. They came together in the silhouette of a man then burst apart, fluttering like butterflies.

Her mouth gaped as they vanished in one blink.

Jasper. She shoved Nick away. Dropping her feet to the floor, she backed toward the double doors.

"Felicity ... wait. No. You've got that look in your eye."

She sputtered, "I—I'm sorry. I gave you the wrong impression. I meant I'm ready to go to bed. My bed, alone. That's why I want to go upstairs. I'm suddenly very tired."

He studied her, narrowing his gaze. "Two minutes ago, you fell over the brink of bliss, and now you're going to shut yourself away in your room——two floors down from me—isolated from the man who took you there."

Felicity struggled to reason things out in her mind. Her

brother's spirit must have drifted into the room at this very moment, in search of the phonograph. He'd heard the music and came to see why it stopped. She needed to go to the tower to check on him but had to be sure Nick wouldn't follow.

She paused at the threshold and opened the doors. "I am so grateful. But also tired. I'd like to walk you to the playroom."

Nick scowled. "So, you're shutting *me* in *my* room." He cast a glance to the pine sideboard on the other side of the table as he shoved one half of his shirt tail into his trousers. "Is it that you're afraid to leave me down here with the laudanum? Perhaps you should hide the bottles elsewhere, since I can't be trusted."

"Stop that! I would never have agreed to this marriage if I didn't have faith in you. I simply need to know you're not going after Landrigan tonight. I want you tucked safely into bed."

"And you're planning to do the tucking?" He looked so appealing in his grumpiness, with his hair unkempt and his clothes disheveled where her hands had run amuck.

Felicity battled to hold her resolve. She held out a hand. "I'll give you a goodnight kiss at the door."

The fulfilled throb between her thighs belied her nonchalance. He'd touched her in a way no other man had ever cared to. And she wanted more. She wanted to shatter in the apex of the holocaust again ... but this time she wanted to give Nick all he'd given so freely—to take him with her. But it wasn't to be. Not tonight.

Her groom flipped off the electric lights, casting them both in utter darkness and shutting down her fantasies.

"Strangest damn honeymoon I've ever had," he said. Then he clasped her hand and led her up the stairs without another word between them.

CHAPTER TWENTY-SEVEN

Nick awoke at the crack of dawn, cradling a pillow in his arms.

He'd dreamt it was Felicity. They were dancing to a waltz drifting from the phonograph, and the music brought her to her knees on the floor. She'd looked up at him with those tragic eyes and confessed everything—all of her feelings, all of her secrets, all of her fears and hopes. Then he'd knelt beside her, laid her down, and made love to her in front of the fireplace until she cried out his name in rapture.

He growled and tossed the pillow, ruffling the bed's canopy. Pink light filtered through the curtain seams and shimmied across the wall.

Bloody delusional subconscious.

But he hadn't imagined the way she'd felt beneath his hands last night—so hot, so receptive. He'd given her a woman's pleasure, that very pinnacle of elation no other man had ever taken the time to offer. And she'd been so beautiful afterward, flushed and basking in her ecstasy. Then she stopped him cold before they could consummate their marriage and both be satisfied.

He'd stayed up half the night painting his finished carving, remembering her expression when release first took her. And as he mused, he ran his hands over the figurine's curves in a pathetic pantomime of the way he wanted to touch his bride—without any barriers—clothing or secrets. While filling in the final lines, he had thought he heard a sound in the corridor ... something scraping the wall. When he'd peered out, he could've sworn there were silhouettes in the darkness going up the turret stairway. Curiosity got the better and he trekked down the long corridor to climb the stairs himself. He'd failed to take a candle and felt his way up blindly with only the moonlight through the tiny windows to guide him.

No one had been there when he reached the broken steps. As he'd passed Felicity's bedchamber on the way back to his own, he wiggled her door knob and found it locked.

It infuriated him. They were married, yet she felt as if she had to bar the door against him.

He'd been so worked up, the only way he finally got to sleep was by rubbing his pillow case with the scent of orange blossom and burying his nose into the cushion. This was what he had been reduced to. A man so desperate for his bride's touch that he kept a bar of her soap hidden in his chamber so he could imagine her beside him.

Well, no longer. He'd found her weakness.

She'd cried last night in his arms as they danced. Then she'd admitted the truth about Landrigan's visit. And—most astonishing of all—she'd become playful, initiating a masterful seduction, almost giving in to their passions before all was said and done.

Music was the way to level her walls, something he never would've guessed. To that end, he planned to play the phonograph again today, every chance he got. He had the perfect excuse with Lia's gala being tonight. Even though no visitors would be attending, the girls wanted to learn every kind of dance imaginable. And he wasn't about to disappoint them. All he had to do was talk Felicity into being his partner. They would teach the girls together. Then later, after the festivities, they would dance alone.

After washing up and donning a grey shirt and navy trousers from Hannah's bundle, Nick stepped out into the corridor. He considered exploring the turret stairs in the daylight to see if any new footsteps were there, but when he passed the main stairway, he nearly tripped over Lia. She sat on the top step, brushing out her doll's long curly hair with her fingers.

Looking up from under her riding hat, she held out a hand so he could help her stand. "Morning, Mister Sir."

"Happy birthday, Lady Lia." He smiled.

"Do you like my attire?" She flung out her long braids and posed in her baggy trousers and blouse, nearly toppling from the step.

Nick captured her arm to help her balance. "Very nice."

"And I'm plenty brightened enough, too."

"Enough for what?" Assuring she had the footing to walk down the steps beside him, he studied her profile, those pale, thick lashes trembling like dandelion fuzz on a breeze.

"To learn to ride Butterscotch. You said if I stayed abed and slept all night you would teach me." Her vivid blue gaze turned on him, drowsy and accusatory. "Did you forget?"

He grinned. "A gentleman never forgets a promise to a beautiful lady. We'll go after breakfast."

One dimpled hand grazed the railing while the other clutched her doll to her chest. "Oh, I've already taken breakfast."

"And what are we having?" Nick paused on the middle step so she could catch up.

"Sausages and pudding. Auntie said it's in honor of you."

His thoughts digressed to their fervid sport on the table and his ears grew hot. "Did she, now."

"Yes, because you bought them for us with your earring."

He rubbed a palm along his stubbled chin, stepping down again. "Has your aunt already eaten?"

"No. She's drinking tea and awaiting you. She says a husband and wife share everything together. It's one of the rules."

Nick huffed. "Would that I could get those in writing."

"Those what?"

"Rules."

Lia frowned up at him with a crinkle stitched between her blonde eyebrows.

"Ah, never mind," he said.

They'd reached the last step and the sprite leapt to the floor while holding her doll upside down. Its brown curls swept the marble tiles. Lia gasped upon noticing and tucked the doll beneath her chin. "Oh, Sasha. We should've left your hair in a bun." She slanted her gaze up to Nick. "Sasha's going riding with us."

"Is she? She looks more primped for a performance than a horse ride."

A proud smile lit Lia's face. "She's an expert ballerina." She fondled the frilly tutu on her doll's velvet leotard. "I wanted to show her that dance you taught us. The minute one."

"The minuet."

Lia scowled. "That's what I said."

He smirked at her impertinence. No matter how foul his mood, bantering with Lia always managed to lift his spirits. "Well, let's go show her then."

"We can't. It's gone."

Nick threw a glance toward the dining hall. From this

angle, he could only catch the tail of Felicity's orchid colored skirt draping her chair. But he had a clear visual of the desk where the phonograph once sat. A bleak foreboding unfurled within his gut. "Gone."

"Auntie says it's broken. Clooney will look at it when he has time." She flashed that pout which softened his heart to putty. "If it isn't fixed by tonight, we'll have no music to dance to."

Nick tapped his hand on the curved edge of the stair's railing. "I'll speak to your aunt. We will have music tonight. I promise."

"Thank you!" Lia hugged his leg. "I love you, Mister Sir!"

Though the proclamation was as casual as her love for rain puddles and mud pies, it brought a softening deep within—and a warmth that spread to his soul.

He patted her hat then watched her skip to the front door.

She twirled around. "We'll be in the greenhouse with Bini and Aislinn, awaiting you."

Nick shaded his eyes from a flare of sunlight when she trounced outside.

A slow burn began behind his sternum as he stepped into the dining hall to find his bride intently studying a familiar ring of keys.

"Does your selfishness know no bounds?" he asked.

Felicity placed the keys next to her silverware with a gentle clink. Her butterfly brooch glittered as she turned toward him. "The cook deigned it best to send her daughter away for the incident with you and the skeleton key. It was not my place to interfere."

"I'm not talking about Rachel or her bloody keys."

Trying to ignore how his bride's skin glowed radiant against the vivid hue of her chiffon gown, trying to discount the sparkle of sated bliss so clear this morning within her lovely dark eyes, Nick poured himself a cup of coffee.

Not sparing her another glance, he strode to the wall to study the girls' artwork. Lia had put up a new picture: stick figures dancing beneath speckled stars and a smiling moon. There were two girls and two boys. She'd scribbled *Mister Sir* beneath the tallest one. His jaw clenched.

He tensed when he heard skirts rustling behind him.

"Nick...?" Felicity placed a hand on his shoulder.

He shook her off, still not facing her. "Have you ever stopped to consider that the girls are innocent in all this? You cry and lament about the distance Donal has put between you and your nieces, when it's you and you alone. Every time, it's you."

"What—"

He rounded on her, holding her gaze. "All their lives, they've been deprived of anything that might give them even an inkling of joy or normalcy. Because of your fears. Your blasted insecurities. Last night they laughed and danced for hours to that phonograph. They were typical children living life, Felicity." He gestured to the empty desk. "Why can't you let them live?"

"Allow me to explain..."

"What, that it's conveniently broken today? Tell me, did you actually render it useless with a hammer, or did you simply put it away somewhere?"

She glanced down and he noticed a pearlescent shimmer to her eyelids. Was she wearing cosmetics?

He shook off the random thought, instead watching the tears that built along her lower lashes. He hated to be the cause of them, but he could see the guilt behind her sorrow. She'd lied to Lia.

"The player still works," he accused.

"Yes," she whispered.

He scowled. "You hid it out of sight because the music affected you. It breached that damnable shell you hide within. We connected last night. You opened up to me after our dance. You wanted me ... touched me like a woman with desires. Then I gave you bliss. But you can't let yourself embrace such happiness. You can't let yourself feel anything at all, so to hell with the rest of us who want nothing more than to *feel*."

A shocked expression replaced her wounded frown. Tears streamed down her face in earnest now, and Nick resisted the urge to kiss them away. He knew that taste: salt intermingled with her floral scent. His mouth watered for wanting it. But the floodgates to his pent up frustration had opened, and he was caught within the torrent.

"Until meeting you, I never realized that a scar could be contagious. A cancer in fact, that slowly eats away its bearer, and threatens to do the same to those who care for her."

She touched her chest. "No. It isn't that. It isn't *only* that..." Her lower lip trembled and it took all his resolve not to touch her, to stop the tremor with the strength of his thumb.

It was then he noticed the stain upon her mouth. She was wearing lipstick. The color was a shade paler than her gown, and made her lips look like petals ... dewy and soft. The memory of last night, of her tongue torturing him with sweetness, came rolling over him.

He tightened his grip on his coffee. Fragrant steam drifted up, scorching his chin. "Well if it's not *only* your scar, then it must be my past. Your disdain of my weakness is causing this distance between us. Causing you to hurt your nieces."

"No, Nick!"

Her intense scowl almost convinced him. But he needed

proof. "You have the keys. Open that sideboard. I want to see the laudanum."

Felicity blinked and a fresh stream of tears trickled down her cheeks. "Please ... don't do this."

Since she made no move toward the table, Nick strode over and got the keys himself. Squeezing them so hard they left jagged lines in his palm, he went to the sideboard, crouched down, and unlocked the door. The hinges squealed open, revealing empty imprints in the dust where the laudanum once was. The vision gored his soul like rusted razor. He slowly stood and looked at Felicity. "You trust me, do you?"

She opened her mouth as if to speak, then pressed her fingertips over her lips.

Nick gritted his teeth. "I made a vow to Lia. And seeing as my truest friend Johnny is gone, and those girls are the only ones here who have any faith in me at all, I intend not to disappoint the child. I promised her she would have music tonight at her party. So, the truth, Felicity. Where did you hide the phonograph?"

Swiping her cheeks, she glanced at the hem of her dress where it swished from her nervous jitters.

"You *hid* Father's phonograph?"

Nick's attention snapped to the doorway.

Aislinn stood there glaring at her aunt, one hand clenched to the knob. "Have you truly become so bitter?" Anger tightened her pretty features and cast shadows beneath her eyes, making her as desolate and pale as a weathered statue. "Fine then! Banish everything that reminds us of him. But you cannot make me give up, no matter how hard you try!"

Wiping her cheeks, Felicity stalked to the fireplace, her long skirt trailing behind her. Nick paused to watch her ... to really *look* at her. Her shimmering hair hung down past her waist with a portion of the front and sides pulled into a knot at her nape. Dried forget-me-nots and lavender had been tucked within the tied strands. The flowers looked suspiciously like remnants from her wedding bouquet.

She'd taken great pains with her appearance this morning, and the result was nothing short of resplendent. A woman didn't go to such lengths unless she wanted to impress a man.

Why would she care, if she despised his past and refused to let him consummate their union?

Massaging his pounding temple, Nick moved to the table and dumped his untouched coffee back into the pot.

"Aren't you going to eat?" Felicity asked without turning around.

Nick studied the curve of her hips, her small waist, and rubbed his knuckle across the table's slick edge where that exquisite body had writhed in abandonment beneath his the night before. "I've lost my appetite."

He thumped the wood then strode toward the door.

"You'll still be joining us for our hike?" Felicity asked, almost too quietly to be heard.

He stalled at the threshold and met Aislinn's bewildered gaze. He squeezed her shoulder, pleating the soft pink cambric of her dress. "I wouldn't miss it. The girls are looking forward to it. Their happiness is more important than my petty sensitivities." With that, he left the room.

In a matter of moments, the castle door slammed shut.

Stinging from Nick's accusations, Felicity fondled her wedding ring and turned to her niece. "Before you say another word ... come with me to the tower."

The turret smelled of warm wax and fragile hope.

Soft light streamed in through the dusty, cobwebbed windows overhead. A candelabra was lit on the wall, illuminating the phonograph and bottles of laudanum which sat beside Isabella's urn on the table next to Jasper's bed. Clooney had transferred his medical supplies to this chamber last night when they brought the player and medicine in.

Felicity glanced over her shoulder. Aislinn waited in the doorway with an anxious frown on her face.

Moving around to the other side of the bed, Felicity felt the gentle heat of the pot-bellied stove off in the corner. She motioned her niece closer to her father.

"I know about the pupas," Felicity said as Aislinn stood opposite her on the other side of the bed.

They both looked down at his motionless body. His eyelids were closed, showcasing an intricate network of bluish veins along the translucent skin.

"I have no regrets, Auntie. I had to try."

"Just like I had to try the phonograph. Clooney and I played music for him last night."

Aislinn's gaze captured Felicity, an apology swimming in the aquatic depths. "What I said downstairs ... I never meant to hurt you." She wiped a tear from her cheek. "Thank you for trying. And for not being angry with me. It wasn't my intention to compromise your caterpillar business."

"Your father's health is more important than any business. It was worth it. For we were successful." Felicity waited for a reaction.

"What do you mean?"

"I know now, what you know. The Dark Raven is real. It's your father's spirit somehow connected to the butterflies. I've seen him, Aislinn. And I've told Clooney. I told him that

I believe with all my heart that your father is trying to come back to us."

Aislinn slapped her hands to her mouth. "Oh!" She gasped behind her fingers, "You saw him, too ... you believe? At last you believe!" Wet lines slipped down her cheeks, streaming faster with each blink. Her hands fell to cover her father's where they rested on the sheet. "Wait ... you said *we* were successful?"

Feeling the burn of happy tears behind her eyes, Felicity cranked the phonograph. A waltz began to play—tinkling and soft. She leaned over her brother, smoothing some black hair off his forehead. "Jasper. Look who's here to visit."

His eyelashes fluttered first—straining to break apart, then his lids followed suit, opening slowly. He seemed to struggle to focus, his eyes rolling in their sockets, but soon his pupils were fixed on Aislinn. The slightest smile turned his lips.

"*Aislinn...*" The word was soundless—carried on a wisp of air pushed from his lungs.

Aislinn fell to her knees beside the bed, lifting his limp hands to kiss them. "Father!" The rest of her stunned proclamations broke beneath a sob.

"He hasn't the faculty of his body yet," Felicity hurried to explain. "He still can't use his vocal cords. He can barely whisper and can't move anything but his eyes and lips. But somehow the phonograph lures him out of his shell. Clooney believes ... if we have faith and continue the pupal treatments, he will be able to speak aloud again. And one day, perhaps even use his arms and legs. That's why we brought the laudanum up. Clooney wants it accessible. Your father is bound to be in pain when he starts trying to move. But our hope is that his body will one day be whole again."

"Yes. It will." Smiling, Aislinn touched her father's

features, tracing his eyebrows, skimming the beard on his chin. "I've been reading your journals, Father. I found the answer there ... you gave me the answer."

He offered another whispered acknowledgement, indecipherable to Felicity.

Her brother's gaze didn't leave his daughter's face, as if drinking in every nuance of her appearance. No surprise his eyes would be starving for her, having not seen his beloved child for three years. Felicity's heart ached at the tenderness and pride which coursed through his expression.

Aislinn kept her gaze firmly on Jasper. "We must tell Lia. And Nick."

Felicity faltered at the suggestion and toppled some books with her foot. "We should wait until he's improved a bit more before telling your sister. And I've ... other secrets I must tell Nick first." She bent to straighten the mess she'd made.

Aislinn tore her attention from her father. "He's your husband. You should have no secrets."

"I've lied to him about some monumental things. Things I should've told him before we married, that could've altered his choice. And once I confess, I fear he'll leave without looking back. After seeing how angry he was over just a phonograph..." *And how hurt over the laudanum.*

The song stopped and Jasper's eyes closed again.

"Father?" Aislinn patted his cheek gently, concern frosting her voice.

Felicity caught her niece's wrist. "Let him rest. Clooney thinks it's best if we leave the player up here in case he awakens on his own. It obviously brings him comfort. His spirit is teetering between this world and the other. He's been trying to find his way back to the living since my headaches three years ago. He was writing through me ... a novel that only a lepidopterist's mind could've crafted. Clooney suggested we may be connected through the cream I wear on my face."

Sniffing, Aislinn stood and smoothed the red satin ribbon at her waist. "The butterfly saliva?"

Felicity nodded.

Aislinn glanced at the urn on the table. "Do you think Mother's there, in that other place where he's been adrift? And that's why it's so hard for him to come back?"

"Perhaps. I think he needs a reason to want to come back to us. He needs to remember why life is worth living. It could be why the music draws him back. It's reminding him. He's forgotten. That happens sometimes with adults, when fate has dealt us a bad hand."

Perception softened Aislinn's thoughtful frown. "I've seen the change in you since Nick has come. He helped you remember."

"Yes."

"You love him."

Though Felicity didn't answer, the heat in her cheeks surely made her feelings blatantly apparent.

"Is it because of your scar that you slept in separate rooms last night? Are you ashamed to let him see it?" Aislinn asked.

"Separate...?" Felicity's flush deepened. "That's entirely too private a thing for you to take note of!"

"It's hardly a secret! I saw him coming down from the fourth floor this morning. Have you told him how you feel?"

"I-I wouldn't know how to begin."

"Why is it so difficult? He loves you, too."

Felicity had earlier hoped that might be possible. Even tried to look pretty for him today ... to show him how happy she was to have him in her life—how grateful for his patience and generosity last night. She'd planned to discuss her barrenness and invite him to share her chambers tonight in hopes that by tomorrow, they'd be so bonded he'd never leave her, even after his father arrived. But now he was beyond angry, and she wasn't sure how to bridge that gap between them without telling Jasper's secret, which wasn't hers to tell.

She fisted a hand in the gauzy chiffon of her skirt, feeling ridiculously overdressed. Everything had backfired. The resentment and pain in his voice when he accused her of distancing herself from him and the girls had hurt almost as much as the slash of the knife on that dark night so long ago. "I'm damaged ... and a liar. Why would Nick feel anything for me?"

"Because you're strong." Aislinn came around the bed to catch Felicity's hand. Felicity caught a breath, realizing her niece was level to her collarbone now. When had she grown so tall? "But most of all, because you're flawed. Nick doesn't want perfection. Do you know what he told me on the way back to the castle that day I snuck out?"

Felicity curled her niece's fingers in hers and shook her head.

"'Frailty moves the heart in a way perfection cannot match.' If you let yourself open up to him, he'll never see your scar. He'll see only you. His greatest masterpiece, shaped by his love."

Felicity almost smiled, wanting to believe the romantic notions. Here in this tower where she'd reclaimed her childhood faith, she could almost let herself. She stroked Aislinn's hair. "When did you become a lady? I must have blinked and missed your childhood. You shame me with your wisdom."

Aislinn leaned into her touch. "Wisdom is learned. And I had a wonderful teacher."

"Dearest heart." Felicity cupped her chin and pressed a kiss to her forehead. "I believe you're so wise because you had more than just one."

They looked at Jasper and the urn. Then they looked at one another and smiled.

"Tell him your secrets, Auntie. Every single one. They won't matter a whit to him. I'm sure of it."

Felicity squeezed her niece's hand. Aislinn's confidence stemmed from the misconception that Felicity hadn't yet told Nick about her scar. It was so much more convoluted than that. He'd told her in the lookout post that he wanted everything he'd lost with Mina. Even if he tried to deny it, he still wanted that son.

Once he learned of her inadequacies as a woman, he would fall back into his obsession over Mina and Christian— a complication which could only be exacerbated by Jasper's discovery about the pupas.

And Nick's father's impending arrival would drive the final wedge between them.

Yet none of that mattered any longer. Nick deserved to know of her barrenness and the investors; he deserved proof of her faith in him—that he would stand by his wedding vows for the girls' sakes, if no other reason. They wouldn't have another private moment together until after the picnic. So, she'd have to speak to him late this afternoon, before the gala. Until then, she'd give him a wonderful day filled with happy memories to cushion the toxic pain, in hopes he would forgive her enough to stay despite all her lies.

Thoughtful, she stroked her butterfly brooch. She would begin by helping him keep his promise of music to Lianna.

CHAPTER TWENTY-EIGHT

The mid-morning hike was long, but the sweet, damp air invigorating. Nick's newly healed muscles thrived with the exercise.

Felicity and Aislinn had braided their hair like Lia's. All the girls donned hats tied beneath their chins, along with trousers, blousy shirts, and boots to ease their trek. Felicity carried a rucksack filled with lunch and flasks for everyone. She had her whip looped around one shoulder. Nutmeg and Dinah trundled beside her. Most cats would prefer to stay home lazing in the sun, but like all the other females living on this Irish estate, this particular tabby didn't fit the typical mold.

Nick grinned as he led Lia on her horse. She'd insisted on riding Butterscotch, being generous enough to give Aislinn a turn once when she'd felt winded.

Along the way, they stopped to admire slugs and fungi on tree branches and the girls picked an abundance of clover to stuff into the canvas bag hanging from the hobbie's saddle horn.

Clouds rolled in as their caravan burst out of the forest and arrived on the moorland. Felicity had told Nick before they left that there was a special reason she wanted to bring him here—to the one bog he and Clooney hadn't explored. It must have been for the stunning view.

Against the gray sky, blue mountains peaked and dipped in the distance, piercing the occasional band of fog. Long grasses waved on the gusts, giving sporadic glimpses of the bog which separated the moor from the cliffs overhead. The tall, rocky formations bordered the ocean far below on the other side. Though the slapping waves couldn't be seen from here, a slight tang of salt attested to their presence.

Nick adjusted his hat and studied the cliffs and the ancient oaks which speared out sporadically from crevices and cracks in the rocks. He couldn't help but compare those craggy heights to the barriers Felicity had built around her heart.

Clooney privately approached him about the phonograph and laudanum before they left for the picnic. As for the phonograph, Clooney said it made Felicity think of Jasper. That's all he offered for an explanation, stating Nick should ask Felicity for any further details, but it was enough to humble Nick. He'd assumed it was all about their stunted relationship when it was in fact grief over her brother's memory. Or something more, considering the way she'd acted last night in the dining hall—as if she'd seen a ghost. He was starting to think she had.

He only wished she would trust him enough to tell him. One thing he'd realized today ... he would never knock down her walls. He would simply have to have the courage and patience to scale them.

The groundskeeper also admitted to being the one who moved the opium tincture. He claimed Felicity had nothing to do with it. This redeemed Nick's hope. He could live with Clooney's distrust, as long as his bride had faith in him.

His bride.

Everything had happened so fast over the past few weeks. He'd hardly had time to stand back and breathe, much less take stock. Now, a surge of possessiveness washed over him—the jarring reality that, as of yesterday, he at last had a family. A beautiful woman and two young ladies who would need his guardianship and loyalty for the rest of his living days.

"A Red Kite!" Lia bounced on her pony's back, pointing to the sky, adding to the warm contentment flooding Nick's heart.

Overhead, a majestic reddish-brown bird spread its white tufted wings, sweeping its feathers with long, deep flaps until it caught a current of wind. It soared with wings held aloft, its forked tail steering with a twist and a flex. From somewhere unseen, a call pierced the skies, shrill and high-pitched like the song of a sea bird. Then another Kite crossed the first one's path, diving and looping until they were on the same course, landing gracefully within a majestic oak on the lowest cliff.

They'd seen all sorts of wildlife on the way here. An assortment of flitting birds, a fox chasing a family of rabbits, three deer, and a handful of large blue butterflies with wings so luminous they appeared to glow as they drifted in and out of the shade. But nothing compared to this.

Nick was reminded of that evening Felicity confessed her desire for wings. Taking a swig from his flask of water, he stole a look and found her staring steadfastly at the birds perched in the oak. Her lovely features, though shaded beneath her hat, held that same fragile sense of wonder and veneration as they had in the moonlit greenhouse. It was then he noticed she wasn't wearing the butterfly brooch her mother had given her. Over his entire stay here, he'd never once seen her without it.

She must've felt his attention, for she turned her dark eyes on him, nearly taking his breath.

"Mates?" he asked, referring to the birds and their entwined flight.

"For life," she commented.

"Made for one another," Nick added.

"Or two broken pieces that found a fit," she said with a gentle smile.

"Broken?" Lia clucked her tongue and reached for Nick so he'd help her off her pony. "You said they're a dangered species, Auntie, like our caterpillars. Not broken."

Nutmeg and Dinah greeted Lia by rubbing her legs as Nick set her feet on the ground.

"No, little goose." Felicity slipped her whip from her shoulder then followed suit with the rucksack. "I said the Red Kites are *endangered*. And our caterpillars are nothing of the sort. In fact, I look for them to be flourishing again within the next few months."

Nick caught the hopeful glance which passed between Felicity and Aislinn. The tension which had been so thick between them this morning, ever since he'd known them for that matter, had vanished. On the way here, they'd laced arms and prattled on about everything from the weather to fashion. It appeared they'd worked things out after he'd left the dining hall. At least one good thing came of that nasty interlude.

Nick turned Butterscotch out to graze on yellow oat grass and sweet clover. Nutmeg and Dinah darted off, chasing some tiny white butterflies toward a lacy spread of flowers a few yards north. Nick couldn't help imagining how Johnny would've loved this ... joining them for the hike ... exploring. He would've made things interesting by chasing Dinah into that blossom field.

Upon that thought, Nick took off his hat for a closer look at the pale blue flowers waving on the wind. His breath caught in his chest. That's what Felicity had wanted him to see. Why she'd chosen this spot. The entire valley was covered with forget-me-nots. A field-full of "I'm sorry-s." They'd have plenty to go around for all the years to come.

A smile broke on his face and he glanced Felicity's way. She looked up with a charming shrug, then proceeded to ready the picnic.

She unfolded a blanket and spread it on the ground, instructing the girls to sit on the corners so the wind wouldn't snatch them. She'd chosen a spot at the edge of the forest where several giant fir trees shared a thick spread of moss. The growth draped the lengths of the middle branches, one tree to the next, forming a cover so dense it provided an umbrella affect. When the mist started to fall, they all gathered beneath to stay dry as they ate. Soft droplets pattered around them—a lulling rhythm which counteracted Lia's uncontained excitement.

"It's like we're in a grass hut, don't you think Sissy? We're pioneers." Lia pushed back her hat so it hung at her shoulder blades.

Aislinn smiled and opened Felicity's rucksack. "I daresay the pioneers never had ceilings this tall." She skirted her gaze up to the mossy cover. "Or cuisine this fine."

From a parchment wrapper, she pulled out something that looked suspiciously like a deformed hand: fleshy and pale pink, with two enormously fat fingers and two miniature thumbs growing off either side of the wrist, like dew claws. She placed it on Nick's tin plate then drew out three identical ones to share with her aunt and sister.

Nick dragged his hat off and lifted the food to his nose. It smelled of vinegar, cloves, and onion, and was firm and cold to the touch. Not a very appetizing combination.

Felicity exchanged amused glances with the girls. "We decided that you should sample traditional Irish picnic fare. These are pickled crúibíns."

Nick frowned.

"Pig's feet!" Lia blurted then covered her mouth to stifle a snort.

"Ah..." Nick set it back on his plate. "And here I thought we had a shortage of pigs." He cast a teasing glance to Felicity.

"Oh, no worries there." Felicity teased back. "Cook has a pantry filled with jars of crúibíns. She also has some knuckles preserved. There'll be no shortage anytime soon."

Nick rubbed his hands together in feigned greediness. "Mmm. What an unmerited stroke of good fortune." He snapped out his napkin and tucked it in his collar. "Where's my fork? Time to dig in."

The dulcet chime of Felicity's laugh sent delicious tremors through his spine.

Aislinn beamed. "There's no need for silverware. We only brought finger foods."

"Would you like to see what we packed in your rucksack?" Lia crawled to the bag Nick had placed beside his thigh. A rain-scented gust of wind caught the blanket corner where she'd been sitting and Aislinn slapped a boot down to hold it in place.

"Hmm." Nick cringed as Lia dug out something wrapped within a towel. "Not sure you'll be able to top pig's feet. Unless..." He opened the towel at Lia's prompting, revealing thick bread studded with dried fruit and cut into triangles. "Surely I can't be so lucky. It's an ear sandwich!"

All of his companions burst out laughing this time, resurrecting that earlier warmth in his chest. He'd thought of Johnny Boy often over the past weeks, but the high he once experienced at the dog's comical responses to his jokes couldn't compare to the giddy rapture these three girls evoked in him.

He looked at each of their flushed, glowing faces as they babbled and plopped an assortment of foreign samplings on his plate. With a quiet rain sweeping across the moorland and a mossy roof over his head, he noshed on fried potato farls, whortleberries, and pigs' feet. For dessert, little Lia popped a bite of barmbrack bread spiced with sultans and raisins into his mouth. She claimed it a delicacy, though it wasn't nearly as sweet as his new family's doting upon him.

The effect they'd had upon his life in such a short time left him reeling. This lovely trio seemed to truly accept him just as he was. But was he worthy of such a gift? He sipped the whiskey Felicity offered from a flask just for the two of them. The drink burned all the way into his chest.

His twin brother had often pointed out how Nick ran at the first sign of trouble; how he was too much of a coward to face his inner demons.

But by living here—isolated in Ireland—he'd never have to face Julian's perfection again. He could finally stop seeing himself through the eyes of past failings. Perhaps his affection for Felicity and the girls would be enough to make him into the man his parents once thought him incapable of being.

Perhaps it already had…

"You ate it all!" Lia pounced into his lap.

Caught up in his meditations, Nick hadn't realized there was nothing left on his plate—short of a pig's ankle bone. He buried his nose in the sprite's milky scented braids. Indeed, his belly felt full, though he couldn't recall a single flavor or texture.

Felicity crouched in front of him. She pushed aside a stray clump of hair from his forehead. "You're far too quiet. Is it not setting well on your stomach?"

Without a word, he caught her chin and pulled her to him, sandwiching Lia between them as he drew his bride into a kiss filled with all the aching tenderness of his epiphany. She dropped to her knees, melting into him with a moan as his hands moved and knocked her hat askew. Lia burrowed her way out from their entwining bodies.

Eyes closed, Nick savored Felicity's response—her petal-soft hands curving around his temples, lips warm and gentle against the press of his. Her scent surrounded him like a comforting blanket.

He felt Lia's heated breath on his cheek and squinted one eye to find her peering over them, entranced.

"Well, I don't think the prince ever kisses the princess like *that*," she scolded.

Chagrinned, Nick broke the kiss. Felicity ducked her head to straighten her hat.

Aislinn tugged her little sister by her elbow. "Certain kinds of kissing can cure indigestion, Lia. Now come here and help me clean the picnic mess."

Felicity's eyes widened. "Wait ... *indigestion*?" She burst out laughing.

Nick joined in.

"Why's that funny?" Lia asked, hands propped on her waist.

Smirking, Aislinn scraped crumbs into the grass before dropping the plates into the rucksacks. "When you're older, you'll understand."

Lia huffed and began to fold the linen napkins. "You always say that."

"Say what?" Aislinn's feigned ignorance set off an argument.

Smiling at their grumblings, Nick rose to his feet and held out a hand to help his bride stand. He hugged her to him a moment longer than he should have, because he'd never before noticed how perfectly her head fit beneath his chin.

Reluctant, he turned her loose. Then holding one another's gazes, they wrapped up the leftover food.

CHAPTER TWENTY-NINE

Dinah and Nutmeg bounded over to lick up the crumbs on the ground, hungry from their romp in the forget-me-nots.

Once the scraps were put away, Lia's sleepy lashes widened on a plea to her aunt. "Is it time?" she asked.

Felicity looked off in the distance. One Red Kite busied itself in the branches of the oak jutting out from the cliffs, while the other flew high overhead. Nodding, Felicity handed over one of the linen napkins to Lia.

"What is that for?" Nick asked, scratching Nutmeg's ear as the dog appeared at his side, panting.

"The Kites are building their nest," Lia answered. "And I want a birthday wish."

"So your wish is to watch," Nick reasoned.

"No," Lia said. "I have to give my wish to the fairies."

Nick felt completely lost now. "Which fairies would that be?"

Lia rolled her eyes. "The reason the Kites are in-dangered is because the fairies have been riding them to Tir-Na-nOg and forgetting to bring them back." Lia balled the fabric in her hand to hide it from Nutmeg's inquisitive nose.

Nick cocked his head, tucking his hat into the rucksack with the foodstuffs. He'd read articles about how the Red

Kites had been wrongly blamed for threatening game bird populations and fallen prey to poisoning by an ignorant society. They'd also lost their habitat on parts of the continent, and egg collectors made it nearly impossible for them to settle anywhere else long enough to replenish their kind. But this tale of the fairies was much more palatable for a child of seven.

He passed a sly glance to Felicity.

She lifted her eyebrows. "What? Folklore has its place. It colors the ugly parts of life just a little prettier."

Nick grinned. Her adventurous and teasing side always fascinated him—glimpses of the innocent girl she once must've been. He knelt in front of Lia, helping her resituate her hat. "Why the cloth? What does it have to do with your wish?"

"The fairies fall asleep in the nests while waiting for the Kites to return," the child answered. "They get cold up there, so high in the trees. They need blankets. If you whisper a wish into a cloth and the Kites pick it for their nest, the fairies will use it to cover up. Then your wish floats into their ears while they sleep and becomes their dream. Everyone knows, anything a fairy dreams will come true."

"Ah." A Shakespearean quote came to mind and he looked up at Felicity. "'When the Kite builds, look to lesser linen.'"

With a twinkle in her eye, she nodded, obviously aware of Shakespeare's referral to the Red Kite's reputation for scavenging cloth for their nests, being particularly fond of linen and ladies' underwear. To think he'd once thought her incapable of imagination. She'd proven him wrong yet again by weaving the bird's trait into her tale.

"So, how are we going to deliver that square of fabric to them ... up there?" Nick motioned to the cliffs.

"We simply have to place it high enough to catch their attention," Felicity said, looping her whip over her arm. "Come along everyone."

They trudged into the clearing toward the bog, leaving the rucksacks at the forest's edge. Clouds gathered overhead and a chilled wind swirled around them, causing the long grasses to clasp their trousers and boots like miniature tentacles. A strange odor drifted on the air—rather like the smell of sweaty feet.

"I think the Kites have been using this pond as their foot bath," Nick teased.

The girls snickered.

"A rare breed of orchid grows here," Felicity said with levity in her voice. "'Tis called dragon's breath. You can see why it earned such a title."

Nick smiled as Nutmeg and Dinah reappeared and scampered ahead. The wind's fingers raked his hair, and he was glad he'd left his hat with the rucksacks. He didn't have ties to hold it in place like the girls did.

The group passed Butterscotch where she'd moved ahead to munch on oat grass.

"Butterscotch!" Lia bolted toward the pony but Nick and Aislinn caught her hands.

Felicity cast them both a grateful look. "Your hobbie's all right," she assured her youngest niece.

"She'll get lost!" Lia refused to take another step.

Acting on an overwhelming surge of protectiveness, Nick hoisted her up and placed her on his shoulders. He held her shins to keep her balanced and she wrapped her arms around his forehead.

Appearing relieved, Felicity trudged onward. "Bog ponies know their way around. They've an excellent sense of direction. In fact, now that she's grazed these moors, she could find her way to the castle and back here again on her own."

"What of Nutmeg and Dinah? They're getting too close to the water," Lia whimpered, her chin settling into Nick's hair.

Nick squeezed her ankles gently. "They're fine. Their instincts will keep them from falling in the bog. You, on the other hand, need to be careful."

Soon the water came into view—a murky lake which stretched around the cliffs from one direction to the next as far as the eye could see. Miniature mossy islands bobbed up here and there, some the size of a wagon wheel, others no bigger than an anthill. They formed a maze in the water, as if a person could use them for a walkway by jumping from one to the next.

"All right." Felicity stalled at the bog's edge, gusts of wind causing her braid to wind and twirl along her back like a snake. She held her hat to her head and looked up at Lia. "Have you planted your wish, little goose?"

Nick set the child down. Lia opened the cloth she'd had wadded in her hand and whispered something into the wrinkled weave. Then she folded the corners together and handed it off to her aunt.

Felicity tucked it into a pocket in her trousers before the wind could catch it. She tightened her hat's ties under her chin. "Aislinn, stay with Lia right here. Nick, would you follow me?" She held out her left hand and the overwrought sky reflected in her ring, coloring the gold a bluish-grey.

"Anywhere." Nick clasped their fingers.

She glanced over her shoulder at him, mahogany eyes warm with tentative hope. "Step only where I do. This is a quaking bog. What might look like sturdy ground could be just a floating mat of organic matter—leaves and stems and rotting vegetation. Not all of them have gathered enough debris on their underside to become stabilized."

Nick arched a brow. "Seems you know more about bogs than I gave you credit for."

"Only what Jasper taught us so we could survive out here if we were ever lost. It isn't that the bog is so deep. It probably would barely cover a grown man's head. But peat is like quicksand. Jerky movements will suck you down deeper into the lake bed. If you fall in, just grab any nearby vegetation attached to solid ground and use it to pull yourself along. The best thing would be to lie flat with your arms and legs spread wide."

"Like a water bug!" Lia injected an example.

Nick glanced at the sprite as she pointed to one of the many bugs skittering atop the water like four-pronged stars gliding on ice.

"A water bug, aye?" He winked at her then turned back to Felicity. "So how long will I be expected to stay afloat?"

"Just until I can cast the whip out to you."

"Hmm. I might prefer to drown. I've been on the wrong end of that whip before."

Shaking her head, Felicity grinned and tapped her boot's tip against a patch of mossy terrain, checking it for soundness. "This one's good."

He moved behind her as she picked their way gingerly to the middle, avoiding the smallest mossy islands. The water rippled each time they stepped from one to the next.

They settled, just short of crossing to a mound built higher than the others. Though it appeared to have more soil on the surface, it wasn't wide enough to support them due to the tall, skinny fir tree growing from its midst. When Felicity stretched out her leg to tap the mound with her toe, the tree swayed, attesting to the precariousness of the floating mat.

"Perfect." Drawing in her foot, Felicity released Nick's

hand and slid the whip from her shoulder. She uncoiled it. "Stand back a bit."

He did as she asked and she snapped her elbow and wrist, sending the whip's tail to the top of the tree where it tangled around the uppermost spike. Giving the cord's handle a tug to secure the knot around the needles, she cast a smug glance to Nick.

He smirked. "Well done. What now?"

"I need you to anchor me."

He eased his arms around her waist and locked his hands over her abdomen, pressing their bodies together. "Like this?" he murmured against her neck. His strong thighs tensed against her hips.

Shivering at the feel of his hot breath on her nape, Felicity froze.

She didn't know what had changed since their argument in the dining hall this morn. But whatever it was, his tender attentions left her feeling even guiltier than she already did.

She turned her head so her cheek touched his whiskered chin. "I didn't hide the laudanum," she said softly. "Please, never doubt my faith in you. And don't be angry with me anymore."

Nick's warm, soft lips glided along her nape. "You've made it impossible to stay angry. You gave me an entire field of mouse's ears. And truthfully, I wasn't innocent in the exchange. I said some things I regret. So, we should share the flowers." His nose rooted around the base of her braid beneath her hat's brim. The contact released a rush of sensation along Felicity's spine which radiated through her womb—a shadow of that racy, placated euphoria she'd experienced last night beneath his deft fingers.

Her legs weakened upon the memory. He tightened his embrace and held her up, his hands pleasurably kneading her abdomen.

"Nick." She gulped, trying to maintain her footing. "We have an audience."

"Who can only see my back. Remember, we're to practice being affectionate today." He pressed a kiss to her neck, balmy and teasing.

"You're already adept enough," she grumbled.

"What's taking so long?" Lia shouted from the banks. "It's going to rain soon!"

Nick laughed against Felicity's titillated skin.

Determined to evade his melting effect on her bones, Felicity started to pull on the whip. The wind kicked up, working against her efforts. The trunk only bent a little. Her joints and sinews strained as she tried to yank harder, arms stretched to their limits.

Abandoning his ministrations on her neck, Nick kept one arm around her and flung out the other to help her tug on the whip. His warm hand covered hers and his stance widened, giving them leverage. As the pressure increased and the leather cord grew taut, the tree slanted and the entire mat tilted, exposing where the fir's roots hung beneath, dripping with water as they lifted partially out of the bog.

Nick whistled. "Would you look at that?"

The girls shouted from the margin, cheering them on just as the rain started. The downpour pelted Felicity's face, soaked her clothes, and dimpled the water.

Blinking her eyes to shake the wetness from her lashes, she pushed down her hat's brim and snagged some branches to draw the tree's tip closer. Nick reached around her with both hands and held the tree so she could tie the cloth in place. Satisfied, she unwound her whip and released the fir.

With a swish, the mat righted itself in the bog and the tree once more stood vertical with the linen waving like a flag high against the drenched sky.

"You've given the sprite a wonderful birthday memory," Nick said in her ear.

Turning into his arms, she lifted to her toes so he could hear her over the spattering droplets. His wet clothes clung to his muscles as he held her steady.

"My birthday memory can't compare to the one you're giving her," she assured him. Thick locks of wet hair plastered his forehead. She pushed them aside and watched the rain glide along his handsome features, wanting to kiss him—to taste the rain on his lips.

"You mean the pony?" he asked.

"I mean your promise."

He wrinkled his brow. "The phonograph?"

"If I remember correctly, you only specified music."

His lips parted on another question, but Felicity silenced him by patting his wet cheek. "Time to get the girls home. We have a gala to attend."

CHAPTER THIRTY

They arrived at the castle soaked to the bone.

Nick's cold clothes stuck to his skin and water dripped from his hems making small puddles on the floor, but he wasn't ready to wash up. He needed to take advantage of the solitude and explore the turret stairway before his bride returned. She had escorted the girls to Aislinn's room so Binata could draw them a joint bath.

A grayish eclipse dimmed the second story corridor. The windows on both ends provided light throughout the day when the sconces weren't lit, but with clouds crowding out the sun and sheets of water coating the panes, illumination waned.

The rhythmic downpour pinged against the glass and drowned out Nick's footsteps as he ventured to the turret stairs. Upon arrival, he noticed not only two new sets of prints in the dust, but a streak about elbow-high where paint had peeled off the wall along the stairway's arched entrance. Rubbing his fingertip across the mark, he pondered the scrape he'd heard the night before, the silhouettes he thought he'd imagined.

Resigned to solve this once and for all, he started up. He'd taken only two steps when someone grabbed his shirt from behind.

He knew who it was by her touch.

Without turning, he peered into the obscured heights. "I understand Jasper asked to have the upmost stairs leveled upon his death," he said. "You left his phonograph on the rubble last night, an offering in hopes to settle his spirit. You've seen him, haven't you?"

"You're still seeking a way to Mina."

Responding to the vulnerable catch in Felicity's voice, Nick turned and stepped down. His eyes drank her in—the silvery-blonde hair, released from the braids and tumbling in damp waves to her waist. *Exquisite.* Her features came next, the fake creases softer in the graying dimness, thick lashes harboring those soulful, dark eyes so full of tragedy and emotion they spilled into his soul. Then her body, wet clothes binding every curve, nipples budded and beckoning beneath her blouse where they peeked out from winding strands of hair.

"Why would I be seeking anyone but you?" He moved toward her, catching her wrist when she tried to back up. "My nurturing, adventuresome, bard of a wife. That tale you told Lia of the Kites was incredible. And how you picked us a path through the bog to that tree. I've never seen anything like it."

"You drank too much whiskey from your flask earlier," she countered with a tentative smirk. "You're waxing poetic."

He grinned. "Oh no. I'm painfully sober. You want poetic? I couldn't keep my eyes off of you on the way home. Watching the rain glimmer on your hair and face … listening to your laugh as you ran through puddles with the girls. You, Felicity, are a princess and a seductress, all within one perfect form."

A fawnlike winsomeness passed over her face—shifting to

an expression of genuine surprise. Nick's chest tightened, to think of how few pretty words she'd heard throughout her life. A sad fact he planned to amend each day from now on.

Glancing over her head to assure they were alone in the corridor, he stretched out a finger to stroke her nipple, his body reacting when it puckered even tighter beneath the chilled cloth. His tongue swelled in his mouth, envying his finger's touch. "You're a dream," he whispered.

Her breath caught and she molded his palm over her fullness. "I'm real. And alive."

His blood simmered. "Show me."

He backed her toward her chamber until they were both inside then shut the door with his heel, pressing her against the wall. Her paleness stood out against the red paint as if she were a drop of cream in a flute filled with wine. Light from the fireplace cast a flickering glow upon her face. Her scent mingled with the burning wood—nectarous and roasted—like a flower field scorched to flame.

He trailed kisses from her forehead to her jaw, cupping her breasts in his palms, unable to resist her softness any longer. She gasped, a rush of warm air against his neck. Her loosened hair clumped between his fingers, impeding the contact and intensifying his lust. "Let me pleasure you again."

With a delightful purr, she lifted to her toes, drew his head down, and kissed him—passionately, deeply—tongue seeking and hot. Just like he'd wanted to kiss her on the hike. It was their audience that had reined him in.

No longer under such restraints, he caught her beneath the arms and lifted her against the wall so they were perfectly aligned, nose to nose. His body pinned her in place, all rigid and taut to her softness and pliancy. Drawing her legs around him, he ached to unbutton her blouse, to taste every facet of her flesh. To feel her breasts bared against his chest—skin to skin.

But respecting her shyness, he settled instead for his lips traversing her jaw line and neck and collar bone. He licked away the floral-sweetened remnants of dried rain and stopped only when he came to a nipple spearing beneath her shirt. She arched upward, as if impatient. Experimenting, he opened his lips over the cloth and nuzzled the swollen nub. A keening cry burst from her throat and pierced through to his groin. He became more fervent, his tongue lapping and suckling. She clutched at his nape, legs tightening around him, her body as weightless as a porcelain doll in his arms.

Wanting nothing more than to sink inside her—to be one with this broken and fascinating woman—he paused to regard her rapt face. "Lord, Felicity. Why are you doing this? It's so obvious you're lying."

A flash of firelight illumined her half-dazed, half-panicked expression. "It is?"

"To pretend our marriage is in name only, when we both want so much more. This union can be real if you'll just *let it*."

Her palms glided along his shoulders, a warm and sultry drag over damp fabric. "I can never compete with Mina. She could give you something I cannot."

"Her innocence?" he scoffed. "She was married before me, though her intimacies with her husband were sloppy at best. But inexperience is highly overrated. I don't want an austere, dewy-eyed bride. I like that you know how to touch me. I like how you respond to *my* touches. What more could any man ask of his wife?"

Honesty and offspring, Felicity said to herself, wrestling for the courage to relay it to him aloud.

As if sensing a rebuttal, he pressed his lips to hers and

swallowed her confession before she could utter even a syllable. How was she to form any coherent thought when his lips and tongue tasted like that? Rain and earth and man—a triad so potent it sparked a yearning deep within her damaged womb.

Her fingers wove into the soft hair at his temples, feeling his desire hard and seeking against her pubis. To know he hadn't been with a woman since his late wife stirred her passion to unexpected levels. This man had waited so long to be touched, to be satiated. She could do that for him.

He was right. She'd been well schooled. She could please him in ways Mina never had, and not even shed an ounce of her clothes. Indeed, she could repay the pleasure he'd given her last night and show him how much she loved him without spending any words or risking rejection.

Such intimacy—such skill—might give him a reason to stay, even after tomorrow.

Empowered by the thought, Felicity's fingers skimmed atop his trousers to wrap around his length. But in that instant the longcase clock began to gong.

She groaned upon realizing the time. "That monstrously large package..." she muttered absently.

Nick pushed himself into her hand. "You can't blame it. It's begging to be unwrapped."

"Not that." Grinning, she forced herself to let go, banking her palms on his shoulders. "I have yet to prepare the last of Lia's gifts—a rather sizeable one. Could you help me with it?"

Nick grunted and set her to the floor, winding fingers through her hair as he kissed her forehead, soft flutters of sensation too tender to be dismissed.

The way he touched her, with such care and veneration, inspired the most far-fetched notion: that perhaps his feelings for her were as real as hers for him, just as Aislinn had said.

"Are you always so easily distracted?" he asked, shattering her musings. "A lesser man could develop a complex."

She pressed kisses to his neck before drawing back to look into his eyes. "Then aren't we fortunate there's nothing 'lesser' about you?"

He stared at her, strong jaw twitching. For a moment, she thought he might refuse to stop ... might lift her into his arms and carry her to bed—initiating the sweet glories of lovemaking he was always telling her about. For a moment, she hoped he would.

The patter of raindrops began to fade.

"The gift is just there, by the window," she mumbled.

Letting strands of her hair slide through his fingers, he gestured for her to lead the way.

The cheval mirror waited, draped in sheets next to the sitting window. Grayish-blue light filtered through the panes from behind and blended to a shaded swirl along the wrinkled cloth, making the form beneath appear haunted and foreboding—as if it were a portal to a world of dreams and shadows. The very thing it represented to Felicity: a doorway to a likeness she'd never have access to again.

She'd kept it hidden in an empty room since her arrival at the castle. Today, for the first time in seven years, she had Tobias and Fennigan haul it into her chamber. But she still refused to look at her bared reflection.

"Aislinn has her mother's mirror ... this one is mine." Standing behind the frame, Felicity pulled the sheets off, nearly sneezing at the dust released on the action. With the cover cast aside, nothing remained but the glass and deep mahogany casing etched with intricate carvings of roses and ivy.

"I wish to give it to Lia since I have no more use for it," she said.

Her husband studied her with a quiet thoughtfulness, his hair and clothes rumpled from the rain and her hungry caresses of earlier.

Instead of waiting for him to ask, she offered an explanation. "The last time I looked upon myself ... fully bared ... was the night of the tragedy. I mean to say, before the stabbing. When I was still whole."

Remembering how she'd had the smallest bulge, the proof of life blossoming within her, she had to choke back a knot rising in her throat.

"Since then, I can't bring myself to..." Gripping the neck of her shirt, she held it closed, missing her brooch terribly. "I've no use for such a thing. Lia wants to be a lady. This"— she stretched her arm over the frame so her fingertips could skim along the chilled glass on the front— "will make her feel like one."

A tortured wrinkle drew Nick's brows together. "You've never seen the scar yourself?"

"Only the tip. But I've felt it. I can't look upon the reminder. Of what I've lost, of how broken I am."

Their eyes held in the semi-darkness. "That scar doesn't make you broken, Felicity. The only part of you that needs fixing is your heart. And I have the means to mend it."

His kind attempt at chivalry wasn't meant to patronize, but it did. A blaze of despondency surged hot in Felicity's cheeks. "No. You can't fix what's broken in me," she said. Then, before she could stop herself, she blurted the ugly fact. "That injury left me barren."

The shock upon Nick's face had her wishing she could gobble up the words and leave nothing but meaningless crumbs. Instead, the truth laid between them, raw and writhing, like a skinned and gutted animal.

Or like the precious baby she'd lost. But she couldn't

share that part of the tale. Not when he was looking at her with such pity in his eyes. Besides, there was still the matter of tomorrow's visitors to discuss.

He swallowed. "Lord. I'm so sorr—"

"No." Her cheeks burned. "You don't get to apologize. You saved my life, and in return, I wronged you. I withheld pertinent information. You can never have another son ... not with me. You should despise me for tricking you. You will, in fact ... when you learn the depths of my deceptions."

Trying to find the courage to tell him everything, she turned to the window seat and opened the hinged cushion, yanking out a long length of silver satin and an even longer strip of pink ribbon. Looking only at the back of the mirror, she proceeded to wrap the satin and ribbon around the glass. When she attempted to hold the ribbon in place to form a bow, she felt his strong frame behind her.

A large, capable hand came around to hold the knot. Together, they formed a tie worthy of any hat maker. His mother would've been proud. Before she could pull away, he laced his fingers through hers, twirled her around, and pulled her close for a hug, snuggling her beneath his chin.

His hot breath stirred the hair on top of her head. "Felicity."

She pressed her ear to his steady heartbeat. So lulled by the reassuring thud, she prepared to confess the rest of her lies, but footsteps slapped down the corridor toward the room. They both glanced at the door.

"Did you lock the latch?" she asked.

He released her. "No. I keep forgetting your children roam—"

"My *brother's* children," Felicity interrupted, awash in grief.

The door slammed open, revealing a tiny slip of a silhouette. "Auntie?"

"I'm here, little goose."

Lianna tumbled in and stalled next to the covered mirror. She wore nothing but a rumpled chemise and a frown—her hair fuzzy with wet tangles. In spite of the ill-timed interruption, the vision amused Felicity. The child looked like a pixie caught in a windstorm.

"Bini wishes to put my hair up," she whined. "But I'm old enough to wear it down with flowers tucked in. Like yours this morn."

"Yes, you are old enough." Felicity assured. "You can tell her I said so."

"Is this my gift?" Typical of her nature, the child slammed into another subject, gawking wide-eyed at the satin and bows.

"It is. But you must wait," Felicity answered, sweeping Lianna's tangles into some semblance of order. "I shall have Fennigan and Tobias move it to your room and after dinner you can open it there."

Lianna's gaze caught on Nick as if just noticing him. "Mister Sir. Is your tummy rocking?"

Felicity glanced in his direction to see what Lianna referred to. He was pale—almost green. He appeared sick enough to retch.

"Yes." He ran a hand through his messy hair. "I suppose I need to eat something."

Felicity turned away, sharing his nausea. What had possessed her to tell him? Now, of all times? No doubt he was already planning a way out of their vows. It wouldn't be so difficult. After all, they hadn't even consummated.

How would she ever get him to stay after this?

She knew the answer. Ask him to uphold the charade for the safety of the girls. But how unfair to put him in such a position. To guilt him into being responsible when he'd only known them one month ... when she was still harboring the lie about his father's looming visit.

She cast about in her mind, fishing for a way to get Lia out of the room ... to give them just a few more moments of privacy.

Another set of pounding steps shook the corridor and Aislinn appeared in the doorway, panting. "There you are, tiny slug. You're so slippery." She saw Nick and her eyebrows shot up. "Oh!" A smile wrestled to break free. "I tried to catch her."

"Tis all right," Nick answered. His broad shoulders drooped slightly along with the corners of his sensuous lips, belying his nonchalance. "I was helping wrap a gift. I should prepare for the gala." He strode toward the door.

Lianna cast an imperial gaze to Aislinn. "He's quite famished."

"Ah." Aislinn's teasing smile broke loose. "We'll have to get accustomed to such spells. Princes are notorious for their gluttonous appetites. Isn't that right, Auntie?"

Before Felicity could even scold Aislinn for her brass, Nick dismissed himself and left the room. The distractions had saved her from confessing everything, leaving the truth of Nick's father hanging heavy and uncomfortable, like a wet shawl draping her shoulders.

If Nick was physically ill over her admission of barrenness, she shuddered as to what his reaction would be tomorrow—when both their pasts came crashing down around them.

CHAPTER THIRTY-ONE

Shaved, scented with sandalwood soap, and wearing a russet colored shirt and brown cravat with matching vest and trousers, Nick descended the stairs.

He cast a glance to Felicity's chamber down the hall. Sympathetic misery clung to his heart—a constant aching sting—as if a knife had splintered within, leaving shards of tarnished steel behind. He'd always known the repercussions of that violent attack by Hayes went far deeper than a flesh wound. But he never realized how deep.

Though the lie didn't set well, Nick understood why she'd been hesitant to confess. Unbeknownst to her, he had no qualms with a barren wife. For him, the thought of losing another child during birth was unthinkable. He hated how much agony Felicity was in, but she was better off to never feel that kind of loss.

He'd left her thinking he was angry and disappointed. That had never been his intent. Her confession leveled him to the bones, bared his inability to stop that monster before the stabbing could take place.

Nick had wanted to comfort as a husband should. To soothe. Was trying to find the right words when the girls burst into the chamber. As a man, he couldn't imagine how such hollowness would feel to a woman ... as bleak as any death sentence.

Something told him in this case, words just weren't enough.

His palm skimmed the stair railing.

Speaking of words, what had she meant, he would despise her after learning the depths of her deceptions? Was there more she'd lied about? What else could there possibly be? Her brother ... the ghost.

He didn't care about any of that. His concern was for her now. She was weighed down with guilt, worried he wanted an heir. Tonight, after the party, he would offer her the gift he'd crafted along with his promise that all was well. It was time his wounded bird got her wings.

He touched the carving where it waited, secure and hidden in his right pocket, then resumed his trek down the stairs.

The sound of the girls' happy chattering led him to the dining hall. He looked forward to their bright, shining faces, eager to embrace the bliss of their innocent oblivion. He now knew why Felicity was so fiercely devoted to them. They were the only children she would ever come close to claiming as her own.

A bittersweet sadness entrenched him, and he paused at the threshold. The clouds had thinned enough that sunset passed through the long windows and hazed the room to the soft ruddy hue of a ripened watermelon. The electric lights overhead and the fireplace cast a warm glaze across the glossy table and furniture. Nutmeg and Dinah wrestled on the floor beside the hearth.

A chiming melody, tinkly and mechanical, drifted from the desk where the phonograph had once sat. Now a music box sat there—new and expensive. It boasted a porcelain stand no bigger than a cigar box supporting a miniature white gazebo. Tiny latticework doors synchronically opened and closed to the melody, alternately revealing a ballerina rotating in the center.

Lia and Aislinn held hands and danced a minuet, though it didn't fit the song playing.

Upon spotting Nick, Lia scrambled for the door. She threw herself against him, hugging his knee so tight the blood stumbled for passage in his veins.

"You kept your promise!" Her nose nuzzled him and hot tufts of breath warmed his leg. "Thank-you thank-you thank-you!"

"You're ... welcome?" Nick smoothed her hair—shimmering like spun sugar around her shoulders and interspersed at the crown with dried flowers. He glanced about the room, seeking Felicity and some answers.

Aislinn shut off the music box then came to his rescue.

"Lia," she said, plying the little sprite from Nick's leg, "go see if Cook has finished icing your cake."

"Oh!" Lia looked up at Nick, her eyes sparkling beneath a curtain of white lashes. "Your empty belly will be all better soon. Cook made a plum pudding cake with honey frosting!" She started to bounce away but stopped at the door. "You'll bump my noggin, won't you, Mister Sir? Clooney used to, but I want you this time."

Nick raised his brows helplessly in Aislinn's direction.

She nodded and strands of her glossy dark hair captured hints of the fading sunset, like embers coming alive amongst coal black ashes. "An Irish tradition. You hold her upside down and bump her head on the floor for each year of her life, giving her one extra for luck. It takes a strong hand to do the lifting and still be gentle."

"Ah." Grinning, Nick turned to the sprite. "I would be

honored, Lady Lia. So long as you return the favor on my birthday."

Lia rolled her eyes and snorted. "You're such a jolly monkey." Then she skipped from the room with Nutmeg at her heels.

Dinah purred and rubbed herself against Nick's ankles. Aislinn bent to pick up the cat. "Lia wasn't supposed to open the gift until you and Auntie both came down. But the moment she saw your name on it, she couldn't hold her curiosity at bay."

"*My* name?" Nick scratched the cat behind her ears as Aislinn buried her nose in its gray-striped fur. "I haven't had time to get her a gift other than Butterscotch."

"Auntie sent Clooney to Carnlough while we had our hike."

Nick studied Aislinn's eyes. "How could she afford it?"

She wrapped the cat's tail around a finger. "I suspect she traded something. Perhaps ... a special piece of jewelry?"

Remembering the absence of Felicity's precious brooch earlier, Nick gulped back an odd flavor on his tongue—it tasted sweet yet sad, like some rare confection made of tears. He couldn't believe she'd part with her heirloom merely to help him save face with Lia. "Where is she?"

"She's getting ready. While the rest of us cleaned up, she decorated."

Nick regarded his bride's handiwork. A white lace runner graced the table, and fresh flowers, snipped off their stems to float in crystal bowls, provided simple yet elegant centerpieces. She'd strung the clover the girls had collected onto long threads and draped the shamrock garland from one corner of the ceiling to another, adding color and the subtle scent of the outdoors. A rainbow of satin ribbons crowned each of Lia's masterpieces on the wall, and her dolls—seated along the settee and wing backed chairs—sported their finest gowns and hair adornments, some of them holding gifts yet to be opened.

He'd never seen any woman with a more giving heart. She would've been a wonderful mother.

Damnit. She already was. Couldn't she see that?

Someone cleared their throat from behind and Nick turned on his heel.

Tobias waited in the doorway, hat in his hands. "Lord Thornton. I-I know Her Ladyship desired we should keep Mister Landrigan outside the estate should he come. But..."

Nick's entire body tensed, alerted by the sound of the name. "Go on."

"He made his way into the courtyard. And he's set on being heard ... by your wife."

Nick sneered. "Is he now?" He glanced at Aislinn. "Tell your aunt nothing of this. I don't want her upset."

Aislinn sat Dinah upon the floor and nodded, her lips pressed tight as she and Tobias exchanged concerned glances.

A charge of dark anticipation electrified Nick's veins. He was going to relish this. Not only because of Donal's mistreatment of Felicity, but because that man was the spawn of the earl—the demon who had degraded and wounded his bride in inhuman and incomprehensible ways before leaving her womb desolate and parched for all eternity.

Nick thrust off his vest and tossed it to a chair. Then thinking better of it, he went to the chair and withdrew his carving knife from the vest's inner pocket. He then brushed past Tobias who fell into step behind him, mumbling an explanation as their footfalls echoed in the marble corridor.

"We were to keep him outside the gate, Sir. He said he

didn't want to cause trouble. That he came only to drop off Miss Lia's gifts. They were too heavy for him to unload alone, so he asked that we should help him carry them in, then he would leave upon seeing them safe within the confines of the fence." Tobias gulped as Nick swung open the door and they stepped into the damp evening air. "He lied, Sir."

"Shocking," Nick said. He started to place his knife in his right pocket for easy access, then remembered Felicity's carving waited there and chose the other instead. Sunset had slipped behind the horizon. Another storm rolled in, casting everything in deep purple shadows. As they stepped from the castle stairs into the courtyard, Nick unbuttoned his sleeve cuffs, pebbles crunching beneath his boots. "Where is he?" A pine-scented gale caught his hair and slapped it about his face.

"With the carousel ponies, waiting just inside the gate. Fennigan stayed to watch him."

Continuing to walk along the pebbled path with the servant, Nick took off his cravat to tie back his hair, already anticipating the taste of blood in his mouth upon the first punch. He'd let the maggot have one hit for the sake of sport ... but that would be all. "Felicity didn't want those horses delivered in the first place."

"I wasn't aware, Sir." Tobias shifted his hat in his hands nervously. "To pacify him, I told him I'd fetch the lady. But I came to you instead."

Nick slapped the boy's shoulder. "I knew there was a reason I liked you." Even in the dimming light, Nick could make out the stable hand's reddened ears.

"Fennigan and I can assist—"

"No. I'll send Fennigan your way." Nick gestured for Tobias to stay put as he stepped off toward the latticework tunnel which would lead through the trumpet vines, past the greenhouse, and to the gate. "I'll require no help. Except to carry out the broken pieces when I'm done." He folded his shirt sleeves up to his elbows. His knuckles fidgeted, craving the crack of Landrigan's jaw.

"You're to destroy the ponies then?" Tobias called over the rattling of branches and leaves in the forest.

"No." Nick strode onward and unbuttoned his collar to relieve the sensation of steam rising from his chest. A brutal smile plucked at the corners of his mouth. "I'm going to kill the Irishman."

✦

Felicity stepped into the dining hall, hoping to find her new husband with the girls. Instead, she found Aislinn and Tobias alone with their heads together, whispering in front of the fireplace.

"I thought I told you two to always have a chaperone."

Their heads popped up simultaneously at her scolding. Guilt darkened their faces.

Felicity frowned. "Where's Nick? I know he'd never leave you unsupervised."

Aislinn and the stable hand exchanged a meaningful glance. Aislinn started to speak but he shook his head vigorously, flushed from neck to brow.

Felicity smoothed the lacy cuffs of her fuchsia gown, worry stilting her movements. Had Nick left already? Was he so disappointed over her inability to bear heirs that he'd told everyone goodbye, even the servants, without giving her the same courtesy? "What's this all about?"

Aislinn scowled at Tobias, clutching her skirt as she spoke. "Nick asked us not to tell you. But we're concerned—"

The stable hand cleared his throat.

Aislinn's eyes rolled. "Fine. *I'm* concerned that if we don't tell you, there will be bloodshed."

"*Bloodshed*?" Dread wound to a nauseous knot in Felicity's stomach. "Whose?"

"Mister Landrigan's," Tobias chimed in reluctantly.

Lianna arrived just in time to catch the name. She clapped. "Uncle Donal has come?" She practically danced over. "Auntie, the Kites must've found my cloth! My wish came true!"

Felicity felt her face drain of color. It was over. Landrigan would tell Nick about the guests. Once her husband knew the extent of her betrayal, he would leave and her nieces would be lost to her.

And she would be lost without them, and him.

She rearranged the flowers on Lianna's head, moving trembling fingers in a monotonous rhythm, all the while trying to catch a breath so she could think. Her pulse thundered in her ears and muffled Aislinn and Lianna's arguing, as if their voices drifted from afar...

"Your wish was for Mister Landrigan to come to your party?" asked Aislinn.

"No. For him to stay in the castle forever. Just like Mister Sir. All of us together ... a family."

"Well that's a doltish thing to wish for, Lia."

"Why? He's Bini's nephew. And there's lots of rooms. They just need furniture."

"Nick and Mister Landrigan aren't friends. They don't even like one another. Tis like asking the dragon to move in with the prince and princess. Ugh. Never mind. What are we to do Auntie? *Auntie*?"

Felicity snapped back to herself.

As angry as her husband was with Landrigan, Nick would most likely knock him out cold before he could get a word in.

If she hurried, she could intervene before their uninvited guest roused enough to talk. It was her place to tell Nick the truth about his father—hers and no one else's—and she had planned to do so tonight after the gala.

She only prayed she hadn't already lost her chance to do right by the man she loved.

CHAPTER THIRTY-TWO

By the time Nick arrived at the gate and saw Landrigan lounging against one of three carousel ponies, his pulse had escalated to a steady and maddening drumbeat in his ears.

Sending Fennigan away with a flick of his head, Nick sized up the situation. Tiny mirrors bedecked the brightly painted flanks of the ponies, sparkling as they reflected the moonlight piercing the clouds overhead. The horses' tails—made of real hair—waved with the wind. Nick was taken out of the moment, back to his past ... the last time he'd seen his twin in person. Years ago, when they had a scuffle on their family's carousel. Nick had left the ride broken and in shreds, and he'd done the same to his relationship with his brother.

It felt odd and ironic, to be in such a similar situation. Yet there was a big difference tonight, for he'd feel no remorse for the damage he intended to inflict this time.

He met Donal's gaze. A peppermint stick hung from the Irishman's mouth, standing out in the dimness against his dark coloring. Offering a cocky sneer, he reached to take out his candy so he could speak.

Nick stepped up. "Not a word. I know that you touched her. I know how you shamed her. Now you answer to me."

371

In the shadows of the storm, Donal's features shifted from gloating to cautious. He stood and dropped his candy to the ground, crushing it beneath his boot, all the while keeping Nick in his sights.

"You get one chance." Nick bared his jaw, jutting it out in offering as cool wind sluiced through the placket of his shirt and ruffled the hair along his nape. "I'll let you throw the first punch."

Eyes narrowed, Donal set aside his jacket and rolled up his shirt sleeves, a strained hesitation to his movements. He was obviously caught off guard by Nick's swift recovery and the absence of his frilly cane. No doubt he wondered if he'd bit off more than he could spit out.

Hell yes you have.

The drumming pulse in Nick's ears grew to a pounding roar as they stared each other down, muscles coiled to spring.

With every blink, Nick became an unwilling prisoner to his mind's eye: forced to watch Donal rip Felicity's dress, violate her with ugly words and harsh touches, ridicule her most sensitive flaw with all the compassion of a bloodthirsty lion taunting its crippled prey.

The image grated his core and decimated any attempt at sportsmanship.

"Time's up," he said.

Donal's eyes widened, but too late. Nick lunged, aiming the heft of his weight in toward opponent's midriff. His head collided with the Irishman's chest—the pounding knock against his skull an intense yet coveted burst of pain which shook loose the tortured images of Felicity.

Donal grunted as Nick plowed them both sideways into the pony's flanks. The horse spun and hit the stone side of the fence, its mirror designs busting and cracking. Shattered glass rained all around.

Nick and Donal fell into the mud. As Nick rolled to get back on his feet, a sensation of heat leaked out of tiny cuts in his nape. He trailed his palm along the abrasions. Tiny shards prickled his skin where the wind chilled his oozing blood to an icy wetness.

Wincing, Donal rose and glanced at his own forearm. A spatter of cuts blossomed to patches of blood along his blue shirt. With a throaty growl, he grappled Nick in a bear hug and rammed his back into another pony that was propped against a tree.

Air shunted out of Nick's lungs when they collided—a bitter-hot rush bursting from his lips. Scalding jabs shot from between his hips to his spine. Gulping a breath, Nick braced his lower back and elbows on the pony for leverage and cuffed a knee into his opponent's abdomen to shove him off. The effort jarred Nick's leg from ankle to thigh and cast Donal into a backward sprawl. His bag of candy slipped from his trouser pocket and scattered to the ground.

Trying to regain balance, the Irishman stumbled toward the iron gate. The peppermint sticks rolled beneath his boots and tripped him. He landed, wedged between the busted pony's hind legs. The tail draped like a curtain from Donal's brow to his chin.

Dazed, Donal raked off the long straggly strands and shook his head to refocus.

Before his opponent could gather his bearings, Nick clasped his lapels, tensing to lift him. Hot red fury lapped at his soul. "You've been bullying her for months. Now she has me. And I'll see you dead before you'll ever hurt her again."

"Wait..." Donal caught his wrists. A trickle of blood crept down to stain the corner of his mouth. A small gash marked his lip; he must've bit it during the fall.

Nick paused, an exertion which strained every muscle

and tendon in his body. "Give me one reason..." He drew a measured breath into his lungs. "One reason not to pound you against those bars until your teeth fall out and I bag them up with those peppermints you're so fond of."

"Ye'll make balls of yer Da's visit if ye've killed a man."

Stunned, Nick let his fingers go limp and eased back, allowing the Irishman to crumple at his feet. "My Da? You mean my *father*? The hell you say." Nick looked around— half expecting his father to step out of the shadows and berate him.

"So ye don't know." Donal's statement grounded him. "I suspected such. See, I've done some checkin' on ye, Nicolas Thornton. I know ye nigh on ruined yer family's reputation by knockin' up an investor's wife. But yer not the only one who has a penchant for secrets. Seems yer wife has been lyin' to us both."

"What are you talking about?" Nick asked.

Donal gulped some air, his smug demeanor returning along with the deepening wash of color in his cheeks. "Fennigan tells me ye've bog workers on the way soon."

Nick gritted his teeth. "Right. To appease your bloody condition so you'll sign the contract about the peat bogs."

"I ne'er asked for a condition. Ne'er agreed to sign anythin'."

The angry roar hazed Nick's hearing again and he started toward Donal. "Backing out, are you?"

The man scooted on his haunches toward the fence, scuttling out of Nick's reach. "Yer wife's been lettin' on the malarky with everyone! It be the patrons of her caterpillar business comin' for a tour, and it be on the morrow." Groaning as he shoved onto his feet, Donal leaned against the gate and ran his palms along his thighs and arms, as if checking for injuries. "I stole her list ... sent the wires to bring 'em here. It was to force her hand, ye see. But she forced yers instead."

Nick froze, a sick thud starting at the base of his throat. Could this be what Felicity had meant earlier by *deceptions*?

A glint sparkled in Donal's amber eyes, as if he not only sensed but savored the ugly speculations going on inside Nick's mind. "Mayhap I'm mistaken, since ye'd already agreed to marry her when I made me last visit. She said ye were in town that very day to get a marriage license; it's why she was alone here, with the girls. That weren't a lie too, was it?"

A fine mist started to spatter all around—a cold awakening—as if raining down reality. Bits and pieces started snapping into place in Nick's memory. The guilt on Felicity's face at their wedding when she said she hoped he wouldn't have regrets, her discomfort each time they spoke of the bog workers, the extra hours she'd spent in the butterfly consortium the past few days and nights—as if readying things for inspection.

He swiped the rain from his face, blinking hard. No. Not Felicity. She'd lied to him about her barrenness, but not this.

She knew of his determination to never see his father again. She wouldn't betray him. Not her. Not the woman who understood him on a level no other human could.

Not the woman he loved.

Love.

The untimely epiphany lumped, mute and knotted, in his throat. He'd been lusting after her since the first day they met. Had his feelings evolved? Was he—a rogue, an addict, and a thief—capable of reaching such noble heights of sentiment?

This wasn't the time for such debate. One thing he knew: he trusted Felicity with his life. The Irishman was trying to put a rift between them. And that he wouldn't stand for. "You're a lying son of a—"

"Nay there." The rain had ceased and Donal wiped watery streaks of blood from his chin. "I can see ye have some issue with yer Da comin'. Must be why she kept it secret. But I've proof. In me jacket ... yer old man's at the top o' the list." He pointed toward the discarded piece of clothing rumpled on the ground.

Keeping a wary eye on his opponent, Nick bent to retrieve the article, his wet clothes sticking to him with each movement. Bits of glass rolled from the jacket and scattered to the ground as Nick searched in the pocket and drew out a piece of crisp parchment.

He held the paper to the faint moonlight. The corners flapped on the wind, but he could make out the script.

Like the Irishman claimed ... his father's name headed her London clientele.

Nick shoved the folded paper into his waistband. His legs numbed and he sat heavily on the carousel pony behind him, its curves hard and cold beneath his hands.

All along he'd thought their arrangement benefitted them both. He thought she was offering him sanctuary in exchange for him overseeing the bog enterprise. But those weren't the reasons she'd wanted to marry him at all. Men from London were coming. Men who might remember her past.

She should've warned him. In the very least, she could've told him his father was among the visitors.

But he would've turned tail and ran. She knew that. She kept him in the dark because she had no more faith in him than his old man did. No more faith than he had in himself.

"Wise up ye gack. Ye been bein' led by the wrong head. We both know what she is. Whores are good for two things

... lyin' and wettin' a man's stalk. Seein' as she lied to both of us, I think it be only fair I get to sample her other talent like ye have. Look what she did. Made a fool of ye for her own purposes. Reclaim yer pride, man. Turn around and walk away. Leave her to me ... I'll see she gets fair recompense. Just like me old Da wanted, before that bollox Clooney put a gap in his bush and ended his life."

Although Nick's thoughts were tangled up in his wounded ego, somewhere along the back roads of his mind, he remembered the heartrending sound of Felicity's gurgling cries as she sprawled on her back, twisting in agony from a gaping knife wound.

The image spurred a wildfire through his veins. He stood, slowly ... purposefully. "Clooney didn't cause your father's fall," he grumbled, his stomach tight and burning. "I did."

Donal's face contorted in shocked disbelief. "Nay, that not be possible. Ye would've been only—"

"Sixteen. Old enough to visit a brothel and throw that vile bastard down the stairs. My one regret is that his neck didn't snap the instant he hit the bottom. He deserved that and more for all the evil he heaped upon Felicity's life. But there's a saying where I'm from, about the sins of the father being visited upon the son."

Donal cocked his head, suddenly alert.

Oblivious to anything else around him, Nick plowed into the Irishman, propelling them both into the iron gate. They hit so hard the bell on the other side gonged with the jolt. Donal yowled upon impact.

Nick shoved his opponent's squirming body in place against the bars, pressed flush with him—nose to nose, thigh to thigh—to prevent any attempt at escape. He squeezed his captive's neck against the bars, clamping his windpipe. Donal clawed at his wrists. His strength surprised Nick, prompting him to tighten his grip even more.

The Irishman's inhalations threaded to tight whistles beneath the pressure; his peppermint breath stung Nick's nostrils and fed his flame.

He thought about taking out his knife and slicing the man's jugular. But this was much more satisfying. A perverse thrill rushed in as his captive started to flail and plead for release—eyes and veins bulging while he struggled to break Nick's hold. The face transformed to Hayes ... the hypocritical swine who'd stolen a young girl's childhood, raped her, and forced her into a life of depravity before ripping away any chance to claim a woman's dearest joy.

A toxic storm broke loose—his guilt for hurting Mina and the shame he felt when his father found him drugged out of his mind, combined with the helplessness of watching a young courtesan being drained of life. Every part of him, even the sockets of his eyes, pulsed with thunder and burned with venom.

He needed to stop the unending squall inside. To shut it down for good.

He'd once heard that killing someone released a high like no other. Laudanum be damned; he had a new drug now.

Turning Donal's neck loose and easing back an inch, he cinched his fingers through the man's frizzy, dark curls. Even as the Irishman gasped gratefully for breath, Nick slammed the back of his head into the gate—once, twice, three times—then lost count as the bell rang with each tremor.

Nick didn't feel the wetness on his own face until the wind swept across him. From somewhere behind, he vaguely heard Tobias's voice say, "Let him be, Lord Thornton. You're killing him." He barely noticed the shrill barking of a dog or registered the tap on his shoulder—prelude to someone grabbing him beneath his arms and peeling him off.

Enslaved by rage, Nick wrestled against the foreign hands. It took several more grasping fingers folded around his neck and shoulders to subdue him.

He only came back to himself when consecutive flashes of lightning lit up the scene, bringing everything into startling-bright focus.

First Nick noticed the aches in his body he'd been too engrossed to feel earlier. His nape throbbed where the glass had cut. Some must've sliced through his right upper thigh as well, because it was stinging noticeably. Then the surroundings became clear.

Tobias, Fennigan, and Clooney had hauled him a good three feet from the gate. Donal folded over in a slump, his nape slick with blood. Binata was on her knees beside him, crying. Lia was there, too, petting Donal's head and whimpering senseless words.

"I'm sorry Uncle Donal!" She sobbed. "I didn't know you were a dragon. I didn't know!"

Aislinn stroked the sprite's hair, trying to comfort.

Why the hell were the children here? Feeling a gentle touch on his arm, Nick looked down into Felicity's apologetic gaze.

"You should've told me," he accused.

The regret in her eyes only fueled his hurt.

He brushed off her hand and started toward Donal in Clooney's wake, dragging Fennigan and Tobias along with him as they attempted to hold him back.

"Take your sister into the castle," Nick said to Aislinn upon getting closer. "She shouldn't be here. Nor should you." His command came out much gruffer than he intended.

Nodding, Aislinn tugged on Lia's arm.

The sprite stood and stared up at Nick, hands laced

beneath her chin as if in prayer. "Please don't kill him, Mister Sir," she wailed. "My wish was bad! It was bad!" She sobbed harder, tears coating those long lashes.

"Hush now. Don't cry." Nick reached out to smooth her hair but she flinched away. Her reaction ripped him apart at the seams. Then he caught sight of the blood on his hands and understood. Ashamed, he stepped back to wipe his palms on his trousers.

Aislinn propped her sister against her and walk the path toward the castle with Nutmeg trailing them.

Binata glared up at Nick. He stumbled for words. "I-I don't know what came over me."

Clooney helped her lift Donal to his feet. Relief ushered through Nick when the Irishman met his gaze. The man was in somewhat of a stupor, but at least he could stand and walk. He staggered next to his aunt and the groundskeeper as they led him along the path behind the girls, leaving Nick alone with his wife.

She uttered his name—her voice little more than a tremor of air.

Jaw clenched against answering, he turned to look at the bars on the gate where Donal's blood glimmered dark and thick beneath another blaze of lightning. It was the very place Nick had held Felicity for a kiss so intense he lost sight of his shortcomings. Shortcomings that were now blatantly staring him in the face.

He didn't belong here. He'd tainted these people's lives just as he had Mina's and his family's.

Without sparing Felicity a glance, he headed for the castle. He sensed her silently following. Smelled her, tasted her, wanted her even now—despite her betrayal.

Why'd she have to look so beautiful tonight ... all aglow in the moonlight, the fuchsia of her gown reflecting in a rosy hue off her cheeks? He had to be hallucinating. Because she wasn't a rose. She was a thorn—hidden out of sight until one stepped upon her, bare-souled; then vicious and piercing, she drew blood.

His mind attempted to displace her presence, focusing instead on the pangs resonating throughout his injured body.

Still, she was everywhere.

They passed the greenhouse where she first stopped his breath with her childhood dreams; through the latticework tunnel covered with trumpet vines, where he hid and witnessed her bravery when she cracked her whip and left the Irishman's threats and sugary appetites crushed on the ground beneath his feet.

Upon their arrival in the castle, he paused long enough to peer into the dining hall and even found Felicity there, in the decorations so painstakingly set in place for a party which would never be.

He had a passing thought of Lia's request, and his soul twisted like a used rag. She would never ask him to bump her noggin for her birthday again, for she feared him now.

Biting back a groan, he noticed where Clooney and Binata tended Donal's wounds on the settee. The Irishman was talking, responsive to questions. It appeared he would be all right.

Nick started for the stairs, limping.

Felicity grabbed his shirt from behind. "Where are you going?"

His response came swift and biting. "To pack my things and leave."

CHAPTER THIRTY-THREE

Cold terror clawed through Felicity at his words. It wasn't just the statement that chilled, but the bitter resolve edging his voice.

"Nick, you cannot leave. Not like this..."

He turned on his heel. His eyes were as dark and lifeless as tarnished steel—as if the bruises on his soul had seeped into their depths, dulling them.

Bruises born of her actions.

She waited for him to speak, but he held his stubborn lips tight. Daring her to give him a reason to stay.

"We're married," she whispered the lame attempt.

He launched a brittle laugh. "That's a rather lofty claim. We've not even consummated the union. We were *playing* at marriage. Adrift on clouds of pretense and fantasy." His strong jaw twitched as he took off his ring. "The thing about clouds, Felicity. They have a tendency to dissipate. The sun breaks through and bares reality down to its raw, grisly bones."

He offered the ring and she took it, reluctant. Her teeth clenched. If he thought she would give up so easily, he was sorely mistaken.

"You speak of reality? Here is your reality." She forced the ring back on his pinky and curled his fingers closed. His skin felt hot against hers. "Those girls need you now more than ever. Jasper never finalized his will. My nieces are not legally mine. And should my past come out when I've no husband to vie for me..." The possibility stalled in her throat to a grinding lump.

His answering scowl pierced like poison arrows. "Those girls think I'm a monster. They saw me nearly kill a man they consider family. And I'm to be a father to them? You sold your brooch for naught, Felicity. There's no music box grand enough to salvage Lia's faith in me now. Take it from one who knows: trust is impossible to win back once it's lost."

His focus tightened on her and she flinched at the double entendre. "No. She'll forgive and forget in no time."

"She saw my hands covered in blood!" He held up his palms in the light. "The sprite's terrified of me. She thinks I'll hurt her. Me ... who believes her an angel—" His voice cracked. "Damnit! Why the hell did you bring them with you?"

"I didn't realize they were following. My only thought was—"

"Silencing the Irishman," Nick intoned, rubbing a palm across his smooth chin. "My father is on his way to this castle. The one man I've gone to the ends of the earth to avoid. For weeks you've known, yet you deemed it acceptable to keep me in the dark." He looked down at the ring on his pinky. "You've done nothing but lie to me."

Felicity tugged her gaze away. He was right. She'd cost him any chance at an heir and left him bound and gagged at the feet of his most crippling fear. What a fine wife she had turned out to be.

Trying to distance herself from the guilt, she regarded his appearance in search of injuries. She'd never seen a man so overcome with righteous fury that he'd forget his own welfare. But she had once seen a boy of sixteen who shared that characteristic.

Twice now he had fought for her, throwing caution to the wind. Her heart tumbled at his devotion. To think she'd repaid him through dishonesty and selfishness made the regret so palpable it stitched pinholes of fire along her scar, like a needle threaded with flame.

The time had come for him to know everything. Every last secret.

Noting the blood wetting his trousers on his right thigh, she caught his wrist. "Come." She didn't let him pull free. Instead, she led him into the kitchen and sat him on a stool. "We need to see to your wounds."

He slumped in place—broad shoulders hunched as he stared down at the marble floor, the thick muscles in his neck corded and strained. It was apparent he had let her win the battle only on the grounds that he was weary from the war.

Felicity glanced at the birthday meal Cook had prepared earlier. Fried potato farls, whortleberries, barmbrack bread, and pickled crúibíns waited in trays on an island crafted of pine which matched the larder cupboard opposite Nick's stool. The scent of the food filled the room—a taunting reminder of happy memories never to be made.

Lianna's birthday had morphed into a nightmare.

Felicity fisted her hands against an overwhelming urge to check on the child. In her present state of mind, she would do nothing but add to Lianna's angst. Her eldest niece would be the best company for now. If anyone could get Lianna settled and asleep, it would be Aislinn—with her level temperament and soothing ways.

The rain started again. Heavy droplets pelted the

window—a melancholy song that did little to lift Felicity's spirits. Searching within the cupboard, pushing aside preserves and wines, she found a bottle of Irish whiskey, new and unopened. When she worked off the cork, it popped over her head and landed atop Lianna's untouched birthday cake, leaving a dent in the white, fluffy frosting.

"She'll think that was my doing," Nick said with a self-deprecating grimace.

"I shall tell her it was mine." Felicity stepped behind him and coaxed his head forward to a bowed position. She untied the cravat he'd wound around his hair and pushed the loosened golden fall aside. Her fingers glided through the soft strands and she longed to bury her nose in them. To breathe in that scent which left her senses spiraling to heavenly heights.

He stiffened beneath her touch.

Checked by his obvious repulsion, she concentrated on the glimmering bits of glass. Oh, to go back to earlier today, when he touched and kissed her with unrestrained abandon. When he offered to fix her. Before he'd realized how very unfixable she was.

Plucking shards from his nape, she dropped each one with a clink into an empty bowl. Blood bloomed across his skin like miniature petals unfolding. She used a soft washcloth doused with whiskey to dab the cuts.

He hissed and flinched at her ministrations.

In spite of his reaction, she reaped a deep and possessive pleasure in tending his needs. If only she could be the one to nurture him for the rest of his life. After tonight's disasters, she'd be lucky if she had him even one more day.

Upon finishing his nape, she knelt beside him, running her palm over his injured thigh. "How did you do this?"

Shoving long strands of hair off his face, he stared at the

back of her hand so intensely she felt a burn and removed it from his leg.

"The trousers aren't torn." She tried again to engage him in conversation. "So the cut is underneath the fabric ... you didn't have your knife in your pocket, did you?"

His hand drifted to the pocket just above the seeping wound. He lingered there, fingers trembling, as if contemplating what was within. "Wrong side," he muttered absently. "The men coming in the morn. Your patrons. They're more than mere butterfly boomers."

Felicity startled, taken aback by his swift change in subject. "Yes. Three of them were Jasmine's clients."

"My father," Nick murmured. "Was he one?"

Felicity winced. She could only imagine how long that ugly possibility had been twisting in his mind. "Oh, no. No, Nick. I've never even met him. But I know he must be very honorable."

"You know, do you."

"I do. For his son is the noblest man I've ever known."

His lashes drifted up to unveil immeasurable depths of suffering. "According to my father, I'm no man at all."

Laying her palm on his knee, Felicity squeezed. "I don't believe that."

"And I intend to see that you'll never have reason to."

Confused by the cryptic response, Felicity frowned. He tensed against her and she realized he wanted to stand. "No. You need to rest."

He took her hand in his, held it far too short a span, then pushed it aside. "I need to think."

"You're still considering leaving?"

His Adam's apple moved on a swallow.

The tenor of his silence stung like a slap. "So, you're choosing to run again. Just like you always have."

"This from the woman who hides in a castle."

"Fair enough. Then come with me ... come with me to the turret and I'll show you why I hide." She clasped her fingers through his. At this point, she was so determined to keep him with her she'd even share him with Mina's ghost.

He jerked free. "I've no desire to look at those broken stairs again. Just like everything with you, they lead nowhere but an agonizing descent into bleakness and shadows."

The acerbic comment stirred a prick behind her eyelids. Ugly images of her past sins with men tore through her, and she wondered if the same pictures taunted his mind's eye. "At last you see me for what I am. A disreputable, disfigured whore."

He leaned forward on the stool and clutched her mouth. "*Never* say that," he snarled. "Never say those words again." His grip pinched and his gaze penetrated. Coming back to himself, he dropped his hand, face pale in the dim light.

Felicity felt a chill from his abandoned hand, then warmth as blood started to refill the fingerprints where he'd squeezed her. She turned away, ashamed to let him see her tears. Desperate for something to do, she walked to the island. Hands aquiver, she dug the cork from Lianna's cake and cleaned it off. She couldn't help but remember the frosting from the wedding cake—how she'd shared that flavor with Nick in a deep, binding kiss after their dance in the dining hall.

Upon shoving the cork into the whiskey bottle's neck, she held the cool glass against her chest in hopes to stop the scalded swell along her scar.

Before she'd even taken a breath, Nick stood behind her, close enough his body heat taunted and teased. She ached to burrow her head beneath his chin. To absorb his strength. To feel love surround her as he held her in his arms.

But it was all fancy and whim. For he'd never once even mentioned love. That was why he wouldn't stay. He didn't love her.

It doesn't matter. I love you enough for both of us. Her confession remained mute—tightly tethered to her heart. Because however sweet the words, her actions implied otherwise and he would never believe her now.

She felt some movement against her hip and an expectant tingle awakened in her core at his proximity before she realized he was digging in his right pocket. Reluctant to turn around, she faced the island and the neglected food, waiting blindly for his next move. Anticipation and dread cinched her stomach into a tangle.

"You once told me to forgive myself of my sins against Mina," he said as his ribs pressed against her shoulder blades. "It's time you take your own advice."

The fabric of her bodice caught on his shirt sleeve as his hand eased around to place something on the island's edge.

"I made this for you," he said. "In hopes you could finally fly above your sadness and regret. All I've ever wanted was to be your sanctuary. A place of safety where you could light and perch when your wings grew weary." His breath stroked her nape.

When he lifted his palm away, she gaped at what waited beneath.

Never had she seen a more beautiful rendition of a woman. So delicate ... so intricate. Her husband must've worked on the carving both day and night. All at once, she realized: this was his perception of her.

She was naked, her breasts a gentle rise of twin curves, her belly softly rounded, legs long and flawless.

Flawless ... the ideal description. For this woman's figure had been sanded to perfection. She bore no scars, no splinters, no lines to detract from her sensual appeal.

And wings. Butterfly wings splayed out from behind her shoulders—the one part of her which had been painted to a vivid burst of color.

A whimper caught in her chest. This dear, sweet man had given her wings.

In trembling reverence, Felicity trailed a finger along the carving's left appendage where it must have snapped during his scuff with Landrigan. A wet, reddish stain colored the splintered tip.

Nick's blood.

"You know"—his murmur brushed her nape— "I debated about the scar. Left it off in the end to please you. But it's better with her broken. She's more valuable this way. There's a wisdom and depth to her—an aching loveliness which haunts the beholder into his very dreams."

Sobbing quietly, Felicity could look at nothing but her husband's masterpiece. What a fool she'd been. He loved her. Who needed words? His actions had been screaming the sentiment for weeks. She'd simply lacked faith enough to listen. And now ... now she'd trampled those feelings to dust.

"Felicity," he said against the shell of her ear, "there's something you have that I want. Very much."

A hot flush of hope warmed her body.

Yes. Say you forgive me, say you still love me... say you want my heart. My body. They're yours already. They've been yours since the first time I saw you, when you begged for me to live. When you made it possible that I could.

Felicity struggled to turn around, to throw herself into his embrace and sing the admittance like a hymn of praise, beg him to take her upstairs and open the floodgates of their passions. But he held her wedged against the island so she couldn't move. His arm crossed her from behind and he caught the whiskey bottle at her chest, jostling the contents within the glass to assure it was full.

Only then did she understand...

"Don't come looking for me," he said roughly. "I prefer to drink alone." He tugged the bottle from her grasp and left the room.

She squeezed her eyes shut, her erratic pulse tied to the volley of his footsteps and the slamming quake of the castle door.

Tinkling strains drifted from the phonograph—a haunting melody which echoed in the dim turret.

Felicity inhaled the familiar scents of dormancy: the warm musk of Jasper's sleep-ridden body; the sting of stale disinfectants; the heavy weight of dust caked along rain-drenched windows.

Lightning blinked, and thunder rolled through her bones.

Seated on the bed's edge, she waited for the music to invoke her brother's spirit. She studied him in the orange-gold flickers of candle light. Never had she felt closer to him. Dead on the outside—numb and drained of life like a tree in winter. But on the inside, emotions boiled like untapped sap—a constant humming tide of subsistence, clawing to be free.

For so long she'd been going through the motions of living. It took a man like Nick to tap that vein, to show her how much she'd been missing.

The same things that she loved about him, she also envied. His contagious wit and almost dewy-eyed eagerness to embrace the unbelievable. The raging fury of a defender held at bay by the gentle spirit of a lover. The ability to give of himself freely and unreservedly, honest to a fault.

Her lips battled a wry smile. Who would've thought a thief could be honest?

She'd been so blind not to see his feelings for her. Perhaps because they reached far beyond lust or shallow animalistic needs. Love was a depth of emotion she'd never experienced from a man, other than her father and Clooney's paternal affections, and Jasper's sibling adoration.

Unconditional, abiding love wasn't at all about pretty words spoken in the heat of a physical act. It was an execution of silent, selfless deeds played out in the shadows so as not to call attention to themselves.

And it wasn't only her that Nick loved.

He had given away his best friend in the world, just to put a smile on Lianna's face. And he'd sold his diamond—that one connection to Mina—to provide for Felicity and the girls. He did those things believing he wouldn't witness or reap the benefits of their gratitude.

Love was enacting without expectation. He'd done that for all three of them.

She had tried to mimic him. But her attempt paled because her motivations weren't pure. Yes, she'd given away her mother's precious gift. But it wasn't just for him. It was for her, too ... so he might be moved enough by the gesture to stay after tomorrow.

Now that she understood her failing, she would atone. She would let him leave for his own peace of mind, and deal with the consequences on her own.

Jasper's lashes began to quiver, opening slowly. His gaze locked on hers.

"Good evening, dear brother." She sighed. "I hope you're ready to come home. Whatever you have to do to put yourself back in your body permanently ... Tis time to do it."

Delving into the jar of fungal paste she'd made to treat her scar, she smoothed the purple mixture over Jasper's forehead and temples, then smudged a circle atop his sternum, just over his heart.

His eyes followed her movements.

She felt inclined to explain. "I can't decide if it's your head or your heart keeping you away. So, we're trying both."

The idea had occurred shortly after Nick left her crying in the kitchen. If the fungus could rejuvenate passion flowers and heal fresh wounds, perhaps it could bring her brother back to himself. Perhaps that had been what his spirit was trying to tell her all along, by leaving trails of it on the sickly vines in the greenhouse.

Jasper's gaze sat heavy upon her, a question darkening their oceanic blue depths.

She awaited his whisper, but he seemed too drowsy yet to attempt it. To bridge the silence, she took a guess as to what he might be wondering.

"I've made a terrible mess of everything," she said, wiping the purple paste from her fingers and returning the lid to her jar. "I've trapped the man I love into an unthinkable position. The only way I can right this and not lose the girls is for you to return. Then Nick can avoid his past and leave us without any reservations. If the girls' father is here—fully lucid—and can speak for himself, no one will take them away even after my identity is revealed."

Humiliation stuck in her lungs and made her breaths shallow. She would be recognized tomorrow without a doubt. Those three men she'd told Nick of had been monthly regulars to Jasmine. She'd lived up to her name; became their transport to sexual bliss, however much she'd abhorred it.

They would remember her for that—regardless of any shoddy disguise.

Knowing that, she was not to wear the wrinkles tomorrow. Already the lines were fading, and she wouldn't reapply her cream ever again. She was finished with this masquerade. Tonight, her servants would see her for who she was, and tomorrow, so would her patrons.

Nick didn't want to embrace his past any more than she did hers, yet here she'd asked him to do it for the girls' sake without a mask to hide behind. Even if Jasper didn't come back, Felicity would face her guests head on—bared and exposed. Because that's what she had asked of Nick.

All these years she'd deprived her girls of life by forcing them to hide from *her* mistakes. It was time they attended school and mass and made friends their age. The only way that would ever happen was if she finally made peace with her past and moved forward. Just like Nick said. It was time she forgave herself and embraced the woman she had grown to be. Being loved by a man as benevolent and giving as Nicolas Thornton, enabled her to see herself for who she really was.

She was a fighter. Those cruel years had given her the power to fend for herself, but Nick's love gave her the mettle she once lacked. Surely these men coming wished to keep their affiliation with her secret just as much as she did. There was such a thing as blackmail. Should they threaten her family, she would shake them in their high and mighty trees, and let the leaves fall where they may.

"*Your heart...*" Jasper's whisper shook Felicity from her defiant thoughts.

Her pulse jittered. "My heart will survive Nick leaving," she answered her brother's piercing gaze. "As long as I have you and the girls."

"*Lies...*" The muscles in his face twitched to a scowl.

She nearly choked, both thrilled to see her brother find

the strength to defy her and leveled by the wisdom in that one word. "Yes! It's a lie. My whole life has been a lie. Here's the only truth there is: I love him; I need him. I want him beside me from this day forward. But I've brought him nothing but misery and pain. No more. I'm setting him free. Make it simpler. Come back to us tonight."

The turret door creaked open to reveal Aislinn's weary face. "Yes, Father." She padded in her stockinged feet toward the bed. "Come back. We need you."

Felicity wondered how long she'd been listening. "Is your sister asleep?"

Aislinn nodded without turning from Jasper whose gaze had shifted to her.

"Bini promised to check on her." Aislinn stroked her father's beard. "After Clooney is done treating Mister Landrigan's wounds." She studied her father's prone form, focused on the spread of purple at his chest. She didn't even ask. By the way she touched her own healed forehead, it was obvious she understood. "No one has been able to find Nick," the girl muttered, a worried pinch to her voice.

A boom of thunder shook the window panes, as if an omen.

Felicity's body numbed. "I've lost him."

"He's leaving you? Due to his fight with Mister Landrigan? Or was it your secrets? He isn't worthy of you Auntie, if he can't accept your scar."

Before Felicity could jump to Nick's defense, Jasper's gaze began to seek about the room, frantic.

"Lianna's wish..." His whisper—panicked and hissing—stretched louder than the chords of music in the background. *"Heaven ... help her."* His left hand shot out to snag Felicity's fingers, squeezing them. Then the music stopped and his eyes snapped shut.

Mouth agape, Felicity met Aislinn's shocked gaze. The candles snuffed out on a gust of frigid wind, leaving the turret ensconced in darkness.

CHAPTER THIRTY-FOUR

What had he expected? To go through life and never face his old man again? Never face the consequences of all the shame he'd brought upon his family?

Hell yes.

Legs stretched and crossed at the ankle, Nick took another swig of whiskey and let it burn from his esophagus to his belly. Leaning his head against the musty wooden wall, he glanced up at the outlook's low-hung ceiling.

He lifted his pinky to study the wedding ring Felicity had forced back onto his finger. It wasn't just facing his family that stone-cold terrified him. It was the possibility of his bride learning the truth. That her husband was once so weak he nearly sold his body to an abusive man who wished to own him.

She'd be as repulsed as his father—unable to ever wash the image from her mind. Once she knew how low he'd crawled, he'd lose the ability to hide the fact from himself.

Johnny Boy's company had been so much easier to maintain. Such an uncomplicated comfort. One never had to worry about disappointing a dog.

Nostalgic for the pit bull's crooked grin, Nick watched the kerosene lantern sway in the midst of the ceiling. The flame he'd lit flickered within the globe, stirred by the rain-dampened gusts seeping through opened windows. Cobwebs coated the copper framework of the lamp. A spider scurried along the sylphlike lines, repairing one that the gust broke free.

Little blood-thirsty acrobat, setting its trap.

Nick snorted, gulping down another sip. What he wouldn't give to switch places with the insect: his only concern the completion of a masterpiece and the appeasement of appetites.

Then again, it seemed they had more in common than he cared to admit. He fingered the carving knife still at rest in his pocket. He'd used his masterpiece to suck the life from someone tonight. That might've been his blood on the carving's broken wing, but it was Felicity's soul pierced by the tip.

He'd savored it—wounding her with the gift that had been meant to free her. His bitter victory was palpable. He could almost taste the salt of her tears on his tongue.

His stomach seized at such cruelty.

Gritting his teeth, he banged his head against the wall to silence his conscience. He had no reason to be penitent. She was the one who lied. He might've started out as an imposter, but in the end, all his words and actions had been genuine and heartfelt.

Lot of bloody good it did.

Focused on the windows, he sucked down more fiery liquid and hissed as the sky streaked to brilliance on a splay of lightning—illumining glittery sheets of rain.

The memory of Felicity sitting opposite him in this place bit with the vengeance of an asp. She'd laid out her tortured past here. Admitted her walk as a courtesan. Yet he never accepted that as her profession because she did not choose that path. He still didn't accept it, in spite of her treachery.

Hands clenched around the bottle, he shuddered.

He'd clenched her mouth when she'd called herself a whore earlier. His fingers left white streaks on her lips until blood filled the print back in. It wasn't a slap ... not driven by maliciousness or violence; it wasn't enacted out of rage or oppression. He'd wanted to get her attention, for her to realize that those words should never leave her beautiful lips. But emotions had been too intense, and he'd held her a moment too long. He only hoped it wouldn't leave a physical bruise. He'd never forgive himself if he'd marked her.

He winced—the thought unbearable. He should've kissed her to silence instead.

His head tipped back so another trail of liquor could scorch his throat. Lightning flashed and he held up the bottle to find the contents half gone. He'd have to pace himself if he wished it to last.

Closing his eyes, he held his cold ring to his lips and tried to forget the effect Felicity had on him when he braced her against that island in the kitchen. How her hair had caught on his cheek as he leaned over to set the carving on the edge. How his nose grazed her ear when he whispered to her. How the scent of her nigh undid him.

That damn perfume—botanical, citrusy.

Ambrosia.

A blast of thunder forced his eyes open.

Grinding his heels into the floor, he shoved his spine hard against the wall and growled. How could he even consider leaving her? The girls?

The three of them were his world now.

Felicity, who left him beguiled and bewildered each time her face lit up like a dreamy child's while tending her butterflies. Who challenged him at every turn—intellectually, emotionally, and spiritually. Who leveled him to reverence with the maternal nurturing she rained upon her nieces.

At times, she frustrated him. Her stubbornness, her independence, her cynicism and inability to trust. But the tenderness her vulnerability inspired, and his awe at her capacity for forgiveness—a reserve so deep he could drown in it—went far beyond any emotion he'd felt in all his years.

He drained more of the whiskey, not even tasting it this time.

And the girls ... little Lia's tongue, sharp as her aunt's whip yet sweet as clover wine. Her outlook on life, so innocent and untouched. The way she took his hand and made him feel like he could conquer the world and all its dragons—just for her. And Aislinn: her stunning intellect, irreverent wit, and perceptive empathy. Her desire to right every wrong, and her extraordinary devotion to a father long dead.

A devotion Nick envied. For to face his own father, to once more see the look of disappointment in that steady gray gaze would be hell on earth.

The heaviness in his chest threatened to strangle him. Throwing caution to the storm, he sealed his mouth around the bottle's spout. He would drink every last drop—teeter into oblivion and forget everything: this night, his choices, and the weight of responsibility heavy on his shoulders.

If he required another bottle to send him over the edge ... well, there was always more where this came from.

He closed his eyes to let the whiskey glide down, barely aware of a frigid gust until it circled him like a whirlwind. The sensation shook him enough to open his eyes when the gust abruptly changed direction.

As if caught by the wind, the bottle snapped out of his hand. A jolt rushed through his lips as the glass flew to the opposite wall—knocked there by some unseen force. Slack-jawed, Nick chewed his tongue. The remaining liquor leaked onto the wooden floor and drizzled between the slats.

A surge of leaves fluttered around the small space. Weak-legged and woozy, Nick stood, back propped against the wall. He didn't remember there being any leaves earlier. Certainly not such sodden and decayed specimens. They were black as velvet and made no sound.

Not a scrape, not a crackle. Simply ... *swished.*

He realized with a stunned yelp that they weren't leaves at all. They were shadows.

Butterfly shadows...

"Jasper," he whispered, hoping it wasn't the liquor toying with his mind. He'd waited so long to meet the man—the spirit.

Dizziness bumbled his thoughts. If this was truly happening, the professor had succeeded ... he'd somehow joined his spirit to the butterflies. That must mean it was possible to cross into the afterlife...

The shadows came together to form a silhouette. It lifted an arm and pointed out the window in the direction of the storm-shaken trees.

What was it trying to tell him? Was it showing him the way to Mina?

Nick didn't budge, his thoughts still chained to Felicity. A sensation of sandpaper scraped his throat. All those miserable months spent seeking the portal to his dead bride, and here it was staring him in the face. Yet the only thing on his mind was how to cross to his living bride, the one woman who haunted him day and night.

Nick took too long to respond to the silhouette. In a gesture which could only be construed as frustration, the shadows shrugged and burst apart, snuffing out the lantern.

Disoriented by the darkness, Nick pressed his shoulders harder against the wall. A pulsing cold breeze rushed over his skin then caught hold, winding him within its momentum. Falling off balance, air shunted from his lungs upon impact with the floor. The cold wind scuttled over him, dragged him to the opened trapdoor, then tugged him through.

In an inebriated fog, he gouged his fingernails into the splintered edge and held on—shoulders overextended to the point of pain and legs flailing wildly. Sharp pelts of rain sobered him enough to react. He caught the rope with his ankle and managed to ease it over and grasp it. Friction burned his palms as he descended.

Lightning lit up the surroundings the instant his boots met the ground. The silhouette awaited him, beckoning in the direction of the peat bogs. Nick nearly laughed at the irony of it all. A month ago, he would've followed the butterflies anywhere—especially into death. But now he valued life enough to hesitate.

Impatient, the ghostly image motioned for him to follow. Nick sensed desperation in its persistence. His gaze flitted to the tombstone in the distance. Jasper hadn't come back from the dead for nothing. He was trying to tell him something urgent.

Against his reservations, Nick complied ... mud sucking at his heels as he sprinted into the forest's looming depths.

Tree branches scored Nick's shirt as he lifted his arms to protect his face. If he hadn't been in such a hurry to escape Felicity tonight in the kitchen, he might've remembered his rifle-frock coat.

The whiskey's warmth had long since dissipated in the downpour, as had its numbing effects. Moisture seeped from his hair to his shirt's neck, inching across his glass-sliced nape like icy snails. Shivering, he folded up his collar.

His throat scratched, dry from heavy panting. He flitted out his tongue to sample the rain gathered on his lips then continued onward. With each step, his soles tugged against the suction of mud, leaving behind a muck of fallen leaves and heavily scented pine needles. Soggy, foot high grasses reached for his shins. They clung like spindly-fingered children frightened by the storm. His wounded thigh ached with the battle to move forward.

Darkness coated the wooded landscape, deep shadows compounded by heavy trees overhead. The canopy blocked any light from the clouded sky.

He had no idea where he was headed. He'd trekked through the sludge for what seemed an eternity. His body was weary, his head spun—disoriented by the lack of light and alcohol. But each time he lost his way, all he had to do was stop and wait. The ghost ... Jasper ... whatever his guide was, would shove him from behind with a gust of wind.

At last Nick plunged through a fringe of low hanging moss. Lightening rippled through the clouds. In the blink of light, his guide vanished on an explosion of shadows. At the same instant, Nick caught sight of a thousand pale specks floating in the puddles all around, as if it had snowed.

Upon another lightning flash, it registered.

Forget-me-nots.

Jasper had led him to the bog where he'd hiked with Felicity and the girls earlier today. The rains had washed the flowers from their field and deposited them all about the flooded surroundings.

Here in the clearing, the sky opened. The cloud-draped moon shimmered, casting a bluish haze over everything. Nick could recognize shapes ... forms. One in particular startled his breath to stall: a four-legged beast grazing far to his right.

Before he could register what kind of animal it was, a faint, mewling cry lifted from the bog. A boom of thunder muffled the sound, so loud it jolted Nick's heart to pound again—a rampant drumbeat in his chest.

Shivering, he waited, hoping he'd imagined the sound in his drunken state. Praying he was wrong ...

Then he heard the cry once more, louder this time. The animal to his right nickered as if acknowledging a familiar voice, revealing itself.

Butterscotch ...

"God, no. Lia!" Half groaning, half yelling, Nick bolted to the bog's edge. Impossible. She could never have found this place alone.

Mortification knotted in his throat as he remembered Felicity's point that the pony would always know the way to the bog now that it had grazed here.

The memory of Lia's last words scored his soul: *This is my fault. My wish was bad! It was bad!*

That's what she'd meant. She blamed herself for Nick's fight with Landrigan. And she'd come to stop the badness— to take back the napkin with her wish in it ... whatever it was.

No. *No!*

Rain slammed his face. Lightning torched the sky and revealed a tiny blonde head, trying to stay afloat in the peat bog amidst thousands of severed forget-me-nots. His muscles tensed, ready to dive in.

Quicksand...

Felicity's warning came back and stalled him. He had to be smart. To do this right. Or he'd be no help at all. His fingers gouged into his temples. Lord, why couldn't he remember her instructions?

Shaking off his dizziness and cursing the whiskey for thickening his thoughts, he called Lia's name again.

Her answering cry—weaker now—was the only incentive he required. His pulse raged and he sobered immediately.

"I'm coming, angel!" What was it Felicity had told him? *Find nearby vegetation attached to solid ground. No jerky movements. Lie flat with your limbs spread wide.*

"Grab onto something sturdy! Pretend you're a water bug, Lia. Do you hear me? Spread out your arms and legs. You're a water bug!"

A wailing sniffle answered and he thanked God she was somehow managing to stay afloat enough to breathe.

Though he could barely make her silhouette out for the rain and shadows, he waded into the icy depths in the direction of her whimpers. He kept up a stream of constant chatter, his voice gentle in hopes to soothe her, knowing if she struggled she'd get drawn in deeper.

When the frigid depths deepened and the bottom sucked at his feet, he filled his lungs and allowed his legs to drift upward in an effort to float. The stench of stagnancy overwhelmed. Wetness seeped into his clothes and the tiny blue flowers clung to his face and neck. He felt his way with his hands much like Felicity had with her feet, grabbing nearby vines and vegetation connected to mats of solid ground to drag himself along the water's surface.

The rain started to pound harder, slapping the water in a steady rhythm so he had to strain to hear Lia.

Several consecutive blinks of lightning lit up the scene and he saw her hanging onto the very tree that once held her wish at its tip. Its mat had fallen over—a result of the rising water.

"Good girl! Just keep holding on, little water bug." He was almost close enough to touch her now, and his every nerve jumped in anticipation. To embrace her. To keep her safe. That's all that mattered.

At this proximity he should be able to see the glitter of her eyes as her lashes fluttered upward, to see splotches of mud upon her tiny face. But he could only see a bush of matted hair interspersed with soggy forget-me-nots.

"Lia ... look at me, child."

For some reason, she wouldn't turn her head.

"M-m-mister S-s-sir," she sobbed and shook simultaneously. Poor little sprite had to be freezing.

"I'm right here." He clasped at a sturdy mat about four feet away then cast out his free hand, gulping a grateful breath when her cold, pruned fingers clasped his. "Let go of the tree now, baby. C'mon. Come to me."

"I c-c-can't! M-m-my hair..." She sobbed again.

Nick bit back a curse. That's why she couldn't turn her head. Her hair had tangled in the branches. The memory of her asking to wear it down tonight taunted him. He tried to draw her closer ... to pull the tree his way, but it was embedded by its roots.

He considered the knife in his pocket. He could cut her tangles loose. But to get to her, he'd have to relinquish his grasp on solid ground. And if he joined her on the tree, it might sink beneath their combined weight.

Thunder clapped overhead and the horrifying image of his stillborn son, blue and breathless, stamped his brain. He would not let Lia die alone like Christian had. He would not let her die at all.

Turning loose the grounded mat, Nick drifted to the whimpering child.

Her icy body clasped him when he joined her at the tree. With one arm he looped the spiky trunk, and with the other enfolded her.

Her trembles shook his body.

"Shhhh. I've got you now." He spoke into her knotted hair

to shush her cries and tasted the slime and putrid mud coating the strands. Pity engulfed him for all the terrors she'd faced this night. "It's all right, tiny beauty. I won't let you go."

And I will never *leave you.*

She managed to slant her face enough to grind her nose into his neck. Her hot tufts of breath warmed his freezing blood. "I d-d-don't want to be a w-w-water bug anymore."

Surprised by the untimely humor in the statement, he smiled bitterly. His eyes burned with tears. Grateful she couldn't see them, he forced his voice to be strong. "All right. But for us to get out of here, I have to cut your hair with my knife." Remembering how she'd witnessed his rage tonight, he worried she'd resist. "Do you trust me to do that?"

Face still pressed into his neck, she nodded and sniffled "You're the p-p-prince. Auntie's hero..."

Though the words razed his raw heart, her faith gave him hope. But that hope was short-lived, for the tree started to sink the instant he drew out his blade.

CHAPTER THIRTY-FIVE

Nick was determined to beat the odds.

The rain hadn't let up. Wavelets licked his shoulders, rising too fast. He tilted Lia's side of the sinking trunk so it would buoy her out of the water.

He couldn't acknowledge the hopelessness. That even once he got the child free, they had little chance of escaping the bog. Most of the mounds of land he'd used to draw himself here were treading water by now.

Gravely, he sawed at Lia's beautiful hair, cutting as close to the branches as possible. With little visibility, he took extra care to slant the blade away from her. When she'd whimper from the pulls at her scalp, he'd stop and give her quarter for no more than a moment's breath, knowing that each such hesitation cost them precious time.

His fingers grew numb, making it difficult to be accurate. He was finishing the last clump, sawing the blade back and forth, when a splitting sound erupted over the raindrops. It started as a whispering hiss beneath them then escalated to a popping snap all around. Shivering from the cold, he sliced the last of Lia's hair free, dropped the knife, and tightened his grip around her waist.

"Hold your breath!" He shouted just before the tree trunk

buckled in half and the side they held plummeted into the water. Icy depths submerged and separated them.

He lost the knife as Lia's chilled fingers clawed at his body. Blindly he tugged her to him as he kicked his legs, propelling them upward. He broke them out, but Lia leeched onto him and acted as an anchor. They only surfaced long enough to grapple some air before being pulled under again. The descending tree's branches caught his feet, towing him down.

Dark dread cloaked his thoughts. He had to get Lia above the surface or she'd die. Fighting every urge to inhale water, he pried her off of his torso and guided her upward, helping her settle on his shoulders. Her pant legs bunched his nape and billowed around his face in the current. Holding tight to her ankles, he managed to wrestle his legs free of the branches just as the trunk met the bottom and jolted to a stop.

By some miracle, the busted tree landed perpendicular and Nick balanced precariously on its jagged tip. Fully submerged himself, he lifted Lia high enough out of the water so she could angle her nose and catch breaths. The current's undertow threatened his stance. His lungs curled and wilted, craving oxygen.

The knowledge he was going to fail her severed deep.

Just when he started to fade away and lose balance, Lia's legs tightened around his neck, as though she reached for something. He felt her being lifted. Half-dazed, he kept hold of her ankles, and upon emerging, gasped for precious breath. His lungs ballooned and inhaled—hungry for life.

Blinking wetness from his eyes, he could see them being dragged toward the bank. Though the image blurred, Felicity's voice rang loud and clear. Lanterns lined the embankment. Everyone was here—Felicity, Binata, Clooney, the stable hands, Cook, even Donal—towing on the line that Lia held tight in her little hands.

Soon, he and the sprite were pulled into the shallows and aground.

The stable hands and Donal lifted Nick onto the banks and rolled him to his side. Water and sludge spewed up from his lungs with hacking coughs. Clooney and the others tended to Lia who wept hysterically, caught somewhere between elation and horror.

Amidst the fuzz of oxygen-deprived thoughts, it registered Felicity had somehow used her whip to ferry them out. Everyone else had formed a chain with their bodies to extend it far enough. Pale blue flowers clung to his rescuers' drenched clothes in tribute to their efforts.

Everyone started bustling around him and Lia—wrapping them in blankets and holding up lanterns to check for wounds. Nick glanced up as Felicity turned from the child momentarily, her face lit by the soft glow.

"Her hair," his voice came out in a coarse whisper. "Was tangled. Had to chop it…"

Felicity nodded and knelt beside him, her once lovely dress streaked with mud. The sleeves must've torn in her battle to get here through the clutching trees and they fluttered about her shoulders in the wind, like wings.

No other woman but his bride could make rags look like the raiment of a butterfly.

Tears streamed her cheeks … or was it rain? In a knee-jerk reaction, he started to wipe them away. Felicity caught his hand, sandwiched it between both of hers, and pressed her lips atop her knuckles. After one long, gasping breath, her shoulders began to shake with shuddering sobs—and he knew she'd held strong for everyone and only now could let her defenses down.

In a dreamlike stasis, he pulled her closer and rubbed his mouth across her hands. Her wet skin tasted like salt and honey.

Gratitude bridged her gaze to his, so sincere and beautiful every bit of residual anger shirked from its presence. How could he blame her for her choices? Now, more than ever, he understood with cutting clarity the lengths a person would go to protect a child they loved.

"Thank God for you," she whispered, stroking his face from his temple to his jaw. "*Thank God for you.*"

The numbing fog started to lift, and reality overtook. He sat up, allowing Felicity to help him stand.

Tobias, Fennigan, and the Irishman were off in the distance rounding up the hobbie.

"Donal..." Nick said. "He's *helping?*"

Felicity glanced over her shoulder in the direction of the bog pony's stubborn whinnies. "After you left the castle, he broke down in the parlor. I suppose Lia's attention at the gate affected him deeper than he expected. Or perchance you knocked some sense into him. He'd never realized how deeply he was hurting the children by hurting me. He told his aunt of his efforts to poison my passions vines and scare me with a snake. Even admitted the other schemes he's been behind. Could be he thought you might let him live and still have partial ownership of the bogs, were he to come clean. But there was some sincerity there, for when we realized Lia was missing, he insisted he help in the search."

"How did you find us?" Nick asked.

She peeled some flattened forget-me-nots from his neck. His skin buzzed everywhere she touched and he had to step back. He wasn't ready to act on the intensity of his feelings for her. His emotions were too raw, too fresh to trust just yet.

Felicity looked down and crushed the blue petals between

her fingers as he withdrew. "Lia wasn't in her bed," she answered, a tremble in her voice. "She'd tucked pillows beneath the covers to make it appear she was. We looked everywhere for her. But when we arrived at the stable and found Butterscotch gone, we knew. It made sense that she'd come here for her wish."

Weakened by his fight with the bog, Nick struggled to hold balance against weighted legs. He studied his wife's wrinkle-free face, surprised she would let everyone see her bared in such a way. Then again, circumstances had warranted expediency. He craned his neck to look over Binata and Clooney who were bent across the child, tending to her.

The rain had finally ceased, and the sound of the ocean could be heard in the distance over the drips which fell from the cliffs and forest trees. But he couldn't pull his attention from Lia and her quiet whimpers.

Felicity's fingers tightened on his arm for support. "She's going to be fine. You saved her life. You're her hero. How did you know, Nick?"

He stiffened, suddenly remembering what led him here. "Your ... brother..."

Felicity's eyes widened but before she could respond, Clooney lifted Lia and walked over. The child yawned and buried her face in the old man's neck. Her hair stuck out in a cropped, haphazard mess all about her head, and Nick fought a pang of remorse for those shimmering strands floating away in the bog. Truth was, he felt worse for that loss than his own knife.

In his mind's eyes, he saw the child vividly as she'd been this morning—spirited and spritely. Not once in the past month had she looked haggard like she did at this moment. "I should carry her." He tried to step forward but tottered, unsteady. Felicity caught his elbow.

Clooney shook his head. "You've done enough tonight, Son. You're just as worn as her. Need to get you both to bed. Get you warm. You should walk only with help."

Fennigan offered a shoulder for Nick to lean on and he reluctantly accepted. Tobias took the other side, giving support for the hike back. Donal walked ahead with the pony in tow.

"Aislinn." Nick had just realized she wasn't there. "Where is she?"

Felicity fell into step beside him as they ducked through the moss and into the shadowy depths of the forest, following Clooney and the others who were now out of earshot. "With her father. And as you've already met informally … it's time for a proper introduction."

Nick had been prepared to meet a ghost. Not a living, breathing man.

Felicity explained it all on the way back to the castle. About the turret's secret passage and the occupant within. About her brother's strokes and his determination not to be pitied or a burden to his children. About his tie to her through the butterfly cream she wore, and the pupas and the phonograph, and the deception she so fastidiously honored, in spite of the pain and sacrifices it won her. On either side of Nick, Fennigan and Tobias listened in silent awe as Nick asked questions pertaining to the novel Felicity's brother wrote through her with his sister. Felicity assured him only Jasper could answer those. And for that, they had to hope and pray he would recuperate enough to hold conversations again one day soon.

Upon their arrival at the castle, the group was greeted by Aislinn at the door, her face tear-streaked and beaming. Between happy sobs, she said all their prayers were answered just after Felicity and the others left to find Lia. Jasper had fully awakened the moment his spirit successfully led Nick to the bog.

Since Lia fell asleep on the hike back to the castle, it was decided she would be told in the morning of her father's existence. She'd already endured enough for one night. Binata agreed to rest with the little sprite in Aislinn's bed until Aislinn had time to visit their father once more.

Then, Aislinn, Clooney, Felicity and Nick took the secret passage to the turret where Nick now stood at the foot of Jasper's bed—soaked to the bone, exhausted and weary, but excruciatingly aware of everything around him. The scent and taste of ammonia. The subtle crackle of the coke which warmed the room and tossed out a glow from the potbellied stove.

He watched in wonder as Jasper sat up in his bed, eating broth and bread. The bearded professor was propped on pillows and awash in soft orange light. Clooney stood over him, checking the man's pulse and reflexes. There next to them on a table sat the laudanum and the phonograph, explaining all that Felicity couldn't of their misunderstanding earlier that morn.

Though frail and thin, Jasper had a noble and intelligent mien—a mix of Aislinn's dark-hair-porcelain-skin coloring and the vigorous bone structure of a once stalwart man.

Still physically incapacitated to some degree, he could move his upper torso along with his head. His facial muscles appeared completely normal and responsive, but his vocal cords couldn't emit sound and only his left arm and hand responded to his mind's commands. Being ambidextrous, he wrote rough communications on a slate board.

Clooney took the tray of food and left the room, insisting he needed to check on his two patients. Donal was spending the night in the playroom, so he was to be his first stop.

Nick remained with Felicity and Aislinn. In the stale, echoing silence of the tower, the chalk tapped out each question or answer and Aislinn read them aloud, being the most adept at ciphering Jasper's script. Despite his body's insufficiencies, there was no doubting the professor's brilliant mind remained alert and lucid.

"Brother ..." Felicity sat on the edge of the mattress. "Nick has come a long way ... and made many sacrifices ... to understand the truth about these butterflies. He deserves to know. Did they lead you back to Bella, in the afterlife?" Felicity kept her gaze averted from Nick's when he turned to her, both surprised and touched by the query.

Aislinn answered, reading her father's scribblings on the slate.

"He never left this world. Never saw mother. He says his spirit was tied to the castle at first. He floated from room to room, only able to connect with the outer world through Aunt Felicity's quill and ink. He sought a way to escape the castle but couldn't until I intervened with the pupas." She met her father's gaze, then wiped away the chalk with a cloth to make room for Jasper to jot some more.

Her deep blue gaze followed the words while ciphering them. "The longwings are rumored to have spirits. It's what sets them apart from other butterflies. It was when Father's spirit connected with theirs that he materialized, taking their form as shadows, separate from his body. The purple moss was a divergent fungus he'd been experimenting with before his coma—a fungus that had the ability to heal cells as opposed to breaking them down. When he found his new form, he distributed the fungus himself, to treat the passion vines and counteract Donal's effort to poison them."

She paused, erasing the chalk again. Her features softened upon reading the rest of his answer. "It wasn't the fungus that pulled him back into his body. It was love for Lia, me, and Aunt Felicity." Her voice trembled. "He realized that we did need him—whatever state he was in." Upon finishing the final word, Aislinn wrapped her arms around her father's chest, sobbing.

Nick had never seen the girl so innocuous and tender, nor had he ever felt more out of place or extraneous. Overwhelmed by the night's revelations and physical exertions, he started for the door. Felicity stopped him at the threshold with her hand on his shoulder.

"Wait, please. My brother has one thing more he wishes to say to you."

Nick cradled the tips of her fingers in his. He turned on his heel to look down at her tattered dress and smudged face. Why couldn't everyone else just disappear so he and his bride could mend what was broken between them? But would she want to fix it now? Jasper was back. She no longer needed a husband to secure her guardianship over the girls. That was the only reason she'd married him, wasn't it? An arrangement to appease a necessity which was no longer pressing.

Smothering a groan, he released her hand and returned to the bed's edge.

Jasper clacked the chalk against the slate then handed the message off to Felicity this time before curving his functioning arm around his emotional daughter.

Felicity's lips moved silently as she read, then she met Nick's gaze. "He thinks the plan for harvesting the peat bogs is brilliant. He wants to thank his new brother-in-law for taking care of his sister and girls. He says not many children are blessed enough to have two fathers." Felicity's chin quivered upon her delivery of the last sentence.

Moved by the sentiment, Nick stepped up to shake Jasper's left hand. He was impressed by the vigor of the man's grip, in spite of his atrophied muscles, and surmised this man's inner strength had yet to be fully tapped. He believed the professor would one day make a full recovery.

Nick cleared his throat. "The novel ... the one you wrote with my sister." He offered a stern look, from one older brother to another. "She must be told you were her co-author. She deserves to know. But I'm willing to wait until you can tell her yourself."

Furrowing his dark eyebrows, Jasper tipped his head in gratitude. Yet something blazed behind his eyes ... something Nick recognized, having seen it in his own: a desperate craving. Perhaps it was for a life of normalcy, for the use of voice, arms and legs, as they once had been. Or perhaps it had to do with Emilia herself.

Nick bit back the urge to question the man further. This wasn't the time, for he yet had his own inner demons to quell.

Offering a goodnight to Aislinn, Nick turned without a glance to Felicity and took the stairs through the passageway, intent on shutting himself in Lia's familiar chamber—it being the only room that was available. He would throw himself across that tiny bedframe and allow his aching body some rest.

He didn't expect to sleep, having too much to consider. He could leave at sunrise, now, before the guests began to arrive. He no longer needed to stay and face his father or his past since Felicity wasn't in danger of having the girls taken away.

So, where was the sense of relief? Why the hell, on the eve of this magnificent pardon, did he feel as if his world was ending?

CHAPTER THIRTY-SIX

Felicity followed her husband down the stairs yet kept her distance. She pressed her spine into crevices and blended into the shadows each time he glanced behind.

Slinking out from the stairway, she ducked into her room the moment she heard Lia's chamber latch click. Weary from the night's emotional uproar, she glanced longingly at her bed. But she had one thing left to do, and as she teetered between hope and despair, her body released an unexpected reserve of energy, giving her the stamina she needed.

She took time enough to brush out her hair, strip down and change into a chemise which buttoned up the front and place the carving Nick had made in one of its pockets. She didn't wash off with the water she'd had Cook heat up earlier. Instead, she gathered the basin and washrag and came to stand at Nick's closed door, intent to catch him before he went to the water closet.

Her shoulders ached beneath the basin's weight, still strained from pulling Lianna and Nick onto the banks earlier. Her husband knew how grateful she was; she'd told him countless times on the way back to the castle between her confessions of Jasper. But she doubted he would allow her to clean him and dress his wounds.

If nothing else, he would have to let her in to set the water on Lia's tea table. That would barter a moment alone with him. All she needed was a moment.

She suspected he would sleep a few hours then be gone before dawn to avoid his father. Now that he had no obligation to protect the girls, her time with him was short and precious, and she would not squander this last chance to prove her feelings to him. She would not allow him to leave without his knowing.

Alone in the dark corridor, her pulse jittered in her neck and rapid breaths clawed her dry throat—short and shallow. She gulped twice to assuage the sensations before making her presence known.

Tapping the toe of her stocking against the door resulted in little more than a scraping sound, but Nick—no doubt attuned to such indirect signals after all his years with Johnny Boy—heard her. The shuffle of bare feet crossed the room and preempted the door's creaking hinges as it opened.

Something in the rawness of his gaze made him appear younger, like the reckless youth who had saved her life. His hair was rumpled, and he'd already started to undress for the night. Soft candlelight glazed his bare chest, accentuating those broad shoulders, the cut of his muscles, and that fine spattering of blonde hair which disappeared to a "v" at the waist of his trousers. Her attention snagged on the pale petals which clung to several of those hairs at his waist, remnants of the flowers that he'd trudged through during his courageous rescue at the bog.

Bits and pieces of broken apologies, clinging to his skin.

Steam from the basin rose up between them, heating her already flushed face.

A flash of his naked body cavorted through her memory,

a titillating reminder of their first official encounter in the playroom upstairs. Things had been uncomfortable then, but rife with possibility. The chasm that yawned between them now was much wider, carved deep and hopeless by shattered promises and hidden truths—all on her part. Her footing was precarious at best … and impending death imminent if he opted not to catch her when she fell.

Studying the basin, Nick stepped aside so she could come in. She hesitated for an instant, noticing the cheval mirror she'd bound in satin for Lianna's gift. The two stable hands had brought it here before heading out to the gate earlier. Just the presence of the mirror set her inner qualms to spinning, and she would've slunk away like a coward, except for the fact that it still remained covered. With all the excitement, Lianna had yet to "open" it.

Taking a deep breath, Felicity passed Nick and crossed the threshold, the scent of his sweat resonant and sensual beneath the bog's subtle tang on his skin. Her mouth watered in reaction to the palpable masculinity heavy throughout the room—a sharp contrast to the little girl decor.

He nudged the door behind her but left it open a crack. After her past with men, being alone in a room with one should be old hat to her. But somehow, everything about her husband was new and exciting, yet terrifying … all at once. For a moment, dizziness weakened her arms. It caused her to set the water down too heavily. Some sloshed onto her wrists and the small table where Lia used to keep her porcelain dishes.

The water—hotter than expected—made her yelp.

Nick was standing over her in an instant, his strong hands catching her arms. He pushed her wet sleeves to her elbows and turned her wrists to the light. "Are you burned?"

She considered saying that the scalding patches hurt more than they did to prolong his touch. But she'd lied enough to him already. Nothing but honesty would suffice from this moment forward.

She shook her head in answer. "I'm fine. You look exhausted."

He released her and took a step back. "As do you. I'm surprised you're not already abed."

"Oh, I fear I won't sleep tonight..."

They stood regarding one another with the candles popping and flickering in the background—the only cessation to an interminable silence.

"Perchance Cook might make you some warm milk and brandy," he finally offered. His eyes softened to a curious fray—a splash of gray with flecks of gold reflected from the candles—behind long lashes. She knew in that moment that he could see right through her empty pleasantries. He was baiting her, daring her to speak her heart.

She should leave. Back out. She'd never bared her soul to anyone. But sweet heaven, how she longed to now. This man deserved that and so much more.

Fingers clenched in the pleats of her chemise, she blurted out the words she'd been practicing in her head since he first walked out of the kitchen. "I cannot stop worrying that I'll wake up in the morning and you'll be gone." She swallowed against a sob. "You'll be gone, and I'll have never shown you."

His gaze intensified, the dare harder-edged—relentless in its search for the truth. "Shown me what?"

She leaned a hip against one of Lia's chairs to support her tired legs. "That I am capable of being honest, for one."

He motioned to the bed. "Do you want to sit?"

"No. I-I just want to do this, quickly."

"All right."

"First, I need to tell you why I was stabbed. The real reason."

Sporting a cautious frown, he nodded.

She locked her arms around her stomach, hugging herself. "I was with child."

Nick's chin trembled beneath a stunned expression.

"I wasn't sure who the father was. But I was desperate, so I told Hayes it was his, and that I wished to leave the brothel. That it was time for him to make good on his promise and bring me here to the estate where we could raise a family. But he wasn't ready. He had accrued many gambling debts, and I was to help him pay them. He insisted I induce a miscarriage, and said if Clooney wouldn't assist, he'd find a physician that would." A lump caught in the base of her throat, but she pressed on. "I refused. It was the first time I'd ever stood up to the Earl. I had something worth fighting for, you see. I would not harm my baby or raise a child in that debase world." The sob she suppressed cut through, lodging higher in her throat as an aching mass. "He hit me ... he threatened me ... but I told him nothing mattered. Nothing but my baby. Then I started to walk away from him. He couldn't make me stay. That's what I told him ... that's what I said. His knife said otherwise."

"Dear God." Lashes wet with tears, Nick started toward her.

She raised a quivering hand to stop him. "Please, I need to finish this."

The same expression crossed his face that he'd worn upon learning of her barrenness. Grim nausea. He took a seat on the tiny bed, looking rather like a giant amongst all of Lia's miniature things. The bed's frame groaned beneath him as he shifted and stared at her. His fingers had found the petals clinging to that line of hair on his abdomen. He pulled the flowers free, absently, intent only on her.

She played with the ring on her finger and began to pace, the tile floor slick and cool beneath her bare feet. "When I learned that you'd lost a son, I knew your pain—intimately. I wanted you to have other children. So I tried to push you away. Until my nieces' needs overstepped yours. But now, you're no longer obligated to stay for them. You're free. You can leave and make a family for yourself, elsewhere. It would be best for you if you did."

Nick stood, movements measured and tense. His broad shoulders twitched. "Only I know what's best for me." He glanced at the ring on his pinky then looked up, eyes narrowed. "Why are you so bent on being the martyr? You, too, have been set free tonight. You're not defined by the needs of those around you any more than I am. It is your life to live once again. Yours. So, live it for you. What do *you* want, Felicity?"

Candlelight snapped and flickered, casting dancing shadows over his determined face.

"You," she answered, surprised by the volume and strength of her voice. "To love you ... and be loved by you ... until the day I die."

His glare surrendered to arrested suspension, as if it was the very last thing he'd expected her to say. He opened his mouth on a response, but Felicity barreled forward, needing to spill everything at once or she'd lose courage.

"You needn't say it back," she said. "You've shown me every day how you feel. And if you stay, I'll spend the rest of my life finding ways to show *you*. I'll start now. By proving the depth of my faith in you." Her stomach twisted into a thousand knots—screaming at her to stop. To stop before she lost him for good. "By proving I trust you more than I've ever trusted anyone else in this world. More than even myself." She glanced at the cloaked mirror then bit back a wave of nerves.

Before she could change her mind, she worked her top button free, then the next and the next, not stopping until she'd reached her waist. The placket stayed closed within the clasp of her trembling fingers.

Nick watched, rapt and unspeaking, silent tears slipping down his face.

With her eyes shut, she took a shuddering breath then dropped her hands to bare her shame. The fabric rolled open, skimmed off her shoulders to stall at bent elbows. Cool air hit her scar and breasts, ruthless as the sharpest dagger.

She forced her lashes open and gauged her husband's response. Wonder and compassion moved through his expression. But there was no pity. And he didn't turn away in revulsion as she'd once dreaded he might. Instead, he swiped a hand across his wet face and regarded her from abdomen to chest in a slow and languid sweep, gaze stopping upon her breasts.

A wave of regret surged through her, dousing her bravery. Perhaps he stared too long, his intrusive gaze too bold. Perhaps her hideousness held him in its thrall much as a sideshow freak to a curious child. She averted her eyes and tugged the chemise back in place on her shoulders ... buttoned the placket closed ... wanting to crawl inside a pupa and become something else. Something beautiful and loveable.

She was thrust back into her past, crushed beneath the pain of a separation she couldn't bear—losing an unconditional love she'd never merited but wanted just the same.

She backed toward the door. Hot tears gathered along her lips and drizzled from her jaw.

Nick made it there before she could manage an escape, shutting the door. Sparks of apprehension tingled through her spine as she heard him latch the lock.

Her fingers sunk within her pockets and butted against the carving. She drew it out, unable to look at anything but the broken wing. "Can you fix me, Nick?"

Taking it gently from her, he tossed it aside. "No, my love. I cannot."

CHAPTER THIRTY-SEVEN

Felicity wept quietly. Her husband had confirmed her deepest fears. He couldn't fix her.

She's already known that. What hurt was that even he had to admit it now after seeing the extent of the damage. She tried to find solace in the fact she'd done him a favor. Least he could leave without any regrets, knowing that she loved him and wasn't only using him.

"No more crying." Nick had her pressed to the wall before she could regroup her thoughts. He clasped her chin and lifted her gaze to his, using his thumb to blot the tears along her jaw line. It stunned her to feel his arousal hard against her abdomen.

"You want me still?" Her query was more of an awed observance than a question. "Even though I'm unfixable."

"I never said you were unfixable." He worked her buttons open again. As though mesmerized, he watched his fingers trail her scar where purple fungus caked along its length. Perception crept across his face as he realized she'd been trying to fade the flaw. "Perhaps Jasper's fungus will work and erase the scar. But I don't wish it to."

"Why?"

"I don't want you to erase our first meeting," he said, his

deep voice hoarse with hunger and resolve. "That scar is proof I'm worth something, a reminder of how I saved the woman who would one day save me. It's a part of you, Felicity. My beautiful and desirable bride. Whose eyes grow dark with tragic shadows one minute, and shimmer with hope the next. Whose perfect breasts and curving waist bid me to wrap my arms around her and make her mine." He cupped her fullness beneath the chemise—flesh to flesh. Her nipple budded against the hot calluses of his touch and she gasped. His answering groan filled her with a sense of power she'd never experienced before.

Soft, searching lips glided down her chin to her collar bone then found her breasts. She curled her arms around his head and arched into him. He suckled one then the next until she moaned from the exquisite torture. Pulling back, he wound his fingers through the hair at her nape.

"You are the woman I love," he whispered against her brow. "Head to toe, and everything in between. There's nothing about you that I would change."

"Oh, Nick." More tears leaked from her eyes. She felt silly and weak for crying after he'd told her to stop. But more than that, she felt lovely and cherished. And tears of happiness should be embraced and shared, not hidden away. She sniffled, smiling up at him, knowing that he would understand—just as he always did.

Smiling back, he lifted her to tiptoes and pressed their mouths together, a brush of salty warm sweetness against her lips. Her breasts pressed flush with the toned heat of his chest, uniting their heartbeats.

"So ... you will stay?" she asked the question, knowing it was redundant, but needing to hear the words.

He leaned his forehead against hers. "I'm not going anywhere. This castle is my home."

"Yes, it is." Her face grew warm with radiant bliss. "Now kiss me, my prince," she teased.

Their lips touched, sharing the curve of a smile.

This time, as she opened to him, their tongues touched and twined, and her husband's playfulness gave way to more determined exploits.

His mouth shifted to work sensual magic along her earlobe—uncoiling tendrils of wildfire from her breasts to her pelvis. His hands skimmed beneath her gown, hot and seeking. In answer, she skated her fingers across his chest, nails scraping along the copper sheen of his nipples then playing through the hair which vanished beneath his pant waist. She stopped there, trying to work the flap free, spurred to haste by the tremors of his rippled abdomen beneath her touch.

Growling, he forced her wrists over her head and secured them with one hand. "Your pleasure first—always." He used his free hand to find that bundle of nerves between her thighs which ignited at his touch. In only minutes, his ministrations erupted in that same brilliant spark of light she'd encountered the night before, making her bones liquid.

They both broke free from kisses and caresses, gasping for breath. Still adrift in dazed ecstasy, she remembered her bare chest and buttoned the placket again. A habit seven-years in the making was impossible to drop at a moment's notice.

Watching her movements, his gaze grew dark and fierce, and she knew the time had come to become his wife in truth. Thus, it surprised her when he turned aside to retrieve the basin and washrag then coaxed her over to the plush pink carpet leading from the door to the bed, situated at the foot of the cheval mirror. There he set the basin down and stripped the satin and ribbons away from the glass in one smooth movement, positioning the reflective surface to face her.

She studied her unkempt state—face flushed in anticipation, lips still swollen from his kisses, and chemise crinkled and clingy. She caught his wrist as he turned his back and started toward the bed. "What are you doing?"

"I'm going to love you. But first, you're going to learn to love yourself." He nuzzled her knuckles then worked his hand free.

Arriving bedside, he fished something from beneath his pillow.

When she saw the bar of soap, she frowned, befuddled.

"How else could I sleep at night without you beside me?" He dropped the small, creamy block next to the basin and washrag. "Least this way, I could smell you."

Her rash of nerves gave way to astonishment at the depth of his romantic pining. "You can't be real."

He grinned, a sexy turn of lips that torched her skin. "You'll soon feel just how real I am."

As if her heart wasn't already fluttery enough, it sprouted wings and butted against her sternum like a confined bird in view of the sky.

He opened the drapes to coax in the moonlight then blew out the candles, casting the room in deep purple brush strokes and milky sparkles. Then he came to stand before her, his silhouette large and luminous.

"Nick ... I can't do this. Don't make me look."

He pressed a finger to her lips. "Shhh. Your nocturnal butterflies have inspired me. This is your cocoon." Powerful hands dragged across the fabric encasing her.

She braved a glance around him at the reflection, admiring the masculine grace and confidence rippling through his back and arm muscles as he unbuttoned her chemise once more.

"And like the Heliconius," he murmured, breath brushing her forehead, "you'll make your escape in the dark of night to find your mate waiting in the softness of the moon's glow, ready to fight for you … aching to welcome you to metamorphosis."

Dazzled by the words, her focus left the mirror and slipped to his face, watching his ardent expression in the dimness as he separated the fabric. His palms eased between the panels to follow the curve of her shoulders, coaxing the sleeves to glide down her arms. He left behind chill bumps, exposing her breasts and stomach as the gown slid to her torso.

Golden hair waved around his shoulders, eyes too dark to discern. She raked her fingers through the strands and sucked in a breath as he knelt—slowly, in deference to the gash in this thigh he'd garnered during his fight with Landrigan to defend her honor. As his head leveled with her abdomen, his hands guided the fabric's descent, leaving her naked. The lacy chemise pooled around her ankles on the floor. On impulse, she covered her scar with her arms. He noticed but didn't scold. Instead, he took in every inch of her exposed body with a hungry sweep of eyes, then lifted her feet one by one to shove aside the discarded gown.

He looked up at her, holding her gaze. "I have a theory, Felicity. That you've had your wings all along, hidden within your cocoon." The sound of sloshing water broke the stillness as he prepared the rag. "Let me help you shake them free of their bindings, so you can take flight." His husky voice sent shivers of submission up her spine. Her hands fell to her side, immobile.

The scent of orange blossoms clung on the air. Her skin

bristled pleasurably as warm water and suds scraped away the purple residue caked on her scar. She fought the urge to watch—to see his hands on her skin in the mirror. Her disfigurement would be unavoidable without the fungus hiding it. Even when she'd applied the concoction, she'd used only the sense of touch to guide her.

Nick rinsed off the soap with a second swash of the rag and the comforting heat of the water lulled her to a heady sense of peace and wonder.

She gasped as his hands gripped her buttocks and drew her against him. Every doubt faded with the pressure of his lips kissing the damaged skin on her torso, starting above her sternum and working his way—slow and thorough—down to her abdomen. The intimate ministrations left her vulnerable, shaken, and lax.

What other man in the world would revere her scar rather than abhor it?

The desire to see him touching her became too much to resist, and she dared to face the mirror. Her naked reflection absorbed the moonbeams and she glimmered with the pearlized distinction of a statue. Her husband's arms, dark against her porcelain skin, circled her waist. He tasted the scar again, starting at the top to slowly reveal it as he moved down.

She studied the flaw in increments, shocked that she'd ever let it rule her life. It was thin, not nearly as jagged as she'd imagined—a testament to Clooney's masterful stitches. Admittedly, she saw it through a filmy haze of shadows. Tomorrow she would face it in the garish and unforgiving light of day. But with Nick standing behind her reflection, holding her, she would still see it for what it was tonight: A simple red line. A reminder of a beloved child once loved, *never* forgotten.

At last she understood. This was a most profound keepsake. Unlike Nick's earring or her brooch, this one could never be cast away. Nor should she wish it so.

Overcome by the epiphany, she fell to her knees, arms around Nick's neck.

He cupped her face in his hands and kissed her, soft and gentle.

Grateful beyond words, she wanted to thank him. She helped him shed his trousers, hands trembling to know him intimately.

A rumble escaped his throat—low and impassioned—as she curled eager fingers around his naked heat. Both his girth and length enthralled her. Anxiety swept through, at once exhilarating and fierce. It had been seven years since she'd been with a man ... and Nick was larger than any she'd known. But exhilaration won out. He could give her a first time worthy of memory. One to replace the nightmarish deflowering of her youth.

Once they were stripped of all barriers, time seemed to stop. They shared whispers and smiles ... explored one another with kisses and caresses, not missing even the smallest or most insignificant body part. The inner curve of the elbow, the tiny wrinkles along a knuckle, even the diffident bend where the ankle bone surrendered to the heel. It was magical, this unrushed, unselfish loving. This desire to know one another from the outside-in. A forging of trust Felicity had never imagined could take place between two people. She savored Nick's patience in the teaching, until the touches became too heated, and the tremors of need too exquisite.

Then she took him in hand, guiding him as he eased her to lie on the rug and pushed her thighs apart with a knee. His scent tickled her nose and his panting breath tufted around her, a tender, hot pulse everywhere his lips trailed.

All shyness had abated. She felt every bit the new bride: bared and vulnerable, aching for her husband to complete her. But she also had a courtesan's wisdom and could heighten his pleasure in ways an unlearned maiden could not. This she did, until he grunted and shoved her hands aside.

When at last he joined their bodies, she couldn't fault him his rough enthusiasm. He'd waited so long. She wrapped her legs around him, arched upward, and cried out at the splintering pain. But in the same she cherished it—for it echoed that breech a woman feels when her husband has staked his claim on her untouched body.

Cursing, Nick checked himself and apologized. Upon her reassurances, he soothed her with pretty promises and tender caresses, moving slow and deep until the flow of his body within hers yielded the pain to melting passion.

In all her years of experience, she had nothing to compare this ravishment to. For although he was impetuous in his eagerness, he didn't use her as a vessel. Instead, he measured his every move against her reactions, intent on being her partner in both the giving and the taking.

And when she once more teetered on the edge of rapture, she clasped her sweat slicked body around his and held the tension taut.

"Fly with me," she pleaded.

And with a shuddering moan that shook the glass in the mirror's frame, he did.

They'd made love two more times before Nick clad himself in trousers and ventured down to the kitchen to scavenge for sustenance. He'd had her once against the wall, and once more upon a wingback chair in the corner where they'd awakened—wrapped in blankets with Felicity straddling him—unsure how they'd landed there to begin with. No doubt she was every bit as famished as him after the night's exertions.

Who would've guessed, after how much energy he'd expended at the bog, that he would have the stamina or appetite for such sport? But Felicity made him insatiable. He couldn't think of a single drawback to having a wife so knowledgeable in carnal pleasures.

He chuckled quietly while taking the stairs back to Lia's room. He'd packed the tray with two goblets of wine, whortleberries, and barmbrack bread, and had already sampled several berries to assuage his growling stomach. He skipped the last two steps like an eager school boy. Despite the pained kink in his thigh and a few aching muscles, he truly felt young again—the carefree youth before mistakes and regrets.

On that thought, he paused at the bedchamber door he'd left slightly ajar, a niggle of trepidation returning to his chest. In just a few hours, dawn would come. Shortly thereafter, he'd face his father. Face his old man's disappointment and shame.

His mouth dried, a puckering sensation exacerbated by the lingering tartness of the berries. There was something he had yet to tell his bride. And he hoped beyond hope she would understand. After all they'd shared tonight, he had to believe she would.

With a shove of his toe, he opened the door and stepped within. He closed and locked it behind him.

Felicity was still seated in front of the mirror where he'd left her. Moonlight reflected off the glass behind her. That long luxurious hair glistened around her in a diaphanous pool of silver-blonde, and her face glowed with sensual bliss. A fairy princess ensconced in twilight.

She had wrapped her lower half in the satin panel that earlier draped the mirror and positioned the bow seductively just between her bared breasts. The bow's legs cascaded down either side of her scar—doing little to hide it.

It gave him great pleasure that she no longer flinched beneath his intent regard.

"What a tempting gift you make," he said to assure her of her beauty.

One dark eyebrow quirked and she opened her arms, an invitation.

He stalked her, suddenly hungry for something other than food. Placing the tray next to her, he knelt and trailed a finger along her navel. "Do I get to unwrap you now, beloved wife ... or after we eat?"

"After." Smiling, she embraced and kissed him, blanketing him in a dreamy mist of citrus and flowers. She drew back to study his face. "You looked so thoughtful when you first came in. Are you contemplating tomorrow?"

He grappled a handful of berries and dropped them, one by one, into her mouth. "My father."

Her chewing slowed and she wiped her lips. "You needn't stay." Her assurance came from behind the napkin. "Go visit Johnny Boy at Hannah's for the two days they're here. I'm sure she has work for you. Then come home when the guests are gone."

Shamed by her courage, Nick shook his head. "I would not leave you to face your past alone. And I'll not leave you or the girls vulnerable in a castle full of strange men." He gnawed on bread spiced with sultans and raisins, hoping she might change the subject.

Instead, she skimmed a palm along his arm. "So, you ran off with an investor's wife. You made mistakes in your first marriage. But the manor survived, and you grew from those missteps. A parent's love and forgiveness knows no bounds. You've allowed this rift to wedge between you for so long that it's become larger in your mind than it really is."

Nick rolled his eyes and took another bite of bread. "That makes absolutely no sense." He brushed crumbs from his hands.

"You're right. As if anyone could build something up to monstrous proportions in their minds simply by running from it." She opened the legs of the bow to reveal her scar, a smug expression on her face.

Lifting a finger to trace the thin pink line, Nick tried to smile. "Point taken. But there's more than a few failings between my father and me." He paused. "He's seen me at my very lowest. Stopped me moments away from selling my body for opium." The confession caught like a clump of sawdust in his throat and he swallowed some wine to loosen it. "The night he found me, he walked in on the cusp of a transaction between me and a vendor. *A man.*"

Felicity's berry stained lips didn't gape, nor did they frown. In fact, he never would've predicted such a composed expression in response to those words. She seemed to be more thoughtful than anything—turning things over and looking at them from all sides.

"You thought I would condemn you," she reasoned. "Think you weak in your vulnerability. That's why you were so angry for my lie of omission about your father. You were more afraid for *me* to face him, in the chance he might disclose details of your past."

Glancing sideways at the tray, Nick crushed some berries to bloody puddles with his thumb. He didn't want to acknowledge the truth of her epiphany. Not aloud.

Felicity scooted the platter aside and straddled him, her satin wrappings bunched around her thighs. The fabric was cool and slick against his abdomen, but the meeting of their bodies underneath was nothing but luscious heat, even with his trousers between them. She lifted his thumb and sucked away the berry juice, sending ripples of sensation through his nerve receptors.

"Mmm." He couldn't resist. Breaking his hand free of her lips, he glided both palms along the soft flesh of her thighs, bunching the fabric around her waist. He stopped at her naked buttocks and pulled her hard against him to bring a breast to his mouth so he could savor it.

She gasped. Her fingers twined through his hair like a cat kneading her paws. "My dearest husband..." Her voice was breathy and low. "I of all people understand the persuasion of desperation and the dregs of shame. But consider this: after the way you've protected me since that dark night we met"—she snuggled closer to him— "and the way you saved my niece by risking your life ... how could I ever think you anything less than a strong man?"

He halted his reverent exploration of her body, clenching his jaw in astonishment. She understood as she always did. This worldly woman with as many wounds and regrets as him.

Together, tonight, they had put them all to rest.

"So," he teased, almost giddy with this unfamiliar weightlessness in his chest. He untied the bow cinched beneath her breasts, letting the ribbon coil to the floor on whispers of satin. "My prowess is all convincing."

"Yes ... but I could stand more convincing yet."

Nick smiled at the wicked glimmer in her dark eyes. "Were you perhaps wanting some sausage with those berries and bread?"

She huffed in feigned annoyance. "I was rather hoping for scones, but I suppose sausage will do." A surprised snort clipped her lips as he clamped her legs tight around his waist and stood.

He spun around, tumbling onto the bed with her. Before he could initiate a proper seduction, the frame groaned, coming to a jolting crash upon the floor as the legs snapped from their combined weight.

They lay on their backs, startled, bones rattled, staring at the ceiling where moonlight shimmered in waves reflected off puddles collecting on the outer windowsill.

"You're all right then?" Nick asked.

"I-I am."

"Good, because I'm telling Lia that was your doing."

The spontaneity of his bride's response—contagious, tinkling laughter, uninhibited and pure—carried him to new heights of joy. He rolled to his side and caressed every inch of her silken nakedness while kissing her soundly, deep and long, until her laughter gave way to pleading moans, and the taste of berries and wine mingled between them—a feast fit more for a king than a prince.

CHAPTER THIRTY-EIGHT

Nick sat in the playroom, elbows propped on the wingback chair's arms as he attempted to carve. Since he'd lost his knife in the bog last night, he'd had to settle for one from the kitchen. It was a poor substitute, and Nick had garnered his share of splinters. But he didn't dare grumble or make a sound on the chance he'd wake the sprite.

Felicity had cut Lia's hair earlier this morn, smoothing out the jagged lines Nick's blade had left. Yet the child looked anything but boyish. In fact, the chin-length waves made her vivid eyes appear bluer and her cheeks rounder, so she favored an angel even more than before. Especially at the moment, with her hair splayed out on the pillow, framing her face like a gauzy halo. One strand was draped across her rosy pout and vibrated with each breath.

A humming surge of protectiveness fizzed through Nick's blood. He would've died had they lost her last night. Thanks to Jasper, they didn't.

Both girls had been visiting their father in the turret for the whole of the morning, while Nick and Felicity greeted the incoming patrons. It was well after lunch now, and Lia had needed her rest. The only way Binata could convince the little sprite to leave her father for a nap was by promising

Nick would sit with her and hold her hand until she fell asleep. Nick had been more than happy to comply.

Lia's lashes twitched dreamily in pale seams over her eyes, and a tiny snore drifted over the ticking of the pink clock. Nick smiled, basking in memories, awash in his earliest experience in this chamber when he'd first met the exceptional woman who was now—miraculously—his for life.

Looking every bit the lady of the manor, Felicity had greeted each guest this morn as herself without the mask of wrinkles. Encased in velvet and lace, she was a picture of grace and confidence. Even the three clients who would've been her undoing, she handled without the misbegotten flutter of an eyelash.

The first, Lord Treyton, was almost blind now, and had no chance of identifying her since Jasmine had kept her trysts muted for the most part, only responding if spoken to. And what man wants to waste time talking when he's visiting a brothel? The second, Lord Stanford, had been involved in a fox-hunting accident which injured his brain—the very side which retained snippets of the past.

But the third. Lord Rasmuth ... oh, he'd recognized her. Nick had caught the glint of lustful malice behind the man's gaze. Rasmuth had even been so bold as to make an unseemly remark. At which point Nick took him by the scruff of his neck out to the courtyard for a lesson in manners and discretion, then, after insisting Rasmuth apologize to his wife, sent him on his way.

It mattered little what the aristocratic swine might say once he arrived back in London, for Felicity's livelihood and the girls' welfare no longer depended upon her reputation. And even if her butterfly business faltered, she had the Thornton name to cushion her, and beyond that, Nick was here to oversee the peat bog venture. He would assure that she'd never face the upper class or its prejudices alone again.

The sound of steady rain brought Nick's musings back to the playroom. Ribbons of silver streamed down the window pane. He couldn't remember ever being this happy and content. Everything in his life was now perfect ... almost.

Only almost, because his father had yet to arrive. Shaving a long, splintering sliver from the block of wood in his hand, Nick paused. He should be relieved. But after last night's clearing of closets and rattling of bones ... he couldn't shake the desire to be rid of this one last skeleton. If his old man didn't show by late afternoon, Nick would head over to the train station at Carnlough to see why he'd been delayed.

Legs stretched out, he crossed his ankles then concentrated on the knife's blade, watching the wood sliver beneath it. He'd wanted to mend Lia's carousel ponies today, but the rain intervened. So, for now, he worked on carving a miniature merry-go-round for her doll garden in the greenhouse. Over the past few hours, he'd managed a rough horse-like shape, but it was a slow process. Once they hired workers for the bogs and had a steady income, he would buy a new carving knife to etch the more intricate details.

He was just about to get out of his chair and head to the kitchen in search of a better blade when he heard footsteps clomping down the corridor.

A familiar, deep voice thanked someone for the escort before a lighter set of footsteps faded away. The heavier footsteps resumed, alternating with the clack of a cane.

Nick froze, gripping the wooden horse and knife so tight his knuckles bulged. He'd know that sound anywhere...

"Nicolas."

Gulping, Nick stood, feeling every bit the child again. He turned to face his viscount father: the grand Lord Thornton.

A rush of terror trailed the action. This must be what Felicity experienced while facing her scar last night. Other than his old man's darker hair, he might as well be looking in a mirror himself, to see his image in twenty years.

The viscount's broad shoulders tensed in his tailored silver waistcoat beneath Nick's silent regard. He smoothed a red silk puff tie into the lapel of his lime-green embossed vest. Even after all these years, he still preferred the garish style of his Romani heritage. And damned if it didn't tug at Nick's chest—a nostalgic ache that made him feel more vulnerable than he cared to admit.

Steeling his resolve, Nick shifted his gaze to those eyes so like Julian's—steadfast and gray. Though unlike Nick's twin, these eyes were offset by crinkles at the edges, forged over decades of laughter and tears.

"Father." Setting aside his project on the chair, Nick stepped up to shake hands. He pumped once then released, nonplussed by what to say. "Mother. How is she?"

"She'll be weeping in relief, once I tell her you're still among the living." His cane under one arm, his father shifted his weight off his bad leg and raked a palm down his salt and pepper beard. The thick locks upon his head had flecks of white as well, and Nick wondered how many of those hairs he'd caused. "Imagine my surprise, to find you here, of all places. *Ireland?* Why did you leave without any word? Why did you let us think—"

"Because you told me you'd rather see me dead than what I'd become." Nick clenched his teeth upon the biting response. He hadn't meant to say it, but too much hurt and regret had surfaced before he could drag it back down.

His father's full lips pressed to a thoughtful line. "Those weren't exactly my words, son. I said you'd be better off with your dead uncle if you were to follow in his footsteps ... using women, driven by bitterness and rage over losses you couldn't control. Thinking of only yourself and your pain."

Nick snarled. "You're the one who named me after him. What did you expect?"

"I named you Nicolas because I loved my brother. Because, in death, he became a better man. I hoped you'd honor that better side as his namesake and give it new life." His father studied Nick's every feature, as though seeing his brother in that very moment.

Nick struggled for some way to bridge the gap between them.

"Mister Sir..." Lia's breathy voice rescued him.

He looked down to find the little sprite blinking her lashes heavily. He moved his carving articles to the floor then tugged his chair bedside. Taking a seat, he coaxed gossamer strands from her face. "What are you doing awake?"

She yawned. "I ... heard voices." Rubbing her nose, she slanted her sleepy gaze over Nick's shoulder. "That man looks like you."

Nick's father smiled kindly, his beard opening to a spread of white teeth. He'd always been handsome. From as far back as Nick could remember, his mother had called him her gypsy prince. Time had only mellowed his olive complexion to something more regal, like the weathering of bronze statue.

"He's my father," answered Nick, focusing again on the child.

A second yawn broke free and another plump hand appeared outside the blanket to rub her eyes. "Has he been pretending to be dead like mine?" Her voice was as drowsy as her heavy blinks.

Nick tucked her arms beneath the covers once more. "No,

angel. I'm the one who was pretending. Now, take your nap, or Binata will put you to bed early before the sun even goes down tonight. And you promised to count stars with your father and sister, remember?"

Sighing, Lia nodded and rolled to her side. Her eyes fluttered shut and the gentle snore resumed.

"Beautiful child. And quite precocious." The viscount's voice came soft and even from somewhere above Nick's right shoulder.

Nick nodded, feeling a pride that wasn't truly his to feel; still, the observation warmed him all the same.

"I didn't mean to wake her," his father said by way of an apology.

Nick raked a finger across her flushed cheek. "She was more asleep than awake. I doubt she'll even remember the conversation." Nick repositioned in the chair but remained seated in case the little sprite needed him again. "We have two days to hash all this out. Perhaps we might do it later."

"Yes, of course." His father limped around the wingback to face him, the long tails of his waistcoat rustling. "However..." He kept his voice to a murmur. "There's something we need to clear up right now."

Nick shrugged—an effort at nonchalance when inside he felt only dread and self-loathing. "If we must."

His father leaned against the window and used the tip of his cane to touch Nick's carving on the floor. "I met the countess downstairs. I've been in the dining hall for the past half-hour having a private tea with her. She told me of this little one's love for carousels after I asked about the broken horses outside. They reminded me of ours at home. You should bring her to London, so she might see a real one. Let her ride the ponies we made together."

Nick winced beneath yet another bout of nostalgia. So

many months they'd spent working on that carousel, the three of them. Nick carving the intricate forms, Julian tweaking the pulleys and drive belts on the mechanism, their father painting the mounts, and the saddles and bridles. Nick had missed those days, that comradery. "Last I saw that ride those horses were in worse wear than the ones in my courtyard."

"We patched them up as best we could, but it was your sister's contribution that truly gave them life again. She's become quite good at painting. She'll trump me one day soon. She seemed restless after she stopped receiving post from the countess. Wasn't even interested in attending galas anymore, or meeting suitors. We had to find her a new hobby."

Moving his boot to tow his carving away from his father's cane, Nick kept Jasper's secret tightly locked away. No one, other than Nick, Willow, and Julian, had known Emilia was writing the novel with the countess to begin with. His parents had believed it to be correspondences about butterflies. Perhaps they could accept their sweet, young daughter having a penchant for scripting sensual tales. But Nick was sure they wouldn't approve of a widower scientist, some eight-years her senior, exchanging such erotic and intimate passages with her. Despite that Emilia was nineteen now, and of age to marry, she was still their adored and precious girl.

"So, she took up painting to assuage her boredom?" Nick tried to guide the conversation back to safer waters.

"She realized she had a knack for colors and brushwork. She'd be so eager to show you. She misses you. Your brother misses you. He would have accompanied me, had Willow not been so close to her confinement. Their second child will be here within a couple of months. We already see so much of you in their son, Nico."

Nick's brow furrowed. "That's his name?"

"His full name's Nicodemus, but they call him Nico." An intensely proud expression crossed the viscount's face. "In honor of his uncle Nick."

Nick's eyes stung as something new stirred within; no longer envy but regret over time lost. "Uncle Owen, Aunt Enya ... and Leander's family. Are they well?"

"Yes, physically. But emotionally? They're heartsick from worry. Home hasn't been the same without you these past few years," the viscount pressed.

Nick set his jaw in spite of the tenderness gnawing at his heart. "I can never call London home again."

"That doesn't mean you can't visit your family and mend fences. And I'm not leaving this room until you understand that you're always welcome there."

Nick picked up his miniature horse and the kitchen knife, holding silent.

His father propped his cane against the window ledge and embedded a hand inside his vest's pocket. "The countess said you came here a month ago, looking for work. Then you married her two days ago to protect her and the girls."

Nick's pulse pounded. "Yes."

"She also told me her true identity."

Nick ground his teeth. He hadn't wanted his father to know of Felicity's past. Not that Nick was ashamed. He simply didn't want her to be misjudged.

"She's afraid there might be some repercussions in London after your run-in with Lord Rasmuth," his father explained. "She wished to let me know ahead of time, so we'd be prepared. She doesn't want your mother or sister hurt, or for our newspaper or manor to suffer any fires sparked by the man's forked tongue."

"You have some time yet." Tucking the knife and wood

between his thigh and the chair's frame, Nick propped his elbows on his knees. He adjusted the cuffs of his Fairlawn shirt. "I doubt Rasmuth will show his face in society until both black eyes have healed."

His father snorted softly. "That's my boy."

Nick bit back a wave of emotion at the affection in his old man's voice. "So, that's what all this talk of coming home is about. You're going to tell me what a mistake it was to wed a woman of Felicity's …" He cast a glance to Lia, assuring she still slept. "Repute. No doubt you plan to disinherit me unless I annul the arrangement and return to London. Well I don't bloody care. This was no marriage of convenience. I love her and these girls. And that's more valuable than any inheritance or title or lands."

His father's jaw twitched as he pulled a forget-me-not from his vest. "A very charming lady, your bride. I was surprised by her age, obviously. Expected someone much older. But such a wizened heart. To admit something as intimate as her past to her father-in-law—an investor in her business and a man she hardly knows—all in hopes to protect her new husband's family. That takes real courage." He lifted the flower, a puzzled pull to his brow. "She's mysterious, that one … so like your mother."

One side of Nick's lip lifted in surprise. His father had just given Felicity the highest praise that could be afforded any woman, for his adoration for Nick's mother knew no bounds.

"The countess asked me to press this in a book and offer it as a gift to your mother, from you," his father continued. "But she wouldn't explain why. Although she provided the book and circled a passage within."

Nick's half-smile widened to a full grin. "Mark Twain?"

"Forgiveness and forget-me-nots."

Nick met his father's steady gaze. "Mouse's ears, actually."

The viscount held the pale petals to his nose. "Strangest thing about this genus of flower. They can bloom spontaneously out of a marble floor. You mother stumbled upon a harvest once in our manor. She swears by it." His own lips spread to a smile that mirrored Nick's.

A breath locked in Nick's chest. "She told you?"

"Oh, yes. Julian saw you place them; told your mother they were yours, meant for her. She waited for you to tell her yourself, but even when you didn't, she still had hope. That discovery affected her deeply. For she knew that if something so lovely could burst from stone, surely goodness could bloom out of a heart, however hardened it might one day become." Sporting a beguiled slant on his whiskered chin, his father tucked the flower away. "Your bride mentioned your bravery in the bog last night." His focus fell on Lia. "This is the child you saved?"

"It is." Nick swallowed against a sudden bittersweet burn. "So ... am I now man enough to match up to Julian in your eyes, Father?"

The viscount gave him a saddened smile. "You were never in competition with your brother—least not in my or your mother's eyes. And I never thought you less of a man for your choices. Only thought you less than the man you could *be*. I wanted you to do something right for the right reasons." He paused to glance once more at Lia's prone form. "I can't imagine anything more right than this." He gathered his things and limped to the door, his cane leading the way on a swishing scrape. "As to your inheritance, that's something we should discuss over the next two days. Seeing as you now have your own family to support."

Battling a tingle behind his eyelids, Nick stood. "I never thanked you for stopping me that night ... for weaning me off the opium ... for caring for me despite all I'd done."

Back still facing him, his father straightened his silk puff tie. "No need for thanks. That's what a man does. He cares for his own—whether they're his by blood or by marriage. No one can deny how well you've learned that. I'm proud to call you my son. I hope now you can believe it, and be proud of the man you've become." With a thoughtful tilt of the head, he stepped into the hall.

Nick was still standing speechless beside his chair, watching after him, when Felicity appeared in the doorway.

He cleared the lump from his throat. "Good afternoon, my lady." He moved his carving articles once more, took a seat, and motioned for her to join him.

"I don't wish to hurt you," she half-scolded.

"The leg is fine." He caught her wrist and tugged her into his lap—a warm and welcome bundle of swishing lace and velvet.

She settled in cautiously, favoring his left side to avoid the punctured thigh they'd treated earlier with Jasper's healing fungus and bandages. "Did you speak to your father?"

"He spoke to me." Nick followed his bride's gaze to little Lia, slumbering so sweetly in the bed. "He helped me remember."

Felicity's attention returned to him, interest dawning in her delicate features. "Remember what?"

"That it wasn't his stick I was being measured by all those years ago. It was my own. And today, I've met the mark. At last, I am a man of substance." Nick clasped his hands over her abdomen.

"At last, you finally know what I've known all along." She nestled against him.

Nick grinned. "Father showed me the forget-me-not you offered in my name," he baited, his nose burrowing into her orange-blossom hair.

"Ah, well ... I thought perchance, were your mother to read the quote with the word struck out, to see the flower from you, she might recall a time she stumbled over a similar bouquet some years ago."

"It seems she recalled without the reminder."

"Did she now?"

"But you already suspected that, didn't you? You're quite clever. I rather like that about you."

"Merely like?" she asked, pulling back to meet his gaze.

"*Love.*"

"Better," she answered.

They exchanged teasing smiles.

"So ..." Nick ran a finger from her jaw to her neck, absently tracing the lace at her clavicle, wishing they were alone so he could undress her, feast upon her breasts, and trail his finger along her scar. "How did our investors respond to the tour of the greenhouse? Were they duly impressed with the Heliconius?"

"Once I assured them the populous would triple within the next few months, they were putty in my hands. Oh, and they asked how often it rains here. I said almost daily. Then they relayed their surprise about the butterflies' proliferation ... how something so beautiful could thrive in the midst of such dreary gloom."

Nick narrowed his eyes, the storm outside imprinting streaky silhouettes along the chamber walls. "Interesting. It would seem they have little experience with the layers of the human heart."

With a soft, satisfied giggle, his bride wound their fingers together. "Poor sods have no idea what they're missing." She lifted his hand to kiss the ring on his pinky and their gazes met once more. It struck him then, how brightly her brown eyes sparkled today. Not a tragic shadow to be found. She blushed beneath his ardent study, and a deep and contented warmth filled him at the vision.

"I think today has been a grand success thus far," she offered, squeezing his hands in hers. "Wouldn't you agree?"

"Well, let me take stock." He nibbled her earlobe, his hunger deepening when she leaned closer in a bid for more. "I awoke this morning with the most perfect woman in my arms and nothing broken around me but the bed. I'd say it's a damn fine start." He tilted her face up to kiss her.

"And I daresay tonight will be even finer," she whispered against his lips, bringing her arms around his neck.

"Mmmm," he responded. "Perhaps, if we're naughty enough, Bini might put us to bed early."

He captured his bride's resultant laugh by pressing his lips to hers again. They kissed until they were both breathless, until Felicity tucked her head beneath his chin and laid her palm across the thumping rhythm in his chest. As Nick snuggled with his bride in the quiet calm of Lia's snores, he watched the rain drizzle against the glass. The droplets smeared the view of forest and sky to watercolor grays and greens.

Indeed, it was the loveliest shade of gloom he'd ever seen.

EPILOGUE

Felicity had collected her share of miracles since meeting and marrying Nicolas Thornton. But now she was to have one she'd never dreamed possible: bringing new life into the world.

Upon realizing Nutmeg was pregnant after the bog incident nearly six weeks earlier, they had hypothesized Johnny Boy was the sire, considering the pit bull and the setter had become chummy during his short stay.

Today they would see if their suspicions held true.

Fighting a bout of nausea, Felicity cast a glance to the empty dining table behind her, regretting that she had failed to eat. Nick's carving caught her eye, and she smiled upon seeing the new knife his brother had sent a week earlier lying beside it. Already, Nick had put the blade to use, finishing the miniature carousel for Lia. It was bare wood, as Nick hoped to convince his sister to make a trip to Ireland under the pretense she might paint it for Lia.

He hadn't mentioned Jasper to Emilia yet, nor had he or Felicity mentioned the possibility of her visit to Jasper ... but they both felt the two should meet. An intellectual bond had sparked between them during the writing of the novel. Should that spark rekindle, it might help pull Jasper from the malaise he'd been falling into. His physical rehabilitation was proving more daunting than they'd anticipated, and he was becoming withdrawn once more.

Suppressing a surge of concern for her brother, Felicity turned back to the whelping box they'd arranged next to the fireplace. Morning streamed through the windows, gracing everything in warm, white light. A rare sunny day. The perfect setting for a miracle.

Felicity knelt and smoothed the Irish Setter's soft fur. "You're doing fine, sweetheart. Just fine..." Upon hearing a swish of skirts, she glanced up at the new maid.

Abigail—a prune faced spinster—was sweet natured yet pragmatic, wonderful with the children, respectful of Nick, patient with Jasper's enigmatic and varied temperaments, and got along well with Cook and Clooney. But no one had ever imagined they'd be using her expertise as a midwife one day. Felicity was so grateful the woman was here.

"How long?" Felicity asked, trying to breathe through her mouth. The smells were ill-affecting her at the moment.

"Soon. His Lordship should come in now. He does want to be present?"

"Oh, yes! He's already been by twice to check. He's the most eager of anyone." Felicity couldn't stop happy tears from blurring her view. Her emotions had been all askew lately. "He's up in the turret with Jasper and Mr. Landrigan. They're discussing our first two weeks' intake from the bog. Could you please get him?"

Before the spindly limbed woman could even reach the double doors, Nick was there—gray eyes excited and bright— the color of a stream over glossy rocks.

"Splendid timing." Felicity smiled and wiped tears from her cheeks.

Nick nodded at Abigail as he strode in. He dropped to his

knees beside Felicity, kissing her cheek before he leaned forward to rub the dog's ear.

"The girls," Felicity said, relishing the tingles where Nick's whiskers had grazed her skin. He was growing his beard back at her behest, though he'd been kind and understanding when she'd gently refused to return her hair to its original black depths. With the wrinkles gone, she needed to keep that one layer of separation from her prior identity for her own sanity. "They'll be so disappointed they missed this."

Nick chuckled. "Are you joshing? Tis their first day of school. Did you not hear Lia chafing me about how many grand stories she'd be bringing home this eve? Let's see her top this one." He took Felicity's hand and kissed the knuckles gently. "As to that ... how are you holding up?"

Chagrinned, Felicity managed a smile. "Not too well, I fear." She nearly gagged at the stench of blood and wet hair. She'd never expected her stomach to be so fickle about things. Nick was convinced it was a result of nerves from sending Aislinn and Lia to school with Clooney and Tobias ... that she regretted not being there to see the girls off on their first day herself. She smiled—a soft knowing smile.

Nick patted her thigh. "I'm here now. You don't have to—"

"Stay? Yes, I do. I want to share this with you. Besides, it's good practice." She laced their fingers and squeezed.

Nick's gaze narrowed. "Practice?"

"Oh!" Felicity cried out, her attention on Nutmeg again. "I think the first one's coming!"

"Let a midwife do her work." Abigail shooed Felicity and Nick aside to take her place next to the whelping box. The hound was panting heavily. "Dogs her size usually have a half dozen or so. Be ready with the cloths to rub down the pups like I showed you earlier."

Nutmeg delivered the first four ... all female replicas of her redhaired breed. Then a fifth came out, wriggling in the inky birthing sac. Nick tended it while Abigail introduced the others to their mother.

"Is it the last one?" Felicity asked when no other seemed to follow. Abagail nodded in answer.

Felicity inched closer on her knees to look across her husband's broad back. She propped her chin on Nick's shoulder. There, between his bent legs, was the spitting image of Johnny Boy, though teeny with two perfect ears and a brown patch over its left eye.

The room filled with squeals and whimpers, the pup in Nick's lap the loudest of all. He glanced over his shoulder at Felicity, sporting the most charming grin. "It's a boy."

Felicity playfully cocked her head. "Well, it will surely be your responsibility to teach him manners. I'll not have him running about and tormenting his sisters. And no scaring Dinah half to death. She may be a cat, but she's still his grandmother. Most importantly, you'd best assure he doesn't inherit his father's affinity for tug of war, or you'll be getting an earful from Lia."

"Yours to command, fair princess." He kissed her nose, then turned and rubbed the pup's pink belly until its tiny legs paddled as if it were swimming. Its lips curled upward. "Did you see that?" Nick asked, beaming. "He has Johnny's smile."

Felicity laughed. "Yes, he does."

Nick fussed over the wiggly bundle. "Little John. That's your name. We're going to be grand friends, you and I, like me and your old man. He lives close enough you'll get to know him. Why, I visited him just last week. Once you're weaned, we'll head out for a day trip to meet him."

From behind, Felicity curled her arms around her

husband's neck to kiss his cheek. Swaddling Little John in the cloth, Nick gently handed him over to the midwife so the pup could acquaint his mother and siblings.

Nutmeg nosed and licked her babies as they each blindly found a teat and began to nurse. It amazed Felicity, how natural maternal instincts were in each species. Another slow smile crept over her face.

Grinning, Nick stood and offered his palm to help her do the same. "I suppose tomorrow I should send a wire to London. Let my old man know that he and Mother are grandparents again."

Felicity lifted her eyebrows and took his hand. "You might want to wait on that." She stood too quickly and nearly fainted. Woozy darkness faded her vision for an instant.

"Whoa." Nick caught her, his scruffy chin tightening on a concerned frown. He guided her to a chair by the table. "You shouldn't have stayed."

Abigail walked by, dirty cloths in hand. "Nonsense. Your wife simply needs to eat. A woman in her condition should not be neglecting meals so carelessly. I'll bring some tea and toast until Cook can manage something more substantial." With that, she scooted out the door, leaving them in solitude.

Nick stared at Felicity, transfixed. The most beautiful expression of awe swept over him. She couldn't resist picturing that face on a rough and rowdy little boy. Or in the least, his gloriously blonde hair on a fine-boned, pink-skinned girl.

Her husband fell to his knees in front of her, touching her abdomen. She could feel the love radiating through those fingertips, and knew their baby could, too.

"My lord, Felicity." Tear-filled eyes met hers. "How?"

Stroking Nick's hair, Felicity relayed Clooney's perspective as a physician. He said it was possible that though her babe had died, her womb hadn't been as damaged as they assumed. It wasn't as if Felicity had been with another man since the tragedy to test her barrenness. Clooney could have misdiagnosed the extent of the internal damage. Jasper, as the scientist, had other suspicions: that Nick's body had somehow retained the properties of the fungus which had healed his leg, and by her trying to fade her scar those three weeks before they married, she'd also been exposed. Their physical union amplified the medicinal quality of the spores so it could heal her womb.

As for Felicity, she kept her own explanation to herself, for it was as intricate and fragile as a spiderweb's winding tendrils, and mightn't survive the winds of deliberation. She had come to believe that the Creator she'd once thought had forgotten His creation, had in fact been watching all along.

God, fate, magic ... or all three combined. Who was to say? When it came to miracles, explanations mattered naught. A wise person took them at face value, and thanked heaven for the gift.

Felicity basked in the sweetness of the moment as Nick rose and brought her to stand before him carefully, as if she were a rare porcelain treasure.

"A baby—made of us. A product of our love." His hand drifted down to her abdomen once more, seeking a roundness that was only beginning to bloom. Something akin to trepidation and sorrow flickered across his face.

Felicity covered his hand with hers. "I am strong, and we have a midwife, a professor, *and* a physician on hand," she answered his unspoken fear. "You won't lose either of us. I have faith in this."

The worry slowly melted from his features. "So, why did you suggest I wait to wire my parents?"

"I simply meant there's no rush." Pressing her hands over

his, Felicity smiled. "The birth won't be for another seven-and-a-half-months. *If* I conceived the night Jasper came back to us. I can't be sure."

Hard to know, because her menses had been few and far between after the stabbing—sometimes skipping entire years—only to reappear the morning after the bog incident for one day before leaving again. Hard to know because she and Nick rarely fell asleep without making love each night, and often awoke to another dose of passion in the morning.

His strong arms hugged her close. "It doesn't matter when." There was a smile in his voice. "I'm not waiting. I'm wiring them today. They'll want to come for a visit. All of them! We'll have a fortress filled with Thorntons, just like in my childhood." Casting aside all doubt, he waltzed her across the floor, laughing.

Felicity's chest swelled so full it could've housed a thousand butterflies. She joined in his laughter and opened her heart to free the wings—sending with them the ghosts of her and her husband's pasts, up-up into the sunny Irish skies, out of sight … never to darken their castle's doorstep again.

END

Now that you've finished *The Glass Butterfly*, please help support the author by writing an honest review on Amazon, Goodreads, and other online sales sites of your choice. Authors make their living off of sales, and reviews are the most effective way for new readers to discover their books. Many thanks! Also, be sure to watch for the next installment in the Haunted Hearts Legacy, *The Artisan of Light*, launch date TBA!

CPSIA information can be obtained
at www.ICGtesting.com
Printed in the USA
LVHW090329110319
610116LV00003BA/608/P